P9-BYW-537

COYOTE FRONTIER

Novels by Allen M. Steele

Collections by Allen M. Steele

Nonfiction by Allen M. Steele

COYOTE FRONTIER

A Novel of Interstellar Exploration

ALLEN M. STEELE

ACE BOOKS, NEW YORK

HIGHLAND PARK PUBLIC LIBRARY
494 LAUREL AVE.
HIGHLAND PARK, IL 60035-2690
847-432-0216

SF

THE BERKLEY PUBLISHING GROUP
Published by the Penguin Group
Penguin Group (USA) Inc.
375 Hudson Street, New York, New York 10014, USA
Penguin Group (Canada), 90 Eglinton Avenue East, Suite 700, Toronto, Ontario M4P 2Y3, Canada
(a division of Pearson Penguin Canada Inc.)
Penguin Books Ltd., 80 Strand, London WC2R 0RL, England
Penguin Group Ireland, 25 St. Stephen's Green, Dublin 2, Ireland (a division of Penguin Books Ltd.)
Penguin Group (Australia), 250 Camberwell Road, Camberwell, Victoria 3124, Australia
(a division of Pearson Australia Group Pty. Ltd.)
Penguin Books India Pvt. Ltd., 11 Community Centre, Panchsheel Park, New Delhi—110 017, India
Penguin Group (NZ), Cnr. Airborne and Rosedale Roads, Albany, Auckland 1310, New Zealand
(a division of Pearson New Zealand Ltd.)
Penguin Books (South Africa) (Pty.) Ltd., 24 Sturdee Avenue, Rosebank, Johannesburg 2196, South
Africa

Penguin Books Ltd., Registered Offices: 80 Strand, London WC2R 0RL, England

This book is an original publication of The Berkley Publishing Group.

This is a work of fiction. Names, characters, places, and incidents either are the product of the author's
imagination or are used fictitiously, and any resemblance to actual persons, living or dead, business es-
tablishments, events, or locales is entirely coincidental. The publisher does not have any control over
and does not assume any responsibility for author or third-party websites or their content.

Copyright © 2005 by Allen M. Steele.
Text design by Kristin del Rosario.

All rights reserved.
No part of this book may be reproduced, scanned, or distributed in any printed or electronic form with-
out permission. Please do not participate in or encourage piracy of copyrighted materials in violation of
the author's rights. Purchase only authorized editions.
ACE is an imprint of The Berkley Publishing Group.
ACE and the "A" design are trademarks belonging to Penguin Group (USA) Inc.

First edition: December 2005

Library of Congress Cataloging-in-Publication Data

Steele, Allen M.
    Coyote frontier / Allen Steele.— 1st ed.
        p.   cm.
    ISBN 0-441-01331-7
    1. Space colonies—Fiction.   I. Title.

    PS3569.T338425C6925   2005
    813'.54—dc22

                                                            2005050812

PRINTED IN THE UNITED STATES OF AMERICA

10 9 8 7 6 5 4 3 2 1

for
Ron Miller—
the man who painted Coyote

CONTENTS

DRAMATIS PERSONAE

Coyote Colonists

MONTERO FAMILY
Carlos Montero—president, Coyote Federation
Wendy Gunther—Carlos's wife; former Colonial Council member
Susan Montero—daughter; naturalist, Colonial University
Kuniko Okada—Wendy's adoptive mother; former chief physician,
    URSS *Alabama*

THOMPSON FAMILY
Lars Thompson—logging camp foreman
Marie Montero—Lars's wife; Carlos Montero's sister
Hawk Thompson—son
Rain Thompson—daughter
Garth Thompson—Lars's brother; mayor of Clarksburg
Molly Thompson—Lars's and Garth's aunt; owner, Thompson Wood
    Company

DREYFUS FAMILY
Barry Dreyfus—captain, *Orion II*; *Alabama* colonist
Will Gentry—first officer, *Orion II*; Barry's partner
Jack Dreyfus—Barry's father; former *Alabama* engineer

LEVIN FAMILY
Cecelia "Sissy" Levin—musician
Ben Harlan—Sissy's second husband
Chris Levin—Chief Proctor, Liberty, Cecelia's son

CAYLE FAMILY
Bernie Cayle—farmer

Vonda Cayle—professor of History, Colonial University
Dana Monroe—bar owner; former *Alabama* chief engineer
Jud Tinsley—crew member, *Orion II;* former *Alabama* executive
   officer
Paul Dwyer—wagon driver, former *Alabama* crewman
Henry Johnson—astrophysicist
Manuel Castro—savant; former lieutenant governor, New Florida
   colony
Tomas Conseco—Carlos Montero's chief of staff
"Hurricane Dave" Peck—bartender
George Waite—tugboat captain
Tillie Van Owen—logging camp cook

EASS *Columbus*—Crew

Anastasia Tereshkova—commanding officer
Gabriel Pacino—first officer
Jonathan Parson—second officer

On Earth

Jonas Whittaker—physicist, Federal Space Agency
Roland Shaw—director of Internal Security, United Republic of
   America
Maggie Kendrick—physician, Federal Space Agency
Angelo Margulis—chief administrator, Highgate
Dieter Vogel—senior consul, European Alliance, Highgate
Farouk Sadat—secretary-general, United Nations
Marcos Amado—U.N. ambassador, Western Hemisphere Union
Sir Ian Rutledge—U.N. ambassador, European Alliance
Morgan Goldstein—entrepreneur
Mike Kennedy—bodyguard
Joseph Walking Star Cassidy—equerry

PROLOGUE

The next-to-last day of Muriel came as the mellow aftermath of a long rainy season, the morning warm and dry, with a clear blue sky vacant of clouds. Tomorrow was the summer solstice; the students would get the day off to prepare for their finals, but by the end of the week they'd be returning to the farms and ranches from which they'd come, and then Colonial University would close its doors for the month of Verchiel. So today was a day for reflection, for taking stock of the world, and, just perhaps, wondering what lay ahead.

As was her custom, Vonda Cayle decided to hold her final class outside. It would have been a waste of a fine morning to keep her students cooped up; the classrooms were well insulated, of course, and each one had its own woodstove, but they'd never been equipped with fans, and as spring had faded into summer the rooms had gradually become stifling even with the windows thrown open. For this last session she wouldn't need blackboards or maps, though, so Vonda moved the class out to the quadrangle, where they took seats upon the lawn surrounding the small pond that lay in the middle of the campus, while she claimed the bench beneath the shade of a faux birch.

Giving her students a few moments to settle down, she gazed upon them with a certain fondness that she'd never expected to find at the beginning of the trimester. This year's World History class had been a little larger than usual: fourteen pupils, their LeMarean ages ranging from six to eight, with the youngest little more than teenagers and the oldest in early adulthood. The sons and daughters of immigrants, none had been born on Earth, and all were young enough to be her own children. They'd come here from towns as close as Shuttlefield and colonies as distant as New Brighton, their tuition either paid for by their families or, as in the case of a few of the older students, work-study scholarships that enabled them to

live in the dorms while doing all the small but necessary jobs that kept the
university running on a day-to-day basis. The first time she'd met them,
they were all strangers; now she regarded them as friends, even if some of
them didn't think of her the same way.

Very well, she thought. *We've spent the last four months together. Now let's see
how much they've learned.*

"All right, now . . ." Leaning her cane against the bench, Vonda gently
clapped her hands, bringing an end to murmured conversation. "If everyone is ready . . ."

Her lecture book was spread open in her lap, a soft breeze pulling at its
handwritten pages. She gazed down at it for a moment, as if preparing to
deliver another lecture, then she slowly and deliberately closed it.

"And they all lived happily ever after," she said. "The end."

For a few seconds, they stared at her in bewilderment. Pens paused
above blank pages of notebooks, ready to jot down everything she said,
only to find that she was saying nothing. A few tittered laughs, politely
muffled behind hands. An insolent cough from somewhere to the left; she
didn't have to look to know where it came from. She waited, her hands
folded together in her lap, pretending to study the grasshoarder that had
just touched down on the ground beside her.

"Pardon me, Professor Cayle, but—"

"Yes, Aaron?" She didn't look away from the tiny bird as it pulled at a
blade of swampgrass. "Is there something you'd like to add?"

Aaron hesitated. One of her older students, he'd always been shy about
making his opinions known, until she'd carefully coaxed him out of his
habitual timidity. "Well, I mean . . . surely there must be more. After all,
yesterday we only got up to"—he flipped back a page of his notebook—
"Hamaliel '13, when the *Columbus* arrived."

"That's correct, yes. But this material has been covered by Contempo-
rary Politics and Trade, hasn't it? And since I don't want to be redundant
with everything Professor LeBeau has been trying to teach you, I'd just as
soon leave it alone." An offhand shrug. "We all lived happily ever after, and
that's that. The end. Anyone care to argue with that?"

"Nope. I'm satisfied." Raven slapped her notebook shut, started to
stand up. "Thanks, Professor, this has been a—"

"Did I say class was dismissed?" Vonda looked the black-haired young
woman straight in the eye. She froze, then slowly sat down again, not

looking away until she lost the staring match with her teacher. "Like I was saying," Vonda continued, "we all lived happily ever. But then again"—and now she favored them with a coy smile—"I could be wrong."

Some knowing chuckles from the brighter students, the ones who'd become accustomed to her deliberately provoking arguments. Vonda tossed aside her notebook, disturbing the grasshoarder and causing it to take flight. "I've spent all last spring telling you how and why we came here. Day after tomorrow, you get your finals. The ones who are good at memorizing facts and figures are going to do well. The ones who've written good papers will get passing grades, too. And some of you"—she refrained from looking at Raven—"are going to muddle by, and with any luck I won't have to see you here again next fall."

Outright laughter this time, although not from Raven, who was red-faced and seething. "But right now," Vonda went on, "I'm not interested in rote-memorization or writing talent. I want to know what you've actually learned, not just what you're able to parrot back to me. So today . . ."

She paused. "No notebooks. Put 'em away, right now. If I see anyone peeking at them, they get a failing grade for the day."

Near the back of the group, another young woman raised her hand. "I don't understand, Professor," Zephyr said. "I mean, what are we supposed to talk about?"

"Good question." Vonda nodded. "Perhaps we can start with you, then. Tell me, why did I come here?"

Zephyr blinked in surprise. "You? Well . . . to teach this class, I guess."

"No, no." Vonda shook her head impatiently. "Tell me why I came to Coyote in the first place."

Zephyr hesitated. "Umm . . . you were aboard the *Alabama*, the first ship . . . the one that left Earth in 2070, I mean. And you told us that you'd been one of the intellectual dissidents—"

"Dissident intellectuals," Vonda corrected. "Or D.I.s, for short. Go on."

"The D.I.s were a group of radicals that the government persecuted because of their beliefs, so they hijacked the *Alabama* and—"

"Wrong." Vonda looked around. "Anyone want to take a stab at it?"

"The D.I.s weren't radicals," Aaron said. "It was the Liberty Party who were the radicals, not the D.I.s. Once they took control of the government, they renamed the country the United Republic of America, rewrote the

Constitution and the Bill of Rights, instituted martial law, abolished all other political parties, suspended free elections, established reeducation camps—"

"All those things, yes. And Zephyr's correct when she says that the D.I.s were persecuted because of this." Vonda smiled; she had little doubt that Aaron would ace his final exam. "But she got something else wrong. Anyone else?"

"The D.I.s didn't hijack the *Alabama*." This from Carter, idly plucking at the grass between his legs. "That was done by Captain Robert E. Lee, along with members of his crew. The D.I.s were just passengers they managed to smuggle aboard at the last minute, so they didn't have anything to do with . . ."

"Uh-uh." Erik shook his head. "A lot of D.I.s were part of the conspiracy. If it hadn't been for the ones who'd worked for the Federal Space Agency, Lee wouldn't have gotten away with it."

"Absolutely correct." Vonda shifted a little on her bench. "Although it was Captain Lee's plan, he had considerable assistance from many of the D.I.s . . . my own late husband, among them." She frowned, and added, "This is something a few of you are going to have to study a little more closely. I guarantee, you'll get a question about this on the exam." A few students, Raven among them, started to reach for their notebooks; one sharp look from their teacher, though, and they left them alone. "Let's move along. The *Alabama* managed to escape from Earth, and after . . . oh, I must be going senile, I forget how long—"

"Two hundred thirty years . . . or two hundred and twenty-six years, shiptime." This from Snow, the most literal-minded member of the class. "Give or take a few months, of course, due to the time-dilation factor of twenty-percent light-speed, along with—"

"Relative time will do, thank you," Vonda said, to the accompaniment of scattered chuckles; Snow was well liked among his classmates, but he was also something of a hairsplitter. "So the *Alabama* arrived in the 47 Ursae Majoris system on August 26, 2300, and reached Coyote on September 7, 2300."

"First Landing Day," Raven chirped. "Uriel 47, c.y. 1."

Vonda tried not to show her disgust. That particular date was taught to every child almost as soon as they learned how to read; next to Liberation Day, it was most significant holiday of the year. Only the boys who weren't infatuated by Raven's charms didn't smirk at her attempt to curry favor; everyone else glanced at each other and rolled their eyes.

"Yes, that's correct," Vonda said. "And so we lived happily ever after . . . right?" Even Raven's latest boyfriend cracked up at this, and received a glare from her in return. "No, I think not," Vonda continued. "We had quite a few problems, starting with the fact that we had to learn how to live off the land, while at the same time contending with a number of natural predators . . . boids, for instance. The first year here was quite harsh, but somehow we managed to make it through the winter, and by the beginning of Gabriel, '03, Liberty had become a self-sufficient colony. But then . . ."

She barely had time to pause before Aaron's hand shot up. "The Western Hemisphere Union showed up. Their ship, the WHSS *Seeking Glorious Destiny Among the Stars for the Greater Good of Social Collectivism*, arrived on—"

"Would you like to take over for me?" Vonda asked. "I could use a nap."

More laughter, although not as mean-spirited as that which Raven's comment had earned. Aaron was the star pupil of the class, yet no one begrudged him. Except perhaps Raven, who cast a cold look in his direction. Yet Aaron only grinned and bashfully shook his head, and Vonda noted the expression of admiration that crossed Zephyr's face. If Aaron didn't know that she had a crush on him, then he should be spending a little less time in the library.

"The *Glorious Destiny* was the first Union ship, yes," she continued, "and Aaron gets bonus points for being able to accurately recite its full name." She paused. "Come to think of it, I'll reward up to five bonus points to everyone who can tell me the full names of each of the five Union starships . . . on the exam, I mean."

A few appreciative whistles, but most of the class groaned. It was easy to remember the abridged names of those vessels—*Glorious Destiny, New Frontiers, Long Journey, Magnificent Voyage*, and the *Spirit*—but the Western Hemisphere Union had adopted the Chinese-socialist tradition of christening their ships with long, elaborate names, and it took a keen memory to recall that the third vessel, for instance, was properly known as the WHSS *Long Journey to the Galaxy in the Spirit of Social Collectivism*. Aaron could do it, no doubt . . . but Vonda would've bet a wooden dollar that Raven wouldn't be able to earn those bonus points if her life depended upon them.

"Who wants to take it from there? Not you, Aaron, someone else." When no one volunteered, she picked a student at random. "Nestor."

"The Union occupation lasted just over three years, from Gabriel '03 to Asmodiel '06, when Liberty and Shuttlefield were retaken by Rigil Kent guerillas under Carlos Montero. After the Matriarch Luisa Hernandez was killed . . ."

"All true, but that's not what I'm looking for." Vonda let out her breath. "Look, if you think this exam's only going to cover names, dates, and places, then you're in for a rude awakening. A lot happened in those three years you just skipped over, and much of it shaped our history as we know it." She looked around. "Anyone else want to try?"

"Umm . . . are you talking about Midland?" Zephyr wanted to make up for her earlier gaffe, and Vonda encouraged her with a nod. "When the *Glorious Destiny* arrived, the original colonists escaped to Midland, where they established a new settlement in the Gillis Range . . . Defiance, my hometown," she added with a touch of pride. "And after the Garcia Narrows Bridge was built, other colonists . . . the ones from the Union ships, or at least those who got fed up with life in New Florida . . . went across the channel to Midland and set up more colonies. Shady Grove, New Boston, Forest Camp, Fort Lopez . . ."

"Fort Lopez was a Union military base," Carter interrupted, with an expansive sigh, "and it was destroyed on Liberation Day when Robert Lee deorbited the *Alabama* and brought it down on them."

"I knew that." Zephyr gave him a withering glance. "In any case, that was when colonies started being established outside New Florida." She stopped, then added, "Oh, and I forgot . . . Thompson's Ferry, too. But that one didn't last very long, and it was on the New Florida side of the West Channel."

"Maybe not," Nestor said, "but that was how the first bunch of Union colonists got across the channel to Midland, before the bridge was built. It was also where the first battle of the Revolution was fought, when Clark Thompson and his nephews took down a squad of Union soldiers who came into town to—"

"No, Thompson's Ferry wasn't the first battle." Andrew had been quiet until now. "Rigil Kent staged two raids on Liberty and Shuttlefield before then, and that's not counting the sabotage of the Garcia Narrows Bridge. All that happened long before Thompson's Ferry."

"Thompson's Ferry was just a skirmish." Snow shook his head. "The Union raid on Defiance was the turning point. That's when the colonists . . ."

Vonda had been hearing this debate all trimester long. When and where had the Revolution begun. Who'd fired the first shots. Whether it had been instigated by Robert Lee or Carlos Montero or Clark Thompson and his family. Yet, although she'd been an eyewitness to many of the events and known all these people, nonetheless it was difficult for her to form any sort of objective historical viewpoint.

Indeed, her lecture notes formed the core of a history of Coyote she'd been writing for the last four years. She hoped to finish it one day, yet every few months she found herself revising it once more. After all these years, there was still more that she was learning about the times in which she herself had lived. Wendy Gunther's memoirs, for instance . . .

"Enough!" Again, she clapped her hands for attention, trying to bring the discussion back in line before it flew out of control. "All of you are right, one way or another . . . and if there's anything this class should have taught you by now, it's that history is rarely an exact science."

"Ask me why I prefer physics," Snow grumbled.

"If Dean Johnson was still around, I think he'd disagree with you. But that's beside the point." She glanced at her watch. Just a couple of minutes left until the bell rang, then her students would be in someone else's class. So little time left for summation . . . "Look, what happened here wasn't just a series of events, happening one after another. It's a process . . . or rather, a progression, a story that had a definite beginning but hasn't yet reached an end. You can memorize names and dates all you want, but in the long run you have to reach your own conclusions."

"And what's that?" Aaron quietly asked.

"I don't have any." Vonda shrugged. "Or at least none that I'm going to tell you. But as you study for the finals, keep this question in mind, the very first one I asked you today . . . did we live happily ever after?"

No one spoke. A few mouths opened, then slowly shut. From the tower above the administration building, there came the low gong of a cast-iron bell. Vonda slowly stood up, wheezing a little as she reached for her cane. "Thank you," she said. "You've been a wonderful group, and it's been a honor and a privilege to have been your instructor."

Scattered applause as the students gathered their notebooks, hurried away to the classrooms. Vonda waited, watching them leave. As always before, this was her least favorite part of the academic ritual: seeing an-other group of young people depart from her life, often never to be seen again. Oh, she might see a few of them now and then, in chance encounters at markets or the theatre, yet then she'd simply be their old history prof, either revered or scorned in their memory. For now, though, their time together was done.

The days were getting warmer, yet she felt winter closing upon her. Not so long ago, she'd been Zephyr's age. Now her hair was stone-grey, her bones as brittle as cheap ceramic, and almost all the people who were the subjects of her lectures had passed away long ago. Suddenly, another trimester was finished, and once again she found herself wondering if she'd be around for the beginning of the next one.

Well . . . there would be time to think about these things later. For now, she had term papers to read and grade and an exam to write. And af-ter lunch, perhaps a nice cup of tea, and maybe a brief nap at her desk be-fore her afternoon class. These days, this was the most that an old lady could hope for from a perfect day in spring.

Putting her weight upon her cane, she hobbled away from the pond, following the footsteps laid by children too young to remember days when the world had still been a frontier. Lost in rumination, she forgot about the notebook she'd left upon the wooden bench.

The morning breeze riffled its handwritten pages, turning back through time . . .

Book 5

Amid the Alien Corn

The voice I hear this passing night was heard
  In ancient days by emperor and clown:
Perhaps the self-same song that found a path
  Through the sad heart of Ruth, when, sick for home,
  She stood in tears amid the alien corn . . .

**—JOHN KEATS,
"Ode to a Nightingale"**

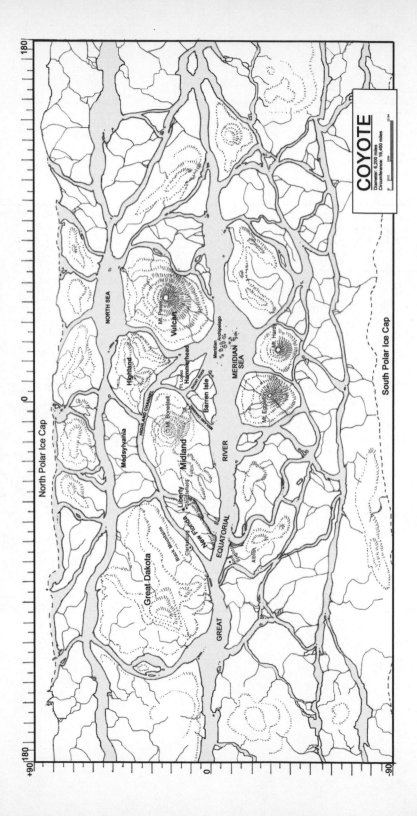

COYOTE

Diameter: 6,200 miles
Circumference: 19,400 miles

North Polar Ice Cap

South Polar Ice Cap

NORTH SEA

Mt. Pesco
Vulcan

Highland

Medsylvania

HIGHLAND CHANNEL

Mt. Bonestell

Pt. Lopez
Hammerhead

Barren Isle

Midland

Liberty
Shutterfield

New Florida

Clarksburg

Black Hills Mountains

Great Dakota

Meridian
Archipelago

MERIDIAN
SEA

Mt. Hardy

Mt. Egbert

EQUATORIAL

RIVER

GREAT

AIDAN

180

180

0

+90

-90

0

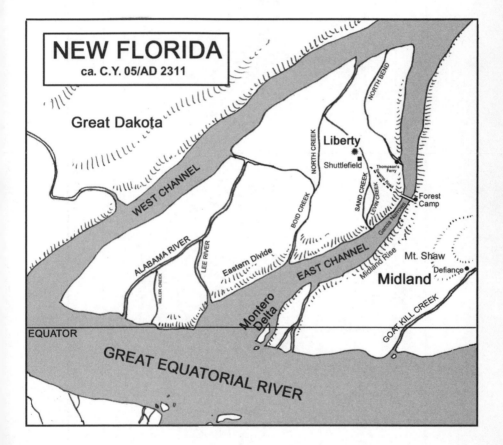

NEW FLORIDA
ca. C.Y. 05/AD 2311

Great Dakota

WEST CHANNEL

ALABAMA RIVER

MILLER CREEK

LEE RIVER

Eastern Divide

BOID CREEK

NORTH CREEK

NORTH BEND

Liberty

Shuttlefield

SAND CREEK

LEVIN CREEK

Thompson's Ferry

Swann Road

Forest Camp

Garcia Narrows

Midland Rise

EAST CHANNEL

Mt. Shaw

Defiance

Midland

Montero Delta

GOAT KILL CREEK

EQUATOR

GREAT EQUATORIAL RIVER

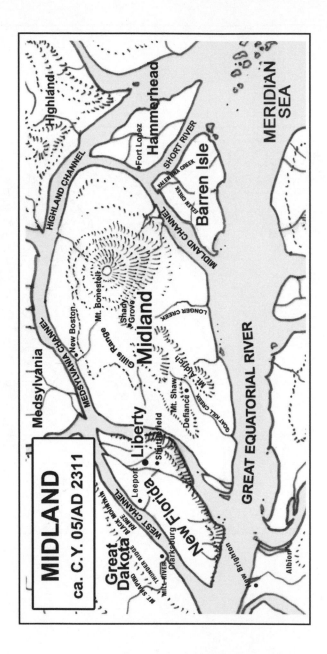

MIDLAND
ca. C.Y. 05/AD 2311

Great Dakota

New Florida

Liberty

Medsylvania

Midland

Highland

Hammerhead

Barren Isle

MERIDIAN SEA

GREAT EQUATORIAL RIVER

HIGHLAND CHANNEL

MEDSYLVANIA CHANNEL

MIDLAND CHANNEL

WEST CHANNEL

SHORT RIVER

VALENNA CREEK

EDEN CREEK

LONGER CREEK

GOAT KILL CREEK

Fort Lopez

New Boston

Gillis Range

Mt. Bonesteel

Shady Grove

Mt. Aldrich

Mt. Shaw

Defiance

Shuttlefield

Leeport

Clarksburg

MILL RIVER

THUNDER RIDGE

BLACK RANGE

MT. SHAPIRO

New Brighton

Albion

Part 1

BRIDGE OF STARS

The midi sent to pick him up at the airport was black as the night itself, with the two-digit plates that designated government vehicles. Once the unmarked jet taxied to a stop at the far end of the runway, the two Prefects who'd accompanied Jonas Whittaker from Huntsville marched him down the boarding ramp. For a moment he envied their grey overcoats and peaked caps; a warm, steady rain pelted his bare head as he walked across the tarmac, and the handcuffs caused him to slouch forward. A third Prefect waiting beside the midi held open the rear door and slammed it shut once Jonas and his escorts climbed in.

There was no conversation as the midi left the airport and hummed onto the outer belt. Although he used the lane reserved for government vehicles and Liberty Party members, the driver didn't turn control over to the local highway system, instead keeping his hands on the wheel. Now and then Jonas caught his eyes when he glanced back at him through the rearview mirror, but no one spoke to him, and Jonas tried to hide his fear by gazing out the window. The city looked familiar, but no one had told him where he was going. It was almost midnight, long past curfew, and so there was little traffic; it wasn't until he spotted a Texas plate on a passing police coupe that he knew where he was.

The driver took an exit south of downtown Houston, and before long Jonas glimpsed a long expanse of chain-link fence surrounding a cluster of featureless buildings. As the midi pulled up to a security checkpoint, he caught a glimpse of a sign: FEDERAL SPACE AGENCY—GEORGE W. BUSH MANNED SPACE FLIGHT CENTER. A uniformed United Republic Service soldier stepped out of the gatehouse just long enough to inspect the ID held up by the driver, then he raised the vehicle barrier and let the midi pass through.

The first time Jonas was here, back when he was a young post-grad fresh out of Cal Tech, this place was still called the Johnson Space Center.

But that was a long time ago; now an entire generation was growing up that had never heard of NASA, and in a few years he doubted that even the United States itself would be remembered as little more than a few chapters in a history book. An enormous flag was draped above the front doors of the headquarters building. Once it had fifty stars; now there was only one. One star, one political party, one government . . . and no hope.

No. This time, Pandora hadn't shut the box quickly enough. Hope had managed to escape, in the form of a starship called the *Alabama*. Which was why he was here . . .

The midi glided to a halt in front of a four-story building, and Jonas barely had time to observe that most of its windows were dark before the Prefect seated to his right opened the door. Jonas climbed out of the vehicle, wincing as the Prefect to his left impatiently prodded him with his swagger stick. If anything, the rain was coming down harder now; his greying hair was plastered to his skull as he was marched up the sidewalk. Another URS soldier awaited them at the entrance; he held open the glass door, silently gesturing to an elevator bank on the other side of the lobby. Just behind a vacant admissions desk stood a large holosculpture—an idealized DNA helix, slowly rotating within a shaft of light—and that was when Jonas realized where he'd been taken.

The medical research facility. He'd never visited this building, even during his infrequent trips here from the Marshall Space Flight Center. His research in theoretical physics kept him busy on the other side of the campus, and once his security clearance was revoked and he'd been fired, no one he knew here had ever spoken to him again, lest they join in the disgrace. By then, of course, it didn't matter; his only regret was that he and his family had been unable to join the others aboard the *Alabama*.

But this didn't make sense. Why had he been brought here? Not just to Houston, or even to Bush . . . but *here*, to a building he'd never set foot in before. He'd kept his mouth shut after he was arrested, but once he learned that the *Alabama* had been hijacked, he'd cheerfully blabbed everything he knew about the plot. Not that his interrogators found anything he said useful; one of the strengths of the conspiracy was that most of its participants were kept in the dark about its ultimate objective, and even who its leaders were, and therefore knew little more than what they needed to know. Jonas was aware that a few of his colleagues from Marshall were involved—Jim Levin, Henry Johnson, Jorge Montero—but he had little doubt that they'd gotten away. Even after being deprived of food, water, and sleep while ISA inquisitors hammered at him under bright lights, he could tell them little in the way of meaningful information. Yes, he'd been part of the plot to steal the *Alabama*. And now the *Alabama* was gone. Any more questions?

Apparently there were. But it still didn't tell him why he'd been brought all the way to . . .

The elevator doors opened, and the two Prefects led him out into a third-floor corridor. He walked between them, barely noticing the framed photos of orbital spacecraft, until they reached a door marked CONFERENCE ROOM 3-12B. The Prefect on the left rapped his knuckles against the door; a short pause, and then it opened.

The room was dark, lit only by ceiling panels that had been turned down low. Their dim illumination was reflected by the polished surface of a long oak table that ran down the center of the room; thick curtains had been pulled across the windows on the opposite side of the room. A wallscreen behind the far end of the table displayed ever-changing images of Mandelbrot patterns, and seated before it was a lone figure, caught in silhouette yet otherwise invisible.

"Dr. Whittaker, sir." The Prefect on Jonas's left spoke, his voice low and respectful.

"Thank you. Wait outside. Close the door." The two Prefects saluted, then turned and walked from the room, shutting the door behind them. A moment of silence, then the figure gestured toward the row of empty chairs. "Sit, please," he said quietly. "I'm sure you must be weary from your flight."

Before Jonas could respond, a form emerged from the shadows behind him. Another Prefect, younger than the others and a bit taller. When he raised his hands, Jonas instinctively flinched; he thought he was about to be struck again, as he'd often been since his arrest. But instead the Prefect did the unexpected: he pulled out the nearest chair and held it for Jonas.

"No doubt you've been treated badly the last two days," the man at the far end of the table continued, as Jonas carefully sat down in the offered chair. "If it helps, I gave orders that you were not to be harmed . . . or at least subjected to physical abuse, at any rate. Anything that might have been done to you was beyond my control, and for this I apologize."

Jonas swallowed, discovered that his throat was parched. He was tired, so tired. "May I have some water, please?"

"Of course." The Prefect behind him quietly moved away, and a moment later Jonas heard liquid being poured into a glass. "I'd offer you something to eat, but . . . well, I'm sorry, but this is the best I can do. And please, don't drink much. It won't be good for you."

The Prefect reappeared at his side, offering a glass with little more than an inch of water in it. Why so stingy about giving him a drink? Perhaps this was the overture to another form of coercion. For every truthful answer, he'd get water; for every hesitation or obvious lie, water would be denied. By the time they collected enough evidence to convict him on charges of high treason, he'd have sold his soul for a full glass.

Yet if this was an interrogation method, it was clumsy, something only amateurs would do. And besides, he'd already told them everything he knew. Even if they didn't believe him, there wasn't much they could do about it. Jim, Henry, Jorge . . . they and everyone else were aboard the *Alabama*, and it was probably couple of million miles beyond the Moon by now.

But his wife and daughter . . .

"My family." He took a small sip, resisting the urge to chug it down. Conserve what little he'd been given for as long as possible. "Where are they?"

The chair squeaked slightly as the man at the end of the table stood up. "Safe and sound . . . or at least as much as they can be under the circumstances. They've been sent to Camp Buchanan, but I assure you that they'll be treated well. If possible, I'll try to arrange for their release at the first possible opportunity."

Camp Buchanan. The government reeducation center outside Valdosta, Georgia. Little more than a concentration camp, from what he'd heard. "When will I see them?"

Silence. The shadowed figure disappeared from in front of the wallscreen, but Jonas could see him slowly walking closer, his hands clasped behind his back. Just as he was almost close enough for Jonas to see his face, though, he stopped.

"Dr. Whittaker, I'm sorry." His voice was very quiet, nearly a whisper. "I don't think you'll ever see your family again."

For a second, Jonas didn't know what to say, even how to respond. He found that he couldn't remember Caroline's face, even though he'd woken up next to her almost every morning for thirty years; he recalled the day Ellen was born, but everything after that was lost behind a haze. It was as if a curse had been laid upon him, one that erased memories of them as well as their place in his life. Just like that, they were gone.

So this was the game. It wasn't water they were going to withhold from him; it was his wife and daughter. "Who do you people think you are?" When he was finally able to speak, his voice came as a hollow rasp. "You think you can just . . . can just—"

"I'm sorry, Dr. Whittaker, but I didn't have any choice except to have them interned. As your family, they're considered security risks as well. I'll do my best to make their stay as short as possible, but—"

"What's the point? You've got everything you want. You know I'm guilty. You can only go through the motions now."

Which was the truth. The best he could expect was a show trial on Govnet, in which the prosecution attorneys would denounce him as an enemy of the people and his government-appointed lawyer would offer only a token defense. A federal judge would determine his fate, without the unnecessary distraction of a jury of his peers, and in the United Republic of America, there was only one sentence for capital crimes. Yet just before he was marched to the gallows, usually within hours of the end of the trial, Govnet would show a quick shot of him hugging his wife and child goodbye. A small, public display of tenderness, demonstrating that the government was not without mercy. To be denied even this . . .

"You're right. Your guilt has already been determined. But . . ." A pause. "There won't be a trial, nor will there be a public execution. Not if you're willing to cooperate."

"What?" Jonas was confused; he shook his head. "I don't . . . what are you—?"

"We don't have much time. Please, you have to listen to me." Then the figure sat down beside him, and for the first time since he'd entered the room, Jonas saw his face.

Roland Shaw, the Director of Internal Security. Next to the attorney general, the highest-ranking law enforcement official in the country. If President Conroy himself had shown up, Jonas couldn't have been more surprised.

Seeing that he'd been recognized, Shaw nodded. "You know who I am. Good. Glad we've got that out of the way." He raised a finger to the ceiling, twirled it slightly. "In case you're wondering, I've already had the room cleaned. No mikes, no cameras. No one's listening, and there'll be no record of what's been said here."

"I . . . I find that hard to believe."

"You're right to be suspicious. I would be, too, if I were in your position." Then he moved closer. "Yet my position is even worse than yours. Your involvement in this affair has already been exposed. Mine hasn't . . . or at least not yet."

If he hadn't been so afraid, Jonas might have laughed out loud. "Oh, I believe you. Of course. The top Prefect, involved in a plot to commit treason. Makes perfect—"

"Robert Lee was the ringleader." Shaw spoke softly, yet there was an urgency in his voice. "It was his idea to hijack the *Alabama*, with the assistance of as many crew members and FSA people as he could recruit. The conspiracy was arranged as a pyramid, with only a few people at the top knowing where all the pieces lay. Lee and his senior officers were at the highest level. I was on the second tier, yet my job was just as crucial, because when all the D.I.'s who went aboard the *Alabama* were rounded up by my people, I was the one who arranged for them to be taken off the prison train to Camp Buchanan."

"I'm not aware of—"

"Of course not. That was the part you weren't told about." Shaw sighed, shook his head. "If you hadn't been so smart, you'd have been aboard that train, and my friend here"—he gestured to the Prefect standing quietly behind them—"would have been able to remove you and your family from the train and put them aboard a maxvee for Cape Canaveral. You were that close to getting aboard the *Alabama*, but—"

"Oh, God." Jonas slumped in his seat. "I didn't know."

When word had come down through the grapevine that the Prefects were closing in, he'd swept up his wife and daughter and they'd fled for their lives. Their home was an old farm on the outskirts of Huntsville, and the dense woods behind their house had hidden them. The rendezvous point was supposed to have been a closed-down restaurant in Titusville, not far from the Gingrich Space Center on Merritt Island, yet they didn't make it nearly that far. Jonas had borrowed a coupe from a friend who lived nearby, and there he'd made his mistake; no sooner had they left when his neighbor had a change of heart and tipped off the Internal Security Agency. A couple of hours later, Jonas found himself spread-eagled across highway pavement, a mere mile from the Florida state line.

That was the last time he'd seen Caroline and Ellen. As a heavy boot against the back of his neck held his face against cold asphalt, he watched as they were bundled into a maxvee just a few yards away. Caroline screamed his name, and then the rear hatch shut behind them and they were gone.

"You were too clever for your own good," Shaw went on. "No one told you that you were supposed to be arrested in Huntsville, because they figured . . . *we* figured . . . that the Prefects would be as efficient as they always were in rounding up D.I.s."

D.I.s—*dissident intellectuals*, the Liberty Party's favored term for the so-called liberal extremists who took issue with the United Republic of America. Jonas had heard it so many times, mainly from people who had the courage and intellect of rats, he took it as a badge of honor. "So we were too late to make the train. Were there others?"

"Two were shot trying to run a roadblock near Atlanta. Everyone else made it. Rather a miracle, although coming up five short resulted in some problems down the line." Shaw impatiently waved a hand. "But that's beside the point. Our problem is more immediate."

"Which is . . . ?"

"Namely, it's the fact that you're still here." Shaw reached forward to push a button, and a touchpad flickered to life on the table's black surface. "Of all the people who should have been aboard the *Alabama*, you were perhaps the most important," he said as he typed in a six-digit code number. "Not because your presence was vital . . . you know as well as I do that it wasn't . . . but because of the work you've been engaged in."

"I don't know what you're talking about." Jonas forced himself to remain calm.

"Please, Dr. Whittaker. We don't have time for this. I'm fully aware of what you've been working on for the last twenty-five years. After all, I *am* in charge of internal security." Shaw moved the tip of his forefinger across the touchpad, accessing and opening classified files. "If you need proof, though . . . ah, here it is."

The image on the wallscreen changed, and Jonas looked up to see something he thought he'd successfully purged from his FSA database: a three-dimensional wire-frame model of a ring-shaped structure, a hundred and thirty feet in diameter. A circular gridwork of red and blue lines collapsing into one side indicated its event horizon; on the other side was the narrow funnel of an artificial wormhole, leading to an identical ring on the other side.

"A spacetime access reactor . . . or starbridge, as I believe you call it. A way of harnessing quantum mechanics to create a Morris-Thorne wormhole." He regarded it with admiration. "Faster-than-light travel. Quite an achievement, sir. If we had one of these today . . ."

"The *Alabama* would've been unnecessary." Along with Henry Johnson and several others, Jonas had been one of the designers of the *Alabama*, yet even that vessel, however advanced it may be, was a mere rowboat compared with a starbridge. With a maximum cruise velocity of twenty-percent light-speed, it would take the *Alabama* 230 years to reach 47 Ursae Majoris, while a ship using the hyperspace tunnel opened by a pair of starbridges could—at least in theory—travel the same distance in a matter of seconds. "You know, of course, that this is impossible."

Shaw sighed, rubbed the bridge of his nose between thumb and forefinger. "Dr. Whittaker, I'm not an idiot. You've spent more than two decades working on this. A man of your intelligence . . . genius, really, because that's how your colleagues regard you . . . wouldn't have wasted his time if he thought it was impossible. Implausible, perhaps, with our current level of technology, but impossible?"

Jonas remained quiet. Shaw was correct. Starbridges weren't impossible; it was just that no one knew how to build them yet. He and the other physicists on Project Starflight had shelved the idea—along with its close-cousin, the diametric drive—in favor of developing a fusion-augmented Bussard ramjet for the *Alabama*. There, at least, the physics were clearly understood, the engineering safely within the realm of near-term possibility. Even so, he'd continued to research hyperspace travel on his own time, in hope that, one day, the technology would be available to manipulate quantum singularities to the extent that wormholes could be created at will. He was confident that it could eventually be done, but for now . . .

"And that's why I've had you brought here," Shaw continued. "The moment I learned you'd been arrested, I knew that you were too valuable to be scarified. If you were hanged, it would be as much a loss as when Giordano Bruno was burned at the stake for stating that distant stars might harbor other worlds."

"Then put me in a reeducation camp." Jonas didn't want to plead, yet nonetheless he found himself doing so. "I can keep my mouth shut. Just let me—"

"No." Shaw slapped a hand against the table, and the display vanished from the wallscreen. "If I do that, then it'll only be a matter of time before someone else discovers what I know about your work."

"Not if you don't let them."

Shaw was quiet for a moment. "I won't be able to protect you much longer," he said at last, not looking at him. "Making sure that Robert Lee got away cost me more than I can say. It may be only days, or even a few weeks, but sooner or later they'll discover my part in all this. When that happens . . ." He gave a resigned shrug.

"You won't be hanged."

"Oh, I most certainly shall. I've made many enemies, and the Department of Justice loves nothing more than to trot out disgraced government figures." He nodded toward the Prefect standing behind them. "We're both guilty of treason, just as much as you. He has his reasons, as do I, and it's only a matter of time before the truth comes out. But before that happens, there's one last thing that needs to be done."

"And that is . . . ?"

"I have to make sure that no one ever learns what you know." Shaw gestured toward the wallscreen, which once again displayed random fractal images. "It'll take the *Alabama* a little more than 230 years to reach 47 Ursae Majoris. In the meantime, it's reasonable to assume that the technology may become available for the construction of a starbridge. Hence, the Republic . . . if it lasts so long . . . could eventually develop the means to pursue the *Alabama*. Perhaps even beat it to 47 Uma."

"If the enabling technology becomes available, yes, this may be possible." Then Jonas shook his head. "But starbridges have to be constructed at both the departure and destination points. So a second ship wouldn't arrive until after—"

"I realize that." Shaw was becoming impatient; once again, he glanced toward the closed door. "There's several variables we have to consider, not the least of which is that someone in the future develops an engine capable of achieving near-light-speed velocity. In fact, I understand you yourself were investigating this, yes?"

What didn't Shaw know about his work? It was frightening to consider how long the ISA must have had him under surveillance, how much they'd learned about his work. "It's possible," Jonas admitted reluctantly. "But if you have my notes—"

"Encrypted files, which can be erased in an instant." Shaw tapped a finger against the touchpad. "However, one copy will go with you . . . and where you're headed, they'll never be found. For that, I can give you my word."

"Uh-huh." Jonas's hand trembled as he picked up the glass, drank what little water was left. "So . . . what is it that you want from me?"

"Let me tell you what I'll do in exchange for your cooperation. As I said, you'll never be able to see your family again. I wish it could be otherwise, but that's simply the way it is. However, I can make sure that they receive good treatment during their stay at Camp Buchanan, and that they're released as soon as possible."

Jonas reluctantly nodded. He was in no position to negotiate a better deal; he realized that now, and the best he could do now was to save Caroline and Ellen. He sighed, shrugged in resignation. "Fair enough. So what do you want me to do?"

Shaw looked past him, nodded his head. From somewhere just behind him, Jonas heard a hollow metallic click. He didn't need to look back to know that the Prefect had just drawn his gun from its holster and cocked it.

"First," Shaw said, "I need for you to die."

CLARKSBURG, GREAT DAKOTA / HAMALIEL 69, C.Y. 13 / 1112

The wind turbine was a slender white pylon rising from a ridge overlooking town. A hundred and sixty feet tall, it towered above the treetops of the surrounding forest, its three paddle-like blades creaking softly as they revolved in the mid-summer breeze. A hundred yards away, an identical turbine rose from another hilltop; another hundred yards farther down the ridge, a third tower thrust upward against the sky, dwarfed only by the rocky peaks of the Black Mountains looming in the background.

They looked out of place, like weird contraptions erected by some alien race. Which, Carlos reflected, they were indeed. Although smaller turbines had been built elsewhere in the colonies, beginning with the ones in Liberty shortly after First Landing, the Thunder Ridge Wind Farm was the most ambitious energy facility yet erected on Coyote, and they wouldn't be here were it not for the presence of humankind.

"Okay, I'll admit it," he murmured. "I'm impressed."

"Nice of you to say so." Marie chuckled quietly. They stood together outside Tower One's control shack, gazing up at the giant machine. "I mean, we knew we had a good plan, but it's so nice of you to vindicate our efforts."

"Cut it out. You know what I'm saying."

"Maybe I don't. Sometimes I don't know if I'm talking to my brother or the president." Then she relaxed; stepping closer, she hugged his arm. "Never mind. I just wanted you to see this." She looked up at the tower. "Awesome, ain't it?"

"It is at that." Carlos gave his sister a kiss on the forehead. "Y'all done a good job."

Nonetheless, he knew what she was getting at, the reason why she'd had him hike all the way up here just to look at something he'd already seen in countless photos. Although the towers themselves were built from Great Dakota timber—mountain rough bark for the support pylons, faux birch for the lighter wood of the blades—much of the construction material had been imported. The concrete blocks of the base structures were made of volcanic ash shipped in from the eastern side of Mt. Bonestell, the electrical cables of copper mined from the Gillis Range and insulated with tightly woven strands of chokeweed vine from New Florida.

Nonetheless, these were all local materials, derived from the mountains, woodlands, and savannahs of this world. Their generators, though, were not renewable resources. Like so many other items upon which the colonists depended, they'd been manufactured on Earth. And it was forty-six light-years to the nearest electrical supply store.

"I know what you're thinking," Marie said. "Three towers, that should give us enough power to run the mills, plus some for the rest of town."

"No question there. That's what you asked for."

"Right. And you delivered." She pointed toward the line of hills to the southwest, where Thunder Ridge continued until it was broken by Mill River, leading into the highlands of the Black Mountain Range. "But we figure that, if we can build three or four more towers—"

"How many?" He looked at her askance.

"All right. Three . . ." She caught his look. "Two at least . . . but even then we'd have enough generating capacity to be able to expand the mills. That way, we could produce more material for the rest of the colonies. More lumber, more paper . . . and not only that, but eventually we might even be able to export surplus power across the channel to New Florida."

"I liked it better when you stuck with lumber and paper. Then I might have believed you." Carlos released her arm. "C'mon, kid. I didn't leave my brains at the door when I got elected. Expanding the mills, that's one thing. But when you start talking about producing power for New Florida, you're talking about putting lines across the channel."

He looked to the east. Below the foot of the ridge, past the narrow coastline of Great Dakota, lay the broad expanse of the West Channel. In the far distance, through the haze, they could make out the western shore of New Florida. "From here to there, that's . . . what? Eight miles? Ten? And most of that's across water. You think we'd be able to lay a cable across the channel? And even if we could do that, then we'd still have to get them all the way to Liberty. That's a lot of line, not to mention the transformer stations that have to be built."

"Okay, then what about Leeport? That's almost halfway to—"

"Have you been to Leeport? Lately, I mean?" Carlos tried not to laugh. "Not exactly what I'd call a boomtown. At least, not unless you're into fried swamper and—"

"Do you have to be so cynical?"

"No. Just realistic." He checked his watch. Quarter past eleven already. Garth Thompson had invited him to lunch at his place before they met with the rest of the town council, and he didn't want to keep the mayor waiting, even if he was his brother-in-law. "Look, it's not a bad idea," he said as he turned to walk toward the path that would lead them back down the ridge. "I just think that your eyes may be bigger than your stomach."

"Jerk!" She playfully punched him in the arm. "Are you making fun of my weight?"

"No, no. Just an expression." Truth to be told, though, Marie had put on a few pounds in recent years; she was in her late thirties, by Gregorian reckoning, and having two kids had cost her the slender physique she'd once enjoyed. Not that he himself had done much better . . . "I'm sure Klon and his people got this all worked out on paper, but even if we could lay electric lines all the way to Liberty, that would mean requisitioning two or three more generators. And you know what that means."

Marie didn't have to be reminded. The generators used for the wind farm's first three turbines had been salvaged from skimmers left behind seven Coyote years ago by the Western Hemisphere Union. One had been severely damaged by Hurricane Bertha, and weardown had rendered the other two inoperative, so it hadn't taken much effort on the part of the Civil Engineering Corps to covert their duct-fan engines into electric generators suitable for wind turbines. But it also meant that, for every new turbine the Thompson Wood Company proposed to build, another skimmer would have to be cannibalized. And she didn't have to check with Jack Dreyfus to know that the remaining skimmers were still in good operating condition.

So which was more important, transportation or more electrical power for the Clarksburg wood mills? Another matter to be taken before the Colonial Council. Another headache he'd have to deal with. Once again, he remembered the hand-carved sign Ted LeMare had given him for his fiftieth birthday, just after he'd won election as president and, sadly, just a few weeks before old Ted passed away. THE BUCK STOPS HERE: something a long-forgotten president of the United States was reputed to have once said. His own chief of staff didn't know what a buck was, yet the message was clear nonetheless.

Time to change the subject. "So how are the kids?" he asked, taking her arm and guiding her around a boulder in the middle of the path. "They getting along?"

"Rain's doing well." Marie snuggled against him. "She's in third grade, and when she's not playing practical jokes on everyone, she's showing signs of becoming an artist. Can't wait to show you her watercolors when you come over for dinner . . . she's got a lot of talent."

"Can't wait to see them. And Hawk?"

Marie became pensive, staring down at the ground as they walked. "Not so good," she said after a moment, her hand slipping from his arm. "He's supposed to be in upper school, but he dropped out two months ago. I only see him when he bothers to come home, and even then he's . . . well, barely there."

Carlos frowned. "If he's not home or at school, then where is he?"

She let out her breath. "Where do you think he is? With his father, of course."

Carlos felt something within him go cold. He'd never liked Lars Thompson; even when they'd fought together during the Revolution, he'd been someone Carlos couldn't turn his back on. Lars's younger brother had been much the same way—and so was Marie, for that matter—but once the war was over, Garth had straightened himself out, in time coming to lead the colony their late uncle had founded on Great Dakota that now bore his name.

Clarksburg—once known as Riverport—had been founded by Lars and Marie six years ago, after the magistrate had exiled them from Liberty. In the aftermath of the Revolution, the two had become violent misfits, and making them leave was the only way Carlos could keep them from spending hard time in the stockade. Together with Manuel Castro, the posthuman Savant who'd been left behind when the Union abandoned Coyote, the three of them had spent the next six months exploring the unknown territories west of New Florida. Everyone expected them to return to Liberty once their sentence was completed, but instead Lars had asked his family to join them in establishing a new settlement at the mouth of a river he and Marie discovered on the southeast coast of Great Dakota. Clark Thompson brought a number of other people with them, most of them people who'd once lived in Thompson's Ferry before it was destroyed during the first major battle of the Revolution, and so Riverport became the first colony west of New Florida.

No one knew what happened to Manny Castro. The Savant had remained with Lars and Marie until the first boatload of colonists arrived from New Florida, then one morning they found his cabin abandoned. He'd disappeared during the night, apparently taking with him only a rucksack filled with a few hand tools and a datapad. To this day, some claimed to have spotted him deep within the Black Mountains, a spectral figure in a hooded cloak, yet nonetheless Manny never again set foot within a human settlement.

It wasn't long before Marie was pregnant with her first child, and one of Clark Thompson's first acts as the colony's leader was to preside over her marriage to Lars. This was also one of the last things he did; less than a week later, the roof-beam of a cabin he was helping build fell on him. Riverport was renamed Clarksburg in his memory, and Lars had assumed the role as mayor.

But Lars wasn't like his uncle. He'd lacked the leadership qualities, preferring to spend most of his time drinking sourgrass ale, and when he wasn't drunk, he railed at people for not working hard enough. It was only inevitable that the townspeople rebelled; during a midnight meeting of the town council—which Lars himself didn't attend, because he'd passed out at the bar of the local cantina—a unanimous vote was taken to remove him from office. His aunt, Clark's widow, Molly, was elected mayor, something which her nephew didn't discover until he woke up the following morning.

Marie stayed married to her husband; she was carrying her second child, and had matured to become a respected member of the community, so she didn't want to leave him. Aunt Molly successfully led Clarksburg to self-sufficiency, establishing the family business, the Thompson Wood Company, as its principal employer; when she stepped down to let Garth become mayor, he and Marie went ahead with Klon Newell's idea to build a wind farm on Thunder Ridge in order to provide electrical power not only to the colony—which, with more than a thousand residents, was now third in population only to the twin townships of Liberty and Shuttlefield—but also to the timber mills that had become the backbone of Clarksburg's economy.

Yet Lars never regained his standing in the community. Embittered by the loss of authority, estranged from his wife and his younger brother, he'd moved up into the nearby mountains, becoming the boss of one of the logging camps that supplied wood for the mills.

"The only time I see Hawk is when he and his father come into town for supplies." Marie stepped over a rotted faux birch that had fallen across the path. "Other than him bringing my son home occasionally, I don't have much use for him. He's the father of my children, but . . ."

She paused to gather her long dark hair and tie it back into a knot. In the midday light, Carlos saw for the first time that it was threaded with grey. It shouldn't have been a surprise; there was silver in his beard, and lately he'd found the beginnings of a bald spot at the crown of his head. Nonetheless it was a shock to see such signs of age in his little sister.

"I married the wrong man, didn't I?" she said quietly, her hands working behind her head. "If I'd known how he'd turn out—"

"Don't beat yourself up." Carlos looked down from the hillside. Through the trees, he could make out wood-frame houses, see smoke rising from the mills. A pair of swoops circled above them, cawing their dismay at the human presence. "You were a lot younger back then. You couldn't have known better."

"Yeah, well . . ." She gave him a sad smile. "You know what they say."

"Time catches up to you when a year is worth three." An old Coyote truism, much like *boids attack when you're not looking* or *don't eat the winter corn until spring.* In this instance, it was a way of saying that time went quickly when you only paid attention to the passing of the seasons. Even though this was only the thirteenth summer he and his sister had spent on this world, they had been here long enough to pass from childhood to early middle age. And yet . . .

His satphone suddenly chirped, startling him.

"Can't get a break, can you?" Marie murmured, watching as he fumbled to unclasp the unit from his belt.

"Goes with the job." Carlos unfolded the miniature dish, held the phone to his face. "President Montero . . . how may I help you?"

"Wow, don't you sound official." Wendy's voice was a low purr in his ear. *"Should I call you 'sir', or is that too much?"*

" 'Sir' will do." Carlos smiled as he heard his wife's voice. " 'Your honor' would be nice, too. Oh how about 'your holiness'? I think I'd like that."

"Holy fool, more like it," Marie said.

Carlos pushed her aside, then turned away. "What's going on? Something important, I hope." Although his annual summer trip to Great Dakota was supposed to be diplomatic in nature, he'd come to regard it as a vacation, or at least a reason to get away from Liberty for a few days. Wendy knew this, and that's why he'd asked her not to call unless it was crucial.

"Important enough," Wendy replied. *"Have you looked at the sky lately?"*

"Huh?" Shading his eyes with his hand, he looked straight up. The only thing he saw was Uma, blazing almost directly overhead. "I don't understand. What am I supposed to be seeing?"

"Are you on high ground?" she asked, and he grunted an affirmative. *"Okay, look due east, toward the horizon. Find Wolf, and then look just slightly above it."*

Carlos peered in the direction she indicated. About a hand's width above the coast of New Florida, through the light blue haze of the sky, he spotted a bright point of light: Wolf, the outermost jovian planet in the 47 Ursae Majoris system, 1.6 A.U.'s from Coyote. This time of year, it appeared as an afternoon star, rising seven hours before Bear and almost invisible in daylight unless you were searching for it.

It took him another moment to find what Wendy was talking about, yet when he did, he felt his breath catch: a tiny, luminescent streak, so small that he could have covered it with an outstretched thumb. It might have been a comet, yet the moment he saw it, he knew what it was.

"Oh, hell," he murmured.

The exhaust plume of a fusion engine. The telltale sign of an approaching starship.

EASS *CHRISTOPHER COLUMBUS* / NOV. 2, 2339 (RELATIVE) / 1532

"MECO in sixty seconds, Captain."

"Thank you, Mr. Pacino." Anastasia Tereshkova nodded to her first officer in acknowledgment. She checked her lap belt to make sure that it was securely fastened, then gently touched the wand of her headset mike to activate the intercom. "All hands, stand by for main-engine cutoff. Repeat, MECO in one minute and counting."

Settling back in her chair, Ana took a moment to glance around the command deck. As expected, the flight crew were already at their stations, watching the screens of their consoles as Pacino commenced final countdown to the end of braking maneuvers. Of course, the AI was fully capable of performing this task automatically, just as it had for all other important functions over the last forty-eight years and nine months. Nonetheless, her second officer, Jonathan Parson, had insisted upon assuming the helm. He was a young officer, though, and this was his first deep-space mission, so Ana wasn't about to deny him the privilege, however unnecessary it may be.

She quietly watched from behind as Parson rested his hands upon the helm, keeping an eye on the master chronometer as the last seconds ticked away. At the instant the clock reached 00:00:00, he snapped a pair of toggle switches. A second later, the low vibration she'd felt beneath her feet ever since she awakened from biostasis faded away, and she felt her body pull slightly against her straps.

"MECO complete. Main engines in safe mode." Parson checked his nav screen, then glanced over his shoulder at her. "On course for 47 Uma B, ma'am. All systems green."

"Very good, Mr. Parson." Ana relaxed a little, savoring the momentary sensation of weightlessness. However much she personally enjoyed freefall, it wasn't a good idea to let it last very long; although most of the crew was accustomed to this, some of her passengers might get ill if it persisted. "Initiate turn-around maneuver, please, and stand by for MCF."

"Yes, ma'am." As Parson's hands moved across his console, Ana turned her attention to her lapboard. Displayed upon its screen was a miniature image of the *Columbus,* the long shaft of its stern pointed in the direction of flight. As she watched, lights flashed along the midsection maneuvering thrusters just aft of the shuttle cradles. She didn't need to study the screen, though, to know that *Columbus* was rotating 180 degrees upon its secondary axis. Brilliant beams of sunlight pierced the rectangular windows and quickly traveled across the low ceiling of the command deck until they reached the aft bulkhead, then formed long shadows as they raced back across the floor before fading out as the windows polarized against the glare of 47 Ursae Majoris.

Ana glanced at Pacino. He met her eye, gave her an encouraging nod. He, too, had been quietly observing the second officer's performance, and was just as impressed as she was. "Turnaround maneuver complete," Pacino said. "Ready to initiate MCF, Captain, on your mark."

"Mark." Although she was watching Parson as he pressed a couple of buttons on his board, she almost didn't notice when the Millis-Clement field was reactivated, restoring 1g gravity to the ship. Her body settled back in her seat, yet she observed this only in an abstract sort of way. For the last twenty hours, *Columbus* had been traveling backward, its fusion engine delivering constant thrust to decelerate its entry into the 47 Uma system. Now that the ship faced forward again, the fat ring of its diametric drive no longer blocked the view; she could see 47 Ursae Majoris as a distant sun, still two and a half A.U.'s away. Yet it was more than just another star. If she looked more closely . . .

Yes, there it was: a ruddy spot of light, bisected by a thin line. Bear, the third planet out from 47 Uma, closely surrounded by a small family of satellites. Dog, Hawk, Eagle, Snake, Goat . . .

And there, just barely visible. Coyote.

Ana's hand trembled as she touched her mic again. "All hands, stand down from maneuvers."

"Captain, we should be able to transmit now." The communications officer turned to her. "Do you wish to do so?"

"Yes, please." Electromagnetic interference from the fusion engine had rendered radio communications impossible until now. "Ku channel, between 15 and 18 gigahertz," she said. That was the band commonly used by older spacecraft; if anyone on Coyote had observed the *Columbus*'s arrival and was monitoring deep-space radio, this was the frequency range they'd most likely monitor. "Use both Anglo and Old English," she added. "We don't know who might be listening."

As the com officer moved to comply, Ana unbuckled her seat belt and carefully stood up. It had been more than forty-eight hours since she'd emerged from biostasis, yet her legs still felt weak. She let out her breath, then walked over to the helm. "Good job, Jon," she said quietly, patting him on the shoulder. "You handled that beautifully."

"Thank you, Captain." Parson barely glanced her way, but when he did there was a guarded look on his face. "Set course for rendezvous with Coyote?"

"Please do, by all means." A brief nod in response, then he turned back to his console, opening a window on his console's main screen that depicted a heliocentric diagram of the 47 Uma system. As she watched, he began entering new coordinates into the navigation subsystem, even though this was a task, like the turnaround maneuver, that AI could have handled just as efficiently.

A strange person, she once again reflected. Of the thirty men and women aboard *Columbus*, she knew Jonathan Parson the least well. Much of that could be owed to British reserve; that, and the single-minded determination of a young man who'd made his way through the ranks to become second officer aboard the second European Alliance starship. Yet even before they'd left Earth, he'd quietly rebuffed her attempts to get to know him better. Like Melville's Bartleby, he seemed to have no life outside his job. He came out of his cabin, did his shift, then returned to his cabin. When he ate, he did so alone; when he bathed, it was when no one else was in the officer PQ. He spoke to no one, and after a while no one spoke to him. Very efficient, and very weird.

Well . . . she had other things to worry about just now. "Carry on," she murmured, then turned to see her first officer beckoning her from the remote-imaging station. "Yes, Mr. Pacino?"

"New pictures of Coyote," he replied, pointing to a pair of flatscreens. "Something here you might want to see."

On the left screen was an optical image of the world, as captured in real-time by the navigation telescope mounted just above the main deflector. Although still fuzzy, it depicted a large moon: a planet, really, a little larger than Mars, its green-brown terrain traced by an intricate network of blue waterways, with white icecaps at its northern and southern poles. It wasn't the first time she'd seen close-up images of Coyote since they'd entered the system, yet once again she was struck by its beauty. A marble in the cosmos, Earth-like yet definitely not Earth.

"Lovely, isn't it?" Once again, it was as if Gabriel could read her thoughts. They'd served together for so long, though, that this wasn't a surprise. Indeed, for a little while during training, they'd indulged in a brief, furtive affair, before deciding that it was better for their respective careers if they no longer slept together. "But that's not what concerns me. Look here . . ."

He pointed to the screen on the right. High-resolution radio inferometry, a little less than fifteen minutes old, depicting an image of the planet as seen by radar beams directed at the planet and bounced back to the *Columbus*. "See something?"

Ana studied the screen. Monochromatic whorls and deep depressions and long lines: a topographic map of the world, more informative than the optical image, yet showing nothing unusual so far as she could see. "All right," she said after a moment, "I give up. What are you trying to show me?"

"Here's a hint. It's not what you see . . . it's what you don't see." Pacino expanded the focal point, allowing her to view the planet from a wider perspective, then waited for her to respond. When she didn't say anything, he pointed to a pair of tiny black dots suspended above Coyote's equator. "Low-orbit satellites . . . communications, possibly meteorological. Much what we'd expect. But if we can see those, shouldn't we also be seeing . . . ?"

"You're right." Ana leaned closer, resting the knuckles of her hands against the console. "Where's the *Spirit*? Or the *Alabama*?"

The first ship to 47 Ursae Majoris had been the URSS *Alabama*, launched by the United Republic of America in 2070. Hijacked, really, and that tale was legend in itself. No other starships had followed it for nearly two hundred years, until the Western Hemisphere Union had sent out five more ships between 2256 and 2260, each using the diametric drive that allowed for near light-speed travel. The last ship launched was the *Spirit of Social Collectivism Carried to the Stars*; it was known that the four previous Union vessels had been ordered to return to Earth once they'd delivered colonists to Coyote, but the *Spirit* had a military mission and was supposed to remain here until further notice. And one would naturally expect to find the *Alabama* still in orbit above Coyote.

Yet as she could plainly see, there were no starships. Only a couple of satellites. "I don't understand."

"Nor do I." Pacino moved a little closer, dropping his voice slightly so that he couldn't be overheard. "It's possible, of course, that the *Spirit* may have headed for home while we were still in transit."

"Perhaps." She absently reached up to push back her hair, before once again remembering that she had none. Like everyone else aboard, her scalp had been shaved before entering biostasis. She ought to start wearing her beret. "We'd have to examine the log to see if the AI registered any ships heading in the direction of Sol."

The *Columbus* had departed from Earth orbit on Jan 19, 2290, thirty years after the *Spirit*, yet more than ten years before the estimated arrival date of the *Alabama*. As fast as the Union ships traveled, or even as late as it had been before the European Alliance managed to develop the diametric drive on its own, the first radio messages transmitted by the *Alabama* still hadn't reached Earth before the *Columbus* had launched.

"Little chance of that," Pacino said, "but we can always check. Yet it doesn't answer the question . . . where's the *Alabama*?"

"Do Italians have to ask so many questions?" She gave him a sidelong glance.

"Are Russians always so obstinate?" He grinned back at her. A private joke, left over from when they'd once shared the same bed. "Look, we've already seen lights from the planet surface, right?"

She nodded. Earlier infrared photos, taken shortly after the *Columbus* had entered the system, had revealed dim sources of illumination scattered in a narrow band across Coyote's northern hemisphere.

"That means the earlier expeditions have established colonies," Pacino continued. "We just don't know what happened to the ships themselves."

A chill moved up her spine. "We don't know what happened to the *Galileo,* either," she murmured.

The smile vanished from Pacino's face. "That's another matter entirely," he whispered. "Don't borrow bad luck. We have to—"

The lockwheel on the hatch next to them suddenly turned clockwise. They looked around to see the hatch ease open, allowing a figure to emerge from the shaft that led up from the ship's lower decks.

"Pardon me." One of the civilian passengers paused on the ladder, uncertain of whether he should enter the command deck. "Is this a bad time to . . . ?"

"Not at all." Ana moved away from the console. "Please, come in. Perhaps you can help us solve a mystery."

"I rather doubt it, but . . ." Jonas Whittaker carefully stepped through the hatch. "Whatever I can do, please let me know."

CLARKSBURG / HAMALIEL 69 / 1200

"The boat's too slow," Carlos said. "I'm going to need—"

The long, sharp blast of the noon whistle startled him, causing him to wince as he clapped his hands against his ears. He glanced in the direction of the timber mill; the vast shed was nearly a hundred yards away, yet the steam whistle mounted on its slate roof was just close enough to deafen him. He waited until the noise subsided, then he spoke into the satphone again.

"Sorry 'bout that," he continued. "It's lunch time. Like I was saying, getting home by boat is too slow, so I need—"

"A gyro to fly out and pick you up." A faint note of amusement in Tomas's voice. *"We've already got you covered. Wendy called the Chief Proctor's office and asked them to send one over. Should be landing"*—a short pause while he cupped the phone to speak to someone else—*"in about thirty minutes. Forty-five, tops."*

"Outstanding. Thank you." Although he should have expected as much. As his chief of staff, Tomas Conseco was responsible for making sure that the president got from one place to another with as little fuss as possible, but the fact of the matter was that the Wendy handled a lot of these details when no one was looking. She'd once served a term on the Colonial Council, so she knew the drill better than anyone else who worked for him. "Tell the pilot to touch down—"

"Near the wharf. Got it. I . . ." A pause; Carlos heard voices in the background. *"Hang on a moment, boss."*

Again, Tomas muffled the phone with his hand. Something was obviously going on back in Liberty. Glancing over his shoulder, Carlos became aware of the curious looks being cast his way by passing townspeople. He stood outside a cheesemaker's shop on River Street, only a short distance from the wharf where the keelboat that had transported him from New Florida was moored. By custom, the president traveled by water when he paid state visits to the colonies. Everyone else did, after all, so why should the president of the Coyote Federation rate special treatment?

Most of the time, Carlos enjoyed the fact that even senior officials received few extra privileges than anyone else. He remembered what it had been like to grow up in the United Republic of America, where the government had become separated from the people and the unwritten rule was that those in power were somehow superior to those who'd put them there in the first place. All this had been rejected on Coyote; indeed, the First Article of the Liberty Compact held that the government existed to serve the public, not vice versa. When he walked down the street, he did so without bodyguards or entourage, and only on formal occasions did anyone address him as "Mr. President."

All the same, standing out here by himself, he was drawing attention that he didn't want just now. Turning away from the street, Carlos headed for the shop behind him. A bell jingled as he opened the front door, and the sharp aroma of fresh cheese surrounded him as he stepped inside. The young woman stacking wheels upon a shelf did a double-take as he entered; the last customer she expected today was the president.

"Pardon me, but is there a place where I can be alone?" Carlos held up his satphone. "Private call. Should take just a moment." Mildly flustered, she hastily ushered him through the beaded curtains of a keyhole door into a back room, where copper pots of goat's milk slowly simmered upon wood-fired stoves and a couple of men stirred curds within barrels. No one paid much attention to them as the clerk led him to an ice block–lined storeroom; she smiled sweetly and favored him with a brief curtsy before closing the door behind him.

A moment later, Tomas came back. *"Sorry to keep you waiting, but—"*

"Never mind. What's going on?"

"We just received a radio message from the ship." Tomas's voice was rushed. *"It's called the* Christopher Columbus, *and claims to be from the European Alliance. They say that they expect to achieve orbit over us by 0200 tomorrow."*

"Who were they trying to reach?"

"The message wasn't . . ." A murmur from somewhere in the background. *"Hold on, I'll put you through to Wendy."*

Another pause, then he heard his wife's voice. *"Carlos, the message was sent to anyone representing either the* Alabama *or the Western Hemisphere Union. Like Tomas said, it wasn't specific, but considering that it was sent first in English, then in Anglo, I guess they don't know exactly who's here."*

That made sense. If the new ship had taken nearly forty-nine years to get here, as had the previous starships using diametric drive, then it would have been launched even before the first radio signals from the *Alabama* reached Earth. "Has anyone sent a response?"

"No. We've maintained radio silence, pending your decision. In the meantime, I've contacted the Council members, along with the chairmen of the Defense and Interior committees. Hope you don't mind, but I knew you'd be out of touch until you got back into town, so—"

"Don't worry. You did the right thing." In fact, he had to admit, she'd done a better job than he would have. Wendy had been involved in colonial politics since she was a teenager, when she was elected to the Liberty Town Council, while Carlos had come into politics only reluctantly, first assuming the mayorship of Liberty following Captain Lee's death, then later being drafted to run as president. But while his wife was a natural-born stateswoman, Carlos's reputation came from being an explorer and war hero; although he was now the leader of the Coyote Federation, in many ways he was Wendy's political protégé.

"So what do we do now?" Even as he said this, he shut his eyes, swore at himself. "I mean, what do you think we should do now?"

"*Carlos . . .*" She took a deep breath. "*C'mon, you can't do this. You're in charge. I can't—*"

"Look, I'm in the storeroom of a cheese shop, all right? I'm making this up as I go along." He sat down on a stool, stared at the wax-encased wheels stacked on the shelves around him. "We've been through this before, and I don't want it to go the same way again. This time, I want the new guys to know where things stand from the beginning."

"*I agree. That's the consensus of the Council members I've spoken with, and same for the committee chairs. No one wants another war, but . . .*"

She didn't say more, nor did she have to. It had been over ten years, by LeMarean reckoning, since the *Glorious Destiny* had arrived from Earth, bringing with it the Matriarch Luisa Hernandez and the armed might of the Western Hemisphere Union. For three and a half years, the Union had maintained an authoritarian dictatorship over New Florida, while the Matriarch sought to assert military control over the rest of the planet. It had taken an armed uprising by the original colonists to overthrow the Union, yet it had come at the cost of many lives.

No one had any desire to repeat that experience. But neither did anyone want to give someone else from Earth the chance to take their world away from them again.

Carlos leaned forward, absently rubbing his forehead. "All right, send a message back to them. Tell 'em we're willing to meet with them down here . . . on Federation territory, not their ship. Give them the coordinates for Shuttlefield and inform that the president will be there to greet them." He thought a moment, then added: "And one more thing. Tell Chris I want him to mobilize the Proctors. Every blueshirt not on leave . . . no, skip that, all leaves are canceled. Put 'em in uniform, and break open the armory. Everyone gets a gun, and everyone gets put on the front line."

"*Are you sure you want to—?*"

"Yes, I'm sure. And get that gyro here as soon as you can."

"It's on the way. Don't stop for souvenirs."

He smiled at that. Wendy had a small collection of handcrafted wood bowls from Clarksburg; he made a point of picking up a new one for her every time he came out here. "I'll IOU one for the next trip. See you when I get back."

Carlos closed the satphone and put it back in his pocket, then left the storeroom. This time, the men working in the cheese shop noticed him, and the clerk was waiting for him just outside the door. Making a deliberate effort not to appear as if he was concerned about anything, he spent a few minutes touring the shop, inspecting their work and accepting a small wheel of smoked gouda as a gift. By the time he made his exit, the gyro from New Florida had appeared, a tiny black dot high above the sapphire waters of the West Channel.

As he waited in a square near the wharf, he took a moment to look around. At midday, Clarksburg went on about its everyday business. Here and there, he saw people moving along the wooden sidewalks, either heading home for lunch or having a sandwich and a mug of ale at one of the pubs along the riverside. Rough bark logs floated in a pond next to the mill, waiting to be loaded into the conveyer that would take them to the saws; a couple of teenagers played on the logs, trying to push each other off as they rolled beneath their feet. From somewhere nearby, he heard a burst of laughter as someone told someone else a funny story.

They'd come a long way in thirty-nine Earth-years: from little more than a hundred settlers struggling for survival upon a dangerous and unexplored world, to nearly seven thousand people in eight colonies scattered across the northern hemisphere. They still had their problems, to be sure, not the least of which was a shortage of advanced technologies they'd once taken for granted, yet their early hardships were now largely in the past. No one was starving; the wilderness had been tamed, and they were at peace.

And yet, on this sunny afternoon of another endless summer, he had the uneasy feeling that all this was about to change.

The skiff shuddered, then took a hard jolt that threw Jonas against his straps, almost knocking the wind from him. Gripping the armrests a little tighter, he took short, deep breaths, yet he refused to shut his eyes, knowing that this would only make him airsick.

"Having trouble?" From her seat on the right-hand side of the cockpit, Captain Tereshkova calmly observed the efforts of her second officer. "If 'you want any help . . ."

"No, ma'am. No problem at all." Parson pulled back on the yoke, then pushed forward on the throttle bar. The engines whined a little louder as the pilot compensated for an increase in atmospheric density. More air, more resistance; more resistance, more drag against *Isabella*'s wings. For a moment, it seemed as if they would encounter more turbulence, yet Parson was keeping an eye on the gauges; there was another jolt, less severe than before, then they found smooth air once more, and everything settled out.

Jonas let out his breath, tried to relax. Tereshkova turned her head to gaze back at him. "How are you doing there, Dr. Whittaker? Not going to be sick, I hope."

"No, no, I'm fine." Which was a lie. Although he tried to pretend that this was just like riding a jet back on Earth, the fact of the matter was that this wasn't Earth, nor had he been on a plane in . . . how long? Nearly 269 years, give or take a few months. Even when he'd left Earth, it had been aboard the New Guinea space elevator: a long, slow climb to geosynchronous orbit, with none of the high-g stress of a shuttle launch. "Doing great, thanks."

He gazed out the window beside him. Now that the *Isabella* had penetrated the thin layer of cirrus clouds, Coyote's northern hemisphere spread out below him, a vast mosaic of islands of all shapes and sizes, separated from one another by a maze of rivers and channels. No oceans to speak of;

the largest body of water was the equatorial river that wrapped itself around the planet's midsection like an immense serpent, becoming broad enough at one point to form a small sea. The enormous blue orb of 47 Ursae Majoris-B hovered above the western horizon, its ring-plane obscured by high clouds as it rose straight up into the deep purple sky.

An alien world. Again, he found himself awestruck by the simple fact that he was here. Although his life's ambition had been to build the first interstellar vessel, never had he truly expected to go to the stars himself. Even when he'd become involved in the conspiracy to steal the *Alabama*, its final destination had been something he'd thought about only in the most abstract of terms. But now, here he was.

Yet Caroline wasn't, and neither was Ellen. Once again, any sense of wonder he felt was suffused by the hollow pain of grief. His wife and daughter, long since dead and gone, lost to him forever. Not for the first time, he felt guilt gnawing at him. He'd cheated death, yes, but only at the cost of their lives . . .

"I'm sorry," he whispered, gazing at ghosts only he could see reflected in the window. "I'm so sorry . . ."

"Pardon me?" Tereshkova gazed back at him. "Did you say something?"

"Just thinking to myself." He drew a deep breath. "Shouldn't we be seeing the colony . . . um, New Florida . . . by now?"

"We're approaching it now." She pointed straight ahead, through the teardrop-shaped forward windows. "In a moment we'll be above—" She suddenly stopped, staring at something far below. "Is that what I think it is?"

Jonas craned his head to look. They were passing over a channel separating the island just ahead of them from the larger landmass to the east. For a moment, he didn't see what startled the captain so much, but then he spotted a dark, slender line that ran straight across the channel, an artifice that closely resembled . . .

"A bridge!" Parson yelled. "There's a bridge down there!"

Nor was that all they saw. As the skiff shed altitude, now they could make out other signs of human habitation. Small settlements lay on either side of the bridge, with a road leading inland through a quilt-like patchwork of farm fields, and even from several thousand feet they could see the regular lines of irrigation ditches.

"Someone's been busy," Tereshkova murmured.

"They've had a lot of time." Yet even so, Jonas was impressed. The farms lay here and there along the twisting road, isolated from one another by vast tracts of marshland, yet as the *Isabella* continued to descend, they saw that the settlements grew closer together until, as they passed low over a wide creek, they came upon a broad expanse of houses, barns, sheds, buildings both large and small.

Thirty-nine years, he thought. No wonder they've done so well. Give people a wide-open frontier and put them on their own for a few decades, then stand back and watch what happens. If nature doesn't kill them or they don't die of starvation, then they'll learn to live off the land. And these people were well-motivated for survival.

"We're coming in on the landing coordinates," Parson said. "I take it this is the Liberty colony."

"Liberty, or else Shuttlefield. I think they're two towns adjacent to one another." Tereshkova glanced back at Jonas. "We weren't given much information by the person with whom we spoke." Then she looked forward again, and pointed through the cockpit windows. "There, Mr. Parson. Landing beacons, twenty degrees port."

"Yes, ma'am. Lowering gear now." Parson reached up to an overhead panel, snapped a couple of toggle switches. A hard thump from belowdecks as belly hatches opened, then *Isabella*'s narrow prow lifted slightly as Parson throttled back the main engines and engaged the VTOL jets.

"Forty meters . . . thirty meters . . . twenty meters . . ." The second officer kept his eyes on his instruments as the skiff slowly descended. In the last few seconds before touchdown, a thick cloud of dust rose around the cockpit windows, obliterating everything from sight. "Ten . . . five . . . two . . ." Another jolt; an alarm sounded and red lamps blazed across his console. "Contact. We're on the ground, Captain."

"Thank you, Mr. Parson. Nice flying." While the pilot shut down the engines, the captain touched a couple of buttons on the com panel. "*Isabella* to *Columbus*, do you copy?"

"*We read you*, Isabella." The first officer's voice came over the ceiling speaker. "*Telemetry indicates you've landed. Do you confirm?*"

"Affirmative, *Columbus*, we're down and safe. Remain on standby until further notice. *Isabella* over and out." Tereshkova switched off the radio, then unbuckled her harness and let the straps retract into the seat as she turned to look at her passenger. "I assume you're feeling better now, Dr. Whittaker."

"Very much so." Jonas struggled with the clasp of the seat belt for a moment until the captain stood up, walked back to where he was sitting, and opened it for him. "Thank you," he mumbled, embarrassed again by his incompetence. "So . . . what now?"

"I believe much of that's going to depend on them."

Still seated, his logbook open in his lap, Parson gestured with his pen toward the cockpit windows. "Seems we have an audience."

Jonas gazed out the side window. Now that the dust had settled, he could see, a few dozen feet away, several hundred people gathered just beyond the landing beacons. No one approached the skiff, though, and it appeared as if the crowd was being held back by several men in dark blue shirts. It wasn't hard to miss the fact that they were carrying rifles.

"Doesn't look very friendly, does it?" Parson added.

"No, it doesn't." Tereshkova started to reach toward the com panel again, then thought better of it. "Let's not jump to conclusions. Dr. Whittaker, if you'll join me, perhaps we can get this straightened out. Mr. Parson, I know this is asking much of you, but—"

"Yes, ma'am. I'll remain aboard, just in case." He nodded toward a locker in the rear of the passenger compartment. "Captain, if I may remind you . . . ?"

"Perhaps we should . . ." She hesitated, considering her options, then shook her head. "No. Keep the weapons stowed. I don't think it'll make a good first impression if we walked down the gangway with guns in hand." She glanced at Jonas. "Agreed?"

"Completely." Nonetheless, the sight of armed men at the landing site was the last thing he'd anticipated. Indeed, he wondered what had happened here that provoked this sort of reception. "Maybe it's time to practice a little diplomacy."

"That's why we brought you." Tereshkova patted his shoulder as she moved past him. "With luck, maybe you'll find a friend or two out there."

I wouldn't count on it, he thought, but he rose to his feet and followed her to the main hatch.

"That insignia . . ." Carlos pointed to the blue-red-green flag painted on the vertical stabilizer of the spacecraft's starboard wing. "European Alliance?"

"It's theirs, all right . . . but they've come a long way." Tomas caught the look on the president's face and quickly corrected himself. "Level of technology, I mean. When I left, the EA didn't have any starships. In fact, they only had a few lunar colonies." He nodded toward the ship. "This is something new."

"This is new to all of us." The spacecraft that just landed didn't resemble the shuttles used by the Western Hemisphere Union: smaller and more streamlined, with down-swept wings and forward cabin extended at the end of a midsection neck, it vaguely resembled a goose. He cast a glance at the Proctors ringed around the edge of the landing field. Thirty men and women in blue shirts stood at attention, their carbines at their sides. He caught the eye of Chris Levin; the Chief Proctor for more than thirty years, his best friend since childhood, he gazed back at Carlos, gave him a tight nod. His people were ready.

"Maybe they should stand down." Wendy stood next to him, her hands nervously fidgeting at her sides. "It's like greeting house guests by pointing a gun to their heads."

"They're not guests," Carlos said quietly, "and I want them to know exactly where they stand." Perhaps this was only a show of force, yet it would let whoever was aboard the shuttle know that their unexpected arrival was being treated with suspicion. "If the Union had been given this sort of treatment when they showed up—"

"Nothing would have been different," Wendy argued. "We're establishing a bad precedent. We don't know who these people are, what they're—"

"Someone's coming out," Tomas said.

The belly hatch opened, revealing a ramp built into its underside. No sooner had it unfolded and lowered to the ground than a pair of boots appeared on the steps. A young woman made her way down the ladder, followed moments later by a middle-aged man. Both wore tan jumpsuits, and matching berets covered their shaved heads, attesting to the fact that they must have recently emerged from biostasis. They stopped at the bottom of the ladder, gazed uncertainly at the crowd gathered around the spacecraft.

"You're on," Wendy whispered.

Carlos took a deep breath, then marched out to the spacecraft. After a moment's hesitation, Tomas fell in beside him. The younger man was still getting used to his role as Carlos's senior aide; indeed, Carlos reflected, it hadn't been all that many years ago when he'd been little more than a boy, setting foot on Coyote for the first time with his parents. No wonder he was nervous.

As if I'm not, he thought.

Carlos stopped in front of the newcomers, extended his hand. "Welcome to New Florida, and to Coyote," he began, speaking in Anglo. "I'm Carlos Montero, President of the Coyote Federation. This is my chief of staff, Tomas Conseco."

The woman accepted his handshake. "Pleased to meet you, President Montero," she replied, and although she also spoke Anglo, he noted a thin Slavic accent to her voice. "Captain Anastasia Tereshkova, commanding officer of the—"

"No . . . it can't be."

She was interrupted by the man standing behind her. His eyes wide with disbelief, he regarded Carlos with open-mouthed astonishment. "You . . . you can't be Carlos," he stammered. "You . . . I'm sorry, but you . . ."

Captain Tereshkova turned to look at him. "Dr. Whittaker, do you know him?"

"I . . . no, but . . ." Whittaker cautiously stepped past her. "Yes, I know him. It's been such a long time, but—"

"I don't believe . . ." Carlos began, then his voice trailed off. Although his first impulse was to deny any previous association, long-buried memories began to resurface. The face was familiar, although in a distant sort of way. And the name . . . Whittaker, Whittaker. He'd heard that name before.

"Do I know you?" he asked. "Have we met?"

"We have. Maybe you don't remember, but . . ." He shook his head. "It's incredible how much you look like your father. If I didn't know better, I could have sworn—"

"You knew my father? There's no way you could . . ."

Before he could finish, he heard someone running toward them. Carlos barely had a chance to turn around before Chris pushed both him and Tomas aside. "Dr. Whittaker!" he yelled, then he dropped his carbine and wrapped his arms around him. "I don't believe it! You're alive!"

For an instant, it seemed as if Whittaker was just as shocked as anyone else. Indeed, it had been many years since Carlos had seen Chris express this much emotion about anything. Then Jonas carefully prized Chris away from him and took a long, hard look at his face, and tears began to seep from the corners of his eyes.

"Chris Levin," he whispered, his voice choked. "Oh, my god . . . how much you've grown up."

And now, all at once, memories returned. Whittaker. Dr. Jonas Whittaker. Another scientist, a physicist who'd once worked for the old Federal Space Agency. Several years older than his father, a senior colleague who'd visited Carlos's home in Huntsville, had dinner with his family. Carlos hadn't known him very well, but once during a summer outing in the park he'd shown him and Chris how to feed catfish from the footbridge. And he'd had a daughter, a few years older than either him or Chris.

"This is impossible," he said. "You should be dead."

He didn't mean for it to come out quite this way, yet it did. Hearing a strangled gasp, Carlos glanced over his shoulder to see Wendy covering her face with her hands. Captain Tereshkova stared at him in shock as mortified laughter rose from those in the crowd who'd heard what he'd just said.

Yet Whittaker simply smiled. "You're right, son. I'm a dead man. But in my case, it was only a temporary condition."

LIBERTY / HAMALIEL 70 / 0945

Although Carlos insisted upon having proctors present when the *Isabella* landed, it had been Wendy's idea to hold a small reception for the *Columbus*'s captain. Carlos had been reluctant at first, but it turned out that his wife's instinct for diplomacy was correct. Once it became obvious that the first contact would be peaceful, Carlos quietly asked Chris to dismiss his proctors, then suggested to Captain Tereshkova that they move the meeting to the grange hall in Liberty. She graciously accepted his invitation and demonstrated her own good intentions by asking Jonathan Parson, her second officer, to disembark from the skiff and join them.

It was a little late for breakfast and still too early for lunch, but nonetheless the chefs had laid out a smorgasbord: redfish fritters, cornbread, fried

tomatoes and mixed greens, along with apple strudel and coffee. Besides
the fact that the newcomers had been in biostasis for nearly forty-nine
years, it had been a long time since they'd eaten anything except ship's rations. Their guests filled their plates, then everyone took seats at one of the
blackwood tables that ran down the center of the room.

Captain Tereshkova was curious about their surroundings, and Carlos
explained that the grange had been built by the original colonists during
their first year on Coyote. He pointed out the mural of the *Alabama* that
hung from one wall and the original flag of the Coyote Federation suspended from the rafters. He attempted to give her a short history of the
colony, yet he didn't get a chance. Although Tomas had tried to restrict the
guest list to those officials who needed to be there—Colonial Council
representatives, the chairs of various committees, members of the Liberty
and Shuttlefield town councils, and so forth—the grange was jammed with
VIPs, and everyone wanted to have a minute—if not five or ten—with the
members of the *Columbus* party. Chris had posted a couple of proctors at the
front door, but when Carlos happened to glance out a window, he saw that
Main Street swarmed with townspeople curious to see the first visitors
from Earth in nearly a generation.

Despite the fact that, as commanding officer of the *Columbus,* Anastasia Tereshkova was the center of attention, Carlos and Chris weren't the
only ones who remembered Jonas Whittaker. There were relatively few
members of the original group of D.I.'s smuggled aboard the *Alabama*
who were still alive, but they had been hastily brought to the grange hall
to meet Whittaker. When Henry Johnson—the oldest surviving member
of the *Alabama* party, now half-blind and able to walk only with the assistance of a cane—laid eyes on a friend whom he'd long since given up
for dead, there were a few seconds of stunned surprise as Jonas found
himself gazing upon someone who'd once been a few years younger than
himself and now appeared old enough to be his father. Then the two men
threw themselves into each others arms, laughing and weeping at the
same time.

Next appeared Sissy Levin, Chris's mother. This was a sad moment, for
it was when she introduced her second husband, Ben Harlan, that Jonas
learned that his colleague Jim Levin was no longer living; like Carlos's parents, he'd been killed by a boid. And right behind her were those whom

Jonas recognized, but knew less well: Bernie and Vonda Cayle, both of whom were alive and well, and Carrie Geary, who'd survived the loss of her husband three years before, and Kuniko Okada, who'd become Wendy's adoptive mother and now served as chancellor of the Colonial University.

And just how had Whittaker himself survived? Once again, Carlos found himself wondering this, as he watched a steady procession of lined and age-spotted faces come forth to meet someone who, for all intents and purposes, had aged little since they'd seen him. Although the question was often asked, Whittaker avoided giving a straight answer, dodging behind platitudes like *clean living* or *good genes, I guess* before changing the subject. And meanwhile Tereshkova carefully eluded the more probing queries, while Jonathan Parson remained noncommittal, saying little to anyone save for the occasional question about the weather or how the colonists had managed to cultivate apple orchards.

Yet Carlos remained patient, allowing the reception to run its course until finally, a couple of hours later, he'd managed to detach Tereshkova, Parson, and Whittaker from the crowd and lead them to the conference room in the back of the grange. Wendy was there, as were Tomas and several members of the Executive Committee; at Whittaker's insistence, Henry Johnson was invited as well. Once everyone was seated and the door was shut, Carlos called the meeting to order and the small talk came to an end.

"I imagine you have quite a few questions," Tereshkova began, "and we certainly have a few of our own, but let me make one thing clear from the beginning. The European Alliance only wishes to open peaceful negotiations with the colonies, for the mutual benefit of both the EA and the Coyote Federation."

A nice start, Carlos thought. Tereshkova had surmised that the *Columbus*'s unexpected arrival was being regarded with distrust, and was trying to defuse this. "I appreciate this, Captain," he replied, clasping his hands together on the table, "and I apologize if you were offended by the way you and your party were received in Shuttlefield. You have to realize, though, that your predecessors didn't have the same . . . well, benign intentions."

"No apologies necessary, Mr. Pres . . . um, Mr. Montero." A quick smile as Tereshkova remembered that he preferred to be addressed in a less formal fashion. "Although my knowledge of your history is still far from complete, I'm fully aware that the Western Hemisphere Union attempted to use force to take over your colonies. Even before we left Earth, my government had received intelligence reports indicating that this was their intent."

"I take it, then, that the Alliance isn't on good terms with the Union?"

Tereshkova crossed her legs. "Although they aren't engaged in active hostilities . . . at least not when we left . . . all the same there's political rivalry between the two blocs. The Alliance is a capitalist democracy, while the Union is based upon collective socialism, so if they had still been in control, we would've had to negotiate with them on those terms. However, since they're no longer here, we're able to deal directly with those who colonized Coyote in the first place."

"Then you're aware that the Union was deposed during a revolution," Carlos said, and Tereshkova nodded. "And I also take it that you've learned that the Federation is composed of eight colonies."

"Liberty, Shuttlefield, Leeport, and Bridgeton on New Florida." Tereshkova gazed up at the ceiling as she recited from memory. "Forest Camp, Defiance, and New Boston on Midland, and Clarksburg on Great Dakota. Not counting several smaller settlements here and there that haven't yet gained sufficient population to be officially represented by the Colonial Council."

"You're a good listener," Wendy said. "My compliments."

A wry smile. "It's my job to listen, Ms. Montero. I'm not only *Columbus*'s commanding officer, but I'm also something of a trade emissary." Her expression became more serious. "So once more, let me assure you, I'm not here to be a conqueror. My government believed that the Union's attempt to take military control was doomed to failure, and I'm only too happy to learn that their predictions were correct."

"I'll take you at your word," Carlos replied. *At least for the time being.* "But if you say that you're here on a trade mission, then that raises an important question. Given the long time it takes for anyone's ships to get here, then return home, how can—?"

"Carlos?" Whittaker interrupted by raising a hand. "If you don't mind, perhaps I can explain?"

"I think . . ." Henry Johnson coughed in his hand, then leaned forward upon his cane. "I think I know what you're going to say, Jonas. But before you get to that part, would you kindly explain just how you managed to get here in the first place? And why I shouldn't be changing your diapers now?"

Muted laughter from around the table, yet there were also nods and murmurs. Although the two eldest members of ExCom had once belonged to the *Alabama* crew—Jud Tinsley, originally the executive officer, and Ellery Balis, formerly the ship's quartermaster—Carlos and Wendy had been in their teens when the *Alabama* was hijacked. Yet now they both were only a few years younger than Whittaker himself, at least in physical terms, while Jud and Ellery could have passed as a pair of older uncles. Henry was joking, of course, but beneath that was a serious question.

"Jealous, aren't we?" Jonas replied, and even though this was received with a few chuckles, Henry wasn't amused. Jonas settled back in his chair, folded his arms together. "Very well, then . . ."

Jonas kept his eyes shut as he felt the hospital cart come to a halt; *he remained perfectly still, keeping his breathing as shallow as possible. Through the sheet that covered his body, he heard murmured voices, some belonging to the Prefects who'd carried him from the conference room. A door opened and shut, and then he heard a pair of footsteps approach him.*

"They're gone," Shaw said quietly. "You can get up now."

Jonas opened his eyes as Shaw pulled back the sheet, blinked hard against the glare of the ceiling lights. The cart had been wheeled into what appeared to be an infirmary; an examination table lay nearby, surrounded by all the customary medical apparatus, with cabinets lining the clean white walls. A short young woman wearing a surgical gown stood next to Shaw, her blond hair pulled back behind a cap; she regarded Jonas with nervous eyes, casting an occasional glance at the closed doors where the Prefect whom Jonas had met earlier now stood guard.

"We need to get him cleaned up." The doctor spoke to Shaw as if Jonas wasn't there, even as she pointed to his blood-drenched shirt. "I know you had to do this, but we can't risk having him contaminated." She picked up a large metal bowl filled with a watery pink solution, placed it on the cart next to him. "Strip, then use this to wash yourself," she said, handing him a sponge and a plastic bag. "Dump your clothes in here. And try not to make a mess."

His shirt buttons were slick with blood, yet although he wanted to get out of his clothes as soon as he could, he was uneasy about disrobing in front of strangers. It was almost as unnerving as having a pint of warm blood squirted on his chest as he lay upon the carpeted floor of the conference room, then having the Prefect fire a blank at him from close range. "What's the rush? I'm dead, aren't I?"

"Yes, you are, but we've got to make sure you're still dead by the time Dr. Kendrick gets through with you." Shaw smiled at him. "It won't be long until an ambulance arrives to take you to the mortuary, and by then we have to switch you for one of the cadavers she's generously agreed to provide." He looked at Kendrick. "You have the body, don't you?"

"In the storeroom." Turning away from them, she walked across the tile floor, her long cotton robe brushing against her ankles. "With any luck, no one will notice the substitution before they've cremated it."

"They won't," Shaw said. "We've done this sort of thing before."

Jonas refrained from asking the obvious questions; it seemed that Shaw had some previous experience with disposing of corpses in the middle of the night. Likewise, he also wondered how many times Shaw had faked someone's death. It was all so perfect; the blood, the gunshot, the story told to the Prefects standing outside the room that Jonas had tried to attack Shaw and that his bodyguard had acted to protect him. This, and the fact that a medical facility lay conveniently close at hand, complete with a doctor who just happened to be working late. And now, another body that would soon be cremated in the interests of national security.

Shaw worked for a corrupt system, yet he'd learned how to manipulate that same system to his own ends. No one would question his version of what had happened, and even if they did, he had witnesses to back him up. A stone alibi. All this might have been comforting, if Jonas hadn't known where it was leading.

Once he'd stripped off his clothes and given himself a sponge bath, Kendrick returned to give him a quick yet thorough physical, all the while asking him questions about his medical history. Apparently satisfied with his answers, she administered a half dozen injections, jabbing his biceps again and again with a syringe gun; she didn't bother to tell him what she was giving him, so he assumed that they were antibiotics of one sort or another. Then she handed him a bedpan and ordered him to relieve himself, right then and there. And the humiliation didn't stop there; while Shaw watched from the corner of the room, Kendrick made him lay down on the cold metal surface of the operating table and, using an electric razor, shaved his entire body, from his head down to his chest and pubic area.

"Clock's ticking, Maggie." Shaw glanced at his watch. "We don't have much time left."

"Don't rush me," Kendrick muttered, yet she was clearly moving as fast as she could. She handed Jonas a cotton gown, then stood back and waited for him to get off the table. "All right, you're done. Now come with me—"

A keycard slipped into an electronic lock opened a sealed door on the other side of the room. A faint whuff of pressurized air as the door slid open, and then Jonas followed the doctor into an adjacent room, as cold and antiseptic as the one they'd just left. "You can't come in," Kendrick said, looking over her shoulder at Shaw. "We have to keep this place—"

"I won't touch a thing." All the same, he stopped just inside the door, his hands in his coat pockets. "You probably don't recognize this place, Dr. Whittaker," he went on, "but I'm sure you know what it is."

Gazing around the room, Jonas nodded, and shivered with a chill that went farther than his flesh. In the center of the room rested three ceramic-alloy containers, faintly resembling coffins save for the tiny windows and the instrument panels at one end. Biostasis cells, used by FSA for testing long-term human hibernation in preparation for Project Starlight. One of the cells was closed, but the other two lay open, their raised lids revealing the gelatin pads within.

"Your ticket to the twenty-third century," Shaw said, as Jonas gingerly stepped farther into the room. "Maybe longer, I don't know. Sorry, but we can't be sure how long you'll—"

"I know. You've told me." Jonas shuddered, took a deep breath. He had a sudden impulse to turn and run for his life, yet there was nothing behind him save for certain death. Indeed, for all intents and purposes, he was already dead; this was merely the anteroom to a dreamless form of limbo. "How will . . . how will they know me? On the other side, I mean."

"They won't." Kendrick nodded toward the closed cell. "That's Test Subject 11. He went in two and a half years ago, and even I don't know who he is, other than the fact that he was a volunteer. All his records have been scrubbed, in exchange for his cooperation in this experiment. You'll be known as Test Subject 12, and you'll be treated the same way. When you're revived—"

"I won't be anyone." Jonas hugged himself. "I'll be nameless, a nonperson. No past, no proof of who I was."

"No. No, that's not true." As Shaw took a tentative step forward, he withdrew from his coat pocket a plastic packet about the size of a manila envelope. He extended it to Kendrick. "Here's all your records . . . personal, private, everything my people *were able to copy from your files. It's all on minidisc. I've been assured that it'll last a few hundred years without noticeable degradation."*

Kendrick took the packet. She quickly examined it, making sure that it was sealed, then brushed away some lint and handed it to Jonas. He studied it for a second. *"And from what you've told me, it also contains my notes for—"*

"Everything we've discussed." Apparently Shaw wasn't willing to trust even Dr. Kendrick with some things. *"It's all there. All you have to do is enter your old passwords."*

Jonas gazed at the packet, then at the open biostasis cell. *"You think of everything, don't you? Except that I'll be alone when I wake up . . ."*

"We're getting down to the wire." Shaw glanced at his watch again. *"Either you go, or . . ."*

"Next time your man shoots me, he'll use real bullets." Jonas sighed, then turned to Kendrick. *"All right, let's get it over."*

So then he removed his gown and lay down in the nearest cell, carefully placing the packet behind his left shoulder. He watched while Dr. Kendrick inserted plastic tubes in the veins of his arms. She did so with the reverence of an ancient Egyptian priest preparing a pharaoh for his entry to the afterlife, and for the first time her touch became tender, her voice soft. And since he never saw Roland Shaw again, he didn't get a chance to either thank or curse him. Yet, as she injected him with the drugs that would put him in a coma for the next two and half centuries, Kendrick leaned close to him.

"Good luck," she whispered. *"I envy you."*

Before he could ask what she meant by that, he fell asleep.

"And you were in biostasis for . . . how long?" Carlos asked.

"Two hundred and twelve years." Whittaker said this as a matter of fact, yet for a moment he closed his eyes, almost as if recalling what it had been like to have slept for almost a quarter of a millennium. "I was revived on August 12, 2282 . . . just about nine years ago." He stopped himself. "I mean, about nine years before the *Columbus* left Earth. Sorry, I'm still getting used to this myself."

"Happens to us all," Henry said drily. "Getting old is a bitch."

More chuckles, and Jonas went on. "By then, of course, the URA no longer existed. On the other hand, since I wasn't even on Earth anymore . . ."

Wendy raised an eyebrow. "If you weren't on Earth, then where—?"

"Shaw apparently didn't want to take any chances with anyone reviving me, so he had my cell transported to a URS military base on the Moon." Jonas picked up a glass of water, took a sip. "A small research installation on the lunar farside. Top secret, and completely off the map. After the Republic fell, it was abandoned and forgotten. I'd probably still be there if an expedition from the International Geographic Society hadn't rediscovered it. And that's where they found me." He glanced at Tereshkova and briefly smiled. "Luckily, the expedition was Russian-led. They brought my cell back to St. Petersburg, and that's where I was revived."

"Lucky, indeed," Tereshkova added. "If Dr. Whittaker had been found by a Union-led expedition, then they would've also found the disk containing his notes. And if that had happened, then chances are that we wouldn't be here."

"All right. Now you've lost me." Carlos held up a hand. "You mentioned that disk, but you didn't say what was on it. And you haven't told us why Roland Shaw went to the trouble of faking your death and putting you in suspended animation. Why did—?"

"Starbridges."

Until now, Henry had remained silent. Now, upon speaking, all eyes turned toward the elderly physicist. "You finally did it, didn't you?" he added, ignoring the others as he stared down the table at his former Marshall colleague. "You figured out how to build starbridges."

"C'mon now, Henry." Whittaker slowly shook his head. "We knew how to build them even before the *Alabama* left. We just lacked the technological capability, that's all." Then he smiled. "But now . . . yes, we have it. It's all there."

Henry's mouth dropped open. He sat up a little straighter in his chair. "You must be joking. You've—?"

"Will one of you please tell the rest of us what you're talking about?" Wendy asked impatiently. "What in heaven's name is a starbridge?"

Before either Henry or Jonas could respond, Tereshkova gently cleared her throat. "This may be a good time for a visual presentation." She pointed to the comp at Carlos's end of the table. "Does that operate, Mr. Montero? And the screen, too?"

"Umm . . . more or less." Like all other electronic equipment left behind by the Union, the comp was an antique, as was the flatscreen behind him. They'd been seldom used, though, so he had doubts that they'd still work. Like so much other Earth-made equipment that had gradually worn out over the years, it was difficult to find even a pad that functioned. He reached forward to switch on the comp, and was relieved to hear a faint beep as its aged hard drive creaked to life once more. "Yes, I think they do."

Tereshkova raised a skeptical eyebrow, but said nothing as she drew a small pad from her pocket and plugged it into the comp's external port. She tapped on the keys, and the wallscreen flickered for an instant before resolving into a grainy image: a three-dimensional wire-model of a ring-shaped structure.

"This is a starbridge," she began.

Henry leaned closer to Carlos. "Watch this," he whispered. "You're going to love it."

HAMALIEL 70 / 1832

Twilight was settling upon the town by the time Carlos and Wendy returned home. The meeting had only lasted a few hours, but after it broke up they spent the afternoon showing the visitors around town. Since Captain Tereshkova had accepted their invitation to spend the night in Liberty, Wendy arranged for them to stay at a small inn near the grange, and once the tour was over Chris escorted them over there.

Yet the day wasn't done yet. Carlos and Wendy had invited Henry Johnson over for supper, so they met the old man back at the grange. The lights of their house were on, and when they came in through the door, they found that Susan had already fixed dinner. Their daughter had briefly attended the reception, but had returned to the university to teach her afternoon class. Once she'd learned that her parents were showing the visitors around town, though, she'd canceled class. She knew her parents would be hungry and decided that her biology students could use an extra day to prepare for their next exam.

"Besides," she said as she laid out another setting at the table, "there's no sense in trying to teach 'em anything today. All they want to talk about is the *Columbus*."

"Fine with me." Carlos sat down to remove his boots and exchange them for a pair of catskin slippers. Their two dogs, Zack and Jake, cavorted around him, competing for his attention. "It was my turn to cook anyway." He looked at Susan askance. "Not leftover stew, I hope."

"Fed it to the dogs. Went to the market and bought a chicken . . . and don't give me that look, Papa. I sprung for it myself." Spotting her mother lifting the lid of the pot simmering on top of the stove, she hastened over to snatch it away from her. "And don't mess with my bird! I didn't put in too much garlic this time."

"Lord, I hope not." Henry wheezed slightly as he settled into a wicker chair next to the kitchen table. "Last time I ate your chicken, I had gas for three days."

"Henry!" Wendy started to scold him, but he and Carlos were already cracking up, so she surrendered to the inevitable and went into the bedroom to change into her robe. Carlos poured some waterfruit wine for himself and their guest, then stoked a fire in the flagstone hearth. It had been a long day for everyone, and it was good to be home at last.

Little of consequence was discussed over dinner, but once Susan cleared the table and Carlos put the plates in the sink, the four of them retired to the hearth. With drinks in hand and the dogs curled up between them, the topic of conversation turned to what had been discussed at the meeting. As usual, Susan was sworn to secrecy, something she'd understood ever since she was old enough to know that most of the things she heard in her living room weren't meant for public knowledge.

"This is beyond me." Wendy pulled a shagswool comforter around herself as she gazed into the fire. "I mean, I understand the concept of wormholes and all that, but the idea that we can create them . . ." She shook her head. "It doesn't seem possible."

"Oh, it's possible, all right." Henry finished loading his clingberry pipe with cloverweed and lit the bowl with a twig from the fireplace. "We understood the basic principles a long time ago. Only thing we didn't know was how to do it at will. Now it sounds like they've got that part licked."

"Let me get this straight." Carlos stood up to crack open a window. He normally didn't allow smoking in his house, but for Henry he made an exception. "You've got two starbridges . . . one in Lagrange orbit between Earth and the Moon . . ."

"Uh-huh." Henry puffed on his pipe as he idly scratched Zack behind the ears. "That one's already been built. Or should be, by now."

"And the other one . . . the one that hasn't been built yet . . . would be in trojan orbit between here and Bear."

"That's correct. Two entrances at either end of a tunnel . . . or a bridge, if you want to think of it that way. Only in this case, one port can't function without the other, because if you tried to enter the tunnel without having an exit on the other side, you'd just fall into a singularity and be crushed to nothingness."

"So that's what they've brought here," Wendy said. "The materials they need to build a second starbridge. The first gate is already . . . should already . . . be in place, and the second one . . ."

"The components are aboard the *Columbus*, right." Henry removed the pipe from his mouth, absently studied the embers of the bowl. "A rather elegant feat of engineering, really. Instead of the vanes used by Union ships, *Columbus*'s diametric drive was built as a torus. So all they have to do is dismantle the ship, then reassemble it in trojan orbit as the starbridge and its gatehouse. Saves on time and material."

"That's what Captain Tereshkova wants to show us," Carlos said. "She's invited Wendy and me to ride back on the *Isabella* tomorrow morning, so she can let us see the *Columbus* firsthand."

"Wish I could come along, but I don't think I could handle it." Henry winced and shook his head. "Damn, I hate getting old. Anyway, once they've rebuilt the diametric drive as the focusing ring, all they'd have to do is activate the swiftgate. They can do that easily enough by reversing the drive's polarity to open a quantum singularity in Bear's gravity well, then thread the aperture with negative energy so that they create a stable wormhole. After that, it's mainly a matter of expanding it to a usable size. They can do that by—"

"Sure. Got that part." In truth, it was over his head, and Carlos was too tired to listen to another lecture in quantum physics. "Let's assume that it works," he said, leaning against the mantle. "Starbridges between here and Earth. Instead of forty-nine years, it just takes a few seconds for a ship to get from here to there."

"Or from there to here," Wendy murmured.

"Right." Susan nodded in agreement with what her mother had just said. "It's not so bad when Earth is forty-six light-years away. But when it's only a few hundred thousand miles . . ."

"Not even that far," Henry said. "Look, let's say we've got a couple of starbridges right here in this house. One here, in front of the fireplace, and the other . . . oh, say, over by the kitchen." He pointed to the next room. "That's about twelve feet, right? But if I walked through the one here, I'd instantly come out through the starbridge over there. You could even look through the wormhole and see me standing in the kitchen. The distance between here and there would simply cease to exist."

"Uh-huh." Susan looked at the others. "Am I the only one here who thinks this might be a bad idea? Do we really want to have a fleet of starships coming through the swiftgate and parking themselves on our front doorstep?"

No one said anything. Carlos found himself gazing at the boid skull that hung from the wall above the fireplace. As a young man, he'd killed that boid while making a solo journey down the Great Equatorial River. Susan hadn't yet been born, but just as his *hegira* had been the pivotal moment of his life, her earliest memories were those of the years when the *Alabama* colonists had lived in a tree house village, her father gone for long periods of time to wage a guerilla war against the Union. She was almost thirty-one now, but her life had been shaped by the revolution. She knew nothing of Earth except distrust for anyone who came from there.

"No one wants to have the Union on our backs again," he said quietly. "Believe me, I'm the last guy to want to fight another war. But if this technology exists, sooner or later someone's going to use it. At least now, we have a choice . . . do we control it, or do we let it control us?"

Susan stared at him. "I don't know what you're—"

"Hush, dear. Listen to your father." Henry exhaled pale blue smoke. "Go on, son."

"What I'm trying to say is, we've got a chance to turn this to our

advantage." Carlos moved away from the mantle, took a seat next to Susan. "Look, what's one of the biggest problems we have now? Or, to put it
another way, what's the root cause of a lot of our problems?"

"Weardown," Susan said.

"Right. Everything we brought with us from Earth is wearing down.
Comps, solar cells, engines, guns, even hand tools . . . they're getting used
up. The last time anything new was brought here was almost seven years
ago. That's by our calendar. Call it twenty-one by Gregorian reckoning . . ."

"And when they've worn out, we've replaced them."

"No. All we've done is make substitutes, or learned how to get along
without. That's easy when you have to . . . oh, say, replace a axe-handle.
But just yesterday I had to tell your Aunt Marie that we probably couldn't
build more wind turbines because we didn't have any generators to spare.
And you saw what happened in the conference room when we switched
on the comp. I thought it was going to fry out on us."

"It's worse than that." Wendy leaned forward in her chair. "Kuniko
told me yesterday that the clinic is running low on antibiotics. We had a
good stockpile left when the Union left, but they're almost used up. In another year or so, we'll be down to using herbal medicines almost exclu-
sively. I don't want to be the doctor who has to treat a case of ring disease
with nothing more than ball plant extract and an ice pack."

"So what are you saying? We give up our independence just to get a lot
of stuff?" Susan looked at Carlos askance. "Me good injun. Want lots of
wampum from white man. Trade lousy island for some trinkets . . ."

"What've you been letting this kid read lately?" Henry leaned forward to
knock out his pipe in the fireplace. "Haven't heard that since I was . . ."

"Got it from a history disk." Susan ignored him. "Papa, you know what
I'm talking about. If we let them build a starbridge, then we'll have ships
coming through by the hundreds, even thousands. They'll—"

"It's not quite as easy as that." Henry put the pipe back in his pocket.
"The starbridges consume a lot of energy. It'll take a while for them to
recharge between each passage. Not only that, but the wormhole is only so
large. Even if we receive only a few ships every year or so . . ." He
shrugged. "I don't think we'll see much more difference than when we received five Union ships in a two-year stretch."

"But each of those ships carried a thousand immigrants," Wendy said, "and none of them ready to be colonists. I don't want to go back to where we were when Shuttlefield was a squatter camp. That was horrible."

"So we negotiate with them. Reach some sort of agreement." Carlos reached for the bottle of wine. "Look, from what we've been told, the EA isn't the same as the Union. They're offering trade . . . raw material in exchange for advanced technology. Earth's resources have been used up, and they're reaching the limits of what they can get from the Moon and Mars. With the starbridges, it will actually be easier for them to transport material from Coyote than it is from within the solar system . . . their solar system, I mean. And in trade, we get—"

"All the things we need here," Susan said. "New comps, and drugs, and machines that haven't been worn out. All right, I get that part. But what if . . . ?"

The dogs heard the visitors before anyone else. One moment, Zack and Jake were quietly dozing next to the fireplace; the next, they scrambled to their feet, growling and barking as they rushed across the room. Carlos barely had time to turn around before there was a knock on the door.

"What in the world?" Wendy asked.

"I have no idea." Shushing the dogs, Carlos stood up, walked over to the front door and opened it. Within the pale glow of the fish-oil lamp, he saw Chris standing on the front porch. And just behind him, Anastasia Tereshkova.

"Good evening. What brings you out so late?" Then he glanced at Tereshkova. "No problems, I hope."

"I hope not," Chris said, "but Captain Tereshkova—"

Before he could go on, Tereshkova stepped forward. In the cool of the evening, she was wearing the wool poncho she'd been given as a gift by one of the merchants in town. Until now, her face had worn a constant smile, yet now her expression conveyed concern, even a trace of suspicion.

"Mr. President," she said, "one of my people is missing."

"I don't . . ." Taken off guard by her abrupt formality, Carlos shook his head. "Pardon me, Captain, but—"

"Jonathan Parson, my second officer. He was supposed to have dinner with us at the inn. When he didn't show up, we checked his room—"

"His stuff's gone," Chris said, interrupting her. "I looked around after she called me, but it's like he wasn't even there. The blanket's missing, and so's some things from the bathroom. Soap, a towel, the toothbrush and razor the innkeeper gave him." He hesitated. "We thought he might have come over here."

"No, no." Carlos opened the door a little wider, holding back the dogs while letting everyone look inside. "Haven't seen him since late this afternoon." He turned his attention to Tereshkova. "You know, he might have only gone for a walk. Wanted to get some fresh air . . ."

"I thought that, too, but . . ." Tereshkova hesitated. "We looked around for him, and when we went back to the inn, we found that Dr. Whittaker had disappeared as well."

SHUTTLEFIELD / HAMALIEL 70 / 2013

Although more than an hour had passed since the sun went down, Jonas was surprised by how well he could see after dark. Bear had risen to the east, and he was astonished not only by how large it was—many times the size of the Moon back on Earth, like a child's balloon held at arm's length—but also by how much light it cast. Once his eyes became night-adapted, there was no need to carry a lamp.

More than a few times after he left the inn, Jonas paused to take in the strange beauty of Bear's rings, the soft blue pattern of its cloud bands. He told himself that he'd gone out to search for Parson, yet the fact of the matter was that he'd used it as an excuse to take a walk. The tour he'd been given this afternoon had been interesting, but more than a few times he'd wanted to get away from everyone, to see this place without having the president or his wife explaining everything to him. In hindsight, he realized that he should have left a note, or at least told someone at the inn where he was going. Yet the temptation to explore alone was too great. He'd crossed forty-six light-years to reach this world; he was entitled to a little time by himself.

His steps had taken him from the Liberty town center down the gravel road leading to Shuttlefield. He was about halfway between the two settlements, surrounded by low marshland cultivated with tall stalks of bamboo, when he was startled by a high-pitched shriek, carried to him from the distance by the cool evening breeze. It sounded like an animal being slaughtered, and when he heard it he felt an atavistic chill. That would be a boid, one of the giant, flightless avians that killed Jorge and Rita Montero only a couple of days after they'd reached Coyote, and later killed Jim Levin during an ill-advised hunting expedition. Carlos had told him that the creatures seldom ventured close to the colonies anymore—they'd apparently learned to keep their distance from human habitats—but nonetheless Jonas quickened his pace, and didn't relax again until he'd reached the warm lights of Shuttlefield.

A few residents were out and about, strolling the dirt streets that meandered between wood-frame cottages, yet no one paid much attention to him. A craftsman in Liberty had gifted him with a shagswool poncho; wearing it over his jumpsuit, Jonas figured that he passed for a local. Enjoying the anonymity, he smiled to himself. In time, perhaps he'd have a little house somewhere on this or that street, perhaps with a small garden out back. Maybe a job teaching physics at the university. Caroline would like this, and Ellen could . . .

No. His wife and daughter were forever lost to him; he had to remember this. They would never see this world, never enjoy the wonder of watching a ringed planet as it rose above bamboo fields on a cool midsummer night.

God, forgive me, he thought. *I never intended to trade my life for theirs.*

Alone in his melancholy, he found himself approaching the landing field where the *Isabella* had touched down. The skiff was no longer surrounded by curious townspeople, yet he was surprised to see light glowing within its cockpit. Intrigued, he walked closer, and now he saw that the ramp had been lowered from the ship's belly. He was certain that Parson had shut it after they'd left.

"Hello?" he called out. "Is anyone there?"

For an instant, he thought he spotted movement inside the cockpit. Then the lights winked out, and now he became wary. Someone had managed to enter the *Isabella*. A looter, perhaps, searching for whatever he or she could steal. Jonas remembered the firearms stowed away in the locker, along with the emergency supplies: spare clothes, rations, flashlights, even a small tent. If there was a black market here, they'd probably fetch a high price.

He shouldn't have gone out by himself. He should have found a Proctor, brought him along. Yet there was no one in sight, and even if he ran back to the nearest house, who would he ask for help? And if Captain Tereshkova found that he'd allowed a thief to escape . . .

"Who's there?" he shouted, his legs shaking as he inched closer to the ramp. "You're not supposed to be there. I'll . . ."

Footfalls from the open hatch, then a figure appeared within the shadows. "Dr. Whittaker? Is that you?"

Parson. Jonas let out his breath. "Damn it, man, don't do that to me. I thought someone was breaking in."

A wry laugh, then the heavy clunk of boots descending the ladder. "Right you are. Only difference is, I used the remote to get in."

As Parson came down the ramp, Jonas saw that he carried a backpack in his right hand, and slung over his left shoulder was a carbine. A wool poncho covered his EA jumpsuit, and he wore the wide-brimmed catskin hat he'd bartered from a shopkeeper. Indeed, Jonas had been embarrassed by how much wheeling-and-dealing the second officer had done during the tour; it was as if he'd used his notoriety to bargain as many items as he could away from the locals.

"Had to come back here to pinch a few items," Parson said, as if this explained everything. "I'm sure no one will mind. Well, perhaps they will, but . . ."

"What are you talking about?" Jonas stared at him. "You know the captain's been looking for you? She even went to find the police."

"Proctors, you mean. Did she really?" Parson set down his pack, then reached into his jacket pocket and pulled out a small unit. A soft beep as he pressed it, then the ramp began to rise, folding itself against the underside of the hull. "Better hurry then. If you found me, then it's only a matter of time before they do, too."

"What are you doing?" Jonas couldn't believe he was hearing this. "You're not . . . you don't mean you're . . . ?"

"A fine old naval tradition." Parson handed the remote to him. "Sailor reaches paradise, decides he likes the scenery, so he grabs whatever he can and jumps ship. Worked for Mr. Christian when he reached Fiji, so why not for me?"

He pulled the carbine off his shoulder. For a second Jonas thought he was going to level it at him, but instead Parson laid it down on the ground, then picked up the pack and pulled it across his shoulders. "Once I'm gone, I'm sure you'll run off to find the captain, tell her what you know. However, I'd appreciate it if you took your time. Give me a few minutes head start. As it stands, I figure I've only got a fifty-fifty chance of getting away."

Jonas hesitated. "I'll walk instead of run if you'll tell me why."

"I just did." Then he chuckled. "All right then. Truth of the matter is that I've planned to do this all along. Even before we left Earth . . . hell, even before I enlisted. I've put a lot of thought into this, and now's my best shot. If I delay longer, there's going to be more of our people on the ground, and once that happens they might be able to stop me. But for now it's just you and the captain, so—"

"That's not what I'm asking."

Parson was bending down to pick up the rifle. He sighed, then straightened up again. "All right, I'll tell you. For as long as I've been alive, I've wanted to find a place I could call my own. I don't mean a house in the country, nothing like that . . . I mean true wilderness, a place where no one has ever been. But that sort of place doesn't exist anymore, at least not where we came from. But here . . ."

He stopped, gazed off into the night. "It's all out there, Whittaker. A whole world for the taking. All I have to do is go walkabout, as they say, and sooner or later I'll find it."

"You're . . ." Jonas shook his head. "Man, you're out of your mind. There's no way you can survive out there on your own."

"Umm . . . yes, well . . ." Parson bent down again, picked up the carbine. "If I was truly mad, you know, I'd shoot you where you stand." Jonas involuntarily took a step back, but Parson laughed again. "Oh, no, don't worry. I've got nothing against you . . . at least, nothing personal. But once those starbridges you devised are built, it's only a matter of time before this place is swarming with people. So if I'm going to find my own private Fiji, the sooner I get started, the better. Before the cruise ships and real estate developers start moving in."

Parson pulled the rifle across his shoulder, then took a little hop to settle the weight of the pack upon his back. "Best be off now. Give the captain my best regards. No offense, but I resign my commission."

And then, without so much as a farewell, Jonathan Parson turned and strode off into the night. He walked fast, but he didn't run, and although he headed in the general direction of Shuttlefield, Jonas had little doubt that this wasn't his destination.

"Good luck," he said softly. "I envy you."

The same words Dr. Kendrick had said to him, all those many years ago. Now he knew what she'd meant by that.

EAS *Isabella* / Hamaliel 71 / 1449

"Mr. President? We're on final approach."

Carlos reluctantly turned his attention away from the starboard side window. It had been many years since he had last seen Coyote from space; indeed, the only time he'd been above the atmosphere was when he was still only a boy, riding down to the new world with his parents and sister aboard the *Plymouth*. Although he'd seen countless high-resolution satellite photos of the planet's surface, he'd almost forgotten what it was like to look down upon his home from three hundred nautical miles.

"Thank you, Captain." He paused, then added, "You know, I really wish you'd call me Carlos."

"Of course. My apologies." Yet Tereshkova didn't smile as she said this, nor did she look away from the controls. Perhaps she was preoccupied with flying the skiff—with the mysterious disappearance of her second officer, she'd been forced to pilot the craft herself—but nonetheless her attitude toward him had become colder since the events of last night.

He glanced back at Wendy, strapped into the passenger seat behind Tereshkova. She caught his eye, quietly shook her head; no words were exchanged, yet she knew what he meant. Although it wasn't their fault, the fact remained that Parson had vanished while he'd been their guest, and for this Tereshkova held them responsible.

The skiff shuddered slightly as Tereshkova fired maneuvering rockets;

Carlos looked back in time to see the limb of the planet swing away as the skiff rolled to port. His stomach clutched at him, and once again he was sincerely glad that he'd taken his wife's advice not to eat breakfast this morning. But once the stars stopped moving, he saw a single enormous object among them.

"Is that it?" An unnecessary question, yet he blurted it out without thinking.

"Yes, it is." A tinge of pride in Tereshkova's voice, and the smile that briefly crossed her face held no hint of patronization. "Perhaps not as large as the *Alabama*, of course, but . . ."

"She's a beauty." And, indeed, from a little more than a mile away, the *Columbus* was awesome to behold. Over 400 feet in length, it was a long, narrow cylinder, segmented here and there by various modules, gradually tapering back to the fusion engine at its stern. Just behind the drum-like crew module at its bow was the giant ring of its diametric drive, a wheel-shaped torus 130 feet in diameter, joined to the axis by three spokes. As Tereshkova said, the ship was smaller than the *Alabama*, yet its design was far more elegant; Carlos couldn't help but gaze at it in wonder.

Tereshkova tapped her headset mike with her right hand, murmured something in Russian. She waited a few moments, then entered commands into the keypad between her and Carlos. A double-beep from the comp; she released the yoke, and simultaneously the *Isabella* made a slight yaw to starboard, aligning itself with the open claws of the docking cradle just aft of the drive ring.

"There. We're on autopilot now. The ship will guide us the rest of the way in." She paused, then added, "I've told Jonathan that he could just as well let the comp handle this, but he always insisted on flying it himself. I suppose I'm not the pilot he was."

Cool silence descended upon the cockpit; no one knew quite how to answer this remark. "I'm sure he'll turn up eventually," Carlos said at last. "Chris has his people making inquiries, and they're also searching outside town. If he's around—"

"Yes, of course." Tereshkova softened a bit. "I'm certain they'll do their best. But still—"

"But still," Wendy interjected, "you said yourself that he appears to have left on his own free will. The survival gear is missing. The main hatch was shut, and you found the remote on the ground. So if he came back here, he must have done it to pick up some things before—"

"Are you suggesting that my second officer deserted?" Tereshkova tilted her head back slightly, almost as if she was challenging Wendy. "I find that difficult to—"

"A fine old naval tradition." It was the first time that Jonas Whittaker had spoken since they'd left the ground. Until now, he'd been oddly quiet, saying nothing to anyone.

"Sorry, Dr. Whittaker." Carlos turned around in his seat to gaze back at him. "I didn't quite catch that."

"Nothing. Just a passing thought." Whittaker continued to gaze out the window. "The stars really are lovely, don't you think? So strange, though . . . no constellations I can recognize."

"We're a long way from Earth," Wendy said. "The sky looks different out here."

"Yeah . . ." Whittaker laughed quietly. "You're right. Everything's different now, I think."

Carlos regarded the physicist for another moment, wondering what he knew that the others didn't. Then he turned back around, watched as the *Columbus* filled the windows.

"You're right," he said softly. "I think everything's about to be different."

Part 2

THE WAYFARING STRANGER

The rain was coming down hard as the stranger rode into town, a midsummer monsoon that turned the streets to mud and filled potholes with tepid brown water. The weather had chased nearly everyone indoors, so few people saw the wagon, loaded with rolls of bamboo and pulled by a pair of shags, as it moved slowly past the wood-frame buildings of the town center, nor noticed the two men seated together on the buckboard, their shoulders slumped beneath the downpour.

The wagon made its way through Leeport until it arrived at the waterfront, where Boid Creek flowed into a shallow harbor upon the West Channel. A sullen grey mist hung low above the tugboats and barges tied up at the piers; the only thing moving was the revolving beam of the lighthouse. The drayman pulled back on the reins, clicking his tongue at the shags until they finally came to a halt. He glanced around once, making sure that they weren't being observed, then looked at the young man sitting beside him.

"All right, here you go," he said quietly. "From here out, you're on your own."

Water spilled from the brim of his catskin hat as the passenger slowly raised his head. Everything looked flat and monotonous, as if the rain had washed all color from the world; his poncho was drenched, and his clothes were soaked all the way to the skin. Yet he wasn't about to complain; despite his misery, he was relieved to have made it this far.

"Thank you. I appreciate it." Reaching beneath the seat, he pulled out the backpack and rifle he'd carried with him since leaving Shuttlefield two days ago. "I told you I'd trade for a ride," he said, once the pack and gun were in his lap. "What can I give you?"

The old man absently rubbed his grizzled beard. "Naah, don't worry about it. Just glad to have the company for a change." He smiled. "Unless, of course, I can talk you out of that nice firearm."

"Afraid I'm going to need it. Sorry." Pulling the strap across his left shoulder, the hitchhiker climbed down off the wagon. "So where's this place you told me about?"

"Right over there." The wagon driver pointed behind him to a log cabin, elevated above the ground by thick blackwood stilts. "The Captain's Lady. Ask for Dana. Just mention my name . . . she'll set you up."

"Thanks again." Slinging his pack over his shoulder, the young man turned away, headed for the cantina. The drayman watched as he walked up the steps to the front porch, then he clicked his tongue again and shook the reins, and once more the shags began to move, hauling the wagon toward a side street leading away from the wharf.

The door made a loud creak as the young man pushed it open, causing everyone to look up as he came in. A single large room, with wood tables here and there and a few chairs in front of a stone hearth where a warm fire crackled. Embroidered wool carpets on the log walls, sawdust on the bare floor, a solid rough-bark bar at the opposite end of the room. A handful of men and women here and there, with a few seated around a nearby table, cards in hand and a small pile of chips between them. The place was quiet, more quiet than he liked; he tried not to notice the eyes upon him as he approached the bar, rain dripping off his clothes.

The man behind the bar was built like a mountain, not much older than himself, yet at least twice his size, his enormous girth pushing against the front of his apron. He studied the newcomer as he set down the beer mug he'd been washing. "Pardon me," the young man began, "but could you—?"

"That gun loaded?"

The young man nodded.

"Unload it and hand it over. House rules."

Silence, save for the rain lashing at the windows. The bartender's gaze never left him, yet his right hand traveled beneath the counter. The traveler hesitated, then reluctantly slipped the rifle off his shoulder, unclipped its cartridge, and laid the weapon on the bar. The big man gazed at the rifle with interest. "Haven't seen one like this before. Where'd you get it?"

"A long way from here." He spoke quietly, trying to subdue a British accent that, he'd come to realize, many people on this world had never heard before.

The bartender picked up the rifle, inspected it carefully. "Doesn't look like a Union piece," he murmured. "You wouldn't be interested in selling, would you?"

"Just put it away, will you?" The young man dropped his pack on the floor, but didn't take a seat. "I'm looking for . . . I've been told to ask for Dana. Is she around?"

The bartender was about to respond when a soft voice spoke from behind the stranger's left shoulder. "Relax, Hurricane, I'll take care of this."

Looking around, he saw that one of the women had risen and walked up behind him. An elderly, dark-skinned lady, with silvered hair pulled back into thick braids, her black eyes narrowed with suspicion. "I'm Dana," she said. "And who might you be?"

The young man groped for words. There were too many people listening, and he didn't want to come right out with the truth. "Jon," he said at last. "Paul Dwyer . . . a friend of yours, I believe . . . gave me a ride here from Shuttlefield. He said I could—"

"Of course." Before he could go on, Dana turned to Hurricane. "An ale for each of us, and some food for him . . . a bowl of chili and a grilled cheese sandwich." She glanced back at him. "Best we can do in a hurry. I imagine you're starved."

"Well, umm . . . sure, if you—"

"Good." She snapped her fingers at him. "Now give me that poncho and hat . . . wear 'em much longer, and you'll catch pneumonia." When he hesitated, she dropped her voice. "Don't worry. I've been waiting for you, Second Officer Parson."

Astonished, he stared back at her, and she smiled a little. "Word travels fast," she murmured, "and right now you need all the friends you can get. So sit down over there"—she nodded toward a small table away from everyone else—"and we're going to put a decent meal in your stomach and maybe give you a place to sleep tonight."

"I . . . I don't have any money."

Dana shook her head. "You don't need any. All I want to know is why the *Columbus* is here, and why you jumped ship."

The bowl of chili Hurricane brought him was unlike any he'd tasted before, made with chicken instead of beef. No cattle on Coyote, Parson reminded himself, although what they called "white chili" was just as good as the red variety, if different. In any case, he wolfed it down, swigging ale to cool his mouth.

Dana waited patiently until he polished off the grilled goat cheese sandwich. "More?" she asked. "That's Dave's recipe, by the way. It's supposed to be secret, but let him take a couple of practice shots out back with that gun of yours and he might let you in on it."

"Who's Dave?" he asked, and she nodded toward the bartender. "I thought his name was Hurricane."

"Hurricane Dave. That's his nickname." She smiled. "If you'd given him any trouble about surrendering your firearm, you would've found out why. Nice guy, but you don't want to get on his bad side." She signaled for the bartender to bring another round. "Okay, now, suppose you tell me why you're here, and why my old shipmate told you to look me up."

Parson wiped his mouth with a napkin. "You were on a ship together? Which one?"

"He didn't tell you?" Dana's eyes rolled upward. "Figures. Sometimes I think he's forgotten himself." She pointed to the fireplace. Mounted above it was a twisted piece of metal nearly as long as his arm, blackened as if it had endured an inferno. "See that? It came from the *Alabama*. There's a serial number on it that identifies it as belonging to Deck H2, the engineering section. Friend of mine recovered it from the wreckage on Hammerhead. Now, ask me why I'd display a hunk of junk like that in my place of business."

Parson's eyes widened. "You're one of the original settlers."

"Lieutenant Commander Dana Monroe, former chief engineer. Paul Dwyer used to be one of my officers, back before he took to driving a shag-wagon between here and Shuttlefield." She smiled again. "Don't look so surprised. Did you really think all of us live in Liberty?"

"Why don't you?"

"Maybe because we enjoy having elbow room." Dana reached up to take the fresh mugs of ale Hurricane Dave had just delivered to the table. "When Liberty and Shuttlefield started to get crowded, some of us decided to pack up and move out here. One nice thing about frontier life . . . if you don't like where you are now, there's plenty of places left to go."

"My feelings precisely. Paul told me that this is a good place to hide out for awhile. Lot of people come through, on their way to Great Dakota."

"Uh-huh. Once the mills got built in Clarksburg, they needed a place to ship their lumber. So the barges come upriver and offload their wood here, and then guys like Paul put it in their wagons and haul back across the island to Liberty and Shuttlefield, then bring stuff we need on the way back. So this is a port town, and since every port needs a watering hole . . ." She shrugged. "Well, there you have it."

"Odd place to find a former starship engineer." Parson smiled as he sipped his ale. "Judging from the name of this place, I take it you and Captain Lee enjoyed some sort of relationship."

"You can take it whichever way you want," Dana said, her voice taking on a certain edge, "but you're going to find yourself on the other side of that door if you don't wipe that grin off your face. And since I'm also the mayor, you'd do well not to make me mad."

"No offense intended." Parson felt his face go warm. "Many apologies."

"Apologies accepted. Besides, you still haven't answered my question."

Parson didn't reply at once. Instead, he gazed around the cantina. It was midafternoon by now, and although the rain continued to patter against the roof, most of the regulars had left, save for a couple of drunks passed out near the hearth. Hurricane Dave moved about, wiping down tables and carrying empty mugs back to the bar. The Captain's Lady was quiet, yet its namesake clearly wasn't.

"The *Columbus* is here to build a starbridge," he said. "That's a means of forming an artificial wormhole between here and Earth, so that—"

"Ships can travel instantly between here and there. I know that part already." Dana absently tapped a finger against her mug. "We may be out in the boonies, but we've got a satphone, and I still have friends back in Liberty. Same ones who told me about you. What I want to know is why."

"It's not complicated, really. Earth's resources are running low . . . in fact, they've pretty much been used up. The colonies on the Moon and Mars helped some, but not nearly enough. The human race needs to expand beyond the solar system if it's going to survive. Coyote's our best chance."

Dana peered at him. "You mean to say no one has found any other habitable worlds? Not even after all this time?"

"Oh, there might be more. I wouldn't be surprised if there were. There's a good likelihood that there may be a habitable planet around HD70642, but that's 90 light-years from Earth." He shrugged. "18 Scorpii is almost as close as 47 Uma, and it has Earth-size planets, but so far as we've been able to tell, they're dead as Mars. Like I said, this is the garden spot of the universe."

"And so you've come here? To take what little we have?"

" 'What little we have . . . ' " Parson gazed out the window. "If only you knew. A storm like this . . . just a minor inconvenience, right? Where I'm from, we've had to build seawalls around much of the southern coast of England, just to keep London from being flooded." He shook his head. "You have no idea what it's like back home."

"This *is* our home," Dana said defensively, then her tone softened. "That bad, huh?"

"I doubt you'd recognize the place." Parson took another sip of ale. "If you have a complaint, though, you're going to have to take it up with someone else. What the European Alliance wants is not my concern anymore. I resigned my commission two days ago. All I want now is a fresh start."

Dana said nothing. Her fingers gently drummed against the table as she regarded Parson thoughtfully, as if trying to make up her mind what to do with him. "Guess everyone is entitled to start over," she said after a while. "That's what we did. But you can't stay here. Not if people are looking for you . . . and they probably are, if you've jumped ship."

"I imagine my captain is rather put out with me just now, yes."

"Then it's only a matter of time before we'll have Proctors knocking on our door. Surprised they haven't already. But since it'd be bad for business if I tried to hide you—"

"I see." Parson drained his mug with one gulp, then stood up. "Well, thanks for the hospitality, but perhaps I'd better move along. If you can tell me—"

"Did I say I was kicking you out? Sit down and shut up." Leaning back in her chair, Dana turned toward the bar. "Hurricane? When's the next boat for Clarksburg?"

The bartender put down the plate he was polishing, walked over to a sheet of paper tacked to the wall at the end of the bar. "The *Helen Waite* leaves at seven in the morning, providing the weather lets up. Everything else is docked till then."

"Thanks." Dana looked back at Parson. "I'll put you up in a guest room tonight. In the morning, you need to find slip three and go to—"

"*Helen Waite.*" Parson smiled. "That joke's rather old, you realize."

"Tell that to the skipper. His name's George Waite. Helen's his wife." Dana grinned. "George is an old friend, and he owes me a favor or two. He'll carry you down to Clarksburg. Don't worry about the fare. You should be able to work something out with him."

"Thank you." Parson hesitated. "But if Clarksburg is as big as I've heard, then it's only a matter of time before someone finds me there."

"If you stay long, sure." Dana prodded Parson's pack with her foot. "Looks like you took a lot of stuff with you when you deserted. I saw the rifle. You got everything you'll need?"

"Bedroll, some clothes, a lamp, and a knife. Everything I could pilfer from the skiff's survival kit, plus whatever else I could barter in Shuttle-field." He gestured to his poncho and hat, now drying on a hook near the fireplace. "Amazing how much you can get in trade, just for a spare data-pad. Figured I was going to be living off the land for awhile."

"You'll need more than that if you're planning to homestead. Winter here is rough." Pushing aside the empty mugs, Dana leaned across the table. "Clarksburg's just your next stop. There's someone farther in-country you need to find. He lives up in the mountains, so it'll be hard to reach him, but I can provide some directions. And if and when you do find him, you'll have to make some sort of accord with him. Sometimes he's hard to get along with. All the same, he may be able to help you."

"Why's that?"

Dana favored him with a sly smile. "Because I said so. And because you're both looking for the same thing."

The *Helen Waite* was a stern-paddle tugboat, sixty feet long and built of wood and iron, its steam engine fired by a coal-burning furnace that belched acrid brown smoke from its top-hat. It looked like something that should be on display in a museum, yet according to its captain it'd been built only three Coyote years ago. Noting his interest, George Waite decided to let his new passenger get a closer look; he was put to work shoveling coal into the firebox, and it wasn't long before the traveler began to miss the sophistication of diametric warp drives.

The tug chugged out of the Leeport harbor shortly after sunrise, drag-ging behind it six flat-bottom barges, empty save for a load of bamboo and several bushels of corn being brought over from New Florida. The monsoon had passed during the night, and the new day was bright and clear, the white sails of fishing boats dotting the blue waters of the channel. When Parson got a chance to take a breather, he sat on a barrel on the aft deck and watched while the coast of Great Dakota slid past, the distant peaks of the Black Mountain Range growing larger with every passing mile. The captain stood within the pilot house, quietly humming to himself as he navigated the channel by memory, turning the wheel now and then to avoid shoals, his only landmarks the occasional bluff or tall tree upon the shore. Again, it was a far cry from everything Parson had ever known; he'd spent years learning how to control the helm of a starship, and only a few days earlier he'd brought the *Columbus*'s skiff to a safe landing at Shuttlefield, yet compared to George Waite's sublime mastery of the channel he felt as innocent as a child.

It took the better part of the day for the *Helen Waite* to make its journey down the West Channel. Besides the captain, there were only two other crewmen aboard: Waite's teenage nephew, and a rather clumsy middle-aged man who, Parson realized after awhile, was borderline retarded. Neither were very curious about their passenger; Donny spent most of his time in the pilot house, learning the river from his uncle, and José was only too happy to let someone else shovel coal for a change. Yet late in the afternoon, while Donny was inspecting the tow-ropes and José took his turn stoking the engine, Parson went forward and spent a few minutes with the captain. George was an easygoing gentleman, with few questions about his passenger. He only knew that he was an acquaintance of his old friend Dana who was down on his luck; by the time the Clarksburg lighthouse appeared off their starboard bow, Parson had learned everything he needed to know.

The *Helen Waite* nudged the Clarksburg pier just as the five o'clock whistle on the millhouse roof blew, signaling the end of the workday. Parson helped José tie down the tug and barges, then he went aft to collect his belongings. He was about to step off when, much to his surprise, Captain Waite stopped him at the railing and put ten wood coins in his hand. Ten dollars, a day's wages for working on his boat, minus passage from Leeport to Clarksburg. It wasn't much, but it would get him room and board for the night at a wharfside inn George recommended. Again, a small act of kindness from someone whom he barely knew.

The Laughing Cat was little more than a flophouse for itinerant millers and down-on-their-luck fishermen, but it offered a single bed, a bath—so long as no one else on the second floor used up all the hot water—and two square meals a day. Parson got his first taste of creek crab stew that evening; it was the only thing on the menu he could afford, and even the fresh-baked corn bread and pint of sourgrass ale that went with it couldn't wash the taste from his mouth. He left the table while the local drunks were still coming in, and later that night he found himself standing in the alley, clutching his stomach and praying that the guy occupying the outhouse would hurry up and die so he could do the same.

He skipped breakfast the next morning, opting instead for a mug of hot coffee. After leaving his pack and rifle with the innkeeper, he walked around the harbor to the mill. Since Captain Waite had told him the fore-man's name, it didn't take Parson very long to land a job, stacking lumber for two dollars an hour.

It was gut-busting, mindless labor that left his arms and back sore, his hands blistered, with splinters in his palms. He was still getting used to Coyote's lower atmospheric pressure, so often he had to sit down and catch his breath. It paid his rent at the Cat, though, and once he bought a pair of shag-hide gloves the job went much easier. While he worked, he remained quiet, picking up bits and pieces of local lore from the other guys on the line; it didn't take long for him to learn how to imitate the local drawl, which effectively masked his British accent. He'd taken the name John Carroll—a misspelling of his first name, along with his mother's maiden name—and whenever anyone asked him where he'd come from, he told them that he was originally from New Boston; he was young enough to pass for a second-generation Coyote native, and the northern Midland colony was far enough away that no one ever made any uncomfortable as-sociations.

During his lunch hour, he ate redfish sandwiches on the wharf while gazing across the Mill River at the foothills of the Black Mountains. Every day, carts bearing cut timber came down Thunder Ridge; he knew where the roads were now, and how they led to the logging camps deep within the mountains. The wilderness beckoned to him, yet he went on collecting his daily pay, spending only as much as he needed to get by and hiding the rest inside a hole he'd cut inside the mattress of his bed. When the time was right, he'd buy the supplies he needed, then head for the high country.

Parson originally intended to stay in Clarksburg until the end of summer, but circumstances forced his hand. He'd been there almost four weeks, well into the month of Uriel, when one day he heard at the mill that a gyro had landed in town earlier that morning. Word had it that several proctors from Liberty were in town, along with the first officer from the starship that had arrived last month, and that they were searching for a crewman who'd gone missing.

Not wanting to attract attention to himself, Parson waited until the lunch whistle blew before he returned to the Laughing Cat. After gathering his belongings, he left what he owed the innkeeper on the dresser, then he made his exit through the window. He took the risk of stopping by a general store a few blocks away, where he spent his savings on various items he needed: woolen socks, dried fruit and jerked meat, a fire-starter kit, a small axe, and a couple of water bottles. He then made his way through the alleys and side streets until he reached the outskirts of town, where he managed to hitch a ride on a timber wagon heading back into the mountains.

The road led up the eastern slope of Thunder Ridge. Sitting in the back of the empty wagon, his feet dangling over the side, Parson gazed down upon Clarksburg for the last time in what would be many months to come. For a few moments, he almost regretted his decision; the town had been good to him, and more than once he'd been tempted to stay through winter. Yet he valued his freedom more than the comforts of civilization, and he knew that, if he remained here, it would only be a matter of time before he'd be arrested as a deserter.

The town vanished behind the trees, and before long he couldn't even see the smoke rising from the mills where, only a few hours earlier, he'd been stacking boards still warm from the saw blades. At the top of the ridge, a half mile past the high towers of the wind turbines, he spotted an abandoned logging road. He called to the drayman and asked him to stop, then he hopped off, taking his pack and rifle with him. The driver regarded him with curiosity, but didn't ask questions; he merely shrugged and shook the reins of his shag team, and the wagon slowly trundled up the road, leaving his passenger behind.

Parson took out his compass, checked his bearings against a hand-drawn map of the mountains. He pulled his pack and rifle across his shoulders, then he took a deep breath and started walking up the road, following directions Dana Monroe had given to him several weeks ago.

Somewhere up here was another person who sought the same thing as he did. The time had come to find him.

The old logging road led several miles northeast along the top of Thunder Ridge before it ended in a steep trail descending into a deep valley that lay between the ridge and Mt. Shapiro, the easternmost flank of the Black Mountain Range. It didn't take long for Parson to discover why the road wasn't being used any longer.

Making his way downhill, he came upon a broad expanse where every tree larger than a sapling had been felled. Acre upon acre, mile upon mile, of old-growth rough bark and blackwood, chopped down and carried away, leaving behind only a wasteland of stumps and brush. Deep furrows in the ground showed where shags had hauled logs to the ridgetop, to be loaded aboard wagons. From what he'd learned while working at the mill, he knew the loggers had abandoned this part of the mountains after it had become more trouble than it was worth to harvest wood from this particular area; by then, they'd found other sites closer to the Mill River, from which they could pump water to fill the flumes they'd built to carry logs most of the way down from the mountains.

Yet it was one thing to hear of such a thing, and another to see the results. A forest, ancient long before humankind had learned how to build starships, had disappeared. In its place were stumps large enough to serve as dinner tables for parties of eight, and heaps of decaying ashes where smaller limbs had been burned. A pair of swoops circled high upon him, screeching their dismay at his intrusion, but otherwise the mountainside was quiet and still. For the first time since he had begun his journey into the mountains, he didn't hear songbirds, or detect the furtive movements of small animals. The forest inhabitants had long since fled this side of the valley, seeking refuge in places which hadn't yet felt the hand of man.

And so you've come here, to take what little we have? Again, he heard Dana Monroe's voice; not accusatory, simply stating a bald fact. And to this he'd replied with some blithe remark about the rain.

How arrogant he'd been. How stupid he must have sounded.

It was late afternoon, and he hadn't eaten since early that morning, yet despite his hunger and fatigue, he couldn't bring himself to rest here. This place felt too much like a cemetery. Instead, he continued hiking down into the valley, hoping that he would escape this place before the time came for him to make camp for the evening.

Fortunately, the desolation ceased before he reached the bottom of the valley. Now the trail was much narrower, becoming little more than a footpath. Near a shallow brook that meandered across the valley floor, Parson came upon the remnants of a logging camp: rotting platforms where tents had once been erected, with a couple of abandoned outhouses standing nearby. Although Uma had disappeared behind Mt. Shapiro and dusk was beginning to settle upon the valley, he didn't want to camp here, so he searched the brook until he found a place where he could step across on dry rocks without getting his boots wet.

Within a small hollow surrounded by tall trees, he made camp for the night. It was more difficult than he'd imagined. Although he'd taken a course in wilderness survival while training for the *Columbus* mission, the fact remained that it had been little more than a weekend camping trip in what remained of the French Alps. This time, though, Parson didn't have the luxury of a heated tent or a bottle of wine to go with a dinner of processed rations. He struggled to tie a plastic tarp across a couple of trees, and once that was done he had to scrounge in the darkness before he found enough dry tinder to build a fire. Even then, the fire he made cast more smoke than heat; it went out twice before he learned that simply shoving more twigs and leaves upon the embers did more harm than good, and in the end he had little more than a weak blaze by which to warm his feet while he chewed some dried fruit.

Even as he huddled against the cool wind that drifted through the valley, though, he gazed up at the night sky. Bear had risen above Thunder Ridge, its rings casting a silver halo across the tree branches, the planet itself a giant blue eye that stared down upon him, not with malevolence, but with godlike curiosity. The high clouds disappeared, exposing stars so brilliant that it seemed as if he could reach out and touch them. He easily located some of Coyote's companions—Hawk, Snake, Eagle—but it took a while for him to find a wan white star, unremarkable from any of the lesser suns in the firmament.

Somewhere near Sol, invisible to the naked eye, lay Earth. Not for the first time, Parson found himself having second thoughts about what he'd done. It was one thing to desert the *Columbus* once it reached Coyote, yet now that he'd actually carried out his scheme, he'd come to realize that heading off into the wilderness to live off the land was far more difficult than he'd expected. It wouldn't be long before summer came to an end, and by then he'd have to learn how to survive by his own wits. Shelter, food, warmth: all the simple things he'd once taken for granted, he would now have to . . .

From somewhere to his left, a twig snapped.

He froze, remaining perfectly still as he listened to the darkness. For a few seconds, he heard only silence. Then there was a faint rustle, as if something was moving through the underbrush.

Careful not to make any sudden movements, Parson slid his hand across the ground, searching for his rifle. Locating it, he slowly pulled the gun into his lap and disengaged the safety. The rifle made a faint *beep* as he switched on the infrared sight; the sound apparently startled whatever lurked nearby, for there was another furtive sound among the leaves, this time a few yards closer.

Holding his breath, Parson silently counted to three. Then, in one swift movement, he leapt to his feet, bringing the rifle stock to his shoulder and aiming the barrel to his left. Squinting through the scope, for a half instant he caught an amber-filtered glimpse of a tiny face, almost monkey-like, peering at him with enormous eyes through the foliage. A high-pitched *ka-cheep!* and then the face vanished, leaving behind only a couple of branches that whisked back and forth where it had once been.

For an instant, Parson was tempted to fire. Then he took a deep breath, and his finger relaxed within the trigger guard. Still holding the rifle to his shoulder, he searched the perimeter through the scope. He saw nothing, though, save for trees and overgrowth. Whatever had come to visit him had been scared away.

Parson lowered his gun. At least it wasn't a boid. He'd heard stories about these giant avians, how they hunted by night and were capable of ripping a man apart with their beaks and claws. They were supposed to be indigenous mainly to the lowlands, though, and unlikely to be encountered up here in the mountains.

Yet the same people who'd told him about boids, at the mill or over drinks at the Laughing Cat, had also told tales about something else that infested the high country. Creatures that looked a little like monkeys, but were far more intelligent. Gremlins, treecrawlers, night-thieves . . . they had many names, and sometimes they visited the campsites of those who ventured into the mountains, and took whatever they could carry away.

Before he went to sleep, Parson took the precaution of closing his pack and placing it behind his head. Once he'd wrapped his blanket around himself, he rested his rifle next to him and put his hand over it; his hat and poncho, he laid against his side. Everything he had in the world was within hand's reach; if anything crept up on him, he'd know about it.

Nonetheless, it took a long time for him to fall asleep. He gazed at the dying campfire until his eyes finally closed of their own accord. His first night in the Black Mountains was uneasy, his dreams dark and disturbing.

Morning came cold and damp, with slick dew upon the ground. He woke up thirsty and craving a hot cup of coffee, and cursing himself for having neglected to buy any before he fled Clarksburg. Yet the first thing he noticed was that his tarp was missing. Sometime during the night, it had simply vanished; even the cords with which he'd tied it to the trees were gone.

The loss of the tarp was a nuisance, but worse was the realization that something managed to get so close to him without waking him. There was nothing he could do about it now, but he swore to himself that he'd be more careful in the future. His fire had long since gone cold, and there was little reason to start it again; he had a meager breakfast of jerked lamb, and wondered again how he'd feed himself once it and his supply of dried fruit was gone. Then he packed up his bedroll and headed out.

It didn't take long for him to find the trail he'd followed since he entered the valley; it led to the west, away from the abandoned logging camp he'd found yesterday. As it wove its way through the woodlands, once again taking him uphill toward Mt. Shapiro, it became apparent that the path hadn't been forged by loggers. It was much too narrow, nor were there any indications of anything having been cut down; no stumps, no signs of brushfires. It didn't look like a game trail, though; if animals had made it, they would have left scat, yet as hard as he looked, Parson didn't see anything that looked like turds.

This made him wary, so after a while he took his rifle from his shoulder and carried it in his hands, its safety cocked but never far from his right thumb.

By midday, the trail had led him up the lower slopes of Mt. Shapiro. Stopping to look back, he could see the way he'd come, the eastern side of the valley marked by the ragged scars of the logging operations. Again, he was blessed by dry weather; the day was bright and cloudless, with Uma casting its warmth upon him. He'd stopped to remove his poncho and rest his back against a granite outcropping when he heard a new sound.

From somewhere not far away, someone was singing.

He couldn't make out the words, yet it was definitely a voice, carried through the trees by the warm summer breeze. Not quite believing what he was hearing, Parson followed the sound, keeping his rifle at the ready.

The trail led uphill for another few hundred yards, then leveled out on a narrow plateau. Here he came upon a clearing where the trees had been taken down. About an acre in size, it had been cultivated as a small farm field; tall stalks of corn grew chest-high, and nearby were rows of other crops; soybeans and potatoes, from the looks of them, and also trellises upon which tomatoes ripened in the summer sun. At the far end of the clearing was a compact log cabin, with a cord of wood stacked against the stone chimney, and a porch out front upon which a large brown dog sunned himself.

A short distance away, a lone figure worked the field. At first Parson thought he was a scarecrow; hunched over, his back turned to Parson, he wore a long black robe, its cowl pulled up over his head. As the garden hoe in his gloved hands swung up and down, digging a long furrow in the soft ground, his song came to him:

> I'm just a poor wayfaring stranger,
> A-traveling through this world of woe,
> But there's no sickness nor toil nor danger,
> In that bright world to which I go . . .

Coming closer, Parson's foot came down upon a discarded corn husk. It made a loud crunch beneath the sole of his boot. Aware that he was intruding, he halted. On the cabin porch, the dog raised his head; he searched the clearing until he spotted Parson, then jerked to his feet and bayed a warning.

The lonely farmer stopped singing. He gazed first at the dog, who'd come down off the porch and was now running across the field, then turned to look at Parson. He didn't straighten up, though, nor did he drop his hoe. He regarded his visitor for a moment with what seemed to be only passing curiosity, then he turned around and resumed his work. As the dog stopped at his master's side, once again Parson heard the farmer's voice:

> *I know dark clouds will gather round me,*
> *I know my way is steep and rough,*
> *But beauteous fields lie just beyond me,*
> *Where souls redeemed their vigil keep.*

Parson ventured closer. "That's a nice song," he said. "Did you . . . I mean, is that your own?"

"You could say that." Standing erect, the farmer rested his hands upon the handle of his hoe, but otherwise kept his back turned to him. "If you're asking if I wrote it . . . no, I didn't. I don't think anyone knows that anymore. It just belongs to anyone who sings it." He paused. "If you've got a reason for being here, tell me. Otherwise, I'd appreciate it if you'd leave. We don't like trespassers."

Parson stopped. "Sorry. I didn't know this was private property."

A queer buzzing sound, like static from a mistuned radio. "No, it's not private property. But it's my home, and I don't encourage visitors." He glanced down at the dog. "Oscar . . ."

The mutt growled deep in his throat, his ears flattening against his head as his mouth pulled back to reveal sharp teeth. "No need for that," Parson said, remaining as still as he could. "I'm just looking for someone. A friend of mine told me I might find him up here. His name's Manuel Castro . . . Manny Castro. Maybe he's a neighbor, or someone you know."

The farmer said nothing for a moment, yet his head turned ever so slightly within his cowl. "Depends. Who's your friend?"

"Dana Monroe. She owns a place in Leeport, a bar called—"

"The Captain's Lady. Yes, I know her. And you say she told you to find me?"

"You're Manny Castro?" No answer. "Look, I don't wish to bother you, but Dana told me that you might be able to help me. Or rather, she . . ."

The farmer turned around, and now Parson clearly saw his face. Within the shadows of the cowl was a metal skull, its plating like tarnished silver, with a grill where his mouth should be. A black patch covered his left eye;

the right was a glass orb that caught the sunlight and reflected it with a multifaceted red hue.

Parson gaped at him. "Oh, hell," he whispered, "you're a Savant." Then he swung his rifle up. "Stay where you are, or . . ."

"Or you're going to do what?" Castro dropped his hoe, then opened his threadbare robe, revealing a mechanical body pitted with dozens of small dents. "I've been shot before, by better marksmen than you."

Oscar growled again, but now his tail was between his legs; he obviously knew what a rifle was, and despite his willingness to protect his master he was clearly frightened. "Easy, boy," the Savant murmured, and his right hand stole down to pat the mutt on the head. "Shoot him," he added, "and I swear my next chore will be digging a grave for you."

Parson weighed the situation. He had no desire to kill the dog; he was simply being loyal. And despite the fact that Manuel Castro was a savant, he was also the person whom Dana had sent him to find. Not only that, but Castro was right; this was his land, and Parson was a trespasser.

"Perhaps we ought to start all over again," he said.

"Perhaps we should." Castro pointed to his gun. "If you put that down, Oscar will understand. And I might be inclined to invite you in for a cup of coffee."

Parson didn't know which was more surprising; that Manuel Castro would be willing to forgive him, or that a savant would have coffee. "You'd do that?"

"Certainly." Again, the electronic buzz that Parson now recognized as a simulation of laugher. "If Dana has reason to send you my way, then perhaps you're a person I should meet."

Parson hesitated, then he bent down and carefully laid his rifle on the ground. He didn't take his eyes from the Savant, but Castro made no motion other than to reassure his dog with a gentle pat on the head. Oscar stopped growling, and his tail wagged a few times as he cautiously stepped out from behind his master.

"Very good," Castro said. "Now let's see about coffee, and you can tell me why you're here."

The cabin hadn't been built with human habitation in mind. Only one main room, with a small storeroom in the back; although it had a potbellied stove, there was no kitchen, only a small metal sink with water hand-pumped from an artesian well. A couple of coarse rugs on the floor, and two chairs and a table, but no bed save for a small mat where Oscar could curl up next to the stove. Four windows, one for each wall, and a few cabinets and shelves containing Castro's belongings: hand tools, some utensils, a handful of books and some writing materials, an old datapad attached to a solar recharger. No privy, although Manny told him he could use the compost heap out back if he needed to relieve himself.

"Every now and then I find myself receiving guests." Castro poured water he'd boiled in an old kettle through a paper sieve filled with ground coffee into a chipped ceramic cup. "That's why I have this stuff. But the only food I keep is the kibble I make for Oscar . . . sort of a mush of ground corn and soybeans."

"Never knew a dog that was vegetarian." Parson looked over at Oscar. Having tentatively accepted him as a visitor, the mutt had finally calmed down, yet Oscar still studied him warily from his nest beside the stove. "Where did you get him?"

"Took him in trade from the loggers for a couple of pounds of coffee beans . . . this is some of what I grow, by the way. He was the runt of the litter, and they weren't paying much attention to him." Castro brought over the coffee, set it down on the table in front of Parson. "A dog'll eat anything so long as you show him some kindness and respect. So he keeps me company, and we look out for each other. I think I got the better end of the deal."

"So that's what you do? Grow food for your dog and loggers?"

"Only for Oscar. Now that the loggers have moved on, I don't see much of them anymore. But I find use for what he doesn't eat." He watched as Parson took a sip. "How's that? Not too weak, I hope."

"It's fine." Truth was, the coffee was stronger than he usually liked, but Parson figured that Castro had long forgotten what it'd been like to taste anything. Savants were once human themselves, of course, but they'd had their minds downloaded into the quantum comps deep within their mechanical bodies. If he'd come here aboard one of the Union ships, it had probably been at least—what, seventy years? eighty? even more?—since the last time he had savored a good cup of coffee. "But if you're only feeding the dog, why—?"

"Because I like to." Castro continued to study him through his one good eye. "Dana didn't tell you I was a posthuman, did she? You reacted rather violently when you saw me."

The abrupt change of subject caught him off guard. "Sorry. I apologize for that. It just took me by surprise. Yeah, Dana kept that bit of information from me. She just told me your name, and told me that if I followed the old logging road to Mt. Shapiro I might be able to find you." He hesitated. "She said we had a lot in common."

"I sincerely doubt that. On the other hand, Dana is a good judge of character, so perhaps I should reserve my own judgment. Last month, I saw a starship arrive in orbit. My guess is that you're from it."

Parson hesitated, then nodded. "The EASS *Columbus*." He suddenly realized that he hadn't yet told Castro his name. "I'm Jonathan Parson. Former second officer."

"Well, well . . . now there's a tale in itself. But first things first. The registry of your ship . . . I take it that it's from the European Alliance?" Parson nodded, and once again Castro emitted that strange laughter-buzz. "Makes sense. The Savant Council estimated that it was only a matter of time before the EA would be able to construct its own starships."

Parson looked away. "Probably the last thing the Council was ever right about," he muttered under his breath.

"Explain your remark, please? No need to repeat it. My hearing is quite good. In fact, I heard you coming long before you saw me. I simply chose to ignore you. But, please, tell me more about the Savant Council."

"You've been out of touch, haven't you?" He was unable to keep the edge from his voice. "Oh, I forgot . . . a half century or so since you left Earth, plus another twenty-odd years. And meanwhile, you've been up here, growing corn and—"

"Mr. Parson, you're beginning to wear out your welcome." Manny took a step closer. Hearing the change in his master's voice, Oscar raised his head, a growl rumbling deep within his throat. Parson had left his rifle out in the field, but nonetheless he refused to be intimidated; he remained in his seat, staring back at the Savant.

"Very well," he said. "Back in 2270, the Council of Savants completed a long-range assessment of Earth's condition. After taking everything into consideration . . . environmental factors, remaining natural resources, census projections, so on and so forth . . . they reached the conclusion that, within the next century, Earth would not be able to support its current population of eight billion inhabitants."

"I'm not surprised. The Council was studying this even before I—"

Parson held up a hand. "Let me finish. The Council made several recommendations, one of which was that humankind had to develop interstellar resources . . . namely, this world. That part was made public, and that's why the Union sent ships here." He paused. "But they also reached another conclusion, one which they kept to themselves. In order to stabilize the global environment and use its remaining resources for as long as possible, Earth's population had to be reduced. Quite drastically, in fact . . . by as much as one-third."

Castro said nothing for a moment. "And how did they propose to do that?"

"Oh, they proposed nothing. Or at least not to us baseline humans." Parson stared at Castro. "The plan called for the eventual extermination of three billion people."

"No. This couldn't . . . they couldn't have—"

"Oh, yes. It was very precise, very logical. One out of every three persons on Earth were secretly marked for death, by whatever means necessary. Starvation of the poor and indigent, introduction of deadly diseases within major population areas, termination of life support for the critically ill, random shutdowns of vital energy systems leading in turn to—"

"I didn't know. I wasn't . . ." Although he was incapable of displaying facial emotion, Castro was visibly shaken. Turning away from Parson, he walked to the open door of his cabin, resting a hand against the frame as if to steady himself. "Did they succeed?"

"Fortunately, no." Parson picked up his mug, found that the coffee had gone cold and put it down again. "When people started dying in large numbers, a few individuals found out why, and they managed to put a stop to it. It's a long story, believe me." He paused. "But over thirty-five thousand people perished before the savants were stopped."

"I see." Castro continued to gaze out the door. "And the Savant Council . . ."

"Dissolved by emergency act of the Union Proletariat, its members rounded up and arrested. In the end the Proletariat decided that the savants . . . all savants, in fact . . . were too dangerous to be allowed to exist.

The ones they managed to capture were . . . well, terminated, to put it in formal terms."

"Executed." Castro's head bowed slowly. "One form of genocide in exchange for another." A metallic rasp that might have been a sigh. "I suppose it was justified on grounds that posthuman life posed an imminent threat to baseline humans."

"Not all were terminated. A few managed to escape by stealing a Union Astronautica freighter and taking off for the outer solar system. Last I'd heard, they hadn't yet been captured." Parson hesitated. "So how many savants are here? On Coyote, I mean?"

"I'm the last." The Savant didn't look at him. "The rest returned aboard the Union ships. They're still on their way back to Earth. I expect they'll be . . . terminated . . . upon arrival."

"That's a likely assumption." Parson was quiet for a moment. "You weren't part of that, though. It happened after your time. You can't be held accountable."

"I rather doubt your kind will see it that way." Castro didn't look at him. "On the other hand, it may take a while for them to find me, so I suppose I'm safe, at least for the time being."

"Uh-huh." Parson said nothing for a moment. "So why are you here, anyway?"

"As you say, it's a long story. To make it short, after the others of my kind left, I didn't feel very comfortable among baseline humans." Castro turned away from the door. "I lived in Clarksburg for a few months, but eventually I got tired of being regarded with suspicion, so I packed up what little I needed and moved up here. I told Dana how to find me, just in case I might be needed, but other than a few loggers whom I've encountered now and then—"

"I'm the only one who knows."

"Yes." He looked back at Parson. "You're the first person Dana has sent here. I assume she must have had good reason for doing so."

"Maybe there is." He slowly let out his breath. "Truth is, I jumped ship. It was something I intended to do before I left Earth . . . even before I put in for this mission, in fact. I figured there had to be a better world somewhere out there, and if there was, it was worth trying to get there."

The Savant studied him for a long moment. "Is it? Is Coyote a better place than Earth?"

Parson didn't answer at once. "I think so," he said at last. "At least it has the potential. I don't know how much longer that's going to last, though. They've invented something called the starbridge . . . a means of opening a stable wormhole between here and Earth. *Columbus* has the equipment necessary to build one end of the tunnel. Once it's completed—"

"More ships, and more people." Castro picked up Parson's mug, peered inside. "I'm afraid my coffee wasn't very good. You've hardly touched it."

"It was a bit strong for my taste, to be honest."

"I appreciate honesty." The Savant carried the mug over to the sink and poured it out. "You may stay."

"Pardon me?"

"You may stay for as long as you wish." The Savant pumped some water into the sink, used it to rinse out the mug. "This house isn't big enough for both of us, of course, but we have enough time left in the summer for us to build a dwelling of your own. The crops I raise are more than sufficient to feed both you and Oscar, and still have enough left for . . . well, my own purposes, shall we say."

"I wasn't asking for—"

"No, you didn't. I'm offering it to you anyway. Believe me, you won't survive out here without my help. Winters on this world are quite long, and up here in the mountains they're particularly brutal. Even the loggers return to Clarksburg once the snow comes. If you tried to make do on your own, you'd almost certainly perish. And since I imagine that your captain is probably irate with you, if you went back into town it would only be a matter of time before you were arrested for desertion. Am I correct?"

"Well . . ."

"I thought so." Castro turned away from the sink. "Let me finish. In exchange for room and board, I expect you to help me with the chores. Most of it involves tending to the crops, but we also need to keep the cabin in good repair, and once we build another for you, twice as much effort will be required. It's hard work, and it keeps me occupied for most of the day, but with another person here this will give me more time to devote to my studies."

"What are you studying?"

"You'll find out eventually. Let's just say that it's something I've been doing on my own for the last three years. In time, I may decide to reveal my findings to others, but until then it's imperative that I conduct my research in secrecy." He paused. "Can you agree to those conditions?"

Parson considered the question for a few moments. When he left Clarksburg, his plan had been to find a place where he could live on his own. Even if he hadn't found Manny Castro, he would have eventually built his own homestead somewhere in the Black Mountains. Yet his first night alone had taught him that he didn't know nearly as much about living in the wild as he thought he did, and he had no desire to face starvation or freeze to death in the depths of a long, cold winter.

He had little reason to trust a member of a subspecies that had once plotted the annihilation of one-third of Earth's population. Nonetheless, the Savant had been open and honest with him; there was also little reason for Castro to murder him in his sleep. And he could do worse for companionship, if only none at all.

"Sure. I can live with that."

"I rather hoped you would." Castro gestured toward the field. "Perhaps you'd better fetch your rifle. It'll be dark soon, and it might disappear."

"I know. I lost my tarp last night."

"Really? Was it stolen from your campsite?"

Puzzled by this sudden insight, Parson nodded, and again Castro emitted his strange approximation of a laugh. "Then maybe I can get it back for you."

The sun had gone down, and once again Bear was beginning to rise to the east. With the coming of the night, grasshoarders cried softly as they settled in for the evening; a gentle breeze drifted in from over the mountains, cooling the sunbaked field and causing the cornstalks to sway gently back and forth.

"How much longer?" Sitting in a chair he'd carried out onto the porch, Parson peered into the darkness.

"Not long." Castro's voice came to him as a thin whisper. He stood next to Parson, a motionless black figure nearly invisible within the shadows of the porch. "Be quiet. They won't come out if they think they're being observed."

Now that Castro had extinguished the oil lamps inside the cabin, the only sign of their presence was the amber glow of the Savant's right eye, and even that was shrouded by the cowl of his robe. He'd wanted to use his rifle's scope, but Manny had cautioned him against it; he suspected that the creatures' eyes were infrared-sensitive, and the rifle's IR beam would frighten them away. The Savant had even taken the precaution of leaving Oscar inside the house; the dog had scratched and whined at the door for a while, before curling up on the floor in disgust.

They waited in silence for a long time, watching Bear as it ascended above the trees, its luminescence bathing the field with a pale blue light. Parson was starting to nod off when Castro tapped him on the shoulder; without a word, he pointed off to the right.

Sitting up a little straighter, Parson stared at rows of corn. For another minute or so, he saw nothing. Then there was a dry rustle among the stalks, and a moment later a small man-shaped form emerged from the cropland, less than thirty feet from the cabin.

Parson watched as the tiny figure hesitated at the edge of the corn. In the wan bearlight, it appeared to search the area, its small head turning first one way then another; it looked straight at them, and for an instant, he had a fleeting impression of a pair of oversized eyes meeting his own.

He thought the intruder would retreat, yet it didn't. Instead, it made a small sound—*keecha quireep cheeka!*—and then it darted forward, keeping low to the ground, its hands almost touching the soil. Once in the clear, it stopped and looked back. *Cheeka! Hoo-reep keecha!* And now two more figures came out of the corn behind it, the larger of the pair dragging something on the ground behind it.

The trio moved toward the wheelbarrow half-filled with green tomatoes that Castro had left out in front of the house. They gathered around it, picking and sniffing at the vegetables, making small chirps, hoots, and whistles. At first, Parson thought they might steal the barrow, but instead the first one overturned it, then played curiously with its wheel, while the other two gathered as many tomatoes as they could carry in their small arms.

The one who'd scouted the terrain watched them go, then it reluctantly abandoned its examination of the wheelbarrow, grabbed an armload of tomatoes, and hastened after them. A few more excited cries—*cheeka! kaka-sheek! woo-weet cheeka!*—and they'd vanished as quickly as they'd come, leaving behind only the wheelbarrow and the object they'd brought with them.

Once more, the field was silent.

"All right, they're gone." For the first time in nearly two hours, Castro moved. "Now let's see if they've reciprocated our generosity."

Parson followed the Savant down the porch steps and across the field to where the wheelbarrow lay upon its side. "Too big for them to steal," Castro said in reply to Parson's unasked question. "The big one continues to be intrigued by it, so I expect he may eventually try to take it away. But maybe not, if they don't have any immediate use for it."

"And you say you've been doing this . . . how long?"

"The last two summers. Intentionally, at least." Castro bent down to pick up the barrow and set it upright. "Before then, they just stole whatever they could get their hands on. After I figured out their system, I let them know I'd rather trade than sic Oscar on them. Since then it's worked out pretty well. Here, look . . ."

Bending down again, he picked up the object the creatures had brought with them. Parson saw that it was his tarp: torn in a couple of places, its cords missing, yet it had been returned, just as the Savant had predicted.

"They didn't want the tarp itself," Castro said. "Anything made of plastic doesn't interest them very much. But something they can use, like elastic cords . . ."

"And you knew they'd do this?"

"Not really. Just a guess based on a hypothesis. They're called the *chirreep* . . . or perhaps a mountain tribe called *reep-chirreep*, although I'm not certain of that yet. They've been spotted here and there all over Coyote. Carlos Montero found them first on Barren Isle northwest of the Meridian Sea. Later, another tribe was located on Midland, just south of Mt. Bonestell. They've been given a lot of different names. Sandthieves, treecrawlers . . ."

"So I've heard. And you've been studying them?"

"That's why I'm here." Castro waved a hand toward his crops. "In fact, that's the main reason why I took up farming. If you want to study a primitive species in the wild, start by offering them food. Once they learn to trust you, perhaps you can establish some sort of communication. Barter is usually the next step."

Parson examined the tarp in his hands. It could still be repaired, if he cared to use it again. "An interesting line of research. Think you could use an assistant?"

"Perhaps." The Savant started pushing the wheelbarrow away. "This world has enough settlers and soldiers and developers. What it needs is a few more students."

Parson watched him go, then turned to gaze at the woods around him. Perhaps life had a higher calling than mere survival. He'd found freedom; now he had something to do with it.

"Sounds like a bargain," he murmured, then he followed the Savant back to the cabin.

Part 3

THE BLACK MOUNTAINS

The supply wagon that carried her into the Black Mountains was drawn by an aging shag that looked as if it was going to drop dead any moment. Grunting within its harness, it hauled the wagon the last few hundred feet up the steep dirt road, while the drover shook its reins and muttered obscenities under his breath. Feeling pity for the poor creature, Susan stepped off the moving wagon almost as soon as they were in sight of Mill Creek Camp; if the shag noticed the slight lessening of its burden, though, it gave no indication, save perhaps to emit one more of the farts that had threatened to make her ill during the long journey from Clarksburg.

Noticing that she'd jumped off, the drover reached back into the wagon bed and pulled out her duffel bag. "Here y'go," he said. "Ain't much further, but if you insist on getting your exercise . . ."

"No, wait, I didn't mean for you to—" Susan began, but before she could stop him he carelessly flung the bag in her direction. She couldn't catch it, though, before it fell into the road. Susan heard the drover laugh as she rushed over to retrieve it. She had no idea what she might have said or done to deserve this sort of treatment; the old codger was being mean only for its own sake.

Sighing, she picked up the bag by its strap and slung it over her shoulder, then followed the wagon up the road, swatting at the skeeters that purred around her face. Nearby was a log flume, elevated upon stilts a few feet above the ground. The camp was only a couple of hundred yards away; it was late afternoon, the early autumn sun beginning to set behind Mt. Shapiro. Still time enough for her to locate her uncle and find out where she was supposed to stay.

From somewhere through the trees, the sound of something like rolling thunder. Susan looked around in time to see a massive rough bark log, seven or eight feet long and twice as thick as her own body, making its descent down the flume. Carried along by a rush of water, the log bumped against the sides of the trough as it hurtled to the bottom of the mountain, where the flume spilled into Mill Creek. There it would be lashed together with other logs, then floated down the creek to Clarksburg and the mills, where it would be cured, cut, and sawn into lumber.

Interesting, but not her concern. She was here on business of a more scientific nature. Or at least that was how she perceived it; she had no idea whether her uncle would see things the same way.

The logging camp had been established on a saddleback on the south-western slopes of Mt. Shapiro, a couple of thousand feet below the summit. A dozen canvas tents erected on wood platforms; ten were large enough to sleep a half-dozen people, while the other two had been joined together to form a mess tent. Clothes hung from lines strung between the tents. A couple of privies at the edge of the woods, and a small shack that, judging from the adjacent water tank, served as communal bathhouse. Nearby was a corral where a couple of shags grazed on hay bales; the wagon she'd ridden up the mountain was parked next to it, but the drover was nowhere in sight. Indeed, the camp appeared to be deserted, yet wood smoke drifted upward from a tin flue poking through the roof of the mess tent, and that was a good sign that someone was inside.

The screen door creaked on rusty hinges as she pulled it open, slammed shut behind her as she stepped inside. The tent was dim, the fish-oil lamps hanging from the rafter beams as yet unlit. A long blackwood table ran down the center of the room, with benches on either side; a potbellied stove stood off to one side, a pile of tree knots beside it, and the air was warm with the aroma of baked bread. From behind a closed flap at the far side of the room, she heard faint voices.

"Hello?" Susan left her bag next to the door, cautiously ventured closer. "Anyone here?"

The voices went silent, then she heard a chair moving back. The flap moved aside and a heavyset woman, starch-fed and with snarled blond hair, peered out at her. She said nothing for a moment, examining Susan with eyes narrow and suspicious, then she glanced behind her. "Yep, it's her," she said to someone else, then she looked back at Susan. "Well, don't just stand there. He's waiting for you."

Susan hesitated, then walked across the dining room, ducking her head a little as she passed through the flap impatiently held open by the woman. The kitchen was cramped: crates and barrels stacked against the walls, a wooden cupboard, a bunk bed, a small table upon which someone had been cutting vegetables. Skillets and pots hung from hooks along the rafter, and a large kettle simmered atop a brick oven.

Two men sat in wicker rocking chairs next to the oven. One was the wagon driver; he favored her with a wily told-you-so smirk as he took a drink from the earthware jug in his lap. Susan didn't recognize the other man until he turned around, and even then it took her a moment to realize that he was her uncle.

"Would'a gotten here a lot quicker if you'da let James bring you the rest'a the way." Lars Thompson's tongue was thick with alcohol; she could smell the bearshine on his breath from ten feet away. "Hope you enjoyed your constitutional."

"Just thought I'd stretch my legs." James cackled at this, and she decided not to mention the rest. "Good to see you again, Uncle Lars."

"Well, hell . . ." Lars rose from his chair, stomped across the kitchen to wrap his arms around her. "Good t'see you too, Susie," he said, using a childhood nickname she'd long since outgrown. "Been a long time . . . a long time."

Drunk or not, at least he got that part right. It had been many years since the last time she'd seen Aunt Marie's husband. There was no blood-relation between them; her father's younger sister had met Lars when they'd served together in the Rigil Kent brigade during the Revolution. That was back when they'd all lived in Defiance, and although Susan had only been a child then, she remembered how much Carlos had disapproved of his sister taking up with Lars; indeed, only a few months after Liberation Day, after he'd become mayor of Liberty, her father had exiled both of them from New Florida, after they'd come close to killing someone in a brawl.

As a condition of their punishment, he and Aunt Marie, along with the savant Manuel Castro, had been sent out to explore the frontier. Their mission had succeeded, in spades; after several months of exploring the southern coast of Great Dakota, the trio established a camp on its southeastern shore, just across the West Channel from New Florida. Great Dakota offered vast forests that didn't exist on New Florida and were more accessible than the ones on Midland, and so it wasn't long before Lars and Marie were joined by his Uncle Clark and Aunt Molly. Together with Lars's younger brother Garth, they founded Clarksburg, thus setting up a family-owned timber company that would soon become the colony's main industry.

All lamb on Coyote bore white wool, yet nonetheless Susan knew the expression "black sheep of the family," and how that applied to Lars Thompson. Clark Thompson had been the colony's original major, but after he was killed in an accident, his elder nephew had assumed the role. Lars was a drunk, though, and his incompetence nearly led the colony to ruin before his own family had deposed him. Aunt Molly assumed the task of leading the new colony, but only for a short while; by then, Marie had straightened out her act, and it wouldn't be long before even Garth, once as wild as his older brother, was responsible enough to take over the job of mayor.

To keep Lars satisfied, Molly Thompson gave Lars the job of running the family's logging operations in the Black Mountains. On the whole, it was a wise decision. Lars was never a good politician, but he was a pretty good boss, and considering that the Thompson clan derived its power and fortune from the timber business, the position of camp foreman carried considerable responsibility. Yet it was no secret that his family would have little to do with him otherwise; he seldom spoke to either his aunt or younger brother, and his wife remained married to him in name only.

So here he was, her wicked Uncle Lars: tough and lean as a faux-birch sapling, hair cropped short by a careless pair of scissors, beard long and coarse and tinged with grey. No more than forty by Gregorian reckoning, nonetheless he looked much older; he might have been pleasant to look upon, were it not for a couple of missing teeth and the hollow look of someone who'd spent far too many nights with a jug in his lap.

"Good to see you, too." Susan gently prized herself from his arms. "Sorry it took awhile to get here."

"Well, y'know . . ." Lars stifled a burp behind his hand. " 'S'cuse me . . . I understand you're a teacher now. Spendin' your time lecturin' and writin' and all that, don't s'pose you get much a chance to see your kin." He turned to the others. "James, Tillie, this here's my niece. Susan Montero. Come all the way out here to help with our l'il pest control problem."

"Hope so. 'Bout ready to make me lose my mind." Tillie had settled down on a stool next to the table, where she resumed dicing potatoes and carrots. "Have to keep a light on all night, just so they won't swipe any-thing. Can't hardly sleep a wink."

"Yeah, well, least you get some." James took another swig from the jug. "Gotten to the point where I have'ta post night watch on the corral. Spook the shags one more time, they're liable to break down the fence."

"They harass the shags?" Susan became curious. "Never heard of *chirreep* doing that."

"That your name for 'em?" Lars took the jug from James. "Treecrawlers is what we call 'em. 'Course you'd know better, considering how you've studied 'em."

"You study these things?" James gave Susan a bleary-eyed stare. "Thought Lars just said you were a teacher." He looked at Lars. "Shee'it, thas' what she tol' me. If 'n I'd known better . . ."

"I'm a naturalist. I teach biology at the university, when I'm not doing fieldwork." She tried to make it as plain as possible, yet no one seemed to understand what she was saying. "I study *chirreep* . . . treecrawlers, I mean . . . in their natural habitat."

"Been doing this all her life." Lars draped an arm around her shoulders. "In fact, when she was a little girl, she—"

"I'm sorry, but I'm really tired." Susan knew what her uncle was about to say, and it wasn't something she liked to discuss, least of all with strangers. Not only that, but there was something in the way he touched her that made her uneasy. "It's been a long day," she said, quickly stepping out from beneath his arm. "I could use a nap. If you could show me where I'm going to stay . . ."

"Sure, 'course." Stroking his beard, Lars made a pretense of pondering the question. "Now that I think of it, there's a spare cot in my tent. Private quarters, too, so you wouldn't have to—"

"My upper bunk is empty." Tillie didn't look up from her work. "Joe, my husband, he's gone into town for a few days, so I'm sure he won't mind. Gets a little busy at mealtime, but if you'd like to lend a hand . . ."

"Love to. Whatever I can do to help." Susan hoped that she hadn't spo-ken too quickly; from the corner of her eye, she could see Lars glaring at the cook. "It'll give me a chance to meet everyone here. Might help me as-sess the situation a little better."

Tillie laughed out loud. "You're going to be assessing biscuits and ham at five in the morning, but that's all right with me. Get that bag of yours, then you can grab a little shut-eye." Rising from the table, she gathered a double handful of diced potatoes and dropped them into the kettle. "You men need to take your cocktail hour somewhere else. I've got dinner to make, and our guest would like a little time to herself. Now shoo."

It seemed for a moment that Lars was going to argue with her, but when Tillie looked back at him, there was something in her face that made him reconsider. "Well, awright then," he murmured, then he headed for the back door, motioning for James to follow him. "See you later, Susie. We'll talk some more at dinner . . . and I got someone I want you to meet."

"Looking forward to it." Susan watched as the two men wandered out of the kitchen. The screen door slammed shut, and she sighed and sat down on a barrel. "Thanks," she said quietly. "I appreciate the save."

"Think nothing of it." Tillie dropped some carrots into the kettle. "Half the women in camp have had to be saved from him."

Susan had been looking for an excuse to get rid of Uncle Lars, but once she climbed up on the bunk bed, she realized how tired she really was. So she dozed for an hour or so, listening to Tillie humming to herself as she moved around the kitchen, and as the daylight seeping in through the cracks in the tent began to wane, she got up and asked if there was anything she could do.

Tillie put her to work in the dining room, setting the table for dinner. Plates, mugs, and flatware were stacked in the kitchen cupboard; once they were laid out, the cook showed Susan how to stoke a fire in the potbellied stove. Once it was hot, Tillie brought out a pan of fresh-baked corn bread and placed it on top to keep warm; she placed jugs of sourgrass ale on the table, then stepped outside to ring the dinner bell. By the time she brought out the stew, the loggers were coming through the front door.

They were big men, hard as the mountain upon which they worked, their faces and clothes filthy, their boots caked with mud and wood chips. A few women as well, but they were nearly as muscular as the men; in a couple of instances, Susan had to look twice to make sure they were female. They stamped their boots on a mat just outside the door, then took off their jackets and hung them from hooks on the support posts as they made their way to the table, taking places to which they'd long since become accustomed. As they filled their mugs with ale, Tillie quietly showed Susan how to ladle the thick vegetable stew into serving bowls and pass them down the table along with platters of corn bread. Only a few loggers seemed to notice that there was a new face among them; most were too tired to care.

Uncle Lars was among the last to arrive. He came in with a young man little more than a teenager; like most of the woodcutters, his hair was shoulder-length, tied back and kept out of his eyes by a bandana. A good-looking kid, despite the layer of grime on his face. Lars gave her a wave, then pointed to a couple of seats left open at the end of the table. Susan nodded and let Tillie finish serving dinner.

"Making yourself useful. Glad to see it." Lars wasn't nearly as dirty or exhausted as the men who worked for him, she couldn't help but notice. "Thanks for helping out. Tillie needs a hand when Joe isn't around."

"Least I could do." It appeared that her uncle had sobered up a bit; perhaps he'd taken a nap, too. "Thanks for offering a bed, but she said I could stay with her if I—"

"Think nothing of it." Lars's face went red, and the teenager glanced first at her, then at him. "Might as well get some of that stew while there's still some left." As she took a seat across the table from the young man, Lars motioned for Tillie to pass them the serving bowl. "Wanted you two to meet," he went on. "This here's my boy, Hawk. He's been working up here this season, learning the family trade. Hawk, this is your cousin Susan. She's come here to—"

"See if she can help us get the treecrawlers under control." Hawk took the bowl as it came to him, politely offered it to Susan. "Know all about it, Pop. You told me last week, remember?"

"I did?" Lars's brow furrowed as he searched his memory. "Umm, well, I guess I . . ."

"You were drinking at the time." Hawk ladled some stew onto his plate, then handed it to Susan before helping himself to the corn bread. "Long trip from Liberty?"

"Umm . . . yes, it was." Susan took some stew and corn bread, then passed the bowl and platter to her uncle. "Took a wagon to Leeport, then bought passage on a keelboat to Clarksburg. Stayed with your mother and sister in town last night, then caught a ride up here. Got in late this afternoon." Catching the look in his eyes, she realized that she'd mentioned places he'd never been. "I'm sorry we've never met until now."

Indeed, until yesterday she'd never laid eyes on either one of her cousins. It was only last night that she'd met Hawk's sister, Rain, for the first time, a sweet little girl who'd proudly shown off her watercolor sketches of the Clarksburg harbor. Aunt Marie had said little about Hawk, though, except that he'd recently dropped out of school to move up into the mountains with his father. The only pictures she had of him were from childhood, and they bore scant resemblance to the young man who sat across the table from her. It was as if her aunt had written off her older child as a loss to her estranged husband, and now doted upon the one who'd stayed with her.

"We don't get into town much," Lars said, as if this explained everything. "We come up here soon as the snow melts and stay until it gets too cold to work. Beginning of each season, we move camp to another part of the range, wherever we find a good stand of timber we can—"

"Pop tells me you know a lot about 'crawlers." Hawk passed the serving bowl to his father. "Did he ask you here, or did Mom?"

Lars scowled. "I told you . . ."

"Your mother did," Susan said. "She got in touch with the Colonial University, told them that the company was having trouble with *chirreep* . . . treecrawlers, I mean . . . and asked if they had any experts who could come out here to study the problem." She shrugged. "As it turned out, they did . . . me."

"Like I was saying," Lars continued, "I knew your cousin was studying this sort of thing, so I told your mom, 'Y'know, you oughta get 'em to send out Cousin Susie, 'cause she's—' "

"Sure you did." Hawk barely glanced his way. "Hey, lucky break for us. A scientist in the family, ready to drop everything and come all the way out here to—"

"Watch that tongue, boy. Gonna get you in trouble." Lars didn't look up as he shoveled stew into his mouth, yet for the first time Hawk didn't respond to his father. "Yeah, we've had a helluva time with those *chirreep*." He mispronounced it as *shire-reep*, not *sure-reep* as Susan had said. "First it was them stealing stuff, and that wasn't so bad so long as we locked everything away, but lately they've taken to sabotage."

"Really? What do you mean?"

"Trying to knock down the flume, for starters. Pulling down one of two support beams so that the trough collapses when we send down a log. Done that three times already. And once they pried a hole in the spill dam, so . . ."

From the other side of the room, a sudden crash as a plate shattered on the floor. Someone bellowed an obscenity, and Susan looked up in time to see one burly logger hurl himself across the table at another man. The next instant, the mess tent was filled with the sounds of a fistfight; men and women stood up, either to get out of the way or see what was going on.

"Oh, hell." Lars leapt to his feet, rushed toward the brawl. "Awright, damn it, break it up, break it up!"

"Don't worry 'bout it." Hawk scarcely seemed to notice the fight. "Happens all the time. Just their way of saying how much they love each other."

Susan regarded him quietly as he daubed a piece of corn bread in his stew. No more than five or six Coyote years; too young to be so cynical. "Pardon me for saying so," she said, keeping her voice low, "but I have a feeling you don't get along with your father very well."

"Oh, no. We're best friends. So long as he isn't drunk, that is." Hawk didn't look up at her as he swirled a spoon through the stew on his plate. "So tell me . . . did he try to get you to sleep with him, or did you ask Tillie to put you up just because you wanted to learn how to make this crap?"

Susan didn't know whether to laugh or slap the kid across the face. "Neither," she said at last, doing her best to muster a reply. "I figured I'd sleep with you, and let your father teach Tillie how to cook."

His eyes slowly rose. He stared at her for a long moment, as if trying to determine whether she was joking or not. A smile twitched at the corners of his mouth. "Are you sure we're related?"

"Oops, I forgot. I'm your cousin, aren't I?" She shrugged. "Sorry, offer rescinded."

"No problem." He chuckled, then the smile faded. "Not that it wouldn't have stopped Pop. He's already made moves on most of the women in camp, even the wives of guys who work for him." He blushed and looked away. "Why draw the line at his own niece?"

"Sorry." She didn't know why she said this, yet he nodded all the same. "If you don't like him so much—"

"Why am I here?" Hawk gazed across the room. His father had stopped the fight, and now he was seated at the opposite side of the tent, talking with the loggers who'd been at each other's throats only a few minutes ago. They were passing around a jug of ale, and there was no sign that he was returning anytime soon. "I dunno . . . kinda figure my options are limited. Stay with Mom and paint pretty pictures like Rain, or come up here and learn the family business." He glanced at Susan. "What do you think? Do I look like an artist to you?"

No, she thought, *you look like a kid who doesn't know what he wants from life.* And more the pity, because he was obviously a more intelligent person than one who should be spending his time splitting logs. She gazed at the wood-cutters seated around them. They were the sons of starship engineers, the daughters of pioneers, yet through the years of learning how to survive on this world they'd forgotten their legacy, until now all they had were splinters in their hands and dirt under their nails, and only the most vague memory of the cosmos. And in this way, one generation became less than those that had come before it.

She tried the stew, discovered that it was awful. An idea occurred to her. "How long have you been up here? Since last Machidiel?"

"Pretty much." A suspicious look. "If you're going to tell me I should go back to school . . ."

"No, no." Although that was her first thought, Hawk obviously wasn't interested in having another adult giving him well-meaning advice; he'd clearly rejected completing his formal education as much as he'd rejected his mother's efforts to make him more like his sister. "Look, you know the mountains, right? Well, I don't, and I'm going to need a guide."

"So why don't you ask someone else?" Not a snide comment, but an honest question.

"Like who? Your father?" She raised an eyebrow. "If I'm going to do my job right, I've got to get as far away from camp as possible. That's where I'm going to find the *chirreep*. But I don't want your dad to get me out there alone . . . you said that yourself."

"No." Hawk shook his head. "No, that's not such a good idea."

Susan gestured to the men sitting around them. "Maybe some of these guys know the woods," she went on, "but I don't know them. Unless you want to introduce me to—"

"I know what you're saying." Hawk seemed to think about it a moment. "Look, I might be able to get away for a couple of days, but what am I going to tell him?"

"What's wrong with the truth? I've hired you to be my guide . . . my research assistant, if you want to put a fancy name to it." She paused. "There's money in it. The university gave me a small grant for expenses. Call it . . . say, thirty dollars a day."

"Thirty?" He shut his eyes in disgust. "Try again, cuz."

"All right, forty."

"Sixty."

"Fifty. High as I go."

He sighed. "All right, fifty . . . but you carry your own pack."

"Did I say I wouldn't?" Fifty dollars a day was steep—she knew the loggers earned that much for a week's work—but she needed him, and he knew it. The kid was sharp, all right. "Don't worry, I know how to hike backcountry."

"Didn't say that you didn't. So when do we start?"

Susan didn't reply. As they were speaking, she'd gazed down the table. Uncle Lars was drinking with his guys; the plates had been shoved aside, and they were working their way through another jug. Yet, in that moment, he happened to look straight at her, and there was a certain glint in his eyes that caused a shiver to run down her back.

"Soon as possible," she murmured. "First thing tomorrow."

She awoke to the sound of Tillie humming to herself as she stirred flour and eggs into batter for the breakfast biscuits. It was still dark outside, yet coffee was already brewing in an urn on top of the oven. Susan's first impulse was to roll over and go back to sleep, but Tillie would have none of it; she prodded her awake and made her get dressed, and once Susan returned from the privy, Tillie put her to work setting the table. Susan had barely finished when the loggers started coming in; they drank coffee until Tillie brought out the biscuits and gravy, then reappeared a few minutes later with a platter of sliced ham. No one spoke much; it was too early in the morning for conversation.

Hawk showed up while she was helping Tillie prepare sack lunches for the crew. He gave her a quiet nod, but otherwise said nothing to her; at his insistence, they hadn't told anyone where they were going. The sole exception was Uncle Lars, and only because he had to know that Susan had hired his son to be her guide. All the same, Susan noticed that Hawk said little to his father when he finally showed up. Not that he was in a talkative mood anyway; with his eyes swollen and his shoulders slumped, he was obviously nursing a hangover.

After she helped Tillie clean up, she found Hawk waiting for her outside. He'd brought a small pack, into which he'd stuffed a canteen, a map, a compass, and a flashlight. Susan had her own pack, in which she carried, along with a canteen and lunch for them both, a camera, a satphone, and a pair of binoculars.

Dawn had painted the sky with wispy slashes of crimson and gold as they began hiking up the trail to the logging site. The crew had already left camp, and Susan and Hawk followed the timber wagons into the forest; from far ahead, they could hear voices coming through the trees, breaking the cool silence of the morning. Scarlet pikes cawed at them from the lower branches of the trees, as if threatening to impale them on clingberry thorns as they did with the leafbugs upon which they preyed. Susan caught a brief glimpse of a pair of shy brown eyes peering at her from a hole beneath a faux birch, then a root rat scurried back into its lair. The woods were alive, its inhabitants spying on the intruders.

"Not a bad place to spend a year," she said, and Hawk gave her a skeptical look. "Here, I mean. I'm rather envious."

"Thought you grew up in the mountains."

"I did, but Great Dakota has a different ecosystem from Midland. There's species here you don't find on the Gillis Range." She smiled. "You know, we've been on this world almost forty years, Earth-time, and yet we've explored less than a quarter of it."

"Yeah? So?"

"Aren't you curious? About what we haven't seen yet?"

"I guess." He shrugged. "If you weren't busy trying to make a living."

She was trying to figure how to respond to that when there was a sharp crack from somewhere up ahead, followed by a loud crash that echoed down the mountainside. "Hey, they just brought down a big one," Hawk said, quickening his pace. "C'mon, you want to see this."

Susan followed him up the trail until, all of a sudden, they emerged from the woods; there were no more trees around them, and a vast clearing stretched away as far as the eye could see. A short distance away, several loggers stood around a giant blackwood they'd just felled. Its lower branches had already been trimmed away, and now the trunk itself lay upon the ground, like a titan brought low by a gang of dwarves.

"They've been working on that one all week," Hawk said. "These old ones, they're pretty hard to bring down. Guess someone got up here early to make the final cut."

Susan didn't answer. She was awestruck by what she saw. Where there had once been old-growth forest were now mile upon mile of barren slope. Scraggly undergrowth surrounded vast acres of raw stumps, with granite boulders now laid bare beneath the sun. She'd seen logging operations before—quite a bit of Midland's rain forests had been harvested, particularly on the western side of Mt. Shaw—but the sheer scale of the clear-cutting being done here in the Black Mountains boggled the mind. Blackwood, mountain rough bark, faux birch, swoops-nest briar: all leveled indiscriminately, with nothing larger than the smallest sapling left standing.

"Good God," she whispered. "What are you people doing?"

Hawk looked at her. "What do you mean, what are we doing? We're cutting down trees."

"I don't . . . you don't . . ."

"We started on the other side of the mountain," he went on, oblivious to her shock as he pointed to the northeast. "About eight seasons ago, back in a valley the other side of Thunder Ridge, then began making our way over here. Trick is finding a good stand where you can put in a road. Last spring, we moved the camp over to this side, to get us closer to the creek. Took us a while to put in the flume, but since we did, we've been moving out twice as much timber as we did last year."

They began making their way through the clearing, stepping over dead branches, passing stumps sawed low to the ground. Here and there, men and women used crosscut saws to cut trunks into logs, which were then anchored together end-to-end by thick chains fastened to iron hooks hammered deep into the wood. Shags dragged the logs to nearby wagons, where they were loaded aboard and carried to the flume. The larger branches were pulled aside to be trimmed to size, the smaller ones thrown upon massive piles where they would be burned.

"We're using hand equipment, for the most part," Hawk explained, "but look over there." He pointed to where a couple of men were carefully mounting a yellow-painted instrument upon a tripod. "That's Big Lucy, our particle-beam laser. Used to be a Union Guard weapon until Pop managed to swing a deal for it. Takes a lot of juice, so we only use it for—"

"And you're not replanting." Susan stared back at the ground they'd just crossed. Already there were signs of soil erosion, deep furrows in the mud where rain was washing away what remained of the ground cover. "You just cut everything down, then move on."

"Umm . . . yeah, sure. There's plenty of trees left."

Susan looked at him, saw nothing in his face save for ignorance. "I've seen enough here," she said quietly. "Let's go."

Leaving the site behind, Hawk led her across the clearing to a trail that went farther up the mountain. It had been made by an exploration team, he said; if they continued to follow it, they'd eventually reach some cliffs at the base of the summit. After that, they would have to bushwhack it; nonetheless, they might be able to make it to the top of Mt. Shapiro by noon, and still be back in camp by sundown.

"That sounds good," Susan said. "The *chirreep* might use this same trail, and it could lead us to their habitat."

Hawk seemed puzzled. "We always figured they live in the trees."

"If that were so, don't you think you would have found them already?" She shook her head. "*Chirreep* usually build their dwellings on the ground. The ones on Barren Isle live in sand-domes, and the group we found on Midland burrowed holes in the side of a cliff." That was getting close to something she didn't like to discuss, so she went on. "This tribe might be arboreal, sure, but I'm willing to bet that if you haven't found any abandoned tree houses in the blackwoods you've cut down, then that's not where they're living."

"If you say so." He shrugged. "You always figured they're . . . y'know, like apes or something."

"They're not animals," Susan said quietly.

The trail brought them to the top of the log flume, where a stream trickled down the side of the mountain. It had been diverted to a small pond just above the flume where a spill-dam had been erected; a rotary winch positioned on top of the wall raised and lowered a narrow gate above the mouth of the flume. Hawk explained to her that, when the crew was ready to send logs down the mountain, they opened the dam's gate and allowed the pond to flood the trough. "Can't use the flume when we've had a dry spell," he said, "but after we've had enough rain, we can send logs all the way to Mill Creek . . . provided, of course, that the treecrawlers haven't played with the flume again."

"Your father said something about that last night." Susan studied the dam; about eight feet high, it was built of mud-packed logs, the pond behind filmed over with floating algae. "Have they ever sabotaged this?"

"Once." Hawk pointed to a place at the bottom of the dam where a small hole had been patched. "They pried open a couple of logs here. Didn't do much damage, except for causing the water to drain out. We found the hole and plugged it up, and they've stayed away ever since. It was after that when they took to knocking down support beams."

Susan frowned. "Doesn't make sense. *Chirreep* are usually shy of people . . . they only come around when they think we have something worth stealing. This is the first time I've heard of them trying to destroy anything we've built."

"You said this was a different tribe. Maybe they do things differently. Of course, you're the expert."

"No one's an expert on *chirreep*. Except maybe another *chirreep*." She patted the side of the dam, then turned away. "C'mon, let's go. Maybe we'll find something farther up the mountain."

The woods became more dense as they climbed uphill, and before long they couldn't hear the sound of the loggers at work. The trail followed the stream for a while, then gradually cut away, making a series of switchbacks that meandered up the mountainside. The slope gradually became steeper as well, and by late morning they found themselves approaching a line of sheer granite bluffs, sixty to a hundred feet high, that loomed over them as a vast wall of rock. The summit was now less than a thousand feet away, but here the trail came to an end; if they wanted to reach the mountaintop, they would have to find their own way.

Susan found a large boulder near the base of the bluffs; she climbed on top, then sat down and pulled out her binoculars to study the escarpment. As carefully as she searched, though, she couldn't find any indications of cliff dwellings. Of course, the *chirreep* might have concealed their homes behind tree branches, but still . . .

"Ever seen any smoke coming from up here?" she asked.

"Now and then, sure." Sitting beside her on the boulder, Hawk took a drink from his canteen. "We get lightning storms up here all the time. Sometimes they cause brush fires." Then he looked at her askance. "Oh, c'mon, you can't be saying . . ."

"They know how to make fire. That might have been what you saw, and just didn't know it."

"You've seen that?"

"Uh-huh." She trained her binoculars on the top of the bluffs, search-ing for signs of chimney holes.

"Y'know, I've heard—" Hawk stopped himself. He was quiet for a minute or so before he went on. "Mom once told me that you were kid-napped by them. A long time ago, back during the Revolution."

Susan lowered her binoculars. Damn. She should have known this was coming. Aunt Marie had been there, after all, and this was a story she would've told her children, perhaps late at night when she was putting them to bed. No sense in denying it. In fact, maybe it would help him understand.

"It happened, yeah," she said. "On Mt. Bonestell, just outside Shady Grove. I was a little girl then, about Rain's age. Your Uncle Carlos and Aunt Wendy brought me there, along with the rest of the children from Defi-ance. They were trying to keep us safe from the Union Guard, but when we got to Shady Grove—"

"I know the rest. Some treecrawlers . . . *chirreep*, I mean . . . grabbed you just outside the stockade and took you up the mountain. Your folks came to rescue you." He peered at her. "You mean it's true? It's not just a story?"

"No, it really happened," she said, yet that wasn't all that had occurred. Hawk didn't know how that tribe of *chirreep* had fallen under the sway of Zoltan Shirow, the leader of a religious cult who'd come to Coyote. When his original flock had perished on Mt. Shaw, Zoltan had fled into the Gillis Range; eventually he'd found the *chirreep*, who'd come to worship him as a god. Her parents had kept this part of the tale from everyone, and had sworn her to silence, because one of their best friends was Ben Harlan, who'd been Zoltan's guide during their doomed trek across the Midland mountains. Ben had lost the woman he loved on Mt. Shaw, and Susan's parents wanted to let him continue to believe that Zoltan was dead. Not that it mattered much in the long run, for Zoltan had doubtless been killed during the eruption of Mt. Bonestell, along with the *chirreep* tribe, yet his involvement in that incident was something of which very few people were aware, even to this day.

"That's how I got interested in the *chirreep*." She pulled out her can-teen, unscrewed its cap. "When they took me inside their cliff dwelling, I got a look at how they lived. Not much, of course. I was a little kid, scared out of my wits. But I saw tools, clothes . . ."

"Oh, c'mon."

"You still think they're animals, don't you?" She took a sip of water. "Far from it. More likely they're much like hominids, early predecessors to homo sapiens, except maybe a little more advanced. They know how to fashion tools, control fire, build dwellings . . . it even appears that they have some sort of language."

"Yeah. Right." He looked away. "Next thing you're going to tell me, they're building starships."

Susan let out her breath, gazed at the forest surrounding them. "You know," she said after a while, "you're a pretty smart kid." Hawk smirked, but she went on. "No, I mean that, really. There wasn't enough in Clarksburg to hold your interest, so you moved up here with your father, but it's pretty clear that you've seen through him as well, and I don't see you becoming a lumberjack."

"Logger." He scowled. "We don't use that other word."

"Logger, okay. But is that what you really want to do with your life?" She put the cap back on her canteen. "As for the *chirreep*, I'm beginning to wonder about why they've taken to knocking down—"

"Shh!" Hawk suddenly held up a hand, hushing her. He cocked his head, as if listening to something in the forest. "Just heard something."

Susan held her breath, quickly glanced about. She had little doubt that the boy's senses were more attuned to the mountains, yet so far as she could tell, nothing had disturbed the late-morning solitude save for an autumn breeze rippling through the trees. When she looked back at her companion, though, she was surprised to see that he'd drawn a weapon from his pack: a flechette pistol, the type once carried by the Union Guard during the occupation. Hundreds of firearms like this had been left behind when the Union was forced off Coyote, yet nonetheless she was surprised to see one in the hands of someone so young.

"Are you sure?" she whispered. "I didn't—"

"I did." Hawk squatted on the boulder, gun clasped in his right hand as his eyes darted left and right. "Thought it was behind you, but—"

"But maybe it was behind *you*," a new voice said.

Startled, Hawk twisted around on his hips, almost losing his balance as he swept his gun toward the figure who'd just come from behind a briar only a few yards away.

"Easy now," the stranger said, slowly raising his hands to show that they were empty. "No reason to get excited."

"What . . . who are you?" The pistol trembled in Hawk's hands. "What are you doing here?"

"I was about to ask you the same." A quick smile as the stranger's gaze traveled to Susan. "On the other hand, I pretty much know that already. If you're looking for *chirreep,* you might try to keep your voices down. I heard you a hundred yards away. If I could, so can they."

"Sorry. Weren't expecting to find anyone else up here." Susan relaxed a little, but not much. The newcomer was about her age, tall and lean, with dark brown hair beginning to grow long and a beard that looked as if it'd been only recently cultivated. He wore a homespun serape and a wide-brim catskin hat, and a rifle was slung over his right shoulder. There was something about him that seemed vaguely familiar, yet she couldn't quite put her finger on it. "If you know so much about us . . ."

"Only said I know why you're here. Like I said, your voices carry." He glanced again at Hawk, who was still pointing the gun at him. "That's rather rude, you know. Put that away before you hurt someone."

"Hawk . . ." Susan glared at the boy, and he reluctantly lowered the pistol. If she'd known he'd packed a gun, she would have made him leave it behind. "I'm Susan Montero," she went on. "I'm a naturalist, conducting research for the Colonial University. This is my cousin Hawk Thompson. He's my guide."

"How interesting." The stranger put his back against the tree, folding his arms together as he casually studied them. "You're related then . . . and I take, Master Thompson, that you're of the same family that owns the timber company."

"Uh-huh." It was plain that Hawk still didn't trust him, for he didn't return the gun to his pack. "I didn't catch your name."

"That's because I didn't give it." He regarded them both for a moment, as if trying to make up his mind whether to explain his presence, then he stepped away from the tree. "Very well, then. Pleased to make your acquaintance. Just wanted to know who was making all the racket." He started to turn away. "I hope you have a delightful hike. Now, if you'll excuse me . . ."

"Wait a minute." All at once, Susan remembered where she'd seen him before. A couple of months earlier, shortly after the new starship from Earth had arrived. The first group from the ship to land in Shuttlefield had included a senior officer who'd mysteriously vanished that same evening. Susan had met him only briefly, but all the same . . .

"You're Jonathan Parson," she said. "The second officer of the *Columbus*."

The stranger stopped. "You're mistaken. Name's John Carroll. I used to work at the mill before I moved up here to homestead."

Susan looked at Hawk, and he shook his head. "I haven't heard of anyone homesteading on this side of the mountain," he said. "You got that satphone?" Susan nodded, then reached down to take it from her pack. "Shouldn't take but a minute to check with the company office," Hawk continued. "They've got records for all former employees."

"Good idea." Susan handed him the phone. "While you're at it, call the blueshirts, too. They've been looking all over for Parson since he—"

"Okay, all right." Turning to face them, Parson held up his hands. "No need to get smart about it."

"And so the truth comes out." Susan took the phone back from Hawk. "So what are you doing up here? Besides hiding out, I mean."

"I don't know what you—"

"C'mon. You know something about the *chirreep* . . . you just said so yourself." He feigned a confused shrug as if to deny this, but she shook her head. "You called them *chirreep*, not treecrawlers. That's pretty specific knowledge for someone who's been here for . . . what, little more than two months?"

"Yeah. Not only that, but you also said they could've heard us coming." Hawk nodded toward the bluffs. "Makes me wonder if you know where they live."

"And if I did, why should I tell you?" Parson gave him a stern look. "Your family is destroying their habitat. All I have to do is go down the trail a couple of miles, and I can show you—"

"Seen it already," Susan said, "and I don't like it any more than you do." Hawk stared at her, but she ignored him. "Look, I'll be straight with you. My school sent me out here to investigate reports that *chirreep* have been attacking logging operations. The company wants to put a stop to this, but I'm more interested in finding out the reason why. If you can help us—"

"Why should I?"

"Then I'll make sure you're left alone." She held up the satphone. "No calls to the blueshirts, and the company doesn't have to know one of their former workers is where he ought not be." She glanced at Hawk. "Isn't that right?"

Hawk was quiet for a moment, then he nodded. "Sure. Doesn't matter to me."

"So your secret is safe," Susan went on. "And if you know something we don't, maybe we can work together to find a way to protect the *chirreep*. If you heard everything I said, then you know I mean them no harm." She paused. "So what do you say?"

Parson gazed at the silent forest around them. For a moment, it almost seemed as if he was listening to voices only he could hear. "Let me think about it," he said at last. "I'll get back to you later."

"If you need my satphone code . . ."

"I've got other ways. Now, go back to your camp. You'll hear from me later . . . if you hear from me at all."

And then he turned away once more, walking back the way he'd come. Susan tried to observe which direction he was headed, yet within moments he was lost among the trees, disappearing into the forest as if he'd never been there.

"Oh, man, that's weird." Hawk let out his breath, then he looked at Susan. "You really think he knows something?"

She slowly nodded. "Yes, I do." In fact, she was counting on it.

That evening, once she'd set the table and helped Tillie serve dinner, Susan ate alone in the kitchen. She didn't want to talk to anyone, lest they ask her what she'd found on the mountain that day, and she'd made Hawk swear not to tell Uncle Lars about meeting Jonathan Parson. Besides, she had work to do.

So she sat cross-legged on the upper bunk of Tillie's bed, nibbling at a plate of goat cheese and sourdough bread as she studied her pad, reviewing reports her colleagues at the university had previously written about the

behavioral patterns of the *chirreep*. As she suspected, there was precious little useful information. Even after all these years, not much was known
about the *chirreep;* most of their knowledge had been derived from chance
encounters in the wild, and even then much of that was hearsay and
rumor.

Four years ago, before she'd joined the university, the biology department had sent an expedition to Barren Isle, where her father had discovered what he'd then called sandthieves. According to Zoltan Shirow—the
first and, so far, the only human known to have successfully communi-
cated with them—this tribe was known as the *chirreep-ka;* as Carlos Montero had later observed, they were smaller and more primitive than the
ones who'd abducted her from Shady Grove. Yet they were just as elusive;
although the expedition had no trouble locating their sand-domes, the
chirreep-ka remained in hiding the entire two weeks the expedition spent
on the island. Remote cameras and motion detectors were set up, camou-
flaged hunter's blinds were built near the domes, food and trinkets were set
out as bait, and then the scientists waited for days and nights on end for the
tiny aboriginals to show themselves. Yet save for two or three brief instances when the scientists happened to spot a small form scurrying
through the brush, the *chirreep-ka* went unseen. It was as if the sandthieves
had known they were coming and had resolved not to reveal themselves,
even if it meant facing slow starvation. In the end, realizing that they were
causing harm to their subjects, the expedition had left Barren Isle with little more knowledge of the *chirreep-ka* than they had before they'd arrived.

No. The answer to this mystery didn't lie in previous research, or in the
academic theories of her colleagues. She had to dig much deeper than that.
Like it or not, she had to return to the nightmare she'd endured as a child.

Ignoring the boisterous voices coming from the other side of the mess
tent, Susan straightened her back, clasped her hands together in her lap,
and shut her eyes . . .

*Wandering away from Shady Grove. Curious to see what lay outside the stock-
ade walls. She's a little girl, and it's a lovely morning in late winter. Her mother and
father aren't around, but what harm could come from taking a walk by herself? So
she slips away through the front gate, heads for the woods near the settlement. But
she's not alone, and she doesn't know this until she suddenly finds herself confronted
by a brown-furred creature almost as tall as she is . . .*

Harsh laughter from nearby. Distracted, Susan briefly opened her eyes, then shut them. Go back. Back through the years. Be brave; they're only memories, shadows of the past . . .

A surge of panic. Trying to flee, only to find another one blocking her path. And now a third, coming in from behind to put a hairy hand around her mouth before she can scream. A brief struggle, an attempt to escape, but they're stronger than she is, and finally all she can do is let them take her.

A forced run through the forest. The cold winter sun slashing through the branches. Small hands shoving her, pushing her, never letting her rest. Climbing the base of Mt. Bonestell, leaving the settlement far behind, even as she hears voices calling her name somewhere far behind. She loses her cap by the side of a frozen creek, but when she bends down to retrieve it, strong hands pick her up, bodily carry her across the ice. Strange voices gibbering at her, a tongue she doesn't recognize— kreepha-shee kashe chee!—*then her tormentors drop her on the other side of the creek, and now more running while her tormentors hoot and chirp all around her, ignoring her tears and pleas to be let go . . .*

The back door creaked open. Probably Tillie, taking out the garbage to the compost heap.

The long sprint up the mountain. Branches lashing against her face, cold and fatigue sucking what little strength is still left in her small body. Fear. An overwhelming sense that she's about to die, and the dark hope that it'll happen soon so that it'll be over and done and she can go to Heaven.

But death is not her destination. Instead, she suddenly finds herself at the bottom of a vast grey cliff, an enormous escarpment in which dozens of holes have been bored. Figures prance around her, tugging at her hair, her clothes, pushing her toward an opening at ground level. She has to duck her head to go inside . . .

Yes. There's something there. Concentrating, she screwed her eyes shut even tighter, struggling to recall.

A labyrinth of tunnels, a maze within the rock, seemingly without end, the only light coming through windows and chimneys. The odor of mildew and rot. Brief glimpses of tiny burrows. Miniature axes no larger than her hand, little beds of woven grass, a dwarf-size fireplace in which coals smolder. A female cowering within a room, staring at her with oversized eyes, her infant suckling at her breast. And now, an upward climb, scrambling up wooden ladders, relentlessly prodded and pushed until she enters a narrow shaft through which sunlight gleams down . . .

Something tugged at her memory.

Climbing the shaft, the frail wooden ladder bending beneath her weight,

desperate to reach the light far above. Yet now, from somewhere far away, she can
hear her mother's voice, desperately calling her name . . .

A small, warm hand touched her foot. Susan opened her eyes, and found a *chirreep* crouched beside her on the bed.

Startled, she immediately jerked away from the small creature. Almost as surprised, it snatched away its hand and drew back from her. Yet it didn't leap off the bed, as she expected, but instead regarded her with its enormous black eyes, more curious than frightened.

The *chirreep* was only a couple of feet tall, scrawny yet muscular, almost like an oversized spider monkey. It was covered head-to-toe with coarse black fur, save for a thick silver mane around its neck and chest, yet it wasn't quite naked; it wore a small loincloth, and a small piece of quartz hung from around its neck on a length of woven grass. Earlier observations by other researchers indicated that such jewelry was worn by tribal leaders, but no one could be sure.

Susan held her breath, fought to remain calm. It had been many years since she'd been this close to a *chirreep*. Indeed, this was the first time she'd ever known one to enter a human dwelling, although she remembered Tillie mentioning something about keeping a lamp burning in the mess tent to keep them from stealing things. This one must be particularly brave to come in through the back door while the lights were on. Not to mention extraordinarily quiet; it had managed to climb up on the bed without her noticing.

Laughter from outside the kitchen, as someone in the dining room presumably told someone else a funny story. The *chirreep* darted a nervous look in that direction, and it tensed on its hind legs, ready to spring away. Why had it come here? If it meant to steal something, then why make its presence known to her?

"*Chirreep,*" she said quietly. It was the only word of their language she or anyone else knew; no harm in using it now. "*Chirreep,*" she said again, and pointed to her visitor.

The *chirreep* returned its attention to her. "*Chirreep-sha katoom,*" it rasped softly. "*Kreepha-shee shon-shee koot.*" It advanced cautiously toward Susan, until it was close enough for her to pick up the rank odor of its pelt, then it reached beneath its loincloth.

Another burst of laughter, then footsteps just outside the kitchen. "You're going to have to do better than that!" Tillie said loudly, then she swept aside the flap. "Lord, these men, they're going to . . . oh my God!"

The *chirreep* was already off the bed. Pausing only long enough to drop something in Susan's lap, it dove headfirst from the top bunk, grabbing a skillet hanging from the ceiling rafter, and using it to swing across the room. Tillie barely had time to snatch a pot from the oven and hurl it after the creature before the *chirreep* lunged through the back door. The pot missed it by several feet, and black bean soup sprayed in all directions.

What happened next was a blur. Tillie shrieking, throwing more cookware at the open door. Loggers charging into the kitchen, demanding to know what was going on. Scattered gunshots outside the tent, while men and women yelled at one another. Uncle Lars managed to get Tillie to calm down and tell him what she'd seen, then he asked Susan for her side of the story. Still sitting cross-legged on the bed, Susan pretended innocence; she'd seen the treecrawler, too, but not until she'd woken up to find it trying to steal her pad. No, it hadn't taken anything. No, it hadn't bitten her. Yes, she was fine, and, no, she didn't want to spend the night in his tent. She caught a glimpse of Hawk, standing just outside the kitchen. There was a sly grin on his face, and for a second she thought he winked at her. Then his father ushered everyone out of the tent; they needed to double the watch tonight and keep a sharp eye on the corral and the flume. Where there was one of these little bastards, there had to be more.

Once everyone was gone, Susan helped Tillie clean up the mess. The cook was a wreck, and it took a couple of shots of bearshine before she was calm enough to climb into bed, yet even then she insisted on putting a paring knife beneath her pillow. So it wasn't until much later, when the camp had finally settled down and Tillie was snoring away in the bunk beneath her, that Susan dared to retrieve the object the *chirreep* had tossed to her, which she'd hastily shoved beneath the blankets of her bed.

A scrap of paper, human-made, wrapped around a small rock. Upon it was scrawled a short message:

> TOMORROW, SAME PLACE/TIME. NO PHONE, NO GUNS—CAMERA OK. BRING GIFTS—THEY LIKE FOOD (VEGGIES) AND FLASHLIGHTS. COME ALONE. TELL NO ONE.—J.

> P.S.—MY FRIEND'S NAME IS KATOOM (I THINK). PLEASE TREAT HIM WELL.

Susan reread the note several times, her mouth open with astonishment. It wasn't until she was sure that Tillie was asleep that she dared speak aloud the thoughts in her mind.

"I'll be damned," she whispered. "He's learned how to communicate with them."

Slipping away from camp the following morning was easier than expected. After she set the table for breakfast, Susan pretended to have trouble getting a fire started in the dining room stove. When Tillie came out to help her, Susan went back into the kitchen and stole a few carrots and potatoes, tucking them into her pack along with her camera and a spare flashlight. She then waited until the work crew showed up, and while Tillie was bringing out the coffee and biscuits, she made her exit through the back door, being careful to sneak around behind the tents so as not to be seen. No one spotted her, and by the time first light was breaking upon the mountains she was heading up the trail to the logging site.

The morning was cold, the sky overcast with grey clouds that foretold of rain later in the day. Susan was glad that she'd worn her jacket and cap. She had little trouble retracing her steps from the day before; all she had to do was follow the log flume back to the dam in order to locate the path Hawk had shown her. She was well ahead of time, but she didn't allow herself the luxury of taking it easy. Someone would eventually notice her absence, and although she'd taken the precaution of destroying the note Parson had sent her, there was always the chance that Hawk might figure out where she'd gone.

She felt bad about not taking the boy into her confidence. He'd proven himself to be a reliable guide, and he'd demonstrated a certain willingness, however reluctant, to open his mind to the possibility that the *chirreep* were

COYOTE FRONTIER

127

more than mere animals. Yet the fact that he'd packed a gun without telling her made him less than completely trustworthy, and Parson had specifically stated that she was to come alone and not tell anyone where she was going. And although she was wary about venturing up the mountain on her own, she didn't want to pass up the opportunity to discover something new about the *chirreep*.

By midmorning, she'd returned to the cliffs, and was mildly surprised to find Jonathan Parson waiting for her almost exactly where they'd met yesterday. He sat on top of the boulder, as if he hadn't gone anywhere since she'd last seen him.

"Good morning," he said, chewing on a piece of lamb jerky. "Glad to see my letter got through."

Susan bent over to clasp her knees and catch her breath. "You mean . . . you mean your little friend . . . didn't tell you?"

Parson considered the question as he took a drink from a catskin flask. "Who do you think I am? Tarzan, lord of the *chirreep*?" He caught her baffled expression, shook his head. "Sorry. Obscure literary reference. Look, it took a couple of hours just to make him understand that I wanted him to deliver that note to you, and he ate the first two before I got it across to him. So I'd appreciate a little—"

"Thank you." Susan sat down on the ground, then took off her pack and pulled out her canteen. "My apologies. It's just that . . . well, I've got a thousand questions to ask you."

"No doubt." Parson capped his flask, then slid down the rock until he was standing in front of her. "I have a few of my own. Did you bring treats for my friends?" She pulled some carrots from her pack and showed them to him. "Good. They'll like those. And you're not carrying a gun, and you didn't tell anyone?" She shook her head. "And you're sincere about wanting to learn more about them? This isn't about finding a way to exterminate them?"

She looked him straight in the eye. "I'm a scientist," she said evenly. "I've been studying them all my life. I don't know what I can say or do that would convince you that I mean them no harm."

Parson said nothing for a moment, then slowly nodded. "I believe you," he said at last. "About not wanting to harm them, I mean. And so does my teacher. I spoke with him last night, and he told me that he's aware of you, if only by reputation."

"Your teacher? Who's that?"

"Later. Right now, I'd like to put a little more distance between us and the camp." Parson stepped away from the boulder. "Think you're ready for some more climbing? It gets pretty rough after this."

Susan gazed at the bluffs towering above them. "We're going up there, aren't we? That's where we'll find the entrance to their dwellings." She glanced at him again. "A cave of some sort, leading into the mountain. Right?"

Parson stared at her. "How did you know this?"

"You're not the only one who's made contact with the *chirreep*." Standing up, she placed her pack once more upon her shoulders. "Take me there."

Leaving the trail behind, they made their way uphill through the woods. Once they reached the base of the cliff, Parson led Susan to the north, picking their way across heaps of broken talus that had sheered away from the granite wall, season after season of relentless erosion. The escarpment rose above them like a time-lost fortress, spotted with lichen and spongy moss; their footfalls echoed quietly off the trees below, resounding against the stones of years.

"This is where it gets tricky," Parson said at last, pausing to rest his back against the opening of a crevice. Looking up, Susan saw that it formed a narrow crack leading up to the top of the bluffs. "Think you can handle it?"

Susan stepped back to examine it more closely. A vertical ascent of nearly forty feet, yet there were plenty of handholds, along with chimneys where she could wedge her back and legs against the wall. "Sure. Just gimme a second to rest."

"Hoped you'd say that." He uncapped his flask, took a sip, and then passed it to her. "Ever heard of Manny Castro?"

The unexpected question caught her off guard. He'd been the Savant who'd come to Coyote aboard *Glorious Destiny*, the first Western Hemisphere Union starship to reach the 47 Ursae Majoris system; her mother had met him way back then. Later, once the Union took control of Liberty, Castro had been the colony's lieutenant governor, serving under the Matriarch Luisa Hernandez. He'd been captured during the battle of Thompson's Ferry and thrown into the West Channel, only to reemerge once the Revolution was over; a short time later, he'd accompanied Uncle Lars and Aunt

Marie during their forced exile, yet had disappeared again not long after Clarksburg had been founded. A figure of near-mythic proportions, much like Zoltan Shirow. Children liked to frighten each other with stories about the evil savant who would creep into their homes and steal them away if they weren't good.

"Of course," she said. "Why?"

"You asked who my teacher is. Now I'm telling you."

She stared at him. "Manuel Castro? C'mon . . ."

"I find it difficult to believe myself. Back on Earth, savants . . ." He stopped himself. "A long story. Let's just say, they're not very popular. Nonetheless, I've become . . . shall we say, associated with him . . . and he's been something of a teacher to me. We live on the other side of the mountain, and I've assisted him with his research. Which coincides quite a bit with your own."

"You've been studying the *chirreep*," she said, and he nodded. "And you've learned to communicate with them?"

"After a fashion." He took the flask back from her, took a drink himself. "For instance, my friend Katoom . . . I'm not sure whether that's his name or his position within the tribe, but nonetheless that's what he calls himself. But his people call themselves the *chirreep-sha*, and to them we're *kreepha-shee*, which we think means 'aliens.' We've been trying to understand their language, but it's been one word at a time, and only after we've established peaceful relations with them."

"I'm impressed you've gotten that far. The university has been studying them for years."

"Yes, well, you didn't have a savant living up here. That's all Manny's done the last three years . . . observe the *chirreep-sha*, gain their trust, take notes. After he took me on as his student, I've been doing much of the legwork, so to speak. Lately we've made an interesting discovery." He gestured to the mountainside below them. "That's what I was doing when I . . ."

Parson suddenly stopped, as if he'd heard something. Susan was about to ask him what was wrong, but he quickly raised a hand, motioning for her to be quiet. A moment passed, then he signaled her to follow him deeper into the crevice. Together, they moved out of sight, and there they waited for several long minutes, remaining still and not saying a word to each other.

The sound of talus sliding underfoot, then a shadow fell across the slope. A figure stepped into view, only a few yards away. For a second, it seemed as if he might pass by without spotting them, but then he turned to peer into the crevice, and they saw who it was.

"Good morning, Master Thompson," Parson said. "Out for a stroll?"

Caught by surprise, Hawk slipped on the broken rock, nearly falling over before he caught himself. "I didn't know . . . I thought . . ."

"Oh, come now. If you've come this far, then you must have been tailing us for quite some time." Parson stepped out of the crevice. "You're quite the woodsman, though, I'll give you that. Being able to track her all the way from camp, I mean."

Susan paled. "Jonathan, I didn't know he was—"

"I don't think you did." He glanced at her, then returned his attention to the teenager. "You realize, of course, that you're not welcome here. If she'd wanted you to come along—"

"She would've told me . . . I know, I know." Hawk looked embarrassed. "But it wasn't hard to figure out where she'd gone. All I had to do was catch up. And when I saw you head up here . . ."

"You followed us to see where we'd go." Parson was visibly impressed. "Quite the stalker, you are. You'd have made a good spy. Well, now, off you go."

"Jon, wait a minute." Susan stepped out from behind him, confronted Hawk. "If you go back now, what are you going to do? Tell your father what you've seen?"

Hawk hesitated, then shook his head. "I only wanted to find out where you're headed. You hired me to be your guide, remember?"

"Uh-huh. And if I told you that we're going to find the *chirreep,* could you promise to keep this to yourself?"

"Oh, no, hold on just a moment." Parson held up a hand. "When I said that I wanted you to come alone, I meant it. No guns, no satphone."

"Not carrying 'em." Hawk pulled off his pack, extended it to Parson. "Look inside. My canteen, a map, and a flashlight. Go ahead, see for yourself." He gazed at Susan again. "And if you want me to make a promise, then I will. Nothing I see here gets back to my dad. Or the company, or anyone else. I promise."

Unwilling to trust him at his word, Parson opened Hawk's pack and rummaged through it. "Well . . . we could use the extra flashlight, at least." Then he looked at Susan again. "But if you bring him along, there's a chance the *chirreep* might not accept us. Two's company . . ."

"And three's a crowd." Susan considered her predicament. Until now, Hawk had done nothing to earn her distrust except carry a gun; she should have anticipated that he'd follow her, considering that she'd slipped away from camp without any explanation. Indeed, she had less reason to trust Parson, a relative stranger, than her own cousin. And hadn't she wanted to impress upon him the fact that the *chirreep* were more than simians? "Well . . . we'll just have to take that chance, won't we?"

Parson didn't reply for a moment, but a look of disgust crossed his face. "Right," he said finally. "Very well . . . but I can't promise you how this is going to turn out." He thrust the pack back into Hawk's hands. "And you . . . do what I say and keep your mouth shut, and we'll get along just fine. Understand?"

"Sure. Whatever." Hawk shouldered his pack once more, then peered up at the crevice. "So . . . I guess we're about to climb this thing?"

"We are indeed." Parson cinched tight the straps of his own pack. "And let me tell you . . . if you fall, I'm not coming back to save you."

"Wasn't expecting you to," Hawk mumbled.

Despite appearances, the ascent wasn't nearly as difficult as it seemed from the base of the cliffs; the rock was stable and didn't crumble when they put their weight upon it, and there were plenty of small ledges for them to grasp as handholds. They took their time, resting whenever possible, helping each other if they could do so without losing their own balance. Nonetheless, it took over an hour for them to climb up the narrow crevice, and once they reached the top of the bluffs they had to stop to catch their breath.

They'd emerged upon a broad shelf above the tree line, with only a few scraggly bushes growing here and there. The summit rose above them as a naked pinnacle, like a giant granite thumb thrust up against the heavens. Grey clouds scudded across the sky behind it, and Susan had the illusion that the rock was teetering, about to fall upon them. Looking away, she hastily zipped up the front of her jacket; without any trees to break the wind, she felt a chill.

"Not much farther, I hope," she said.

"Not at all. In fact, we're almost there." Parson looked around, as if searching for something, then turned to her and Hawk. "All right now, this is important," he said, his voice low. "From here on, you two need to do exactly what I say. No arguments, no questions . . . just do it. Any mistakes now could get us in serious trouble."

"How do we know you—?" Hawk began.

"Keep your voice down." Parson glared at the boy. "I mean it, kid. Start fooling with me, and I'll pitch you over the side."

Hawk started to object, but Susan interceded. "All right, you're in charge," she said. "What do we do now?"

Parson pointed to the left, where the shelf led alongside a steep rock wall. "We're going that way. Walk single file, and try not to talk if you don't have to. And watch your step . . . it can get rather dicey after this."

Susan followed him along the top of the bluffs, with Hawk close behind her. Parson was right; the shelf gradually became narrower, until less than four feet of sand-covered rock separated the escarpment on their right from the sheer vertical drop on their left. She tried not to look over the side as she made her way along the path, being careful where she put her feet. From somewhere many miles away, she heard the distant rumble of thunder. A storm was approaching. She prayed that they wouldn't be caught up here; high winds could easily toss them over the precipice.

Yet then they came around a bend, and suddenly the shelf became wider, almost as if it was a small hollow, with the mountainside forming a concave half-bowl that curved around them. Parson stopped; he put a finger to his lips, then silently pointed to the center of the hollow. Looking more closely, Susan saw an opening in the middle of the floor: a sinkhole, formed over time by rainwater trickling down the slope and carving a vertical shaft where it'd found a fissure.

Yet it was far more than that. Here and there around the sinkhole, small piles of sticks had been placed, as if stacked as . . . yes, of course, firewood. And even farther away, deep within the hollow, lay a circle of stones: a fire pit, filled with black ashes and charred pieces of wood. This was the place where the smoke seen from the logging camp had originated.

"Give me the food and your second flashlight," Parson whispered to Susan, then he looked at Hawk. "Yours, too. We're going to need to give 'em everything we can spare."

Hawk hesitated, but surrendered his light after Susan prompted him with a nod. She removed from her pack the carrots and potatoes she'd lifted from the kitchen, and added one of her flashlights. Parson cradled the vegetables and flashlights in his arms, trying not to drop anything. "All right, now, follow me. Stick close, and don't say a word."

Hunched over by his burden, Parson slowly walked across the hollow, Susan and Hawk right behind him. No one spoke as they approached the sinkhole, yet as they drew closer, Susan spotted something sticking up from the opening. It looked like two tree branches laid side by side, until she recognized it for what it was: the top of a ladder.

"Stop here," Parson said, once they were a dozen yards from the sinkhole. Susan and Hawk watched as Parson carefully laid the offerings upon the ground a few yards from the hole. He took a few seconds to separate the carrots from the potatoes, then neatly placed the two flashlights next to them, switching them on as an afterthought.

"All right," he said, "come with me." Then he stood up and walked away. They retreated another few yards, then Parson sat down, crossing his legs and beckoning for them to do the same. "Keep your hands in sight at all times," he whispered, "and don't make any sudden moves. When they appear . . . if they appear . . . don't look at them straight on. And no one say anything, for God's sake."

"How do they know we're—?" Hawk began.

"They know. Now shut up and wait."

And so they sat in silence, almost as if in meditation, as they watched the sinkhole. The storm was closer now; the day had darkened, and the thunder was no longer quite so distant. The wind was picking up, and Susan felt shy drops of rain against her face. Gazing toward the summit, she saw that it had all but disappeared within the grey smudge of low clouds. They were exposed to the storm; when it hit, and doubtless it would be soon, there would be no place for them to seek shelter.

Like everyone who'd grown up on Coyote, she'd learned to respect the elements. Her eyes sought out an overhang within the far side of the hollow. It wasn't very large, but it might offer some protection, if they huddled together and put their jackets over their heads.

She felt Parson prod her shoulder with his elbow, and she looked around to see a small form emerging from the sinkhole. Stepping off the ladder, the *chirreep* crouched low, its hands nearly touching the ground as it stared straight at them. A young male, Susan decided; it wore a loincloth, but no jewelry. It moved a little closer, examining the gifts but not daring to touch them. After a few seconds, it retreated to the ladder and disappeared again.

"So much for that," Hawk whispered. "Nice try, but—"

"Quiet," Parson hissed. "That was just a scout. Whatever you do, stay—"

"Here he comes again." Susan saw the same *chirreep* come up the ladder once more. This time he wasn't alone. Two more were behind him; the last to appear seemed to be the same one who'd shown up in camp last night. The three *chirreep* stopped at the top of the ladder, no longer crouching but standing upright; they didn't move away from the sinkhole, though, but instead carried on a brief conversation, a rapid succession of soft-pitched chirps and hoots.

She glanced at Parson. His head was cocked slightly as he listened intently, yet when she caught his eye, he shook his head. He couldn't understand what they were saying either.

An abrupt flash, and Susan looked up in time to see a wand of lightning strike just on the other side of the mountain peak, followed a couple of seconds later by a sharp crack that startled even the *chirreep*. Their leader snapped something at the two younger ones, and they scurried over to the food and flashlights. Yet, as they quickly gathered the gifts in their arms, Katoom calmly moved toward the three humans seated nearby, until he was only a few feet away.

"*Chirreep-sha kasho haka,*" he said, looking directly at Parson. "*Katoom hoota kreepha-shee, heep! Hona shaka heet!*"

"He's thanking us for the offerings, I think," Parson said softly. "There's something else, though, but I can't tell what . . . never mind." He pointed to the sinkhole. "*Kreepha-shee hoota, Katoom,*" he said slowly. "*Haka hoota.*"

Katoom peered at him. "*Hana hoota? Kreepha-shee?*"

"*Kreepha-shee haka.*" Parson pointed again toward the sinkhole. "*Katoom hoota?*" He gestured to the sky, then fluttered his fingers around his face, as if pantomiming rain falling down upon them. *"Kreepha-shee hoota,"* he repeated. *"Katoom haka."*

Susan got it. Parson was telling Katoom that the *kreepha-shee* had brought *haka*. Now he was asking if they could be allowed into their *hoota*, to get out of the rain. She desperately wished she could take notes, but that was out of the question just now; the best she could do was try to commit everything to memory.

Katoom seemed uncertain. The other two *chirreep* had picked up everything and had disappeared back down the hole, but he remained with the visitors. Another growl from the sky, and now cold rain came pelting down upon them. That seemed to help him make up his mind. *"Kreepha-shee hoota kasha, koot!"* he exclaimed, then gestured to the sinkhole. *"Koot! Hoota koot, kreepshee-koot!"*

"I'll take that as an invitation," Susan said.

"Yes, it is." Parson pushed himself to his feet, then helped her up. "We've given them something, and they're offering us something in return. It's their way."

"Have you ever done this before?" Hawk asked as he stood up.

"Once." Parson paused to look at him. "I just hope you'll remember what you see here."

The ladder was rickety, barely able to sustain their weight; they went down one at a time, testing each rung before they made the next step. The sinkhole was nearly twenty feet deep, and when they reached the bottom, they found themselves in a narrow tunnel only four feet in height, forcing them to bend over double.

Yet, although the tunnel was dim, it wasn't completely dark. There was a pale green glow from the rock walls, vein-like and irregular, yet just bright enough to light their way. Susan probed one of the veins with her fingertip, felt a sponge-like substance. Bioluminescent lichen, like some sort of moss that grew upon the cave walls. She wondered if it had been deliberately cultivated, decided that it was so; the tunnel itself seemed to have been excavated by patient hands over dozens, perhaps even hundreds, of years.

Katoom waited patiently until all his guests had made their way down the ladder, then he scampered down the tunnel, holding aloft one of the flashlights he'd been given. "It's okay," Parson said, switching on his own flashlight as he bent down upon his knees to gaze back at Susan and Hawk. "I know where he's taking us. Just stay together, and we'll be all right."

"Sure, but what if we . . . ow!" Hawk winced as he banged the back of his head against the ceiling. "Damn! Why'd they have to make these things so small?"

"Because they weren't made for you." Parson began shuffling forward. "And don't worry about getting lost. We're not going very far."

Parson was exaggerating; the tunnel may have been less than sixty feet in length, but it seemed twice that long. Susan felt her thighs and calves beginning to cramp, and more than once her skull connected painfully with the ceiling until she pulled out her remaining flashlight and switched it on. And yet, despite her discomfort, she found herself experiencing déjà vu; this place was very much like the cliff dwelling she'd seen as a child. Only this time, there was no fear, only the thrill of discovery. She was entering the heart of a mystery; soon, all her questions would be answered.

The passage took a sharp curve to the right, and suddenly the tunnel came to an end in a larger cave. Standing upright, Susan gaped at what she saw; their flashlights revealed a cavern nearly a hundred yards across, the size of a small amphitheater. Stalactites hung from between the cracks that ran across the ceiling fifty feet above their heads, and the broken remains of formations lay here and there across the clay floor. The air was cool, but not cold, and their footfalls echoed softly off the smooth rock walls.

They weren't alone. From all around them, *chirreep* stared at them. They squatted on the cavern floor and stood upon high ledges and guarded the openings of small niches that had been carved into the walls. Although they maintained a respectful distance, their eyes reflected the glow of their lights, and their subdued voices were a constant babble of hoots and clicks and chirps.

"Oh, crap, we're surrounded." Hawk nervously glanced left and right. "Look, I'll take my chances with the storm. Let's just get out of here."

"If they wanted to harm us, they would have done so already." Parson nodded toward Katoom, who calmly stood only a few feet away. "He's accepted us as friends. So long as nobody panics, we're fine. And we can leave anytime we want."

"We can? Great." Hawk took a backward step toward the tunnel. "Tell him thanks, but we need to—"

"Cut it out." Susan aimed her flashlight at the cave walls; the *chirreep* flinched, raising their hands against the glare, and she hastily swept it away from their eyes. "What are all these holes? Their sleeping places?"

"Sort of. But it might also be where they hibernate." Parson searched the chamber until he found one that was vacant, and shined his light within it. Now she could see that it was packed with matted grass, with what looked like bags stuffed along the sides. "This far underground, the temperature probably remains constant year-round. I'm guessing that they sleep most of the winter down here, consuming food that they've stashed away."

Susan nodded; his theory made sense. With the exception of marine life, all of Coyote's native fauna were warm-blooded. During the planet's long winter, those species that didn't migrate to the equatorial regions, like the swoops and the boids, or survive by foraging, like the shags, had evolved as hibernating animals, burrowing deep underground or building nests inside fallen trees and ball plants, with smaller creatures like root rats freezing solid. Since no one had ever spotted a *chirreep* during the winter, this had led biologists to speculate that they holed up within their dwellings. Here was proof that this theory was correct.

"That's not what I wanted to show you, though." Raising his flashlight, Parson aimed its beam toward the far wall of the cavern. "I found it over there, the first time I came down here. But that was pretty much by accident. I don't know if they'll let me see it again."

He lowered the light, looked at Katoom. *"Kreepha-shee hoota shak,"* he said haltingly, and the *chirreep* cocked his head slightly, as if trying to divine his meaning. *"Hoota shak,"* he repeated, then pointed toward the far wall. *"Kreepha-shee . . . um, shak. Shak."*

Katoom hooted with what couldn't be interpreted as anything but amusement; the *chirreep* surrounding them responded the same way.

"Guess you got their funny bone," Susan said. "They probably think we're idiots."

"*Kreepha-shee shak koo-shoo heeka!*" Then Katoom darted away, gesturing for them to follow him. "*Shak koo-shoo! Heeka sha! Kreet!*"

"Sounds like an invitation to me," Parson said, then he led the others across the cavern, heading for the place he'd indicated that he wanted to see.

The far wall of the cavern hadn't been tunneled out, save for a narrow opening that appeared to lead farther into the mountain, yet wan sunlight crept down from a crack in the ceiling high above, from which water dripped into crude bowls placed next to what looked like a fire pit dug within the cave floor. Yet this wasn't what attracted Susan's attention; it was what was on the wall above the shallow pit.

"Oh, my God." Stopping dead in her tracks, she stared in disbelief at what her flashlight beam revealed. "Paintings. Cave paintings."

Dozens of pictographs, crude yet unmistakably deliberate, rendered by alien hands grasping pieces of charred wood to etch primitive drawings upon the smooth granite. They covered much of the wall from the floor to as far as their arms could reach: jagged lines depicting mountains, Bear represented here and there by a larger circle bisected by an oval half-ring. Tiny stick-figures went in and out of holes, danced around flames, lurked beneath trees . . .

"They're not animals." Behind her, Hawk's voice was low with astonishment. "You're right . . . they're not just animals."

"Rather settles the issue, doesn't it?" Parson gazed at the wall with admiration. "For all I know, it might just be their version of graffiti. But I think it may be more than just that."

"It is." Pulling off her pack, Susan removed her camera. "This is their history," she murmured as she raised its flash and adjusted the lens for maximum exposure. "I could spend days . . . months . . . studying this thing."

"You don't have that much time. There's a limit to their hospitality. Get what you can before they throw us out." Parson walked to the far left corner of the wall. "Here's what I thought was important. Look."

Bending low, Susan studied the drawings with her flashlight. A blaze above wavy horizontal lines seemed to represent mountain peaks; beneath it, several figures appeared to be rushing away. Next to it, another picture: choppy lines that could have been water, with a half-moon-shape floating upon it; three large stick figures sat in the crudely drawn boat, and nearby a couple of small figures watched from behind trees. Another picture: more tall figures, marching up a slope, while tiny figures hurried away. And yet another image: a row of triangles, and beside them tall figures pushing over trees, hauling them away . . .

"It's about how we came here." Susan found herself barely able to breathe; ignoring the camera in her hands, she pointed to the first pictograph. "Look . . . that's got to be a ship arriving. Probably the *Alabama*. Look how frightened they were. And then, here . . ." She shined her light on the second pictograph. "The first time they saw us, when a boat came across the West Channel." She looked at the stick figures hiding behind the trees. "They knew about us before we became aware of them. They must have been terrified."

"Can you blame them? We were invaders from the sky." Kneeling next to her, Parson pointed to the third and fourth sets of drawings. "Then we came up into the mountains. They ran away, but then we set up the camp, started cutting down trees."

"Hey, y'all, look at this." To their right, Hawk was bending down beside another row of pictures. "Is this what I think it is?"

Susan moved closer to him. Captured by her flashlight beam was another etching: two long parallel lines, tilted slightly downward and held up by shorter lines. Yet near one end, the parallel lines had been broken in half; *chirreep* beat upon them with sticks, while larger figures ran toward them.

"That's where they broke the log flume," Susan said. "They did this even though we tried to chase them away." She glanced at Hawk. "Do you see? We began to destroy their forest, so they acted to protect what they considered theirs."

Hawk turned to stare at the *chirreep* gathered behind them. They'd become quiet now, silently observing the humans they'd allowed into their hideaway. "They want us to see this, don't they?" he said quietly. "They're not afraid of us anymore, and they want us to know that."

"Oh, they're still frightened of us, all right." Parson shook his head. "And that's what you should be worried about."

Susan didn't respond; she was busy taking photographs, praying that her camera was sensitive enough to record the images in the weak glow of their flashlights. "This changes everything, you know," she murmured. "Nothing's going to be the same again."

"Uh-huh." Parson gently tapped her arm. "And you should be worried about that, too."

Uncle Lars was drunk, as usual, yet he wasn't so far gone that he couldn't understand what was being shown to him. With a glass of bearshine resting on his camp desk, he peered at the images downloaded into his battered comp from Susan's camera. He examined them one at a time, not saying anything while Susan patiently explained the pictographs to him; on occasion he clicked back to study one or two of them again, but otherwise he remained quiet as his niece told him what she'd seen. When she was done, he picked up his glass, knocked back the shot of bearshine, hissed between his teeth, and delivered his verdict.

"Yeah? So?"

"Do you know what this means?" Susan fought to stay calm. "They're intelligent creatures. They make tools, gather food, practice art . . ."

"Yup. Those are some pretty pictures, all right. Imagine the people at your school are gonna be real interested to see 'em." He shrugged. "Don't mean crap to me."

Susan regard him with disbelief, then turned to gaze at Hawk. He was sitting on a cot behind them, still reluctant to speak. Night had fallen by the time they'd returned to camp; although they had missed dinner, Tillie grilled some cheese sandwiches for them, which they'd eaten before going over to Lars's tent. Susan had asked Hawk to come with her, yet he'd apparently decided to let his cousin do the talking. Now he simply looked away, as if this had suddenly become none of his business.

"It should," she went on. "You saw for yourself . . . the reason why the *chirreep* are causing you trouble is that you've invaded their territory. At first, they just went in hiding. It's even possible they might have stayed away if you'd carried out your logging operations somewhere else. But then you came farther into the mountains, and at some point they decided that you posed a threat. And so they took to knocking down the flume—"

"And I'm supposed to do what? Go 'way, leave 'em alone?" Lars shook his head. "Besides, weren't you supposed to tell me how to get rid of 'em?"

"That's never what I agreed to do. I came up here to study them and recommend what steps you should take based upon my findings. Now I'm telling you—"

"Fine. You've told me." He burped, his breath even more sour than it'd been before, then he leaned closer to her. "Now, c'mon," he said, laying an affectionate hand upon her knee, "you gotta see this my way."

Susan felt her face grow warm. "I've seen it your way," she said, unapologetically pushing his hand off her leg. "You're destroying their habitat."

"Maybe so." Rebuffed, her uncle's eyes narrowed. "But my business here is the family business, and the family business is what keeps all these people employed. So far as I'm concerned, this is my mountain, and that gives me the right to do whatever I want."

This was getting her nowhere. Not that she'd ever really believed that she could appeal to his better nature; so far as she could tell, he had none. "All right," she said as she stood up, "then I'll take it up with the rest of the family. Aunt Marie may see things a bit differently, and so will Molly, once they find out what you're doing up here. And if they don't—"

"Who are you going to tell? Your father?" Lars smirked at her. "Go right ahead. Tell everyone. Show 'em your pictures." He reached for the half-empty jug of bearshine next to his desk. "By the time they make up their mind, I'll have taken care of this little problem myself."

"What are you saying?"

"What d'ya think I'm saying?" Lars leisurely poured himself another drink. "These drawings . . . you found them in a cave somewhere on the mountain. Well now, all I have to do is take a few of my men back up there. Hunt 'em down, smoke 'em out, shoot 'em down . . . problem solved."

"You won't be able to do that. You don't know where they are." Indeed, she'd been careful not to reveal the whereabouts of the dwellings, other than to vaguely say that she'd found them somewhere on Mt.

Shapiro. Nor had she told him about Jonathan Parson, or how he'd led her to the *chirreep*. "If you think I'm going to—"

"Girl, you think I need you anymore?" Lars looked past her. "He's going to show me . . . aren't you, boy?"

Susan looked at Hawk, sitting in silence upon the cot, his hands clasped together between his knees. He gazed at the floor, not looking up at her, and it was then she realized she might have made a fatal error. He'd sworn to both her and Parson that he wouldn't tell his father anything about what he'd seen, yet his loyalty was not to her, but to his family. If he decided that one was greater than the other . . .

"Hawk . . ." she said softly.

"Now you just mind your own business." Uncle Lars regarded his son with smug satisfaction. "Where are they at? Tell me, and I'll make sure you get cut in for a nice bonus."

"Really? Wow, that's generous of you." He took a deep breath, then shrugged. "Sorry . . . don't remember."

For a moment, Lars stared at him. Then he put down his glass and slowly rose to his feet. "Don't try my patience," he said, his voice filled with quiet malevolence. "You either know or you don't . . . and you're not stupid enough not to know."

" 'Not stupid enough not to know.' " A smile ticked at the corners of his mouth. "Now there's something guaranteed to make me feel pretty good about—"

"Boy, you're rubbing me the wrong way." Lars pushed past Susan, advanced upon his son. "Are you going to tell me, or aren't you?"

Hawk slowly raised his face to stare his father straight in the eyes. Even though Lars blocked her way, she could tell that the boy was trembling. "No," he said at last. "I'm not going to."

Lars's right hand came up, slapped his son across the face. The blow was hard enough to knock the boy off the cot; Hawk sprawled across the wooden floor. Susan tried to scream, but the only sound to come from her throat was a tight gasp; shoving Uncle Lars aside, she rushed to Hawk's side.

"Okay . . . I'm okay." Raising himself up on one elbow, Hawk lifted a hand to his nose. It came away streaked with blood; more seeped down his lip and into his mouth. He spat it out, then looked up at his father. "Is that . . . that your best shot?"

Lars stood over them, his fists clenched at his sides. He seemed to shake with rage, and for a moment Susan thought he'd launch another attack. But then he saw something in his son's eyes—contempt, fearlessness, perhaps even pity—and it was as if all the anger had been sucked out of him, for he simply staggered back.

"G'wan," he mumbled as he lurched back to his desk and slumped down in the chair. "Get outta here, both of you."

Hawk started to say something, but then reconsidered. Instead, he let Susan help him to his feet. Holding a hand against his swollen nose, he shuffled out of the tent. Several loggers, attracted by the commotion, stared at them as they walked away, yet no one spoke to them.

"Is it broken?" Susan stopped to examine his face in the glow of a lantern. "I have a first-aid kit in my bag. Let me—"

"It's okay. Nothing worse than he's done before." Hawk snuffled a bit, then spat a clot of bloody saliva onto the ground. "Forgot the old man could hit so hard."

There was something here she hadn't heard before, but now was not the time to ask. "You were very brave," she said softly, brushing his hair aside to gently kiss his cheek. "I'm proud of you."

"Yeah, well . . ." He took a deep breath. "Tillie will put me up tonight. Tomorrow I'll find you a ride back into town." A wan smile. "Maybe I'll go with you. Think I have a shot at getting into the university?"

"You might." Susan took her cousin's hand, led him toward the mess tent. "In fact, I think your education has just begun."

Parson was waiting for them by the back door. He'd left them just outside camp, and now he was sitting on the woodpile behind the mess tent. "I heard," he said quietly, standing up as they approached. "Apologies for eavesdropping, but I wanted to know what he'd say." He looked at Hawk. "I'm sorry it came to this, but if it means anything—"

"Don't worry about it. Had to be done." Hawk glanced behind them; no one was observing them, yet he seemed anxious. "Look, it's not safe for you to be hanging around. Either of you. When my dad gets like this—"

"You're right. We should leave." Parson nodded in the direction of the woods. "There's a way to get from here to Manny's farm. It's just around the other side of the mountain. If we start out now, we can be there by morning, and I think he'd like to meet both of you."

"Are you sure?" Although she was no longer comfortable with the idea of remaining overnight in the logging camp—she shivered at the memory of the way Uncle Lars had touched her that last time—the notion of travel-ing by night made her equally as nervous. "What if we get lost?"

"Trust me . . . we won't." Parson smiled at her. "We've got friends out here, remember?"

Susan peered into the darkness. She couldn't see anything, yet she had the distinct feeling that they were being watched, by eyes that became ac-customed to nights in the Black Mountains long before humankind had come to this world. Until today, she'd thought of them as alien, but now she realized that it was she herself who was the outsider. If Parson was right, though, then she'd made friends with a force of nature; if she pro-tected it, then no harm would come to her.

"All right. I'll get my bag." She took a step toward the door, then some-thing occurred to her. "You know," she added, stopping to turn back to him, "there's one more thing. I didn't notice it until just a few minutes ago, when I looked at the cave drawings again. They showed pictures of the *chirreep* knocking down the flume . . . but I didn't see any of them trying to destroy the dam. Why do you think that is?"

Again, a smile stole across Parson's face. "As I said, we've got friends," he said quietly. "Now let's get out of here. We've got a world to save."

Part 4

A DIALOGUE CONCERNING THE TWO CHIEF WORLD SYSTEMS

The clatter of distant rotors woke him from his siesta. Carlos Montero sat up from his resting place against the mast of the *Orion II,* shaded his eyes with his hand; a gyro was flying in from across the Midland Channel, a silver dragonfly against the pale blue sky. Standing up, he watched as the aircraft made its descent; it circled the beach once at low altitude, the pilot searching for a place to set down, and Carlos pointed toward an area that he and Barry had cleared of scrub brush. Propwash rippled the canvas awning above the keelboat's upper deck as it came in for touchdown; the men on the shore turned away from the sand kicked up by the rotors, then the gyro was on the ground.

Carlos walked across the gangway to the beach. The gyro's blades were gliding to a halt when its rear hatch slid open; Anastasia Tereshkova climbed out, her long legs unsteady as her boots touched ground once more, and she unnecessarily ducked her head as she darted out from beneath the rotors. Carlos smiled to himself; Tereshkova might be the commanding officer of the EASS *Columbus,* but when it came to being a passenger, it was obvious that she was a nervous flier. Or maybe it was the age of the aircraft itself that disturbed her; he had to admit, these old Union Guard gyros didn't offer the smoothest of rides any longer.

"Welcome," he said. "Hope you had a good flight."

Tereshkova gave him a dour look. "As well as I should expect," she replied. "The trip was longer than I thought it would be."

Carlos nodded; Midland looked small on a map, but it was actually a couple of thousand miles across. "Takes a while to get here from Liberty. At least you picked good weather."

"Pretty much so, yes." She turned to gaze at the beach surrounding them. Her hair had grown out in the past three months, and now she swept it back from her face. "Still, I don't understand why we couldn't have used my skiff to come here. It would have taken much less time. An hour, perhaps less."

"As I said, this is a protected area. We try to disturb it as little as possible." Carlos gestured to the gyro. "That's as far as we let any sort of aircraft come. Even then, I had to pull some strings to get you here. Otherwise, you would've had to take the long way . . . on the boat with the rest of us."

Tereshkova gave a distant nod; it was plain that she didn't quite appreciate the special privilege she was being afforded. They'd left Liberty that morning, flying east across Midland, but after a brief stop in Defiance to take on more fuel, there was nothing but wilderness. Carlos had to wonder what she'd thought when she'd gazed down upon the highlands of the Gillis Range, the vast forests of the Pioneer Valley, the ash-covered steppes of Mt. Bonestell. There was nothing like this on the Moon or Mars; indeed, from what he'd been told, there was little like this even on Earth anymore.

Behind her, two more passengers had disembarked from the gyro. Gabriel Pacino, the *Columbus*'s first officer, helped the pilot unload the bags; unlike his captain, he appeared unruffled by the flight. Neither did Jonas Whittaker, despite his years; indeed, he seemed fascinated by his surroundings. Indeed, from the moment he'd first set foot on Coyote almost three months ago, Whittaker took an inordinate amount of pleasure in every new experience he had. Not that he blamed him, Carlos mused; after all, if he'd collectively spent almost three hundred years in biostasis, as Jonas had, he, too, would probably treat every moment alive as a blessing.

"You haven't set up the tents yet." Raising a hand against the midday sun, Tereshkova looked around. "Aren't we going to make camp here?"

"Nope. We're going straight onto the boat." Carlos pointed to the south; about a quarter mile up the shore lay the mouth of the broad creek that led into the island's interior. "We've got six, maybe seven hours of daylight left. Way I see it, we can get a couple dozen miles downriver before we have to stop for the night. So why waste time here?"

Tereshkova didn't reply, yet she gazed back at the gyro, as if regretting her request to visit Barren Isle. Once again, Carlos wondered why she'd asked to be shown this part of the world. Only a handful of people had come here since humans had arrived on Coyote; in fact, this was the first time he himself had returned to the island since he'd discovered it . . . how long ago? Eleven years, by the LeMarean calendar; a little more than thirty-three years by Gregorian reckoning. Last time he was here, he'd been a teenager. And now . . .

"We could camp here tonight," Tereshkova said. "Perhaps explore the coast for a day or so."

"Uh-uh." Carlos roused himself from his reverie. "There's probably more interesting places than this once we get inland."

"But if you've never explored this part of the island . . ."

"You can't learn anything from sticking close to the coast. You have to go into the interior if you want to find anything new. And that's the point of us coming here, isn't it?"

Tereshkova glared at him, and once again he had to remind himself that she was a starship captain, and therefore used to having her way. Nonetheless, this wasn't her expedition; Carlos was in charge, both in his official role as president of Coyote Federation and, less formally, as leader of this expedition. The sooner she learned to accept this, the better.

Be tactful, Wendy had warned him just before he left. *You've got to think like a diplomat.* Easy for her to say; she was accustomed to being a politician, while this was a job he'd taken only with great reluctance. Yet he stared back at her, refusing to be intimidated, and after a moment she finally nodded. "If you say so," she murmured.

"Thank you. Now, if you'll excuse me . . ." Carlos turned away, walked back to the gyro. Pacino had unloaded the rest of the bags, and the pilot was eager to leave; he had a long flight back to New Florida ahead of him, not counting another landing in Defiance to refuel. Carlos thanked him, then the pilot climbed back into the cockpit. The gyro's engines coughed, then its props gradually spun to life and the aircraft slowly lifted off, heading west toward the distant coast of Midland.

Once they carried their bags aboard the keelboat, Carlos introduced the passengers to her crew. Barry Dreyfus, the *Orion*'s captain, one of Carlos's oldest friends and another original colonist. Will Gentry, the first mate, also Barry's partner; once again, Carlos found that he still had trouble thinking of them as a couple, even though it'd been many years since Barry had finally revealed his sexual orientation to his family and friends. And Jud Tinsley, once the executive officer of the *Alabama,* now content to spend his golden years sailing aboard whatever boat needed a crewman; although he'd grown old and grey, he still had the energy of a man half his age, and when Barry had told him that an expedition was being made to Barren Isle, Jud had practically begged to come along.

So here they were: three original colonists and a Union immigrant, escorting three new arrivals—one of whom would have been aboard the *Alabama*, too, were it not for bad luck—on a trip into the frontier. Carlos couldn't help but reflect upon the irony of the situation as he watched the *Columbus* officers stow away their belongings and *Orion* crew pull up the anchor and unfurl the sails. Captain Tereshkova had wanted to see more of Coyote, and he'd wanted to revisit a place that had made a profound impact upon him in his youth. And so here they were. Coincidence, perhaps, yet he couldn't help but wonder if something else lay beneath the surface.

Sails catching the warm autumn breeze, wheel creaking softly as Barry turned the rudder to starboard, *Orion II* glided across still waters, hugging the coastline as it headed for the inlet. A leisurely sojourn down an unexplored river; not a bad way to spend the last week of Barbiel.

Nonetheless, he had a feeling that it would be more than that.

Barren Isle was a small, diamond-shaped island between Midland and Hammerhead, straddling the equator about a hundred miles northwest of the Meridian Archipelago. Carlos first visited it in c.y. 2, when he'd set out on his own to explore the Great Equatorial River in a handmade canoe—the original *Orion*, after which this fifty-five-foot keelboat had been christened—yet although he'd spent nine days upon the island, he had only paddled along its southern coast and never gone farther ashore than the beach. It wasn't until several years later that anyone set foot on Barren Isle again, and this time it was a research expedition from the Colonial University, sent to investigate the aboriginal species he'd called sandthieves and which they now knew as *chirreep*.

"So you were the first to find them." Sitting on a barrel on the forward deck, Pacino munched on an apple as he watched the riverbanks drift by. "Why did it take you so long to tell anyone?"

Carlos didn't answer at first. Crouched on his knees in the bow, he slowly let a plumb line slip through his hands into the creek, carefully counting the knots tied at regular intervals along its length until he felt the lead weight at its end touch bottom. "Mark twain!" he yelled back to Barry, then grinned at Pacino. "Ever heard of Samuel Clemens? American writer? He took his pen name from that call . . . means we've got two fathoms below us."

"Fascinating." Pacino took another bite from his apple. "But you didn't answer my—"

"Same reason I called this place Barren Isle. Name like that, I didn't think anyone would be interested in coming here." Carlos hauled back the line, rolling it around his elbow as a tidy coil. "If I had my way," he reflected, "no one would still know about them. Would've been my own little secret."

"Didn't last very long, did it?" Pacino had gnawed the apple to the core; he pulled back his arm, flung it toward shore. It didn't reach the ground, though, before one of the swoops that had followed the keelboat since it entered the creek dove down from the sky to snag it in midair. The other birds shrieked in avarice, then circled the boat even more closely, hoping that the intruders would discard another tasty morsel. "Damn," Pacino said. "Hungry little buzzards."

"Everything we do here has an effect." Carlos dropped the line into a wicker hamper, brushed his wet hands on his trousers. "That swoop you just fed, for instance. It'll digest your apple, and somewhere nearby it'll crap out the seeds. If they land in the right place, then apples might grow somewhere on the island."

"Glad to make a contribution."

"Maybe . . . but what sort of long-term effect do apples make upon an ecosystem where there's never been any apple trees before?" Standing up, Carlos gazed at the landscape slowly moving past them. Sandy lowlands, bleak and dun-colored, devoid of forest; desert country, seemingly lifeless, save for scrub brush and small, stunted trees. "That's why I didn't tell anyone about the sandthieves . . . the *chirreep*, I mean. This is a new world. We've got to be careful what we do here."

"So how did—?"

"Things happened that were beyond my control." It was a long story, and Carlos didn't feel like repeating it now. "Watch what you throw overboard, all right? Excuse me."

Stepping past Pacino, he went aft. Will and Jud were minding the sails; Whittaker sunned himself on the mid-deck, his arm draped across his eyes as he took an afternoon nap. Climbing the short ladder to the upper deck above the cabin, he found Barry at the rudder, studying the river with a wary eye; Tereshkova sat on a bench next to him, quietly observing every move he made. Two captains: one accustomed to traveling by water, the other intrigued by a form of transportation that didn't require an AI.

"So far, so good." Barry's gaze never strayed far from the river. "I'll need another sounding before long, though."

"No problem. Maybe we can teach our first officer to handle that." Carlos glanced at Tereshkova. "Think Mr. Pacino is up to it?"

"He can learn." She hesitated. "May I ask which way we're going? Our course, I mean."

"Certainly." Carlos bent down to open a cabinet and withdraw a rolled-up chart, which he spread out across the bench next to her. Like most maps of Coyote, it was a montage of high-orbit photos; although overlaid with grid lines for latitude and longitude, there were very few place-names, and those were for the major waterways that surrounded the island: the Midland Channel to the west, Short River to the east, and the Great Equatorial River and the Meridian Sea to the south and southeast.

"We entered here," Carlos said, pointing to the inlet just south of the northern tip of the island, where the Midland Channel split off from Short River. "The creek we're on now will take us about sixty miles to this other creek." He tapped a finger upon the Y-shaped confluence of a longer waterway that flowed southwest from Short River. "And then we'll follow it due south until it empties into the Great Equatorial. Another two hundred miles or so."

Tereshkova studied the map. "And this will take us how long?"

"About five, six days. Maybe a little longer, if we get hung up."

"Hung up?" She shook her head. "I don't understand."

"*Orion*'s got a five-foot draw." Barry didn't look back at them as he spoke. "That means we need at least five feet of water beneath us before we drag bottom. If that happens . . . say, we run aground on a sandbar or something . . . then we've got a choice. Either get out and push, or abandon ship and walk the rest of the way."

Tereshkova blanched, and Carlos caught a sly wink from Barry. "He's just putting you on," Carlos said. "We've had a lot of rain lately, so the creeks are running high. And even if it did, I'll just call for a gyro to pick us up. We've got the satphone."

"Unless you throw it away, of course." Barry meant that as a joke, but then he caught the sour expression on Carlos's face and quickly shook his head. "It'll never happen."

"So long as it doesn't." She didn't notice the silent exchange as she studied the map more closely. "You don't have names for these creeks. Why not?"

"Sort of a tradition." Carlos shrugged. "Most of this world is still unexplored. There's many islands and waterways we haven't yet visited, and we've only named the major land masses and channels near New Florida."

"Not exactly," Barry said. "There's the Northern River, and the North Sea, and Medsylvania and Highland and Vulcan. And the major volcanoes . . ." Again, Carlos glared at him. "But that's just because they're pretty obvious and we needed to call them something."

"So we reserve that privilege for those who see them first." Carlos paused. "You're our honored guest. Would you like to name this creek?"

This caught Tereshkova by surprise. "You . . . you can't mean that."

"Sure I do." He grinned at her, then pulled a pen from his shirt pocket. "Name it, and I'll put it on the map. When we get home, I'll have the university add it to the official atlas. Simple as that." He didn't tell her that whatever name she chose would have to be ratified by the Colonial Council; so long as she didn't pick anything obscene, though, it would probably pass muster.

Absently touching a forefinger to her lips, Ana pondered the question for a moment. "Valentina," she said at last. "I'd like to call this Valentina Creek."

"Sure. Nice name. Any particular reason?"

"For Valentina Tereshkova, the first woman in space." Embarrassed, she looked away. "My ancestor, at least so I've been told."

Carlos glanced at Barry, and his friend raised an eyebrow. History repeating itself; Robert Lee, the commanding officer of the *Alabama*, also had a famous ancestor. Carlos nodded, then he inscribed VALENTINA CR. on the map. A simple act of diplomacy, he told himself, but one that he hoped would break the ice.

It seemed to work, for a smile briefly appeared on Tereshkova's face. "Thank you," she said, then she excused herself and went forward to join Pacino.

"Nice idea," Barry murmured. "Now maybe she'll talk to us."

Carlos shook his head as he returned the pen to his pocket. "Talking to us isn't the problem," he said quietly. "It's what she's going to say when she does."

By evening, they had traveled nearly thirty miles; the river had become a little more narrow, but not so much that it hindered navigation. Carlos waited until the shadows grew long across the brown waters, then he asked Barry to pull over at a dry bank on the east side of the creek, a likely looking spot for a campsite. Will and Jud lowered the sails, then picked up long-handled oars and began maneuvering the keelboat over to the bank. After watching them for a minute or so, Pacino picked up another oar and came to their assistance; Carlos had taught him how to use the plumb-line earlier that afternoon, and he seemed to enjoy learning to do things in such an old-fashioned way.

On the other hand, the expedition wasn't going to rough it as much as Carlos had eleven years ago. No need to build lean-to shelters or erect tarps; the *Orion II* carried four two-man dome tents, each with its own heat-cells. Nor would they have to go fishing for their evening meal; coolers stowed below deck contained enough fresh food to last them a week, and a portable stove to cook it on. There were folding chairs, and although they had battery-powered lamps to supply light for the campsite, Jud took it upon himself to gather wood for a fire. All things considered, they'd come equipped with all the comforts of home . . . even rolls of toilet paper, to be conveniently placed next to the latrine Will had dug a short distance away.

There were also a couple of tripod-mounted automatic guns, rigged to a motion-detector system, which they could set up to guard the perimeter. Yet Carlos decided not to do so. "Not necessary," he said, kneeling next to the stove as he stirred the pot of curried chicken he'd prepared. "I can tell you for a fact that there're no boids on this island."

"How can you be so sure?" Standing close to the fire, Tereshkova nervously eyed the sandy grasslands surrounding them. "You said yourself that you never went farther inland than the beach."

"Because I didn't hear them at night, that's why." Carlos raised the ladle to his lips, took a taste. A little bland, perhaps, but he doubted the others would like their curry as spicy as he did. "And since the last expedition didn't report any, I think it's a safe bet that they're not indigenous. Probably not enough game to support them."

"Too bad." Sitting in a chair nearby, Whittaker warmed his feet by the fire, a glass of waterfruit wine in hand. One more luxury item they'd brought with them. "I'd sure like to see one up close."

Barry laughed out loud, but the metal plateware in Jud's hands rattled as he unpacked them from the kitchen box. Carlos stared intently at the pot. "No, you don't," he said softly. "If you're close enough to see a boid, then that's too close."

Too late, Whittaker realized the faux pas he'd just committed. "Sorry," he said. "I forgot. Your folks . . ."

"Don't worry about it. Happened a long time ago." Carlos used the ladle to lift up a small piece of chicken; he nibbled it and decided that it was cooked well enough to be edible. The rice in the other pot was already done, so he gestured for Jud to hand him a plate. "Even if boids once inhabited this island, our guess is that the *chirreep* probably took care of them long ago. So far as we've seen, they don't coexist in the same place at the same time. Probably because the *chirreep* locate their nests and destroy their eggs, denying them the ability to reproduce. After a while, the boids get the message and move on."

"Like we did on New Florida." Barry took a plate from Jud, put some rice on it, let Carlos spoon some curry on top of that, then passed it to Will. "Once we learned how to control their population around Liberty, they migrated south and stayed there."

"And good riddance." Carlos caught a questioning look from Tereshkova. "My parents were killed by boids," he added. "Two days after we landed. So I . . . well, I'm not a big fan of them, if you know what I mean."

"I understand. And I'm sorry." Ana accepted the plate handed her, then sat down in the empty chair by the fire. "But these *chirreep* . . . if they're here on the island, and they're capable of killing boids . . ."

"I'm not going to worry about sandthieves . . . *chirreep*, I mean . . . too much." Carlos continued to serve dinner. "Not enough to set up the guns, at least. Before we go to bed, though, everything either goes back on the boat or into the tents with us. They'll steal anything they can carry away if you give 'em half a chance."

"So you're not threatened by them." This from Pacino, and not as a question.

"No. They're just a nuisance. They don't go after humans."

"I've heard different." Pacino accepted the plate Barry handed to him. "The timber operations on Great Dakota . . . haven't they had problems lately? *Chirreep* sabotaging the log flume, attempting to break a dam."

"We're still looking into this." It was something Carlos was reluctant to talk about. His daughter Susan was the naturalist the university had sent into the Black Mountains to investigate the reports, and she'd returned adamant in her belief that the *chirreep* had to be protected at all costs, even if it meant shutting down the logging camps. As her father, Carlos believed her without reservation, yet as president he had to weigh preservation of the *chirreep*'s natural habitat against the necessity of allowing timber to be harvested in the Black Mountains. This had led to more than a little friction between father and daughter lately. "That's an exceptional situation," he went on, carefully picking his words. "The *chirreep* aren't dangerous. They're just . . . something we didn't expect."

"So what did you expect?" Tereshkova asked.

"Not this," he replied.

No one said anything for a while after that. They sat around the fire, dining on curried chicken and washing it down with glasses of wine. It was a clear evening, cool but not uncomfortable; Bear was beginning to rise above the eastern horizon, the leading edge of its ring-plane a silver spear thrust into the autumn constellations. Preceding it, though, was a new object; a tiny spot of light, so small that it could easily be covered by an outstretched thumb, yet brighter than either Fox or Raven, Bear's closest satellites.

"There's your namesake," Jud said, prodding Jonas with his elbow as he craned his neck to stare up at the sky. "Whittaker Station . . . almost finished, isn't it?"

Jonas coughed as if something had just gone down the wrong way; he nodded as he hastily took a sip of water from the flask next to his chair. "I wish . . . *harrumph*, 'cuse me . . . I'd just as soon they don't call it that."

"False modesty," Tereshkova said.

"No, ma'am . . . not at all. I'm rather honored, actually. But if the long-term objective is to construct a network of starbridges, then wouldn't it be better to name them after the places where they're built? Starbridge Earth, Starbridge Coyote, Starbridge Kuiper . . ."

"Starbridge Kuiper?" Carlos gave him a sharp look. "You didn't tell me that a starbridge had been built in the Kuiper Belt."

For an instant it seemed as if Tereshkova and Pacino exchanged know-ing looks. "Well . . . um, yes, there is," Ana said. "K-1X. But it was a test fa-cility, built mainly to see if starbridge technology actually worked. It did, but it hasn't been used since then."

"So you've sent a ship through a starbridge to the Kuiper Belt." In-trigued by this revelation, Jud leaned forward in his chair. "Fantastic! What did you find there?"

Tereshkova shrugged. "Nothing, really. A lot of asteroids, but none of any great interest."

"So you've been there." Carlos gazed at her from across the fire. "Even if you didn't find anything, that's something we haven't heard before now. What did you—?"

"Actually, we haven't been there personally," Pacino said quickly. "K-1X was constructed by a different vessel. Once it was complete, our sister ship, the *Galileo,* undertook the initial mission. So none of us were aboard."

"Oh . . . well, that's too bad." Jud was disappointed. "So what did the *Galileo* report?"

Uncomfortable silence. "As I said, nothing of consequence." Ana rose from her chair. "If you'll excuse me . . ."

"Certainly." Carlos watched as the *Columbus*'s captain walked away from the fire, her flashlight winking on as she made her way through the tall grass toward the latrine. Pacino paid a small compliment about the ex-cellence of tonight's dinner, and Carlos commented that it was his wife's fa-vorite recipe, yet it was obvious that he and Jud had just hit a sore spot.

They're hiding something, he thought. *What aren't they telling us?*

They awoke early, shortly after sunrise, and after a quick breakfast of cereal and dried fruit they broke down the tents and boarded the *Orion II* again. By midmorning, they came to a bend in the river, where Valentina Creek turned due south; consulting the map, Barry estimated that they would reach the confluence of the longer, as-yet-unnamed river by day's end.

Although the creek remained deep enough to permit them easy pas-sage, it was also becoming narrower, sometimes less than thirty feet across; the banks became higher as well, often making it difficult for them to see very far ashore. The topography had changed, too; where there had once been only trackless landscapes of sand and high grass, they now caught glimpses of low mesas and dry arroyos, patched here and there by swatches of brush and small, scruffy-looking trees. Jud remarked that it resembled parts of the American Southwest, or perhaps the badlands of Alberta, Canada, where dinosaurs had once roamed. The others scoffed at this, with Tereshkova in particular chiding him for being just a little too imaginative, yet Carlos could see what Jud meant; although reptiles had never evolved on Coyote, it wasn't hard to visualize the fossilized bones of ancient monsters lying somewhere out there in this wasteland.

As it turned out, though, it wasn't dinosaurs they had to worry about. Late that afternoon, as Uma was beginning to hang low to the west, Carlos and Barry were studying the map and discussing whether they should make camp here or wait until after they reached the confluence, when Jonas let out a shout from the bow.

"Smoke!" he yelled, pointing to the east. "Over there! I just saw smoke!"

Stepping out from under the awning, Carlos peered in the direction he indicated. Just as he said, a slender tendril of brown smoke was rising from the other side of a high riverbank. He couldn't see exactly where it was coming from, but he had little doubt what was causing it. "Pull over!" he called back to Barry. "Anywhere you can!"

Ana had been dozing in the cabin. Now she came out to join him and Jonas. "I don't understand," she said. "What's so significant about a wild-fire?"

"Grass doesn't catch fire all by itself." Carlos turned to help Will lower the sails; Jud and Jonas had already picked up oars and dropped their blades over the port gunnel. "Takes a lightning storm to do that, and we haven't had one in the last two days." Glancing back at her, he saw that she didn't get it. "You wanted to see *chirreep*, didn't you? Well, here's your chance."

Barry managed to locate a spot on the east side of the creek where the riverbank fell to a small, muddy beach. Once they dropped anchor, Jonas hopped over the side; landing in thigh-deep water, he slogged through the shallows, carrying the bow-line over his shoulder. Once he was ashore, he looped the rope around the base of a bush and knotted it tight, but when Jud tried to lower the gangway, they found that the plank wasn't quite long enough to reach dry ground.

"Sorry, Captain," Carlos said to Tereshkova, "but I'm afraid you're going to have to get your feet wet." She scowled, but said nothing as he picked up a pair of binoculars and slid over the keelboat's starboard side. All the same, though, she hesitated as he gallantly offered a hand to help her off the boat. "It's just water and mud," he added. "Nothing to worry about."

"I can see that," she said stiffly, insulted by his belaboring of the obvious. "But shouldn't we arm ourselves?"

Behind her, Pacino was already pulling a weapon from his bag: an EA particle beam pistol, sleek and silver in the waning light of the day. "Put that back," Carlos said. "We don't need it." Pacino hesitated; then, ignoring Carlos's request, he tucked the gun in his waistband of his trousers, staring back at him in defiance. Tereshkova stayed where she was, not making a move to get off the boat. Carlos sighed, "All right then, suit yourself . . . but leave it where it is."

The water was warm, but the mud below it was deep; it slopped around their calves and sucked at the soles of their boots. Ana didn't let go of Carlos's hand until they'd come ashore. Then, with Pacino and Jonas on either side of them, they scurried up the riverbank on hands and knees, clinging to crumbling red soil and half-buried roots until they reached the top.

From here, they saw more of the same sort of broken landscape they'd been seeing all day: narrow canyons, tabletop hills, dry creek beds. The smoke spiraled up from the other side of a small mesa a few hundred yards away. "Over there," Carlos said to the others. "When we get closer, stay low. And whatever else you do, be quiet. They've got a very sharp sense of hearing."

They nodded, and then he led them toward the mesa, careful to avoid stepping on any sticks or brush. Fortunately the air was still, so there wasn't any wind to carry their scent. Once they reached the mesa, he bent low, motioning for the others to do the same. It was only a couple hundred feet high; once they reached the top, Carlos dropped to his hands and knees, and in this way they crawled until they could see the source of the smoke.

On the other side of the mesa, within a gulley surrounded by low hillocks, were eight dome-like mounds, each about fifteen feet tall, nearly indistinguishable from the natural formations around them except for entrances and windows burrowed into their sides. The smoke they'd spotted emerged from a hole bored into the top of the central one; here and there were small piles of wood, and what looked like racks with pieces of woven grass draped across them.

And amid all this, dozens of small dark-furred creatures, none larger than a small ape, each going about their daily business: carrying wood from the stacks in the domes, squatting together in circles and chipping at small rocks, weaving cloth. A couple of children chased each other around the domes; a few older ones sat by themselves, observing their antics with sublime disinterest.

Even from the distance, they could hear the voices of the *chirreep*: a babble of hoots, clicks, and chirps, with the occasional whistle for emphasis. They might have been mistaken for random animal sounds, as Carlos had when he'd first heard them, but when he listened closer he found that it was possible to make out a distinct pattern; consonants mainly, with few vowels. A protean form of language. Susan had taught him a few words, yet just how she'd come by such knowledge, she'd refused to tell him.

"Fantastic." Tereshkova's voice was a faint whisper; she lay on her belly next to him, watching them with wide-eyed astonishment. "Absolutely incredible."

"You'd almost think they're intelligent." Pacino was less impressed; apparently he thought he was watching a group of trained monkeys. "Wonder how they got that fire going."

Carlos ignored him. He pushed his binoculars across the ground to Ana. "Each dome belongs to a family," he murmured, "and the central dome belongs to the tribal leader. It's his job to stoke the fire and keep it going all day, and when evening comes he lets the others carry embers back to their own mounds so they can make their own. Or at least that's how we think they work it out."

Tereshkova studied the village through the binoculars. "An alien civilization."

"A native civilization," Jonas corrected. "We're the aliens."

Pacino smirked. "I'd hardly call this . . ."

Suddenly, a sharp, high-pitched shrill: a *chirreep* standing on top of a mesa on the other side of the gulley, screaming at the top of his lungs. The *chirreep* in the village below stopped whatever they were doing to stare up at him. Another warbling cry, then the *chirreep* raised a staff and pointed it straight toward the mesa where they lay.

"Aw, crap," Carlos murmured. "We've been spotted."

"What?" Ana was just as surprised as he was. "How did they—?"

"Like I said, they've got great hearing." Within seconds, the village had gone into a panic. Alerted by the sentry, the *chirreep* rushed to their domes, dropping their belongings as they gathered their children. Carlos had no doubt that the sentry had heard them; damn it, he should have obeyed his own advice and kept his mouth shut. "No sense in pretending," he added, pushing himself up from his prone position. "Let's go before we . . ."

A beep, then a high whine from somewhere beside him. He looked around, saw Pacino standing erect, his pistol clasped between his hands. He was taking aim at the nearest *chirreep*, an adult who'd frozen in his tracks to stare at the intruders. Pacino's finger was curled within the trigger guard, and he was squinting down the barrel. In another instant . . .

"Stand down!" Tereshkova yelled. "That's an order!"

For a moment, it didn't seem as if her first officer would obey. Then she shouted something else in Russian, and he relaxed his grip on the gun. The *chirreep* at whom he'd been aiming sprinted for the nearest dome; he was among the last to disappear.

Suddenly, the village was deserted. Save for a few items scattered here and there across the ground and the smoke wafting upward from the central dome, there was no sign of life. Carlos rose to his feet, let out his breath. "Well, now you've seen some *chirreep*," he muttered, offering a hand to Tereshkova. "Hope you enjoyed the experience."

At first, it seemed as if Ana was going to ignore his offer to help her to her feet. Upon catching her first officer's eye, though, she glared at him, then took Carlos's hand. "I did, yes," she said. "Thank you very much. And my most profound apologies . . ."

"Sorry, Captain." Pacino put away his gun. "I thought they were going to . . ." Tereshkova said something else in Russian. It sounded like an insult, and his face went red before he turned to look at Carlos. "My apologies, Mr. President. My actions were rash and unwarranted."

"Yeah, well . . ." Carlos wanted to chew him out as well, but it looked as if his commanding officer had just done that. "No harm done," he finished, and let the matter drop. "Let's head back to the boat."

The hike to the *chirreep* village cost them an hour of daylight; it was dusk by the time they reached the confluence. Barry was leery about entering strange waters at night, so they pulled a half mile up from where the rivers came together. As a further precaution, they set up camp on the west bank of the Valentina, across from the side where the *chirreep* lived; no sense in tempting the locals to pay them a late-night visit.

Dinner that evening was lamb stew, which Will served up along with sourdough bread and another jug of wine. They ate sitting around the fire; high clouds were moving in from the west, obscuring the stars and causing a thin, luminescent ring to form around Bear. Carlos used the satphone to call Liberty and check the weather forecast; as he anticipated, it was already raining in New Florida, so they could expect to receive much the same sort of weather in their part of the world, beginning either late tonight or early tomorrow. Hearing this, Jud took a few minutes to go back to the boat and make sure that it was firmly tied down.

The topic of conversation turned to the *chirreep*. "I can see why you think they're a native civilization," Pacino said, leaning forward to turn his waterlogged boots so that the fire would dry their toes. "They build shelters, they tend fires, they care for their young, and so forth. Fine . . . but I wouldn't exactly call them civilized."

Carlos nearly choked on a mouthful of stew. "What do you want? Malls? Netcasts? I can't see what more proof you need to show that they're an intelligent race."

"I said civilized, not intelligent." Pacino favored him with an indulgent smile. "They're not necessarily one and the same. Birds build shelters and care for their young."

"Do birds make fires? Do they have their own language?" No longer hungry, Carlos laid his plate aside. "My daughter showed me photos of cave paintings she found in the Black Mountains a few weeks ago. Pictographs of what look like starships, at least as much as the *chirreep* understood them. Also boats, which the *chirreep* don't know how to build, and humans coming ashore to—"

"I don't quite understand," Tereshkova interrupted. "If the *chirreep* don't know how to build boats, then how did they get from here to Midland and Great Dakota? And why aren't there any on New Florida?"

"I don't know." Carlos shrugged. "We think that the islands of the northern hemisphere may have been closer together at one time, perhaps even forming one great landmass. Sort of like Pangaea back on Earth, before it was separated by the movement of continental plates. If that's the case here, then the *chirreep* might have evolved in one place, then migrated to other parts of Coyote before channels divided the major landmasses. As for the other, we can only guess that the *chirreep* tribes on New Florida lost out to the boids and were wiped out."

"That's quite a bit of conjecture, don't you think?" Ana wasn't being snide; she was simply unconvinced of his theory.

"Perhaps . . . but that's not the point I'm trying to make." Suddenly restless, Carlos stood up from his chair. "If a race is capable of recording its own history, doesn't that make them civilized? Granted, the *chirreep* we've found on Great Dakota may be more advanced than the *chirreep* you saw today, but still they belong to the same species."

"It might," Pacino conceded. "But still . . ."

"Look, we can't judge an alien race . . . I mean, a native race . . . by our own standards. Perhaps they can't build boats, let alone starships. So what? From what you've told me, even after three hundred years, there's been no indication that intelligent life exists elsewhere . . . or at least intelligent life as you define it, on a par with human civilization. Right?"

Pacino uneasily shifted in his chair, absently turning his boots once more. "That may be the case," Tereshkova said. "We still don't know for sure."

"Exactly. So far as we know, humankind may be the most advanced race in the galaxy. Compared to the *chirreep*, we're like gods."

"If we are like gods, then we'd better get good at it." Jonas had said little since they'd left the *chirreep* village; now he sat in a folding chair, nursing a glass of wine. "Someone said that once. I forget who . . . never mind. Look, until about the seventeenth century or so, everyone believed Earth was the center of the universe, and all the stars and planets revolved around it. That was Ptolemy's model, and the church held to it because it proved that Earth was God's chosen place and all that. Fit right in with their doctrine. But then Galileo came along, and he built a telescope to study the movements of the planets, and he discovered that, no sir, the planets revolved around the sun, and there were even tiny moons revolving around Jupiter."

"Are you making a point?" Pacino was becoming impatient with him.

"Let me finish, okay?" Jonas was mildly drunk; he drank some more wine, went on. "So Galileo . . . good ol' Galileo Galilei . . . took it upon himself to publish his findings. Only he knew that, if he went outright and said it, then the church would put him on trial for heresy. So instead he wrote it up as sort of a story, just a chat between two guys, and he called it . . ." He shut his eyes for a moment, seeking to remember. "*A Dialogue Concerning the Two Chief World Systems* . . . and, y'know, the rest is history."

"Galileo was eventually put on trial by the Vatican, anyway." Barry's voice was quiet. Will sat on the ground beside him, and he fondly stroked his shoulder. "He recanted his statements, if only to avoid being put to the stake, and after that he spent the rest of his life under house arrest."

"Right." Jonas raised a finger. "But enough people paid attention to his theories that he overturned the idea that Earth is the center of creation, and that's what I'm trying to get at. The more we learn, the more we have to change the way we look at things. Ever since Galileo, we've searched for life on other worlds . . . intelligent life, I mean. All well and good, but somewhere along the line we managed to persuade ourselves that, when we finally met these aliens, they'd be just as smart as we are, maybe even more. But Carlos is right. It may be possible that we're the most intelligent race, the most advanced, the only ones capable of building starships."

"God help us," Will murmured.

"Then help yourself . . . because if we've become like gods, that means we should recognize the responsibility that puts upon us." He looked straight at Pacino. "Keep that in mind, the next time you get trigger-happy."

Pacino's face turned red. "I only intended to . . ."

"All right, that's enough." Carlos didn't like the way the conversation was headed; they still had a few more days to spend together, and he didn't want everyone at each other's throats. He stretched his back, then bent over to pick up his plate. "It's getting late, and we've got a long day ahead of us. My turn to wash the dishes. Will, if you'd help me gather everything, I'd appreciate it. Everyone, make sure your tents are properly staked and there's no leaks . . . we'll probably get rain later tonight."

And that was the end of the discussion. Yet, as Will collected the cookware and Jud folded the chairs, Carlos observed that Tereshkova and Pacino had walked away from the others. Although they seemed to be having a quiet discussion between themselves, Ana kept glancing in his direction. Carlos pretended not to notice, but it seemed as if they were talking about him.

Another mystery. Or maybe just the same one as before.

*   *   *

Just as the forecast predicted, the next day was wet and miserable, with heavy rain coming down from an overcast sky and a bitter wind from the northwest. They broke down the tents and stowed the gear; a breakfast of hot oatmeal was served in the *Orion*'s cabin, with Jud brewing a pot of coffee on the portable stove, but that was their only source of warmth. No one was dry, and everyone was cranky, and for five dollars Carlos would have gladly used the satphone to summon a gyro to pick them up. But he reminded himself that he'd been through much worse; besides, it was time that his VIPs got a taste of what frontier exploration was really like.

So they pulled up anchor and, with the men handling the oars, they let the current carry the keelboat the rest of the way to the confluence. As it turned out, the passage was easier than expected; the new creek was wider than the Valentina, and once *Orion* rounded the point, it was easily swept along by the current.

And so it remained for the rest of the day. The rainstorm continued, lightening up for a while now and then before returning with a vengeance. Barry had Jud and Will raise the sail, but he became concerned about the wind ripping the sheet, so after an hour he asked them to lower it once more. They could see little of the countryside around them; all they could make out through the downpour were low hills and the occasional mesa. When evening came, they rowed the boat close to shore, then dropped anchor and tied up against a couple of small trees. A cold dinner of ham and beans was served in the cabin, and there was little conversation before they unrolled their sleeping bags and slept, side by side, in the cramped confines of the keelboat.

The sky was clear again the following morning, with a light but steady breeze from the west. The one benefit of the storm was that it raised the water level by a few inches; Pacino dropped the plumb-line from the bow, counted the knots, and announced that it was fourteen feet to the bottom. Smooth, swift water, with little chance of them running aground. The river still hadn't been named, though, so Carlos extended the privilege to Jonas; he thought about it for a moment, then quietly suggested that it be called Ellen Creek, in honor of his late daughter.

Once they got under way, they made good time. Now that the storm was over, they could see that the landscape had changed. Although it was still desert, it was even more chaotic than before, with steep buttes on either side of them separated by twisting canyons; now and then they spotted sharp pinnacles rising high above the sands, around which swoops soared upon thermal updrafts. At one point, they observed a sandstone arch, forty feet tall and nearly twice as long, joining two mesas as a natural bridge. Strange and beautiful country, silent save for the lonesome wind that moaned through the canyons, the eerie cries of the birds; no one said anything, but simply stood on the deck and watched as it rolled past, like a scene from a weird dream.

Early in the afternoon, a few miles after the creek made a bend to the south, once again they saw a slender tendril of smoke, this time to the west. Another *chirreep* village, but farther away. They briefly discussed going ashore to look at it, but decided that it probably lay several miles from Ellen Creek, and so instead Carlos marked its approximate location on the map for future reference. Secretly, he was relieved that no one had insisted upon visiting it; he was in no mood to have a repeat of what had happened a couple of days ago.

They pitched their tents that night on a riverbank. Although it was the first time in two days that they were able to enjoy a cooked meal and a night on dry land, the atmosphere was oddly subdued. Even when Barry brought out his guitar and played a few songs by firelight, it did little to break the somber mood. No one wanted to talk. It was as if Ellen Creek haunted everyone's private thoughts.

The next morning, while the others were loading the gear aboard the *Orion*, Carlos and Barry met together in the cabin to study the map. They were approaching the confluence of another creek, a minor tributary that flowed down from northwest and, after briefly merging with Ellen Creek for a short distance, would branch off again to the southeast. If *Orion* continued traveling due south, though, Ellen Creek would carry it straight to the island's southern coast.

"The current's strong," Barry said, "and we've got the wind at our back. At this rate, we may be able to reach the coast by the end of the day." He looked up from the map. "Unless, of course, you want to spend another night here."

Carlos considered the question. It had already been decided that, once the journey was over, he and his guests would fly back to Liberty aboard a gyro while Barry, Will, and Jud would sail back along the Great Equatorial River to New Florida. Yet, despite the fact that they'd run into some bad weather, they were slightly ahead of schedule; there was more than enough food to last them for a couple more days on the island, and they hadn't even exhausted the reserves of wine that had been stocked aboard.

He was tempted to stay longer. Once back in Liberty, he had only his duties as president to look forward to: paperwork, committee meetings, reports from one department chief or another. At best, a courtesy visit to a greenhouse farm, or a brief inspection of the silos to make sure that enough corn had been put away to feed the livestock through the long winter ahead. Yet here, at least for a few days, he'd been able to recall his youth. True, perhaps now he traveled in greater comfort, without any of the risks he'd faced when he was seventeen, but still . . .

Something crashed on the deck outside. Gazing through the cabin's open door, he saw that Pacino had dropped the crate containing the cookware. Pots and pans lay scattered across the mid-deck, yet instead of picking them up, Pacino had turned to swear at Jonas, who apparently had bumped into him on the gangway. The older man glared back at him, then said something that Carlos didn't catch but which only made Pacino even angrier. They were on the verge of yelling into each other's face when Jud stepped between them.

"No," Carlos said quietly. "Perhaps we ought to head home." He looked at Barry. "These people have had enough. Two more days out here, and they'll be ready to kill each other."

Barry nodded, yet there was a sad look in his eyes. "Well, we tried. But they don't get it, do they?"

Carlos sighed. He was almost ready to agree when he glanced through the door again. Sitting on a barrel near the bow, ignoring the quarrel behind her, Ana Tereshkova gazed at the river. Her hands were folded together in her lap, and the morning breeze caught her hair and pulled it back from her brow, and in that instant Carlos realized that she was seeing the same thing that everyone who'd fallen in love with this world had ever seen.

"I don't know," he murmured. "Maybe they do." He tapped his finger on the map. "Take your time. No need to rush."

By midday, they reached the new creek, and this time Pacino was allowed to christen it. In keeping with tradition, he gave it a woman's name: Bettina Creek, after his mother. Yet it was narrower than either the Valentina or the Ellen, and after a couple of miles it branched off once

more, flowing to the southeast. Leaving Bettina Creek behind, they continued following Ellen Creek as it meandered south.

Although the creek was now much wider and a bit more shallow, the
terrain had gradually become less interesting. Gone were the mesas and
pinnacles farther north; now there were only low hills and shallow gulleys,
windswept and barren, like ancient floodplains. Swoops followed the keelboat for a time, and Carlos noted that they were now the broad-winged
subspecies that nested in the Meridian Archipelago southeast of the island.
Another indication that they were approaching the coast.

Barry checked the compass bearings against the map and confirmed
this; they'd reach the coast shortly before sundown. By then, however, it
would be too late in the day for a gyro to pick them up; the expedition
would have to spend one more night on the island. No one complained, although it didn't seem as if anyone was pleased by the news. It had been a
long trip; everyone aboard was ready for a hot bath and a bed that wasn't
on bare ground.

Late that afternoon, Carlos was sitting alone in the bow, watching Uma
as it began to sink to the west. The sun had been out all day, and the heat
made everyone lazy and sluggish. Will had taken over the rudder for Barry
while he dozed on the upper deck; Jud was minding the sails, but Pacino
and Jonas were napping in the cabin. So he was mildly surprised when
Tereshkova suddenly appeared at his side.

"Mind if I join you?" she asked.

"Not at all." He moved to one side, making room on the sail cabinet for
her to sit down. "Thought you were catching a few winks yourself."

"I was, but . . ." She left it unfinished as she took a seat next to him.
"Such a pretty sunset. Thought I'd come up and enjoy it with you."

It was beautiful: a pale orange disk, painting the western sky in hues of
magenta and gold, with the moons of Dog and Eagle already appearing as
bright stars above the eastern horizon. For a long while they were quiet,
content with simply watching twilight settle in, until abruptly Tereshkova
spoke up.

"I envy you," she said softly.

That startled him. "Why?"

"To be able to have all this." She cocked her head toward the river. "An
entire world, all to yourself. Fresh air, clean water. No war, no crime, no
poverty."

"It hasn't always been this way," Carlos reminded her. "During the Union occupation . . ."

"That's in the past. Now you and your people . . ." She shrugged. "You have paradise. Or at least as close to paradise as anyone back on Earth could possibly imagine."

Carlos frowned. "Is it really that bad back there?"

Tereshkova said nothing for a moment. She glanced over her shoulder, as if to make sure that they were still alone, then she leaned forward, resting her elbows upon her knees and clasping her hands together.

"Listen to me." Her voice had become very quiet, almost a whisper. "There's something you need to know . . . something I shouldn't be telling you, but that you should hear."

Carlos felt a chill that didn't come from the afternoon breeze. He leaned forward, mimicking her posture. Another glance behind her, then Ana went on. "There's forces back home . . . very powerful forces, including my own government . . . who'll want this world for their own, once they learn what's here. After the starbridge is finished, it'll be only a matter of time before they'll come here to claim it."

"They won't get it," Carlos murmured. "We fought the Union and won. If we have to, we'll fight the European Alliance, too."

"I'm sure you will." Then she shook her head. "But you have no idea how terrible things have become. And once they discover what's here, nothing will stop them."

He opened his mouth to object, but then she reached out to clasp his hand. "Please, just hear me out," she went on. "This may be my last chance to talk to you in private. Whatever I can do to help you, I promise you that I will. If you need an ally, you've got it in me. This I swear to you."

Carlos didn't know what to say. One look at her dark eyes, and he knew that she was sincere. It occurred to him that this was the reason why Tereshkova had insisted upon making this trip; she'd wanted to see Coyote for herself, perhaps to make up her own mind how she'd cast her allegiance. One person on her crew had already gone native: Jonathan Parson, who'd jumped ship almost as soon as they arrived, never to be seen again. Now it appeared as if she was considering doing the same, in her own way.

"Thank you. I appreciate that." He hesitated. "Mr. Pacino . . . does he—?"

"Support this?" She shook her head. "No. I've tried to discuss this with him . . . we were once much closer than we are now . . . but he sees his first duty as being to the European Alliance." She hesitated. "Don't let him know. He could make life very difficult for me, once we return home, and it could jeopardize anything that we may do."

"I understand. This is just between you and me."

"Thank you." Again, a long pause as Tereshkova gazed at the river. It was very wide now; the land was nearly flat, and the air held the faint scent of salt. It wouldn't be long before they came within sight of the Great Equatorial River. "There's one more thing you should know," she went on, her voice even lower than before. "The *Galileo* . . . the *Columbus*'s sister ship, remember?"

"The one that went to the Kuiper Belt, sure. What about it?"

She hesitated. "It never returned."

Carlos stared at her. "But you said—"

"There's nothing there, yes, that's true. But that's not the real reason why it went there. They . . ."

Behind them, the cabin door opened. Glancing over his shoulder, he saw Pacino come out. "Am I missing something?" he asked, stifling a yawn behind his hand.

Releasing Carlos's hand, Tereshkova sat up straight. "Only a gorgeous sunset," she said, her voice once again without subterfuge. "Please, join us. It's worth seeing."

"Hmm . . . yes, maybe I will." There was a faint suspicion in the first officer's eyes as he stepped around the mast. Carlos wondered how much he'd overheard, if anything. "It is rather pretty, isn't it?"

"Makes the day worth living." Then she looked at Carlos and smiled. "There, you see? Just as I was saying . . . we're not alone."

And in that brief instant, she gave him a wink, as if to hint at a secret still left unshared.

One last night on Barren Isle, on a narrow beach where Ellen Creek emptied into the Great Equatorial River. So far as Carlos could tell, they weren't far from a place where he'd made camp many years ago. If so, though, time and tide had long since erased all indications of his earlier visit; once more, he was on an alien shore, without so much as footprint or a piece of charred wood to show the presence of humankind.

They tied up the *Orion II* just offshore, then pitched their tents on the beach. There was plenty of driftwood for Jud to gather to build a fire; Will barbecued a chicken and pan-roasted potatoes above the coals. They had dinner while Bear came into view above the black expanse of the river, and after they finished Barry pulled out his guitar again. No earnest dialogues about the nature of intelligent life in the universe this evening; tomorrow morning, the gyro would come to pick up Carlos and the *Columbus* crew, and the rest would sail home, so tonight they celebrated the end of a long journey. No one was sober as they danced barefoot on the sand to the tunes of old songs from Earth, Ana taking turns with each of the men, while sparks rose from the fire to meet the stars far above.

The night finally wore down, and one by one everyone lurched away to their tents, until suddenly Carlos found himself alone on the beach, standing at the edge of the waterline. He was drunk, more drunk than he'd been in many years, a half-empty bottle of wine in his right hand. The fire waned low, little more than a smoky collection of embers; the surf washed up around his bare feet, massaging his toes, and he'd forgotten why or how he'd wandered out here, yet it no longer seemed to matter.

Tilting his head back, he stared up into space. The galaxy filled the sky, billions of tiny lights, a river in the sky . . . and somewhere out there, an island called Earth. So small, so insignificant: invisible from Coyote, undetectable for the slightest of gravitational perturbations it caused upon a wan and distant star. So far away, and yet, very soon now, all too close.

Carlos took another swig of wine, found that the taste had gone sour. On sudden impulse, he hurled the bottle into the river, heard it splash somewhere on the black waters. Cursing himself for his thoughtlessness, he turned to head for his tent . . .

Then he stopped. At the edge of the beach, from within the tall grass just outside the campsite, tiny eyes that reflected the glow of the dying fire peered at him from the darkness. They watched him for a few moments, as if studying him with curiosity, but when he stepped closer they vanished into the night.

Ana was right. They were not alone.

Book 6

Coyote's Stepchildren

A patriot must be ready to defend his country against his government.

—EDWARD ABBEY,
A Voice Crying in the Wilderness

Part 5

EMISSARY TO EARTH
(from the memoirs of Wendy Gunther)

Winter was upon the world, the morning we left for Earth. Although it was the sixth week of Hanael, late autumn by the LeMarean calendar, a light snow had fallen on Liberty the night before. No more than half an inch, but nonetheless a sign that the season was changing. Little did we know that the weather wasn't the only thing that would soon be different.

The sky was overcast, and a cold wind from the north clutched at my cape as I shut the front door of my house. As Carlos and Chris waited for me in the shag-wagon that would carry us to Shuttlefield, I paused to look back at home for what seemed to be the last time. The three of us had only been teenagers when our parents had brought us to Coyote; now we were a middle-aged couple and a family friend, although by Gregorian reckoning we were nearly three hundred years old. Very soon, we'd be back on the planet of our birth; I knew that we'd eventually return to Coyote, but at that moment it didn't seem that way. I remembered that I'd left Carlos's and my bed unmade, and for an instant I had an impulse to go back inside and tidy up a bit so that Susan wouldn't be stuck with that chore, yet I knew that I was just looking for an excuse to delay our departure a little while longer. The ship was ready to leave, and it wouldn't do to keep Captain Tereshkova waiting for very much longer.

So I tried not to let Carlos see the tears in my eyes as I loaded my bags into the back of the wagon, then I climbed aboard and silently took his hand. Chris shook the reins and clucked his tongue, and the wheels creaked softly as the shag lurched forward. Ironic. We'd left Earth aboard a starship; our journey back would begin with a wagon ride.

The *Isabella* rested on the landing field just outside Shuttlefield, a gull-winged spacecraft smaller than the shuttles that had carried us down from the *Alabama* all those many years ago. Cold hydrogen fumes drifted down from its engine vents and drifted around the legs of its landing gear. There were several dozen people waiting for us: friends, family members, members of the Colonial Council, along with curious townspeople who'd come out to watch us leave. Carlos had tried to keep our departure as low-profile as possible, but there was no denying the fact that this was a historic event.

Still, we kept the formalities to a minimum. Carlos took a minute to shake hands with Frederic LaRoux; as soon as we left the ground, he'd assume the position of President Pro Temp, and lead the council until our return. Chris did the same with Juanita Morales, who'd serve as Chief Proctor during his absence. I didn't have any official duties that needed to be filled, but Kuniko Okada gave me a hug, told me that she'd try to care of my patients; that was worth a laugh, since she'd taught me everything that I knew about being a doctor.

And then there was Barry Dreyfus and his partner Will, and Chris's mother Sissy and her second husband Ben, and Bernie and Vonda Cayle. Dana Monroe had come in from Leeport; she'd been the *Alabama*'s chief engineer, and after that, Captain Lee's partner, so her unexpected presence added a certain gravitas to the occasion. My sister-in-law Marie had brought her children Rain and Hawk all the way from Clarksburg; notable in his absence was her husband Lars, who'd apparently decided to remain in Great Dakota. We spoke nothing of this, though; Lars was not a favorite member of the family.

Susan was there, too. Once again, I found myself surprised by just how quickly my little girl had grown up. Coyote's long years had that effect on those of us who'd been born on Earth; although you eventually became used to the fact that a single summer lasted nine months by the Gregorian calendar, it was more difficult to accept that a child could age three years between one winter and the next. I tried not to start crying again as we gave each other a hug, and although she and her father hadn't been on good terms lately, they managed to put aside their differences long enough for a final embrace.

By then, Captain Tereshkova was becoming impatient. We had a narrow launch window to meet if we wanted to rendezvous with the starbridge without burning more fuel than necessary. Our luggage had already been loaded aboard the skiff; looking up at the forward windows, I could see Gabriel Pacino seated in the cockpit, preparing the *Isabella* for liftoff. So I nudged Carlos's elbow, and he finished his conversation with Tomas Conseco, his chief of staff: pretty much politics-as-usual, nothing that he and

Fred couldn't handle while we were away. A last round of good-byes and good-lucks, and then Carlos, Chris, and I walked up the ramp.

The skiff's cabin was small, just large enough to seat the five of us. My hands trembled as I fastened the seat harness around me, and I had to take a deep breath as Pacino powered up the engines. Through the starboard porthole, I could see townspeople backing away from the *Isabella*. I caught one last glimpse of Susan, standing next to Marie and her kids. They'd raised their hands to wave farewell, and I was about to do the same when there was a dull roar, and suddenly the craft rose from the ground.

Liftoff was rougher than I expected. Pacino was a good pilot, and after a minute or so the turbulence eased off, once we got above the clouds. I thought I was accustomed to spaceflight, but as soon as the *Isabella* cleared the atmosphere the bottom fell out of my stomach. Fortunately, Carlos saw it coming; he had a paper bag ready for me, and into it went the hearty breakfast I'd unwisely eaten earlier that morning. Yet my husband didn't get sick, and when I looked over at Chris, he was calmly gazing out the porthole. So much for experience.

My guts finally settled down, though, and after a few minutes I was able to raise my head and peer out the window. We weren't on a low-orbit trajectory, but instead were headed for the recently completed starbridge, established in trojan orbit between Coyote and Bear. So it wasn't Coyote that I saw through the cockpit windows, but Bear itself. Carlos, Chris, or I hadn't seen 47 Ursae Majoris-B from this perspective since we'd been aboard the *Alabama*; we watched in silence as the gas-giant slowly grew in size, its blue cloud-bands and silver rings taking on hues that couldn't be seen from the ground.

It took ten hours to reach the starbridge. Long enough to take a nap, review my notes, chat with the others, even feel a little hungry even though I decided not to put any more food in my stomach. The cabin was cramped, so we didn't unfasten our straps unless it was absolutely necessary, and then only to visit the head. Carlos and I were discussing the terms of the trade proposal when Gabriel announced that we were on primary approach.

Starbridge Coyote consisted of two independent components, both cannibalized from what had once been the EASS *Columbus*. The ship's primary hull was now Station B, otherwise known as the Gatehouse: a long, spindle-shaped structure, over four hundred feet long, which used to be the starship's payload and service modules and now served as a command platform. It was positioned about twenty miles from Station A, which was the starbridge itself: a thick ring resembling a bicycle tire a hundred and thirty feet in diameter, reassembled from sections of the torus that had once contained *Columbus*'s diametric drive.

I don't understand the physics of hyperspace travel, so I won't try to explain how it worked, lest to say that the starbridge created a temporary wormhole between 47 Ursae Majoris-B and Earth by locating and isolating a point of singularity within the quantum foam of Bear's gravity well, then enlarging it to form the hole's mouth. When another starbridge near Earth did the same thing at the same time, a tunnel through hyperspace was created. Eureka: faster-than-light travel.

Jonas Whittaker, the physicist who'd invented the starbridge, was aboard the Gatehouse; he'd flown up last week to oversee its final test phase, which included opening it just long enough to launch a probe into hyperspace. The probe successfully traversed the wormhole; seconds after disappearing from our side of the junction, it beamed back a radio signal, indicating its safe arrival in cislunar space near the Moon. Two days later, the test was repeated, this time with an identical probe launched from Starbridge Earth; once again, it arrived intact. And during each test, brief radio messages had been exchanged; for the first time since humankind arrived in the 47 Ursae Majoris system, people on Earth directly heard from those who'd settled Coyote.

So we didn't need a massive starship to reach Earth; our little skiff was sufficient to make the journey. Nonetheless, it was pretty tense aboard the *Isabella* as it assumed a parking orbit five miles from the starbridge. Through the cockpit windows, we could see it as a small silver ring among the stars, its navigation beacons flashing red and blue. A brief exchange between Ana and the Gatehouse team, then Gabriel entered commands into the comp that slaved the skiff's onboard guidance systems to the Gatehouse AI. A final rundown of the prelaunch checklist, then we commenced final countdown for what was being called "hyperspace insertion maneuver."

It took fifteen minutes for the starbridge to power up. At T-minus two minutes, Ana looked back at us to make sure we'd securely fastened our harnesses; she also warned us not to look directly at the starbridge as we went through. At T-minus one minute, the Gatehouse informed the *Is-*

abella that they'd received telemetry from Starbridge Earth, confirming that the starbridge on the other side of the wormhole had been successfully activated. At T-minus forty-five seconds, the *Isabella* fired its aft thrusters and began moving toward the ring. And at T-minus thirty seconds, I took Carlos's hand in mine and silently began to pray.

I forgot to look away, so the flash nearly blinded me: starlight from the other side of the galaxy, defocused as it entered the mouth of the wormhole, came out on our side like a silent nuclear blast. Dazzled, I yelped as I whipped my left hand in front of my face; even with my eyes tightly shut, my retinas retained a black-on-white negative afterimage of the flash.

By then, though, that was the least of my worries. Everything around me shook violently, and then the craft turned upside down, spiraling around its axial center as if caught in a maelstrom. An invisible hand pushed me back against my seat. Intellectually, I knew what was happening—the *Isabella* had passed the wormhole's event horizon and now was plummeting headlong through the hyperspace tunnel created by the two starbridges—yet in the deepest, most atavistic corner of my little monkey-mind, I knew that I was about to die.

I may have screamed. I can't remember. All I knew was that I hoped death would come quickly, so that I wouldn't suffer much.

Then there was another hard lurch, and suddenly I was pitched forward against the shoulder straps, hard enough to knock the wind from my lungs. Gasping for air, I forced myself to breathe. For a few seconds, everything continued to swirl, then I felt a few quick jolts as the skiff's maneuvering thrusters automatically fired to stabilize our trajectory, and gradually everything began to settle down.

Opening my eyes, I took stock of the situation. Carlos had fainted; his hand still loosely held my own, yet his head lolled back against his seat, and saliva floated upward from his agape mouth. On the other side of the aisle, Chris clenched his mouth as he fumbled for the relief bag beneath his seat; he barely got it to his face before he vomited. Pacino's hands were unsteady as he reached forward to grasp the control yoke; Tereshkova's dark hair was sweat-matted against her forehead and the nape of her neck, yet she managed to touch the wand of her headset and murmur something in Russian.

Through the cockpit windows, I saw stars amid the darkness of space. They didn't seem any different from those I'd seen only a few seconds earlier; indeed, for a moment I wondered if the attempt had somehow failed, and we'd returned to where we had started. But then I turned my eyes toward the porthole next to my seat, and caught sight of something I hadn't seen since I was fourteen years old . . .

Earth.

A marble in the cosmos, a couple hundred thousand miles away: one-third covered by darkness, the rest bathed by the sun. Blue oceans, green continents, white polar icecaps, with everything masked here and there by thin clouds. A world so familiar, and yet so alien.

We'd made it. We'd left home, only to come . . . home.

Nearly as soon as Jonas Whittaker told us that it was possible to reach Earth via hyperspace, we'd begun to make preparations for this trip. True, there were quite a few who were reluctant to have anything to do with our home world; the United Republic of America may have long since collapsed, but the memory of the Union occupation was still fresh for everyone older than seven Coyote years, and some believed that nothing good could come of ending our isolation. During the course of public hearings before the Colonial Council, though, it became clear that this was a minority opinion; a large majority believed that the benefits of resuming contact with Earth outweighed the potential risks.

They had a point. Much of the high-tech equipment left behind by the Union was getting old; weardown had become a common problem as comps failed, machines broke down, and precision tools suffered metal fatigue. We'd learned how to get by through swapping parts or fashioning crude substitutes, but every incident in which a gyro failed to take off or a memory cell crashed was a bitter reminder that even frontier ingenuity had its limits. It wasn't hard to foresee a time, only a generation or two in the future, when our grandchildren and great-grandchildren would be struggling along with bone knives and pieces of flint, while the devices once used by their ancestors rusted away in farm fields.

So while engineers and technicians aboard the *Columbus* began building the starbridge, an executive committee convened to discuss the means by which the Coyote Federation could establish peaceful relations with the governments of Earth. In the end, a draft set of protocols was decided upon, and the members of a diplomatic envoy were selected to undertake the first voyage to Earth.

To no one's surprise, Carlos was tapped to lead the mission. As president, it was only natural that he should represent the colonies; because he'd also once been an explorer, he had the advantage of being able to describe the new world from the perspective of someone who'd seen it as few others had. It took a bit more debate, though, before he managed to convince the committee that I should join him. Several members suspected Carlos was indulging in nepotism by wanting to bring along his wife; they preferred to send a Council member instead. However, Carlos argued that since I myself had once belonged to the Council, I'd be able to represent its interests. And besides, Jonas had warned us that the first flight would doubtless be rough. While most of the Council members were either too old or too inexperienced, both Carlos and I were veterans of the original *Alabama* party, yet still young enough to endure a hyperspace jaunt.

It took a lot more persuasion before the committee decided that Chris Levin should be the third person on our team. Nearly every member wanted to be part of the mission, but what we needed more than another politician was a good right-hand man. Although Ana Tereshkova assured Carlos and me that the European Alliance would treat us as honored guests, we weren't ready to take her word at face value. So while Chris was officially our aide, the fact of the matter was that he was really our bodyguard. He and Carlos may have once had their differences, with me being the girl in the middle, but that was a long time ago; since then, he'd become a trusted friend, and I was glad to have him watching our backs.

So there were the three of us, sitting in the passenger seats of the *Isabella*, quietly watching as Pacino maneuvered the skiff away from the starbridge. Starbridge Earth was positioned at L4, a Lagrange point in a halo orbit near the Moon, about a quarter of a million miles from Earth. Not far away, we could see a small cruciform-shaped space station; at first I thought we were headed for the Gatehouse, but when Ana finished her conversation on the comlink, she said something in Russian to Gabriel. He gave her a questioning look, then shrugged and began entering coordinates into the keyboard.

"We've been instructed to proceed to Highgate," she said, turning to us and speaking in English. "That's the station at L1, in high orbit above the Moon."

"I've heard of it." Carlos raised an eyebrow. "But isn't it controlled by the Union?"

"It was when we left. Apparently it's come under international control since then." She glanced at Gabriel. "I'm not sure what the situation is, but the person with whom I spoke is an Alliance officer, and he insists that we rendezvous with Highgate. A ship will meet us halfway and escort us in."

"If he insists . . ." Gabriel finished punching in the new coordinates, then engaged the autopilot. The aft and starboard thrusters fired; Earth glided away from our windows, and we found ourselves pointed in the direction of the Moon. "I would've thought that we'd head straight for Earth and dock with the New Guinea space elevator instead."

"I asked about that." Ana paused. "I was told that it no longer exists."

Gabriel's eyes widened. "For God's sake, what happened?"

"No idea. It wasn't explained to me." Ana looked back at us again. "It seems that much has changed since we were last here."

Carlos nodded silently, and Chris shifted uneasily in his seat. Nearly three centuries had passed since the three of us had left Earth, yet it'd been almost fifty years since *Columbus*'s departure. I knew that the EA had built a beanstalk in New Guinea, just as the WHU had erected one of its own in Ecuador; if the New Guinea space elevator was gone, then that left only the one operated by the Union . . . and there was no way an Alliance ship was going to dock there.

Ana turned away from us again, her expression pensive as she gazed through the cockpit windows. I'd never warmed to her very much, although she and Carlos had become friends during their trip together to Barren Isle the previous month. To be truthful, it was probably because my husband had established a relationship with a younger woman—however cordial it might be—that I instinctively distrusted her. Long-married couples are apt to suspect one another of having affairs, but Carlos and I had crossed that point many years before. All the same, though, something had happened during the week they'd spent together that my husband still wouldn't tell me about. Maybe he hadn't slept with Ana—and Barry, who'd also been on the boat with them, had positively sworn that he had not—yet nonetheless . . .

Even so, I couldn't help but feel a certain sympathy for Captain Tereshkova. When she'd left home, everything had been a certain way; deep in her heart, she'd probably believed that the world would remain unchanged upon her return. I'd received that same sort of shock when the *Glorious Destiny* had arrived at Coyote; now it was her turn to find out otherwise.

Yet she wouldn't be alone. Many more surprises awaited us.

It was a long ride to Highgate. Once again, I tried to kill time by taking a nap, even though I wasn't tired at all; I just shut my eyes for a while and tried to ignore my sense of unease. At some point, I must have actually dozed off; when I woke up, I looked out the window and saw a small, cylindrical vehicle keeping pace with the *Isabella* off our starboard side. About half the size of the skiff, the tricolor flag of the European Alliance painted on its forward hull, it looked somewhat like a spark plug; harmless, until I noticed the missile rack protruding from its starboard side. An armed spacecraft: not the most comforting introduction to the twenty-fourth century.

But it was Highgate itself that threw everyone for a loop. I'd seen pictures of the original station, from the datafiches brought to Coyote by the *Columbus*. It had been impressive then, yet sometime during the last half century it'd been replaced by something far larger. Almost three miles in diameter, it vaguely resembled an enormous fan, with a saucer-shaped hub and three giant spheres at the ends of long booms that telescoped out from the hub at equilateral distances. Two drum-shaped modules rose from the top and bottom halves of the hub; the spheres were opaque, but light gleamed from hundreds of portholes within the hub and cylinders. Along the curved sides of the spheres were vast hatches; as the skiff drew closer, I peered inside one, and caught a glimpse of a streamlined spacecraft floating within a skeletal dry dock.

Many years ago, when I'd accompanied Captain Lee to the *Glorious Destiny* after it had arrived at Coyote, I'd been stunned by the sight of a vessel that dwarfed the *Alabama*. Yet Highgate made even Union starships seem like toys by comparison. Back home, people considered the Garcia Narrows Bridge a major feat of engineering, yet even James Alonzo Garcia would have been awestruck by the size of this thing.

I wasn't the only one who was amazed. Gabriel could barely keep his attention on the controls, and Ana was so shocked that she had to ask the traffic controller twice where the *Isabella* was supposed to dock. As it turned out, Alpha Dock was the same sphere where I'd seen the ship during our first flyby. Red and blue beacons flashed on either side of a small-craft hatch, and the escort craft peeled away as we slowly entered the sphere. A tethered figure in a hardsuit waved luminescent batons above his head as he guided us toward a small docking cradle; Pacino brought the *Isabella* to a halt, and there was a sudden thump as the cradle closed around the skiff.

Ana slowly let out her breath, then cupped a hand around her headset and listened intently. "We're to disembark through the top hatch," she said after a moment. "A gangway is being extended." Then she frowned as she listened further. "I don't believe this," she murmured. "We're going to be put in quarantine until we pass sterilization procedures."

I couldn't help but smile. "Nothing new here. I had to put up with much the same when I went aboard the *Destiny*." Gabriel gave me a dark look, and I shrugged. "Can't blame 'em for being careful. They don't know what sort of cooties we might be carrying."

"Cooties?"

"Extraterrestrial microorganisms." Carlos grinned. "My wife has a fine grasp of scientific terminology." He gazed out the portside window at the giant spacecraft docked nearby, whistled under his breath. "Will you get a load of that thing?"

I leaned over to gaze past him and Chris. The ship was nearly six hundred feet long: shaped somewhat like a pumpkin seed, its sleek hull gradually expanded back from its narrow bow to where a pair of nacelles on its flanks contained what appeared to be diametric-drive engines. Aft of the nacelles were blunt wings, with vertical stabilizers above and below the wingtips; on the topside of the hull between the wings was what appeared to be a shuttle bay, its hatch doors yawning wide open. At the front of the ship, rising from the upper fuselage just above the bow, was a small bulge that I assumed to be the bridge.

The ship was obviously capable of making atmospheric entry—that alone was a radical departure from every other large space vessel I'd ever seen before—yet its graceful lines weren't the only thing I noticed. Just forward of the starboard engine nacelle, I spotted a pair of horizontal hatches, recessed slightly into the hull. They were in the wrong place for landing gear, and the wrong shape for gangway doors. It took me a moment to recognize them for what they were . . .

Torpedo tubes.

Maybe they housed energy weapons instead, like particle-beam guns. I couldn't tell for sure, but nonetheless this was an armed ship. The fact that the vessel bore the insignia of the European Alliance upon its aft hull didn't assuage my feelings. Until now, every starship I'd ever seen had been unarmed. This one was, though, and that sent a chill down my back. Why would anyone want to put weapons aboard a . . . ?

There was another abrupt jolt, this time from the top of the *Isabella*. The gangway had been moved into position. Ana listened for another second to her headset, then pulled it off. "We're free to disembark," she said, unclasping her harness. "Bring your belongings . . . no one's coming aboard until the skiff's been thoroughly decontaminated."

"They'll probably open the hatches after we're gone," Gabriel muttered as he shut down all systems. "Void the entire ship, just to make sure." Unexpectedly, he fondly patted the yoke. "I wouldn't be surprised if she's hauled away to a museum . . . or maybe to the junkyard."

"Why do you say that?" Chris asked.

He glanced over his shoulder at him, then cocked his head toward the nearby ship. "Take a look at that thing. You really think the *Isabella* isn't obsolete?" He sighed as he unfastened his harness. "I'll be lucky if my next job is piloting a tugboat."

The next couple of hours were humiliating.

We were met at the end of the gangway by two men in isolation suits, who silently led us down a sealed-off corridor to a windowless room that had no furniture, only several cardboard bins stacked along a wall. By now we'd entered that part of the station that had artificial gravity, thanks to a localized Millis-Clement field. Our escorts gave us each a pair of dark glasses, then they left, shutting the door behind them.

A few minutes later, a voice from a speaker grill instructed us—in both Anglo and English—to put our bags in the bins, then undress completely and place our clothes on top of them. This was an uncomfortable moment. Carlos, Chris, and I had seen one another naked before, of course— although it had been quite a long while since the last time I'd seen Chris in the buff—and I had a sense that Ana and Gabriel weren't unaccustomed to each other's bodies. Nudity is a cultural taboo that's hard to break, though, and there was no telling how many other eyes might be observing us through hidden cameras. But we stripped, carefully keeping our backs to one another, and once we put our clothes in the bins with our baggage, the guys in the white suits came back in to take them away.

The voice instructed us to put on our dark glasses, then extend our arms and stand still with our legs apart. Panels within the ceiling and floor slid open, and for the next couple of minutes we were subjected to ultra-violet radiation, designed to kill any cooties we may have carried with us from Coyote. Can't blame anyone for being careful, although I could have done without having deeper shade added to my tan.

Once this was over, our escorts came back, this time to give each of us a robe and a pair of slippers. We were taken farther down the corridor to a row of examination rooms, where for the next hour or so physicians in iso-lation suits worked each of us over. My doctor, a humorless young woman about Susan's age, submitted me to a complete physical; I was poked and prodded and scanned, asked a long series of questions, forced to submit blood and urine samples, and finally given a purple liquid to drink that soon gave me a reason to make a frantic dash to the adjacent toilet.

After she was done, I was taken to yet another room—a little more comfortable than the first; at least this one had chairs—where the others were already waiting for me. We were left alone for awhile. I was beginning to regret leaving the bed unmade this morning—if I'd stayed home, I'd probably be asleep by now—when the door opened once more and our doctors reappeared, no longer dressed in isolation gear. As politely as they could, they administered injections to each of us, then attached adhesive drug patches to our biceps.

They'd just finished when a new person appeared, a thin gent with a chin beard that had begun to go grey and the kindly expression of someone who commiserated with all the indignities we'd suffered. He ducked his head and shoulders in a respectful bow, an oddly Asian gesture for a European, then introduced himself as Angelo Margulis, Highgate's chief administrator.

"I'm very sorry we've had to put you through this," he began, speaking in Anglo once Carlos, Chris, and I let him know that we were fluent with the language. "Please, understand that these precautions are not unusual. They're normal procedure for anyone arriving here from anywhere else than the lunar and orbital colonies, and those coming from Earth have to undergo complete sterilization." A slight smile. "Although, in your case, we've decided to waive the usual ten-day quarantine."

Ana glared at him. "Since when did that apply to—?"

"Much has changed since you've been away, Captain." Margulis held up a patient hand. "In short, though, problems with disease control on Earth have given us reason to enact health procedures to protect our residents. In your case, much of this was unnecessary, since you're headed to Earth . . . but we had to make sure that none of you brought anything contagious from 47 Ursae Majoris."

No point in telling him about ring disease or the effects of pseudowasp stings, or any of the other minor illnesses that Coyote colonists had learned to deal with over the years. Kuniko had given each of us a physical only a couple of days earlier, just to make sure we weren't going to bring any unwanted souvenirs from home. After what we'd just been through, though,

I sincerely doubted that even a single E. coli cell still resided within my lower intestines.

"So I take it we're free to go?" Carlos asked.

"Of course. Your belongings will be returned to you shortly, once they've been decontaminated as well. However, since I understand you're guests of the European Alliance, you'll probably be taken to their sector as soon as you're released. In fact, I believe one of their representatives is waiting for you outside."

"You're not from the EA?" Pacino appeared confused. "I thought you were—"

"Sorry, no. I was born and raised in Florence, but my family left Earth many years ago." Another quick smile, almost apologetic this time, then he went on. "Highgate is neutral territory, established as an interplanetary port for the major spacefaring powers . . . the Western Hemisphere Union, the European Alliance, and the Pacific Coalition, as well as their off-world colonies." He raised his head slightly. "Arthur? Display station chart, please."

"Certainly, Mr. Margulis." The same disembodied voice we'd heard earlier; I now realized that it belonged to the station AI. An instant later, a holographic image of Highgate appeared above our heads, rendered transparent to reveal a complex hive of docking bays, passageways, and interior decks.

As Margulis pointed to one of the three spheres, it lit up in red. "This is Alpha Dock, where we are now. It's leased to the European Alliance, so everything . . . well, almost everything . . . that goes on here is within their jurisdiction." When he pointed to the bottom three levels of the station's upper cylinder, they were likewise illuminated. "That's North Hab. The levels here are also leased by the EA as its consulate . . . I imagine you'll be taken to VIP quarters there. The decks above it belong to the Pacific Coalition, but I doubt you'll hear much from them. They're . . . well, they tend to keep to themselves."

"And the Western Hemisphere Union?" Tereshkova asked. "Where are they located?"

"Beta Dock, with its consulate located on these levels on South Hab." Another sphere lit up, this time in blue; the bottom three decks of the lower cylinder were similarly illuminated. "You're free to visit them as well, although I wouldn't recommend it. Relations between the Union and the Alliance have been rather strained since the destruction of the New Guinea beanstalk."

The fact that the Western Hemisphere Union and the European Alliance were rivals wasn't news to us; we'd learned this shortly after the *Columbus* arrived at Coyote. We were also aware that the Union had a space elevator in Ecuador and the Alliance had one in New Guinea. Yet the revelation that the New Guinea beanstalk no longer existed was just as much a shock to Ana and Gabriel as it was to the rest of us. They burst forth with questions, but Margulis shook his head as he raised a hand again.

"I'm sorry," he said, "but perhaps it's better that your government brief you. That way you'll receive an honest appraisal of the situation." Meaning, he was tactfully washing his hands of the matter. Margulis touched the side of his jaw, murmured something that I didn't quite catch. "As soon as you're dressed, you'll be released to the custody of the Alliance."

The door opened and a couple of orderlies walked in, carrying plastic bags containing the clothes we'd worn aboard the *Isabella*. I almost laughed; it was as if they'd just been brought over from the dry cleaner. Margulis stepped aside to allow another man to push a cart into the room; it held our bags, almost wrapped in plastic. The chief administrator waited until they left, then he turned to Carlos, Chris, and me. "On behalf of Highgate," he continued, assuming a more formal tone, "it's an honor to receive the first delegation from Coyote. I hope your stay here will be pleasant and that you'll think well of us during your negotiations."

"I'm sure we will." Carlos stepped forward to offer his hand. Margulis hesitated, then he gingerly grasped his palm. "Thank you for your hospitality," Carlos added. "We greatly appreciate it."

"My pleasure, Mr. President." Margulis hastily withdrew his hand, then assayed another bow, which Carlos clumsily returned. Then he turned and left the room . . . just a little too quickly, I thought.

"Lesson one," I murmured, as soon the door shut behind the chief administrator. "Handshakes are no longer popular." I glanced at my husband. "Sorry, dear, but I think you committed a social faux pas there."

"How was I to know?" He glanced at Ana, but she only shrugged; this was new to her, too. "Bows, no handshakes. Gotcha. I'll try to—"

"Aw, dammit to hell," Chris muttered, and as we turned toward him he looked up from his clothing. "They took away my gun. My knife, too."

Until now, I was unaware that Chris had been carrying weapons. It made sense that he would; after all, it was his job to look out for Carlos and me. I was about to respond when Arthur's voice came from the ceiling. *"Personal weapons are not allowed aboard Highgate. Your pistol and knife, along with your ammunition, will be returned to you by station security before you leave."*

Another surprise. I was beginning to lose count. Yet I was beginning to detect a certain pattern. Rival powers sharing the same space station, while being carefully kept apart from one another. Quarantine and sterilization procedures for those coming from Earth, with bows replacing handshakes as the socially accepted form of contact. Routine disarmament of visitors. The as-yet unexplained loss of the Alliance space elevator, while the Union's remained intact. And now, an AI that routinely monitored every-one's conversations.

Carlos must have been thinking the same things, for he bent closer to me. "Lesson two," he whispered. "Trust no one . . . because they don't trust each other."

As Margulis promised, we were met outside the quarantine area by an aide to the chief consul, a rather effete young man who seemed to be-lieve that we'd just arrived from the Stone Age. He raised a disapproving eyebrow at my shagswool cloak and seemed repelled by the catskin jackets Carlos and Chris wore, although he treated Ana and Gabriel with a little more respect, probably because he recognized their ESA jumpsuits.

Yet he was polite enough: more bows, then he escorted us down a cor-ridor to a tram station. A small cab whisked us down a long tunnel to a transit center at the station's core; a brief glimpse of a vast central atrium, with tier upon tier of balconies overlooking gardens surrounded by shops and cafes, before we were hastened aboard a lift that carried us up to North Hab.

It was here that we parted company with Ana and Gabriel. As soon as the lift doors opened and we stepped out into a circular corridor, the young man informed them that their presence had been requested by ESA senior officers for a mission debriefing. Ana showed a moment of reluctance—I sensed that neither she nor Gabriel were looking forward to this, particu-larly since one of the things they'd have to report was the disappearance of Jonathan Parson, the *Columbus*'s second officer—but she nodded anyway, and we took a few moments to say farewell. Despite my distrust of her, I gave Ana a hug; after all, she and Gabriel brought us safely through hyper-space, and right now they were the closest thing we had to friends. Besides, it was amusing to observe the disgust on our escort's face as he observed two people getting so close to one another that their bodies actually touched. How barbaric . . .

Our quarters in the EA consulate were spacious: a three-room suite, carpeted and comfortably furnished, with a small lounge separating the bedroom Carlos and I would share from the one Chris occupied. Broad oval windows looked out upon Alpha Dock; from the sitting room, we could watch spacecraft moving around the station. A small fridge was well stocked with bottles of water, soft drinks, and wine, along with packets of some sort of junk food that I wasn't eager to sample, and there was also a wallscreen activated by a miniature remote. Only one bathroom, though; when our escort showed us the shower stall, an ever-so-slight crinkling of his precious little nose told us that he wished we'd avail ourselves of it as soon as possible. I wanted to swat him just then—if he doubted that we were clean, all he had to do was talk to Margulis or the doctors who'd ex-amined us—but I kept my mouth shut and contented myself with thoughts about how long he'd last on Coyote.

Finally, he informed us that Dieter Vogel, the senior consul, had invited us to join him for a late dinner at 2100, about four hours from now. Until then, we'd be left alone to rest, have a snack, perhaps even take a bath; Car-los gently squeezed my arm, preventing a diplomatic incident. If we needed anything, all we had to do was ask Arthur for assistance. Carlos bowed and thanked him, and the young man made his leave, not a second too soon.

We bumbled about the suite for a few minutes, unsure of what to do with ourselves. Chris opened one of the soft drinks from the fridge, took a sip, and made a face; he said it tasted like raspberry-flavored piss. Carlos tried the wallscreen, clicked a few channels: a sporting event that looked like four men in zero-g chasing a ball around a court no larger than our liv-ing room; comedies and dramas utterly meaningless to us; an early-twenty-first-century action movie frequently interrupted by a panel discussion among three academics disapprovingly obsessed with its sexual innuendos. I sat on the couch and watched spacecraft moving around the station until I realized just how exhausted I was. Excusing myself, I went into the bed-room and, without taking off my clothes, lay down in bed. It took a long time for me to remember how to switch off the lights.

"Arthur, turn off the lights," I said.

"*Yes, ma'am,*" the AI replied. "*Sleep well.*" The room went dark, and that's when it occurred to me how many years it had been since the last time I'd done it that way. No oil lamps to be extinguished, no candles to be blown out. Just a verbal command, and the deed was done.

Good heavens. Perhaps I *had* become a barbarian . . .

A few minutes later, Carlos came in. He lay down beside me, and I curled up next to him, and for no reason I began to cry. He stroked my hair and told me that everything would be all right, and after a while I fell asleep.

Dinner was served down the corridor from our suite, in a large dining room whose windows offered a magnificent view of the Moon. Other than that, though, we could have been in a country estate somewhere in western Europe; framed lithographs of foxhunting scenes hung upon wood-paneled walls, and the table and chairs were either genuine nineteenth-century antiques or clever reproductions. White linen drapes, Indian carpets, a crystal chandelier, fresh-cut roses in China vases—no expense had been spared to make the room as elegant as possible.

By comparison, though, the chief consul was rather unremarkable. Dieter Vogel had dressed for the occasion, but even his dovetail morning coat and white cravat couldn't disguise the fact that he was a doughy, bland-faced man who was losing his hair; I pegged him as a mid-level bureaucrat who'd somehow parlayed his way into a comfortable diplomatic position. Or at least that was my first impression; although both Carlos and Chris offered bows as his aide introduced us, Vogel extended his right hand without a trace of reluctance. Apparently he'd done a little homework and knew that handshakes had been the customary form of greeting back in the twenty-first century.

And indeed, Vogel did his best to put us at ease. He seemed to notice that we didn't like his aide very much, so once the young man minced about serving us wine—'81 Mare Crisium, an exceptional lunar Bordeaux, or perhaps we'd prefer beer instead?—Vogel dismissed him, then apologized for his manners once he was gone. He inquired about our jaunt through hyperspace, and seemed genuinely curious about the experience. He expressed interest in our clothing and asked about the wildlife on Coyote from which the materials had been derived. Small talk, of course, but nonetheless it helped to make us feel more like envoys than hayseeds who'd just fallen off the potato wagon.

By this time, stewards had finished setting the table. Once we were seated, they ladled chilled vichyssoise into pewter bowls before each of us. Vogel sipped his soup as he listened to Chris finish an anecdote about hunting boid on Miller Creek in New Florida, then daubed his lips with a linen napkin.

"Quite fascinating, *Herr* Levin," he said. "You must save that story for my colleagues in the diplomatic corps. I think they'll be intrigued by your descriptions of the native fauna, once you meet them."

Obviously he was changing the subject. "We'd only be delighted," Carlos replied. "And this will be . . . ?"

"As soon as you like, of course." Laying down his spoon, Vogel signaled for a steward to take away his soup. "Unless you have serious objections, our present schedule calls for us to board a yacht for Earth tomorrow morning at 1000 hours. If all goes well, we should arrive in London by 1400 Greenwich time the following day." He smiled. "It's not quite as fast as it sounds . . . the entire trip will take twenty-eight hours."

"Of course." Carlos put aside his own spoon. "And I take it that you're going to accompany us?"

"My government has requested that I do so, yes. I've been assigned as your official escort. Since you've come here aboard an Alliance spacecraft, we consider you as our guests." He favored Carlos with a sly wink. "Naturally, we hope that you'll remember our patronage during your negotiations. We believe that you won't find a more worthwhile ally among the members of the U.N. General Assembly."

"We'll try to keep that in mind." Carlos shot me a glance, and I rubbed the corner of my left eye. A prearranged signal: *be careful.* "I'm rather surprised that you're flying us into London," he continued. "Didn't the ESA once operate a space elevator in New Guinea?"

Vogel didn't miss a beat. "Unfortunately, as you may have already heard, our beanstalk no longer exists. It was destroyed by a terrorist action about fifteen years ago . . . a bomb planted aboard one of its climbers, which detonated sixty miles aboveground. We haven't rebuilt it since then."

"Any idea who did it?" Chris asked.

"Living Earth claimed responsibility . . . a terrorist group that wants to put an end to space colonization." Vogel shook his head. "However, we have reason to believe that their action may have been covertly sponsored by another country."

"Such as?"

"It's not my place to speculate." Vogel signaled for the stewards to bring the next course. "However, I will offer the observation that the Ecuador space elevator remains operational, nor has it ever received any serious threats."

Carlos and I traded another look. Even if he wasn't coming straight out and saying so, Vogel clearly meant to implicate the Western Hemisphere Union. And he had a point; it was difficult to believe that a terrorist group opposed to space colonization would sabotage one beanstalk only to leave the other alone.

As if he'd read our minds, Vogel went on. "You can expect that the WHU will do their best to assert territorial rights to Coyote," he continued, as the stewards placed what looked like broiled lamb cutlets before each of us. "I've already spoken with Captain Tereshkova, and she told me that the colonies successfully rebelled against the Union and forced their troops to leave. My congratulations. However, I sincerely doubt their U.N. delegation will accept that prima facie. They'll probably say that the Union still has control—"

"We considered that," Carlos said. "We've brought recent pictures of our colonies, along with sworn affidavits by colonists who came over on Union ships. That should help prove that the WHU is no longer in charge of the government."

It was a weak leg to stand on, though, and we knew it. Our evidence of having achieved independence was tenuous at best. Yet Vogel smiled as he picked up knife and fork. "Good, very good. That should go a long way to convincing the General Assembly." An indifferent shrug. "And if they're not, then we have other means of persuading them."

"How so?" I asked.

A steward interrupted to ask if we wanted more wine. Vogel nodded, then went on. "You may have noticed the vessel dry-docked in Alpha Port. The *Francis Drake,* the first starship specifically designed for hyperspace travel. Since it doesn't have to accommodate biostasis decks, it can transport up to 10,000 tons of freight or passengers in a single run. As soon as it's christened, it'll take very little effort to carry U.N. representatives to Coyote to verify your claims."

Now the reasons for its streamlined hull were apparent; the *Drake* could land directly on Coyote, instead of having to rely upon shuttles to haul passengers and cargo to and from the surface. Chris whistled appreciatively, yet Carlos showed little emotion as he allowed a steward to refill his wineglass. "Quite impressive," he said, "but isn't that quite an effort to make on the presumption that we'd make a trade agreement with the EA?"

"Possibly." Vogel shrugged as he spooned some mint jelly onto his cutlets. They were a little well done for my taste, but on the other hand, I wasn't sure they were lamb at all. Possibly a soybean substitute; the texture wasn't quite right. "But we're confident that you'd rather have us as a principal trading partner than the Union or the Pacific Coalition. And, to be quite honest, even if the WHU had maintained control of your colonies, sooner or later they would've had to negotiate with us. A round-trip journey of nearly a hundred years versus a starbridge jaunt of only a few minutes . . . ?"

"I see your point." Carlos absently ran the tip of his finger around the stem of his wineglass. "But since you have this sort of capability, what prevents you from attempting the same sort of hostile takeover that the Union did?"

Vogel didn't respond at once. He deliberately took time to sip his wine. "Nothing," he said at last. "At least not in military terms. But"—he raised a finger—"I should point out that the EA has a better grasp of history than the WHU does. We're aware that you can't hold a hostile population at gunpoint for very long before they rise against you. Even their Savants tried to warn their Patriarchs and Matriarchs that such a revolution was inevitable . . ."

"And your Savants?" I asked. "What did they advise?"

"The Savants in the European Alliance were never allowed to hold positions of responsibility." Dieter's voice turned cold. "When the Union's Savant

Council turned against them, we told ours to leave . . . and so they did. For the outer asteroid belt." Then his manner thawed. "We don't intend to repeat the Union's mistakes. As I said, we'd rather enjoy a peaceful partnership based on trade and cultural exchange than have to worry about your people staging guerrilla raids and blowing up spacecraft. Wouldn't you say . . . Rigil Kent?"

Carlos's mouth went tight, and I felt my own heart skip a beat. Damn it, just how much had Ana told him? It was obvious that Dieter Vogel was far more than the minor cog that he'd first appeared to be. "Not to worry," he continued, his voice low as he leaned forward. "Your background as a . . . shall we say, a freedom fighter . . . is classified information. No one needs to know about it."

"Not that it makes much difference." Carlos got hold of himself. "I did what had to be done. I won't apologize for that."

I could have kissed my husband. From the look on Chris's face, he was just as proud of Carlos as I was. Unruffled, Vogel slowly nodded. "Very good. I'm pleased to hear that. But for others to know this . . ."

"I fought in the war, too," Chris interrupted. "So did almost everyone else on Coyote. You're just going to have to get used to that."

I shut my eyes. Very patriotic, but now wasn't the right time to wave the flag. Yet Carlos nodded at his old war buddy, and the two exchanged a grin that made me want to kick both of them beneath the table.

"Yes, well . . ." Vogel glanced at the antique grandfather clock in the corner. "I hate to run, but I have other duties this evening. This has been a delightful—"

"One more question, if I may?" I raised a hand, and all three turned to look at me. "The *Drake* . . . when we saw it earlier, I couldn't help but notice something rather unusual about its hull."

"Such as?" Vogel gave me a distracted glance. Perhaps he was expecting me to ask something obvious, like why it had wings.

"There were hatches on either side of its forward section. They weren't cargo doors, and they were in the wrong position for landing gear." I paused. "In fact, they looked very much like weapon bays . . . torpedo tubes, maybe?"

Vogel's face lost color. From the corner of my eye, I could see Carlos covering his mouth with his hand. Chris covered his expression by taking a drink . . . a major thing for him, since he'd studiously avoided the wine all evening.

"You're very observant," Vogel said.

"I try to be," I replied.

"The *Drake* is intended to be primarily a merchanteer. Which means that it will carry valuable cargo. Considering that the EA has been attacked once already, we believe that it's in our best interests to provide protection for its crew and passengers. So, yes, we've installed missile launchers . . . torpedoes, if you will . . . as a means of preventative measures."

Perfect bureaucratese. A Govnet flack from the old United Republic of America couldn't have done better. "Thank you," I said. "Just wanted to know."

Vogel blinked, then once again offered apologies as he stood up. A few bows, then he hastened out the door. One of the stewards offered coffee and dessert, but we declined; it had been a long day, and we needed to get some sleep. Yet once we left the dining room and Vogel's aide—who'd apparently been waiting in the corridor the entire time—nervously led us back to our quarters, Carlos took my arm.

"Nice try," he murmured, "but I wish you hadn't done that."

"Why not?" I was still grinning. "I haven't smelled manure that fragrant since I cleaned out the goat pen last week."

Chris chuckled under his breath, yet Carlos glowered at me. "There's more about this than you know," he whispered.

I darted a glance at him, and he shook his head. "Another time. When we're sure the walls aren't listening."

Next morning, another journey: this time aboard a delta-winged transport twice the size of the *Isabella*. The EAS *Von Braun* was intended to shuttle VIPs to and from Highgate; its passenger cabin was fitted with faux-leather seats with individual viewscreens, a small galley, even a plasma billiards table. A uniformed steward offered us squeeze bulbs of champagne shortly after the vessel undocked from Alpha Port, then handed out menus for what would be the first of several meals.

I passed on the champagne and nibbled at some cheese and grapes as I gazed at Earth through the window beside my seat. From lunar orbit, the planet of my birth was so small that I could easily cover it with my thumb. An impressive sight, to be sure, yet after a little while I started looking for other things to do.

Although the yacht was too small to have its own Millis-Clement field generator, its nuclear engines fired at constant quarter-g thrust that cut our travel time from days to hours, so there was sufficient gravity inside the craft to allow us to walk around the cabin. I shot a couple of rounds of pool with Chris—strange to play billiards on a table that operated in three dimensions, with cues that generated an electromagnetic pulse and balls that were nothing more than colored spheres of light—and let Vogel explain the rules of zero-g handball to me while we watched a game. I took a nap, woke up and had dinner, went over the draft of the trade agreement one more time with Carlos, played another game with Chris . . .

And still, despite my best efforts to distract myself, I kept returning to the porthole, watching Earth as it gradually swelled in size. When we left Highgate, I had to crane my head to see it through the window by my seat, but as the hours went by the planet slowly crawled closer to the center of the pane, slowly waxing as its daylight terminator moved from east to west. I discovered that my seat's viewscreen allowed me to access a close-up view from a camera positioned in the yacht's bow, and it wasn't long before I was able to distinguish the major continents. At one point I was even able to spot the Ecuador space elevator, a silver thread rising in a horizontal line from the equator above South America, reflecting sunlight until it reached its terminus in geosynchronous orbit.

But that wasn't what caught my attention. As the *Von Braun* drew closer, the pilots made midcourse corrections so that we'd be able to land in the northern hemisphere. It wasn't long before southeastern Europe was spread out before us, and certain geographic changes soon became apparent. Italy had lost its boot-like appearance, becoming instead a slender peninsula, with Sicily little more than a speck in a Mediterranean Sea that had become a vast gulf that altered the coastline of much of North Africa.

"Too bad we can't see the South Pole from here," Vogel said. Surprised, I looked around to find him leaning over my shoulder to peer at the screen. "That's where it all began."

"I know. The collapse of the east Antarctic ice sheet." Vogel seemed surprised that I knew about this, and I nodded. "We've already heard. Dr. Whittaker already told us . . . so did the *Columbus*'s crew."

"Then if you're aware of what's happened, there's not much for me to tell you."

"I'm aware only that it happened, not how or why. Go on, please. I'd like to learn more."

Vogel hesitated, then settled into Carlos's seat across the aisle. "It didn't happen overnight," he said, his voice low. "The climate started to change during the late twentieth century, when Greenland began losing its glacial icepack. The trend continued through much of the twenty-first century, but even after the major industrial nations curtailed the use of fossil fuels that discharged carbonic oxides into the atmosphere . . ." He paused, then added, "With certain notable exceptions, as I'm sure you know."

Feeling my face grow warm, I looked away. He didn't need to say it, but one of those "notable exceptions" had been the United Republic of America. One of the dubious achievements of National Reform had been the rollback of every environmental protection program intended to reduce global warming, which the Liberty Party claimed was only liberal propaganda. There had been protests, of course, but it wasn't long before activists and the more outspoken scientists joined the ranks of those sent away to government reeducation camps.

Vogel noticed my discomfort. "I forget . . . you were only a child then," he said, gently patting my arm as if to absolve me of personal guilt. "In your time, the global sea level had only risen by a dozen or so centimeters . . . enough to cause a few beaches to disappear in your country, but not much else."

I gazed at the screen. By now, I could make out the Middle East; the Persian Gulf had swelled to consume the lowlands of the Arabian Peninsula. "All we heard from Govnet was that it was a natural occurrence. A temporary problem, nothing more."

"A temporary problem." Vogel shook his head in wonder. "If only they'd been right . . ." He stopped himself. "Well, be that as it may, ocean temperatures continued to rise through the late twenty-first century and into the twenty-third until, in 2265, one-third of the east Antarctic ice sheet slipped into the ocean."

"So we've heard." But not until much later. By then, the *Alabama* was still on its way to 47 Ursae Majoris, and I'd been in biostasis for nearly two hundred years. The last of the Union starships had already departed from Earth by that time, though, so no one on Coyote would know about this until the *Columbus* arrived. "That was the tipping point."

"That's one way of putting it, yes." A wan smile. "In hindsight, it's fortunate that it happened much later than most climatologists predicted. That gave some countries time to prepare themselves." Then his face darkened. "Coastal regions and river deltas flooded, and the subsequent loss of freshwater supplies afflicted much of the inland regions. Drought caused some regions to become uninhabitable. But that was only part of the problem. The introduction of freshwater from the ice sheet also caused seawater to expand at the molecular level while at the same time growing warmer. And that, in turn, caused the Gulf Stream of the North Atlantic to reverse itself."

As he spoke, I stared at the screen. The southern half of India was no longer recognizable; Sri Lanka had all but disappeared. Vast stretches of Southeast Asia were now separated from one another by bays and channels that hadn't been there before. "That probably had an effect on wind patterns in the Northern Hemisphere, didn't it?"

Vogel nodded. "Europe got colder, yes, while much of North America got considerably hotter. The results were crop failures, deforestation, mass extinctions of wildlife . . ."

"Yet the colonies on the Moon and Mars . . ."

"They managed to hold out." Vogel shrugged. "The Union, the Alliance, the Coalition . . . they'd had the foresight and the resources to build colonies on the Moon, with a few more on Mars. The wealthy migrated there, and they were able to preserve much of human culture. Nonetheless, a lot of people died."

"How many?"

"No one knows for certain. They stopped counting the dead a long time ago." Almost impulsively, Vogel reached forward to switch off the screen. "So far as we can estimate, though, there's less than three billion people now alive on Earth." He shook his head. "What the Savants failed to do, we managed to accomplish ourselves . . . starting three hundred years ago."

Somewhere behind me, I could hear the buzz of one plasma ball striking another: Carlos and Chris killing time at the billiards table. The air inside the cabin suddenly felt cold, as if the flight engineer had decided to adjust the thermostat. "Do you realize now just how important you are?" Vogel said, his voice very quiet now. "Do you now see why Coyote has become our last, best hope?"

Through my window, I could see Earth, a wounded planet for which time was running out. Feeling sick at my stomach, I only nodded.

Night was still upon the west coast of North America as the *Von Braun* raced across the Pacific, rapidly shedding altitude as the darkened limb of the Earth filled the viewscreens. The pilot's voice came over the speaker, informing us that we were on primary approach; by now we were buckled into our seats, gazing out the windows. There wasn't much to see: fewer lights along the California coast, and a dark gap where Seattle once lay.

The first light of morning had just touched New England as the *Von Braun* began atmospheric entry. Just before a reddish-orange penumbra started to form around its hull, I caught sight of the ruined shores of our homeland. A brief glimpse of the Massachusetts coast: Cape Cod was no more, and all I could see of Boston were a few tiny silver pylons rising above dark blue water.

The yacht quaked and trembled as its wings bit air, and I deliberately shut my eyes and clutched the armrests. Then the turbulence ceased, and there was a sudden roar as air-breathing jets cut in. I looked out the window again, saw only the vast expanse of the Atlantic. Then a ragged green peninsula swept beneath us—southern Ireland, perhaps, although it was hard to tell—and disappeared again. More ocean, and then, suddenly, we were above England.

What had once been Wales was now an archipelago of tiny isles, the port cities of Cardiff and Newport long since drowned by St. George's Channel, now extending inland as far as Gloucester. As we came in low, I could see where canals had been dredged in an attempt to alleviate the flooding. I saw deserted English towns, their roads abruptly disappearing beneath swollen creeks, with small lakes where there had once been pastures. The whiskery trail of a small boat moved past the spire of what might have once been a country church.

The others also gazed down upon the devastation, Carlos with his mouth hidden by his hand, Chris staring in stunned disbelief. Yes, we'd known that things were bad back on Earth, yet somehow it had seemed abstract, a matter of statistics. Seeing it firsthand, though, was another matter entirely.

And then, all of a sudden, we were above London.

The city itself had been spared the worst effects of the floods. Unlike that in my country, the British government hadn't ignored scientists' warnings about the long-term effects of global warming. I'd later see pictures of the vast row of seawalls erected along the southern coast of the English Channel; as we flew in, though, all I saw were the massive floodgates of the Thames Barrier, with fortress-like levees rising above either side of the river. Yet even these macroengineering projects hadn't been enough; London now lay below sea level, and time and again the rising waters had breached the levees and barriers. The Waterloo and Hungerford bridges were gone, and a pair of half-collapsed towers were all that remained of the Westminster Bridge. Although Big Ben still rose above the Houses of Parliament, its windows were dark, its ancient walls overgrown with weeds and creeping vine; I'd later find out that the seat of British government had relocated to Buckingham Palace.

Despite its best efforts, London was losing the battle against the sea. Where countless foes had failed, nature was inexorably succeeding. Much of the city had been abandoned; streets once filled with vehicles and pedestrians were nearly empty, and as the *Von Braun* circled low over London, I looked down to see boarded-up shops and abandoned high-rises. Smoke from the fires of squatter camps rose from Charing Cross Road and the Strand; the stub of what had once been the Telecom Tower loomed above the wasteland of Oxford, and a rotting and overgrown hulk was all that remained of the British Museum.

Nonetheless, it became clear that a long row of dikes erected west of Oxford had effectively isolated much of the chaos caused by flooding, for this part of the city looked relatively undamaged. As the yacht's descent jets kicked in, I caught sight of the New United Nations Plaza; the curved half-arch of the Secretariat rose above the enormous white geodome of the General Assembly Building, both built on the former site of the U.S. Embassy at the east end of Hyde Park.

This wasn't new to me. The U.N. had left New York when I was still a child, after the URA had withdrawn from the General Assembly and unilaterally revoked the U.N.'s title to the site on the East River where its headquarters had once been located. The U.N. responded by relocating to London, where the first sessions of the General Assembly and the Security Council had been held in 1946. In the long run, perhaps this had been just as well; London may have been a shadow of its former regal self, yet at least its system of seawalls and levees had held back the waters long enough to save much of the city. Like Washington, D.C., and Boston, Manhattan now lay underwater, inundated after the seawalls the Union belatedly attempted to erect around the island collapsed due to slipshod design and construction.

The *Von Braun* had been given permission to land in Grosvenor Square, on a paved landing pad specifically built for diplomatic aircraft. There was a mild jar as its landing gear touched down, then a low rumble as the pilots throttled back the engines. Luminescent strips along the ceiling and aisle went from red to green; Dieter unclasped his harness and stood up.

"Gentlemen, lady, we're here," he said unnecessarily, as if we'd slept through the whole thing. "Don't worry about your personal belongings. They'll be brought to your quarters. Now, if you'll follow me, please."

I unbuckled my harness, started to stand up . . . then my knees collapsed, and I fell back into my seat. It felt as if someone had suddenly placed a fifty-pound bag of sand on my shoulders. I should have expected this; Coyote's gravity was less than two-thirds that of Earth's, and even the Millis-Clement field aboard Highgate had been adjusted to approximate lunar gravity for the benefit of those born and raised on the Moon. All well and good, yet although I'd spent my first fifteen years on Earth, for the last forty Gregorian years I'd become accustomed to living in .68-g. Sitting in an overstuffed seat during the ride from Highgate, I hadn't noticed the subtle difference . . . but, oh boy, did I now.

And so did Carlos and Chris. Both were in excellent shape, at least for men in their mid-fifties, but my husband grunted as he heaved himself to his feet, and Chris swore beneath his breath as he clasped the back of his seat for support. I couldn't see how Vogel could take the strain with so little effort; perhaps he worked out in a high-gravity gym aboard Highgate.

The steward came forward, offered each of us canes; apparently this was a common occurrence. Although it made me feel like an old lady, I accepted mine and found myself wishing that I'd dyed the grey in my hair before we'd left home. Carlos was even more reluctant; as President of the Coyote Federation, he didn't want to be seen hobbling down the ramp. Yet it would have been even more humiliating if he'd fallen flat on his face, so he took his cane with a scowl. Chris would have nothing to do with it; he took a deep breath, squared his shoulders, and stood erect. At first I thought he was just toughing it out . . . but then I noticed the bulge created beneath his jacket by the holstered flechette pistol, and recalled why he was with us. He couldn't be a good bodyguard if he couldn't reach for his gun.

With diplomatic stoicism, Vogel pretended not to notice our difficulties. He patiently waited until we caught our wind, then he led us through the cabin to the main hatch. It had already been opened, its ramp lowered. Vogel paused for a moment, as if to make sure that we weren't going to have heart attacks, then we followed him as he exited the spacecraft.

At the bottom of the ramp, a dozen members of the Royal Palace Guard stood at stiff-necked attention on either side of a long red carpet, their black fur helmets giving them the resemblance of a double row of exclamation points. Beyond the landing pad, a vast crowd surrounded the yacht; several thousand people had gathered in Grosvenor Square to witness our arrival, held back by portable barriers and dozens of British police officers in security armor. The afternoon sun was bright, and as we made our way down the stairs, I raised a hand against the glare. Someone in the crowd must have misinterpreted this as a wave, for suddenly a cacophony of sound rolled across us: shouts, yells, applause, whistles, like surf crashing upon a rocky shore . . .

I don't know what sort of reception I'd anticipated, but it certainly wasn't this. Startled, I stumbled on a riser. Chris was behind me; he managed to grab my arm before I made a fool of myself. As our feet touched ground, from somewhere nearby I heard a brass orchestra strike up "God Save the King." Which was entirely appropriate, because His Royal Highness awaited us at the other end of the red carpet.

Henry XI was a bit shorter than I expected, yet nonetheless quite handsome. Dressed in a collarless black suit, with the Prime Minister at one side and his consort at another, His Majesty stepped forward to offer a bow to Carlos, then clasped my hand and gallantly passed his lips about two inches above it. A few short, noncommittal words of greeting—"Welcome to the City of London, and the United Kingdom of Great Britain" was all that I remembered—and then he and his entourage were ushered to a row of black hoverlimos that floated away before I had a chance to remember how to curtsy.

Yet even that royal reception, or the crowds or even the red-carpet treatment, didn't make as much of an impression on me as something else far more subtle. Something that everyone there had learned to take for granted, but that instantly struck me as unusual.

The weather.

We landed in London on November 4, 2340. When we'd left Coyote on Hanael 62, c.y. 13, we'd dressed for late autumn. Expecting much the same on Earth, we'd packed warm clothes—catskin jackets, shagswool sweaters and so forth—and although we put on our best outfits just before the *Von Braun* made ready to land, I figured that we'd probably peel off a layer or two shortly after we disembarked.

Yet London was cold as a midwinter day in the Midland Range. Oh, the Palace Guard was comfortable in their red dress jackets, and His Majesty had a red scarf loosely draped around his shoulders, but despite the bright afternoon sun, everyone standing behind the barricades was bundled up in heavy coats, wearing hats and gloves. A harsh wind nagged at us as we walked to the limo waiting to take us for a short ride down Knightsbridge Road to the European Alliance embassy; just before we climbed in, though, I observed patches of snow on the ground beneath the trees. Their branches were barren, without so much as a stray leaf clinging to them, and their bark was brown and lifeless.

Dead trees and snow. A new ice age was approaching. It wouldn't be long before winter was permanent, with summer only a faint memory.

That evening, a reception in our honor was held at the embassy. Vogel had warned us that this had been scheduled, so once we were shown to our suite—larger than the one on Highgate, with windows that looked out upon Hyde Park—we took the opportunity to catch a few winks. We didn't have long to rest, though, before an embassy staff member showed up at our door; pushing a cart laden with sandwiches and coffee, he informed us that, although there would be food at the reception, we'd probably have little chance to eat.

Thoughtful of our hosts to consider this, but our appetite wasn't their only concern. We were still chowing down when a squad of tailors arrived, complete with a rack of formal apparel. It went without saying that *Herr* Vogel considered our homespun clothes a bit too rustic for the occasion. Just as well; none of us wanted to look like Daniel Boone. Carlos and Chris picked out identical tuxedos, while I selected a strapless black gown that trailed to the floor yet complimented my figure. Carlos's eyes bugged out when he saw me in this—the cleavage was deep enough that you could have dropped a coin between my breasts—but he didn't protest as a seamstress took my measurements. The clothiers disappeared, and by the time we'd showered and had a second cup of coffee they showed up again, this time with our outfits, each one perfectly fitted. Don't ask me how they performed this minor miracle; I was still trying to figure it out when Dieter came to escort us downstairs.

The embassy ballroom was crowded to capacity, with several hundred men and women each as elegantly dressed as the next. They arrived two or three at a time, each briefly detained at the door to step through an arch that scanned them for weapons. Chris hesitated when he saw that, but since we'd been brought down to the ballroom via a private lift, no one thought to check to see if he was packing a gun. 'Bots circulated through the crowd, carrying platters of drinks and hors d'oeuvres, while a string quartet in the corner performed waltzes by Vivaldi and Strauss. Ambassadors and attachés and senior aides made their own dance steps, deftly moving from one conversation to the next. No handshakes, only slight bows and brief curtsies . . . and I noted how gloves had come back into style, along with face masks worn by several men and silk veils by a number of women.

No formal announcement was made of our arrival, yet our entrance didn't go unnoticed. As soon as we walked into the room, it seemed as if every eye turned in our direction. And yet there was no rush, but instead the cool aloofness of diplomacy. Carlos and I sauntered into the crowd, with Dieter leading the way and Chris close behind, and before long various dignitaries began to make their way toward us, each carefully maintaining a certain savoir faire even though they were anxious to meet us. Vogel ran interference for us, and soon it fell into a pattern: a brief but formal introduction by Dieter, then we'd exchange bows and curtsies. A few polite words, then on to the next guest. Minor aides and attachés were acknowledged, but weren't allowed to get too close: senior diplomats received a few more seconds of our time, and Dieter would intercept their cards and slip them into his pocket. Every now and then, someone had a floater hovering nearby; Carlos and I would pose on either side of them and let our picture be taken, and sometimes Carlos would sign the print. This amused me the most; even in high society, there were no shortage of autograph seekers.

No doubt about it: we were celebrities. Carlos Montero and Wendy Gunther, the President of the Coyote Federation and his wife. We needed canes to walk, and we may have worn finery that we'd put on for the first time less than a hour ago, yet nonetheless we were visitors from a star so far distant that its light hadn't yet reached Earth. Our lives were the stuff of legend. We weren't just part of history . . . we *were* history.

So we chatted, and we posed, and we enjoyed the limelight as we made our way through the ballroom. But after a while the bureaucrats and minor scoundrels fell away, and it wasn't long before we found ourselves in more rarified company: ambassadors and senior consuls, the men and women who represented the governments of their respective countries and thus weren't impressed by mere fame. Vogel didn't put himself between us and them; a brief introduction, then he'd step out of the way. Most were polite, even charming; they didn't wear gloves, masks, or veils, and some offered handshakes instead of bows. The Russian ambassador went so far as to bend down to kiss the back of my hand. No one had ever done that to me before—not counting His Majesty, who'd only made a polite pass at it— and it was utterly charming. I tried to stifle my laughter, but he must have caught the gleam in my eye, for he favored me with a seductive wink as he stood up, and his eyes never strayed far from my breasts.

Yet all encounters weren't so pleasant.

Carlos and I were about halfway across the room when someone began making his way toward us: a tall, slender gentleman with a grey-tinged goatee, his long black hair tied back in a ponytail. When Vogel spotted the newcomer, a stern look appeared on his face; he murmured something to Carlos, then attempted to guide us in the opposite direction. But the other man was too quick for that; he artfully stepped around a couple of women with whom Carlos had been speaking and, before Chris could intercede, planted himself directly in our path.

"Dieter, my friend," he said, with a smile that didn't have a trace of affection, "aren't you going to introduce me?"

That was when I noticed what he wore: a long velvet robe, dark purple, with gold trim around its sleeves. I'd seen pictures of the patriarchs of the Western Hemisphere Union; this was how they dressed for formal occasions. I instinctively took my husband's hand.

"Of course, *Señor* Amado." Dieter tried not to show his reticence. "May I present to you the Honorable Carlos Montero, President of the Coyote Federation, and his wife Wendy Gunther, former member of the Colonial Council. Mr. President, this is—"

"Patriarch Marcos Amado, ambassador for the Western Hemisphere Union." He offered a bow that was little more than the slightest nod of his head. "Very pleased to meet you, *Señor* Montero . . . although you'll forgive me if I don't address you as Mr. President."

"You can call me anything except late to dinner," Carlos replied. A few chuckles from those standing nearby. My husband had been using that line all evening; it was an old saw, but it helped break the ice, especially among all these stuffed shirts.

The loudest laugh, though, came from a rotund little man with a shaved head who hovered at the edge of the crowd. I hadn't noticed him before; when I glanced his way, he favored me with a grin that was both knowing and warm. I needed all the friendly faces I could get just then, so I gave him a brief smile.

"Very good, sir." A dry smirk appeared on Amado's face. "I trust we'll hear more of your . . . wit, shall we say? . . . when you address the General Assembly tomorrow."

"And until then," Vogel said, "I trust your government will afford the president and his party the courtesy to which they're—"

"Patriarch, I take it the Union doesn't recognize the Coyote Federation," Carlos said. "May I ask why?"

He didn't raise his voice, yet even if he'd shouted it wouldn't have made much difference. A hush fell across the people around us; it seemed as if everyone moved in a little closer. Dieter winced, and even Amado seemed to be taken aback; for a moment, his condescending attitude was replaced by one of respect, however reluctant.

"I appreciate your candor, *Señor.*" The Patriarch's voice was quiet. "I think our negotiations will be . . . interesting, to say the least."

"No doubt they will," Carlos said. "I'm looking forward to them."

The two men silently regarded one another for a moment. Then Amado went on. "You'll hear my government's opinion on this matter when we meet before the General Assembly. Until then, I hope that you and your wife will have a pleasant stay."

"Thank you," Carlos said. "I'm sure we will."

Amado nodded, then unexpectedly he offered his hand. Carlos hesitated, then he accepted the handshake. "One more thing," the Patriarch added. "Regardless of the outcome, my government wishes to extend to you and your wife an invitation to visit the Union. We understand that you were both born and raised in the *Norte Americano* provinces. Perhaps you'd like to see your home country again before you leave?"

We'd received nearly a dozen similar requests all evening. Carlos responded just as he did to all the others. "Thank you. Our time here is limited, but if we can . . ."

"Of course." Amado withdrew his hand. "Consider it an open invitation, at your leisure." A formal bow in my general direction. *"Señora . . ."*

"Señor," I said, with as much frost in my voice as I could muster. A dark look, and then the Patriarch disappeared back into the crowd.

Chris moved closer. "Watch where you step," he whispered. "I think he left a slime trail."

I was too irritated to find this funny. Until this moment, no one had challenged Carlos's standing, either as President of the Coyote Federation or as its designated emissary to the United Nations. Yet Marcos Amado had insinuated Carlos was merely some upstart yokel, representing a province with pretensions of statehood.

I was still seething when a hand gently touched my elbow. "Your husband took care of that quite well," a voice said softly, and I turned to see the short fellow who'd caught my eye a couple of minutes earlier. "I'm impressed. Marcos doesn't usually back down like that."

"Neither does my husband." From the corner of my eye, I could see Chris moving closer to protect me, yet this gent seemed as harmless as Amado had been menacing. "I don't believe we've been introduced."

"Forgive me." An elaborate bow, with head lowered and hands spread aside. "Morgan Goldstein, m'lady, at your service. I suppose you could say that I'm a diplomat without résumé—"

"As always, Mr. Goldstein, you flatter yourself." Vogel appeared at my side. "How did you get in here?" he asked, although he didn't appear to be perturbed. "I thought this was by invitation only."

Feigning insult, Goldstein arched an eyebrow. "But I did indeed receive an invitation, Dieter. The very best money could buy."

Vogel shook his head as he looked at me. "Be careful of this one," he said. "*Herr* Goldstein apparently believes that because he can buy and sell entire countries . . ."

"Only buy," Goldstein added. "I rarely sell." Ignoring Dieter, he turned to me again. "Truth to be told, I'm merely an entrepreneur, and only modestly successful at that." Vogel made an uncharacteristically rude noise with his lips, which Goldstein chose to overlook. "When I heard that you and the president were going to grace us with your presence, I hopped the first suborbital I could find."

"Don't let him fool you," Dieter murmured. "He owns his own fleet."

"True, but they're always committed to something else." Goldstein glared at him. "Dieter, don't you have something else to do?"

For a moment, it seemed as if Dieter wavered. Goldstein said nothing, only waited patiently. Then, much to my surprise, Vogel stepped away, apparently deciding that a nearby ambassador and his wife needed his attention. I was amazed; it was the first time that evening that Dieter had left our side.

"That's impressive," I murmured. "Do you often order chief consuls around like that?"

Goldstein smiled. "My dear lady, I never order anyone around. I merely offer alternatives." He paused. "You're new here, so you don't know better . . . that both Dieter and Marcos are playing the same game."

"And what game is that?" Carlos asked.

I hadn't noticed that he'd come up behind me; apparently he'd been listening the entire time. Yet Goldstein wasn't surprised; his eyes nor his ears missed anything. "Seeking control of your world, of course," he replied, his voice just low enough for us to hear. "*Herr* Vogel seeks to ingratiate himself with you, while the Patriarch believes that he can win through intimidation. Two different means, but ultimately the same objective."

"And you, of course, aren't interested—"

"Oh, but of course I am." Goldstein flagged down a passing 'bot, took a glass of wine from its platter. "The difference between me and them . . . and indeed, everyone else here . . . is that I have a gift to offer to your world, with no strings attached." He took a sip from his wine. "Oh, perhaps just one, but I think you'll find it difficult to reject. As I said, I merely offer alternatives."

"And that is . . . ?" Carlos asked.

"Another time. When we don't have so much company." He paused, his eyes shifting to see who was around us, then he went on. "Marcos invited you to pay a visit to the Union. May I suggest that you take him up on this . . . but when you do, you let me know first, so that I can arrange private transportation."

His left hand went into his jacket, came out again with an engraved card. "This is my private number," he said, handing it to me. "I can be reached anytime, day or night. Please don't lose it . . . you can't possibly underestimate its importance."

Another bow, then Goldstein said good night and drifted away, just as Vogel detached himself from the brief conversation he'd just had. By then Carlos had slipped the card into his pocket. We said nothing of this to Dieter, and shortly afterward Carlos requested that we return to our suite.

I didn't know quite what to make of the mysterious Morgan Goldstein. Yet somehow, I had a feeling that we'd found a friend. I certainly hoped so. Because I had no doubt that we'd also found an enemy.

The next morning, we appeared before the United Nations.

Beneath the cavernous dome of the General Assembly Hall, delegates were seated at oak-top desks arranged in concentric tiers overlooking a circular floor where the U.N. seal had been engraved in blond marble. High above, a ring-shaped array of viewscreens was suspended from the ceiling; although Anglo was the official language, simultaneous translations were offered to the delegates through comps imbedded within their desks. The flags of the member nations hung from the walls, and were also displayed on the front of each desk.

Carlos, Chris, and I were escorted to an elevated dais facing the Secretary-General's podium. The hall was packed; every seat had been taken, and even the public gallery was filled to capacity. Floaters hovered about our table, their lenses constantly trained upon us; glancing up, I saw myself on one of the screens, my face enlarged to giant size. Taking a deep breath, I looked down and self-consciously shuffled some papers, trying to appear more calm than I actually was.

The Secretary-General was Farouk Sadat, a tall, thin Egyptian with slate-grey hair. Dieter had briefly introduced us to him the night before; I'd liked him, even if he was a bit stiff. Once he took his place, he banged his gavel on the podium to bring the session to order. A quick roll call was taken, then Sadat formally introduced us to the General Assembly. It soon became clear that the Secretary-General took unabashed pride in welcoming the delegation from Coyote; he congratulated us not only for undertaking humankind's first expedition to the stars, but also for successfully establishing its first interstellar colony. That made me relax a little; at least he was on our side, or so it seemed.

After offering further congratulations to the European Alliance for having demonstrated the viability of hyperspace travel, Sadat relinquished the floor to Carlos. Gathering his notes, my husband stood up and walked to the rostrum. Despite my advice to wear the formal attire that had been tailored for him only yesterday, Carlos decided that he wanted the delegates to see us for what we really were. So it was in clothes made of hemp, shagswool, and catskin—the same outfit he wore when he presided over formal meetings of the Colonial Council—that the President of the Coyote Federation addressed the U.N. General Assembly.

Carlos began by acknowledging the European Alliance for their hospitality, then offered his appreciation to the U.N. for allowing him to address its General Assembly. Then he gave a brief description of the world we'd discovered. Much of this was pretty dry—facts and figures, some historical background—but we'd also brought a datafiche containing images of Coyote. While he spoke, pictures were projected on the overhead screens, and an awed hush fell upon the hall as the delegates received their first look at our home: the vast savannahs of New Florida, the Gillis Range of Midland, and the Black Mountains of Great Dakota, the broad expanse of the Great Equatorial River, Bear rising at sunset above the West Channel. As Carlos went on to describe the progress we'd made in establishing permanent settlements, there were more images: street scenes of Liberty and Shuttlefield, the Garcia Narrows Bridge, tugboats upon the East Channel, the timber mills of Clarksburg, the towns of Leeport, New Boston, and Defiance.

Thinking back on it now, it may have been unwise to show them all this. Compared to what Earth had become, Coyote must have looked like Eden: forests and mountain valleys, clean air and fresh water, miles upon miles of terrain upon which no one had ever set foot. Paradise, virgin and unspoiled. With every picture they saw, their hunger must have grown; like starving children who'd long gnawed the bones of their world, they were now being shown a proverbial land of milk and honey.

Yet there would have been no point in pretending otherwise. They would've found out for themselves what Coyote was like. And besides, just as much as they wanted what we had, we wanted what they had, too. So while the images were still on the screens, Carlos laid out the basic tenets of our proposal.

In exchange for formal U.N. recognition of the Coyote Federation as a sovereign entity, and Coyote itself as an independent world, we'd be willing to negotiate trade agreements with member nations of the General Assembly. Spacefaring nations could also sign right-of-passage agreements with both the European Alliance and the Coyote Federation, which would give them access to the starbridges, with all parties involved being signatory to their terms. We would allow those countries to establish their own colonies, but only if they agreed to strict immigration limits and also signed a nonaggression pact prohibiting military forces on the new world; those colonies would also be subject to the terms of the Liberty Compact, which ensured basic human rights to everyone who came to Coyote. After a six-year probation period—two years by the LeMarean calendar—new colonies would be allowed to join the Coyote Federation, and thus have permanent representation on the Colonial Council.

It was a hard bargain, and we knew it. Yet this was what the executive committee had hammered out during countless meetings that had lasted late into the night. Although we certainly desired to have relations with Earth, we didn't want a repeat of the Union occupation: invasion by a militant power that sought to impose their social system upon ours, even as it dumped thousands of ill-prepared immigrants on our shores. This time, there would be no Union Guard, no squatter camps, no matriarch with ambitions of empire. We'd fought hard for our freedom; we weren't about to give it away.

All the same, it took a lot of courage for Carlos to stand before the nations of the world we'd once known as home and say these things. Yet he never stammered; his hands didn't shake as he turned the pages of his speech, and his gaze remained calm and unwavering. In the many years I've known my husband, after all the things we've been through together, I've never been more proud of him than I was at that moment. I hadn't known his father very long before he died, but I did know Captain Lee; Jorge Montero may have been Carlos's flesh and blood, yet it was then that I realized that my husband's spirit had come from another man.

When Carlos finished, murmurs swept through the hall. As customary during U.N. meetings, there was no applause. Carlos returned to his seat; beneath the table, I gave his hand a reassuring squeeze. Chris nodded to him, but his expression was stoical. Looking around, I saw aides in whispered conference with ambassadors who peered at their notes. We'd run up the flag; now we'd see who saluted.

The Secretary-General thanked President Montero for his presentation, then opened the floor for comments. One at a time, delegates took a turn at responding to what Carlos had said. Most were carefully neutral—the ambassador of the Pacific Coalition, for instance, reiterated Sadat's admiration for the progress we'd made in colonizing the new world, and stated that his country looked forward to negotiations with the Coyote Federation—but others were a little less forthcoming. The Israeli ambassador told us that, while his country was also interested in pursuing a trade agreement, it was primarily interested in immigration; he expressed hope that small, nonspace-faring countries such as his would eventually be allowed to claim unoccupied islands as colonies. The ambassador from India expressed concern that raw materials imported from Coyote might pose unfair competition with the same materials exported from the Near East; he wanted to know how much we intended to ship back to Earth, and whether it would be subject to tariffs. The South African ambassador stated that, while he respected the Coyote Federation's desire to be recognized as an independent entity, we should take into consideration Article II of the U.N. Space Treaty of 1967, which forbade signatory nations from claiming any planet as sovereign territory; in that regard, in accordance with Article I of the same treaty, Coyote should be considered the rightful inheritance of all humankind.

Yet it wasn't until Secretary-General Sadat recognized Patriarch Amado of the Western Hemisphere Union that things got rough.

"Mr. Secretary General," Amado began, "while the Western Hemisphere Union respects the opinions of our fellow members, my government questions the validity of the statements made by Mr. Montero. In fact, his assertion that the colonies he represents have a rightful claim to Coyote leads us to believe that he intends to perpetrate a deliberate deception. Indeed, we believe that it is nothing but an outright lie."

Low murmurs swept through the room. The Patriarch's pointed refusal to refer to Carlos as "President Montero" hadn't been lost on anyone, and his accusation showed that he'd abandoned any pretense at diplomatic niceties. Sadat clasped his hands together beneath his chin; he showed no emotion as he listened intently.

"First," Amado said, "the historical record clearly shows that the first starship sent to the 47 Ursae Majoris system was URSS *Alabama*, and that vessel was under the registry of the United Republic of America when it was launched in 2070. Since the URA was subsequently absorbed by the Western Hemisphere Union in 2096 . . . two hundred and four years before the *Alabama* arrived at Coyote . . . this means the *Alabama* was the rightful property of the WHU long before it reached 47 Ursae Majoris. Second, since no radio transmissions from the *Alabama* have been received by deep-space telemetry stations, either on Earth or elsewhere in the solar systems, any territorial claims made by its captain and crew aren't legally admissible under international law."

Chris muttered a curse beneath his breath, but Carlos calmly jotted notes on a sheet of paper. "Third," Amado continued, "between 2256 and 2260, the Union Astronautica dispatched five starships to 47 Ursae Majoris, the first of which arrived less than four years after the *Alabama*. With five thousand colonists aboard those vessels, the Union has just as much right . . . and, indeed, even more so . . . to claim Coyote as the *Alabama* party, which numbered little more than a hundred."

Amado paused; now he glared straight at Carlos. "Furthermore, my government has received reliable information that our peaceful efforts to colonize this new world were met with hostile resistance by the members of the *Alabama* party, resulting in the deaths of many Union colonists. We've also been told that the principal leader of this unlawful insurrection was none other than Mr. Montero himself."

This stunned me. How could he have learned this? Carlos's face went pale; his left hand went below the table, found my own. I grasped it, offering what little comfort that I could.

"Therefore," Amado went on, his voice simmering with outrage, "it's our opinion that the so-called Coyote Federation is little more than a guerilla insurgency, bent upon assuming control of territory that rightfully belongs to the Western Hemisphere Union. The WHU also regards any efforts by the European Alliance to open hyperspace travel between Earth and Coyote to be just as intrusive, and views its sponsorship of an illegal government as nothing less than an intrusion tantamount to an act of war."

By now, Carlos was gripping my hand so hard that I was afraid he'd bruise my fingers. Yet he was careful not to show his anger; he stared directly ahead, refusing to let his emotions get the better of him.

"Thank you, Patriarch Amado," Sadat said. I thought he was going to allow Carlos a chance to respond, but instead the Secretary-General looked to the other side of the room. "The chair recognizes the ambassador of the European Alliance."

Dieter Vogel had also introduced us to Sir Ian Rutledge the night before. He'd failed to make much of an impression upon me: an elderly Englishman, stoop-shouldered and rather frail, like some tired old lord who'd been given a diplomatic position a long time ago and left to rot there. Dieter was seated next to him; he whispered in Sir Ian's ear, and the old man listened to him for a moment, then nodded slightly.

"With respect to my collegue from the Western Hemisphere Union," Sir Ian began, soft-spoken and calm, "my government believes that his concerns have been rather overstated. In fact, to put matters as bluntly as he did, they're completely and wholly without merit."

More murmurs from the delegates. Sir Ian let it pass. "When the *Alabama* left Earth," he went on, "it was hijacked by a group of political dissidents led by its captain, the late R. E. Lee. This, too, is a matter of historical record. In doing so, they effectively dissolved all political ties to the United Republic of America . . . and therefore, by extension, to its successor, the Western Hemisphere Republic. So the WHU has no legal claim upon the *Alabama*, its crew, nor any of its passengers."

Chris gently rapped his knuckles against the desk; Carlos shook his head at him, but he was having a hard time keeping a straight face. "The fact that the *Alabama* has failed to establish radio contact with Earth is a simple matter of physics," Sir Ian continued. "Given the limitations imposed by the speed of light, the first transmissions from the *Alabama* won't be received for another"—he paused to check his notes—"five years, eight months, twenty-eight days, ten hours, and some-odd minutes and seconds." He paused. "That's a back-of-the-envelope calculation," he added dryly. "Sorry I can't be more specific, but my watch seems to be a bit off."

Laughter rolled across the room. Sir Ian allowed it to die down before he went on. "Granted, five ships from the Union Astronautica have also visited the 47 Ursae Majoris system, but since their radio signals have yet to be received, either, there's no way to ascertain their own territorial claims." More laughter, and Amado's face turned red, but Sir Ian chose to ignore this as well. "However, our own intelligence reports indicate that the Union's efforts to colonize Coyote were anything but peaceful. Heavily armed Union Guard soldiers were aboard the very first Union Astronautica vessel, along with colonists who had been selected largely by public lottery, as was the case with every WHU starship. In fact, the last ship sent to 47 Ursae Majoris was primarily military in nature, its mission undertaken by the Union Guard upon the recommendation of the Council of Savants . . . and I don't think this body needs to be reminded of the threat posed by the Savants before they were abolished."

More murmurs. Everyone surely remembered what the Savants had once planned for the rest of humankind: selective genocide, with the ultimate goal of reducing the global population. Yet Sir Ian wasn't done yet. "Therefore, any resistance the original colonists may have offered was justifiable. It was occupation by the Western Hemisphere Union that was unlawful, not their revolution. And once the Union Guard was defeated twenty-one years ago, and its forces sent back to Earth, the colonists set about forming the Coyote Federation as a free and democratic society."

Sir Ian gestured toward Carlos. "The very fact that they elected this man to be their president speaks well of their society. They chose neither a terrorist nor a tyrant, but instead one of their own . . . a common man who'd taken up arms to fight for their liberty. And I think we should respect them for this."

Carlos sat up a little straighter; he was no longer gripping my hand, but instead gazing at Sir Ian. I glanced at Amado; he should have considered himself lucky that a floater wasn't focused upon him just then.

"Therefore," Sir Ian continued, "it's the opinion of the European Alliance that the U.N. Space Treaty doesn't apply to the Coyote Federation since, from the very beginning, its colonies dissolved their connections from the governments of Earth. By much the same token, it should also be allowed to reestablish those ties, this time as an independent entity, free to negotiate matters of trade and immigration with whomever it chooses. My government is proud to act as its intermediary to the United Nations, and hopes to sponsor its eventual membership to the General Assembly."

Again, voices rumbled across the vast hall, as delegates quietly conversed with each other. The Secretary-General let it go for a few seconds, then pounded his gavel and called for adjournment. Hearings would continue tomorrow morning; until then, he'd be available to hear any motions for mediation. For now, the General Assembly was in recess.

It took nearly an hour for Carlos, Chris, and me to make our exit; we found ourselves surrounded by diplomats and their aides. The last I saw of Ambassador Amado, he'd gathered his notes and stalked from the hall. He'd made his best shot, and blown it.

I caught a glimpse of Sir Ian. The ambassador left the Assembly Hall without any fanfare; for him, this was just another day's work. But just before he left, I caught his eye. He smiled at me and nodded, and I blew him a kiss.

Thank you, Ambassador. You may have just saved my world.

A hoverlimo took us back to the European Alliance embassy, where we remained for the rest of the day. Yet Carlos and I had little chance to relax. All afternoon, we received visits from various U.N. delegations, each wishing to privately discuss the details of our trade and immigration proposals. The embassy staff allowed us to use a ground-floor parlor near the ballroom for our meetings; Carlos and I sat in armchairs near an ornate fireplace warmed by the holographic projection of burning logs as, two or three at a time, various diplomats and their aides were ushered in to see us.

Every one of them was willing to recognize the Coyote Federation as a sovereign entity, and nearly all were willing to join the European Alliance in cosponsoring Coyote's induction to the United Nations. However, in return for their support, they all wanted certain concessions to be made. The potential for future colonization was the biggest concern. Nearly everyone objected to our insistence that immigration be limited; they saw no reason why their countries shouldn't be allowed to ship as many people as possible to a world that was largely uninhabited. Others were reluctant to accept our stipulation that new colonies would be nonmilitarized; they argued that they needed to protect themselves from their neighbors. Several were less than enthusiastic about having to abide by the terms of the Liberty Compact; they wanted to export their own forms of government, in effect turning their colonies into miniature copies of their home countries.

And there were dozens of questions. What were Coyote's most temperate regions? Which continents and islands had the greatest reserves of natural resources? What was the potential for mining? Were there any rare substances? Was the native animal life dangerous? Were the indigenous plants edible? Who would control access to the rivers and channels? Had anyone yet explored the polar regions? How did we maintain agriculture during the long winters? Had we yet considered building an international spaceport? And, most importantly, was there anything we'd told the last delegate who'd walked in here that we weren't telling them?

So on and so forth, with one ambassador after another coming forth to smile, bow, make noises about how much they respected our courage and pioneer fortitude, then try to wiggle out of us a bargain that would give them an edge over their rivals. Carlos listened patiently to each one; I took notes and occasionally offered a comment or two, while Chris quietly stood off to one side. We offered as much information as we could, except about what we'd discussed with the last delegation with whom we'd met, and conceded nothing but vague assurances that we'd take their issues into consideration. The fine art of diplomacy: take as much as you can, surrender as little as possible, and attempt to make friends or, at the very least, prevent anyone from declaring war.

The last light of day cast long shadows through the windows when we finally put quits to the whole ordeal. We'd received over a dozen dinner invitations, but we'd accepted none; all Carlos and I wanted to do was return to our suite, have a shower and a quick bite to eat, then crawl into bed. My skull pounded with a headache, and Carlos complained that his lower back was sore from having bowed so many times; Chris was the only one of us who didn't seem to have any trouble adjusting to the higher gravity.

We were in no mood for more visitors, so when an embassy aide stuck his head through the door and told us that Morgan Goldstein had just arrived, Carlos was on the verge of an ill-tempered reply before I cut him off.

"Yes, we'll be glad to see Mr. Goldstein," I said. "Please show him in." Carlos scowled at me, and I held up a hand. *Five minutes,* I mouthed, and he gave an exhausted shrug. Five minutes. What difference could that make?

Goldstein entered, casually dressed in a charcoal overcoat and a dark brown sweater. This time he wasn't alone; he was accompanied by a tall, heavy-set gent with long blond hair and a thick beard. Clearly a bodyguard. He and Chris warily gazed at each other, two warriors sizing up a possible adversary.

"Mr. President, First Lady . . ." Goldstein smiled. "Or are you tired of hearing that all day? I can call you something else, if you prefer."

"You can call me anything except . . ." Carlos sighed, rubbed his eyelids. "Naw, forget it. I'm already late for dinner. You want to call me Carlos, go right ahead. I don't care."

"Carlos, then." Goldstein nodded, and looked at me. "And I take it I can call you Wendy? And you, Mr. Levin . . . is it too much of a familiarity if I called you Chris?"

"Whatever suits you." Chris didn't take his eyes off Goldstein's strongman; I noticed that his hand had risen to the lapel of his jacket. "If he's packing a gun, though, he's going to have to wait outside."

"Mr. Kennedy doesn't wait outside for anyone." Yet Goldstein turned toward him. "Mike, if you'll kindly divest yourself of your weaponry, I think it'd go a long way toward instilling trust in our friends."

Kennedy hesitated, then opened his overcoat and carefully withdrew a small, chrome-plated handgun from a shoulder holster. A particle-beam laser; he laid it on a nearby table, then slowly stepped away. Chris picked it up, unclipped the power-pack, then put it back on the table. Kennedy nodded, then picked up his gun and put it back in his holster. Professional courtesy; Chris wasn't disarming his counterpart, just making sure that he couldn't do any harm.

"Glad we're past that." Carlos relaxed a little; he reached for a glass of water on the side table next to him. "Mr. Goldstein, you're going to have to forgive us, but—"

"Call me Morgan, please."

"Morgan, we've had a long day. Wendy and I would rather—"

"Of course. I have no intention of imposing upon you more than necessary." Removing his coat, Goldstein walked to the chair where dozens of delegates had seated themselves; for a moment, I thought he was going to sit down, but instead he tossed his coat on the chair. "You're worn out. I don't blame you. For what it's worth, though, you handled yourselves in an exemplary fashion. I couldn't have done it better myself."

Carlos and I exchanged glances. Who the hell did he think he was? "Thank you," I said. "If that's all, then . . ."

"Well, no. Not quite." Goldstein clasped his hands behind his back. "First, I've taken the liberty of having a local caterer deliver dinner to your rooms. Nothing too elaborate, I assure you. Just a little better than the soup and sandwiches the embassy kitchen would offer."

Carlos raised an eyebrow. "We appreciate that, but—"

"Please. Consider it a token of my admiration." Goldstein walked away, rubbing an imaginary speck from his eye. "You know, that really was a remarkable performance. I have to admit, in fact, that I may have underestimated you. I thought you might have been out of your league, but instead you showed remarkable grace under pressure. And having Sir Ian come to your rescue like that . . ." He chuckled. "Outstanding. My compliments on a fine maneuver."

"It wasn't a maneuver," I said coldly. "We didn't ask Sir Ian to defend us. He did that by himself."

Goldstein darted a sharp look in my direction. "Really? That wasn't prearranged?" Carlos and I both shook our heads, and now it was his turn to be surprised. "Even more remarkable. I didn't think the old duffer still had it in him."

I was quickly getting annoyed. "Mr. Goldstein . . ."

"The other reason I came," he went on, as if I hadn't spoken, "is to offer a little advice. My sources tell me that Patriarch Amado has met with the Secretary-General and requested mediation."

This was unexpected. "What does that mean?" Carlos asked, as we glanced at each other.

"That means, tomorrow morning before the General Assembly reconvenes, you'll meet informally with Farouk, Marcos, and Sir Ian. I don't know the specifics, but I'm willing to bet that Marcos knows that any further attempt to claim Coyote as Union territory is pointless, and that he should try to offer a compromise before his country gets left out."

I almost laughed out loud. Last night, Amado had treated Carlos and me as if we were a couple of hicks. This morning, he'd gone so far as to openly accuse Carlos of being a terrorist. Now that he saw which way the wind was blowing, he wanted to make a deal. Politics . . .

"Sure, we can compromise," Chris said. "I'll bend over if he gets down on his knees, so he can kiss my . . ."

Mike Kennedy apparently forgot he was supposed to be a bodyguard, too, because he guffawed. He and Chris took one look at each other, then they both broke up. Moments like that are infectious; a second later, everyone in the room was howling with laughter, with Carlos and me holding on to one another for support and Goldstein half-collapsed against a table. One of the embassy staff opened the door to peer inside; seeing what was going on, he hastily slammed the door shut. And that just set us off again.

When the laughter finally wore off, Goldstein ran a hand across his hairless head. "Well, I doubt he'll go that far, but . . ." Straightening up, he wiped the smirk from his face. "All the same, I think you should take whatever he offers into consideration. The WHU has enormous clout in the

General Assembly, particularly in matters regarding extraterrestrial resources. If you can work out some sort of equitable agreement between
them and the EΛ, then the Pacific Coalition will probably go with it. After
that, the nonaligned countries will fall into line."

"Makes sense." Carlos was sober again. "So why are you telling us
this?"

Goldstein shrugged. "As I told your wife, I'm a businessman. A venture
capitalist, if you will. I see Coyote as an opportunity for long-term investment. If the three major powers can come to terms, then I stand to make
money."

"Simple as that, huh?"

"Not quite so simple. If money was the sole objective, I'd be at my estate, sunning myself by the pool and waiting to see which countries sign
trade agreements with you so that I can buy stock in the right places."
Again, an offhand shrug. "But after a while, there's little difference between having ten billion and having a hundred billion. A few more toys,
that's all. And eventually, time catches up."

Goldstein went silent for a moment, as if reflecting upon thoughts to
which we were not privy, until he finally went on. "So that's it. Dinner,
and a word to the wise. Please take it as is. Mike?"

Kennedy picked up Goldstein's overcoat, held it open for his boss. "One
more thing," Goldstein added, as he pushed his arms into the sleeves. "As I
said before, I have a gift for you. If Marcos offers you a trip to the Union . . .
and I have no doubt he will . . . please take him up on it. However, allow
me to provide the transportation."

"We'll keep it in mind," I said.

"Please do." A bow, and then he turned away. "Very well, then. Good
night. Enjoy your dinner."

The door closed behind them, and we let out our breaths. For the first
time in hours, we were alone. Or at least in the physical sense; I had little
doubt that the parlor was bugged, and EA intelligence operatives were listening to everything we said.

"So," Carlos said. "Do we trust him?"

I said nothing, but instead raised my hand, twisted my wrist back and
forth. Maybe. Maybe not.

The Mediation Room was a small chamber adjacent to the General Assembly Hall; a round mahogany table dominated the room, beneath a circular stained-glass ceiling fashioned to resemble the zodiac. Marcos Amado was already there when we arrived, along with a senior aide; he offered a formal bow to Carlos, Chris, and me, but said nothing until General-Secretary Sadat and his aide showed up a few minutes later, with Sir Ian Rutledge and a senior consul right behind them.

A few more bows, then everyone took their seats: the Patriarch and his aide directly across the table from Carlos, Chris, and me, with Sadat and his aide to our right, and Sir Ian and his consul to our left. A summit meeting. Yet even though Carlos and I were prepared for another fight, we didn't get one. As Goldstein predicted, Amado had apparently realized that any further attempt to claim Coyote as Union territory would be futile; his best hope now was to try to bargain with us.

So he laid his offer on the table. In exchange for WHU recognition of the Coyote Federation, he wanted assurances that the European Alliance would be granted hyperspace passage to the 47 Ursae Majoris system, and also that the Union would be allowed to establish a new colony on a previously unsettled landmass, along with sovereign control of its government.

We were willing to let the Union establish a new colony, but Carlos was reluctant about letting it have its own government. Social collectivism had already been tried on Coyote, and the results had been disastrous: thousands of immigrants reduced to virtual slavery, while a select few had enjoyed the fruits of their labor. As a result, the Liberty Compact was based upon democratic principles; the colonies that made up the Coyote Federation had already accepted this standard as the foundation of our government.

Therefore, if one colony embraced collectivism, it couldn't be allowed to join the Federation, and we didn't want to have a colony that posed a potential threat to the others.

The Secretary-General pointed out that the United Nations didn't endorse one social system over another. If the U.N. were to legally recognize the Coyote Federation, then it would have to exempt Coyote from the terms of the 1967 Space Treaty; this meant that the Liberty Compact couldn't be enforced upon new colonies established by nations on Earth. However, he quickly added that, if the immigration controls were put in place and outside military forces were prohibited on Coyote, then the other colonies shouldn't have anything to fear from one that embraced social collectivism.

Sir Ian suggested a compromise. If the WHU was allowed to establish a colony, then its citizens should also be given the opportunity to relocate freely to colonies if they chose to do so, or even start their own noncollectivist settlements somewhere else. And if the Union colony abided by those terms, and didn't undertake any hostile actions against their neighbors, then the Union colony would be allowed to join the Coyote Federation as a nonvoting member of the Colonial Council.

Patriarch Amado hesitated upon hearing this; so did Carlos and I. The WHU was looking for another toehold upon Coyote, and we weren't wild about them getting it. But the EA controlled the starbridges; they were anticipating the revenue they'd make from passage fees, and denying the Union would cut deep into their estimated profits. And just as much as these two coalitions wanted to exploit the resources of a new world, we also needed what they had to offer. They were desperate, yes . . . but then, so were we.

So we accepted the compromise.

In hindsight, I can't say whether we were wrong or right. All sides had something to gain; likewise, all sides also had something to lose. There's no perfect black or white when it comes to something like this, and even the shades of grey are hard to distinguish. In the years to come, historians would debate the outcome of what happened in the Mediation Room that morning, and they'd come to different conclusions. All I can say is that Carlos and I did the best we could, and leave it to future generations to determine the wisdom, or the error, of our actions.

When we were done, the Secretary-General told us that he'd present the draft of our agreement to both the General Assembly and the Security Council. We could expect further debate, of course, yet he was confident that this was an equitable solution. He passed his notes to his aide, who left the room while we were still bowing to one another. The delegates had already convened in the hall, so Sadat made haste in departing; Sir Ian made a point of shaking Carlos's hand, then he left as well.

That left us alone, for the moment, with Patriarch Amado. He dismissed his aide, and Carlos reciprocated by nodding Chris to the door. Now there were only the three of us.

"Mr. President . . ." Amado began.

"So pleased to hear you say that," Carlos replied. "Sounds better this way, doesn't it?"

Amado shrugged. "Perhaps it does, now that we've settled our differences. And I certainly hope that you'll no longer consider me your enemy."

"I never did. But friendship is something else we'll have to work out."

"Of course." Amado turned to pick up his notes. Then, as if a new thought occurred to him, he looked back at us again. "It's been suggested to me, by a mutual friend . . . *Señor* Goldstein, whom I believe you've met . . . that you might like to pay a visit to the Union before you return to your world. Perhaps to see your old country?"

"We'd be delighted, Patriarch."

"Very well." Amado smiled. "I'll have my people make the arrangements." A short bow. "Good morning, then. I look forward to seeing you again soon."

He walked out of the room, and Carlos let out his breath once he was gone. "What do you think?" he whispered. "Friend or foe?"

"Do you have to ask?" I suppressed a shudder. "This is Morgan's plan. Let's see where it takes us."

Soon we would know. Five days later, a private aerocruiser belong-ing to Janus Ltd., Goldstein's corporation, touched down in Grosvenor Square. We departed London with little fanfare; Sir Ian and Dieter came to see us off, but other than a few journalists and a handful of embassy staff members, few people watched as Carlos, Chris, and I boarded the aircraft. Its VTOL jets swiveled downward, and a few seconds later it lifted off from the landing pad.

By then we'd concluded most of our business on Earth. Acting on be-half of the European Alliance, Sir Ian had introduced a formal U.N. resolu-tion, officially recognizing the Coyote Federation as an independent entity; once the Western Hemisphere Union withdrew its objections, several non-aligned countries signed on as cosponsors, and even the Pacific Coalition had given its tacit approval. Although the General Assembly had yet to vote upon it, Dieter was certain that it would pass. In the meantime, Carlos had conducted trade negotiations with several countries. The compromise we'd worked out several days earlier with the WHU had demonstrated that Coyote was serious about doing business with Earth; now it seemed as if everyone was lined up at the door, wanting a piece of the action.

We were exhausted. When Carlos and I hadn't been wrangling out the details of trade agreements, either one or both of us had conducted press conferences or granted interviews to individual reporters. And when we weren't doing that, we'd fulfilled promises to attend state dinners held in our honor at various embassies and consulates. By then we'd come to know most of the U.N. diplomatic corps on a first-name basis, along with a good part of London high society. Once our bodies had reacclimated to higher gravity, we didn't need to use canes to walk anymore; so many of our newfound friends had gifted us with clothes, we had a wardrobe of the latest fashions to choose from whenever we dressed to go out. Indeed, we'd become in demand as guests; everyone wanted to meet the President and First Lady of the Coyote Federation, and hear our stories of a world where strange creatures haunted its mountains and rivers.

After a while, though, the novelty started to wear thin, and when it did, I began to notice just how jaded this society had become. Although the embassy area surrounding Hyde Park and Buckingham Palace remained gentrified, sometimes our ride took us north of Mayfair and Bayswater or south of Belgravia and Knightsbridge, and then we'd find ourselves traveling through parts of the city where the buildings were noticeably decrepit. Few lights shone in the windows at night; armored vehicles were stationed at every block, with police officers standing watch, while shabby figures huddled in doorways or against the boarded-up storefronts. Every now and then, while I made small talk with the lords and ladies, I'd glance through a window to see the flickering glow of trash can fires, or spot the searchlight of a gyro flying low over a darkened neighborhood not far away. Yet none of that seemed to penetrate the conscience of the wealthy and privileged; shielded from the unpleasant realities of the world, they nibbled canapés and chatted about their country homes in the highlands, and made the occasional joke about a kitchen servant finding a rat the size of a beagle in the pantry.

So when Patriarch Amado extended a formal invitation for us to visit Atlanta, Carlos and I were all too ready to accept. We'd done as much as we could in London, at least for now, and we were hungry for a change of scenery. Dieter was reluctant to see us go, but he realized that we had to pay a visit to the Union, if only for the sake of fostering good relations. He offered to supply us with a security team, but after some consideration Carlos decided that it might send the wrong signal if we showed up in America with European bodyguards. Like it or not, we had to show that we were willing to trust the WHU just as much as the EA. Besides, Carlos, Chris, and I had all once been Americans; if we couldn't safely visit our native soil, then where on Earth could we go?

Nonetheless, shortly before we left the embassy, Dieter gave Chris a small satphone. It had been preprogrammed with an emergency prefix; all he had to do was enter 010 and the star key, then touch the SEND key. No verbal message was necessary; so long as the unit was kept active, someone would be able track the source of our transmission, and help would be on the way. Chris thanked him and put it in his coat pocket.

Morgan Goldstein's aerocruiser was a flying wing, with a ninety-foot wingspan and hydrogen-fuel turbofan engines mounted on either side of its fuselage. Its main cabin was even more luxurious than the one aboard the *Von Braun*; plush white carpets, swivel-mounted armchair seats, private cabins in the aft section, and a well-stocked bar. Morgan was waiting for us when we arrived; a steward offered us drinks while Mike Kennedy made sure that our luggage was safely loaded aboard, and a few minutes later the aerocruiser took off. A last glimpse of London and the inundated coast of southern England, and then we were airborne above the Atlantic.

"I hope you don't mind that we take the slow way home," Morgan said, "but I wanted us to have a chance to talk. A suborbital could have made the trip more quickly, but . . ." An offhand shrug. "Besides, I like to show off my toys. This one's an antique. Less than a hundred were manu-factured before the company went under."

"Very nice. Nice indeed." Carlos jiggled the ice in the single-malt scotch he'd been given. He'd been drinking a little more often than usual these last few days; he'd never gotten drunk, at least so far as I could tell, but during all the dinner parties and receptions we'd attended he'd developed a taste for liquor more refined than the sourgrass ale and waterfruit wine he'd drink back home. I'd tried to chalk it up to pressure, but still it worried me. "So what do you want to discuss?"

"Nothing in particular." Turning his seat around, Morgan stretched out his legs, then used his toes to pry off his black felt moccasins. "It's just that this is first time we've had a chance to talk about stuff when we don't have to worry about who else might be listening." He glanced at his bodyguard. "Mike, the recorders are turned off, right?"

"We're clean, chief." Kennedy slid open a panel on the armrest of his seat, then turned around to let Chris take a look. "See?"

"We'll take your word for it," I said. "So what is it that you want to know?"

"The question is, what do *you* want to know?" Morgan massaged his toes against the carpet. "The way I see it, for the last week or so, you've been the ones on the spot . . . and, as I've said before, you handled the sit-uation quite well. But I imagine there're things you'd like to know that no one has told you. So since you don't have to worry about anyone listening in, why don't you ask me?"

None of us said anything for a few moments. Carlos looked at me, and

I looked at Chris, and Chris looked back at both of us. Morgan crossed his legs, patiently waiting for one of us to speak. "You like the scotch?" he asked, casually raising his glass to peer at it. "Hard to come by these days. I have it made for me in Edinburgh, but—"

"Whose side are you on?" Carlos asked. "The Union or the Alliance?"

"Neither. I'm on my side. I have substantial business interests in both the Union and the Alliance. That's why I maintain a dual citizenship in both the EA and the WHU, and have legal residences in both North America and Europe." He smiled. "In fact, we're going to pay a quick visit to my New England estate on the way to Atlanta. Hope you don't mind."

"So you're playing both ends against the middle," I said.

Morgan shook his head. "Not really, no. I take care that nothing I do hurts either the Union or the Alliance. That's one reason why I've cultivated contacts with the diplomatic community . . . getting invited to that reception last week, for instance, required little more than a couple of phone calls. But in the end, I'm looking out primarily for my own interests."

"So what's your interest in Coyote?" Chris asked. "You want to add us to your empire?"

Morgan grinned as he swiveled his chair to face him. "You know, Mr. Levin, you're very much like your friend Mike." He nodded toward Kennedy, who sat quietly nearby. "People think that because he's my bodyguard and doesn't say much, he's all muscle and no brain. But still waters run deep, as the saying goes—"

"You haven't answered the question."

"Mike, he's being rude. Break his legs." Kennedy hesitated, then started to rise. Chris's right hand drifted toward his jacket. "I'm kidding," Morgan added, and both he and Chris relaxed once more. "No, I'm not planning to 'add you to my empire,' as you put it. Certainly, I'd like to have my company be involved with whatever trade agreements you make, but that's not my principal goal."

"What is it, then?" Carlos asked.

Morgan didn't reply immediately. Instead, he gazed out the window next to his seat as he absently gnawed at a fingernail. "You've seen how bad things have become here," he said after a moment. "The planet is on the verge of environmental collapse . . . no, not even on the verge. It's already reached that point. Every scientist with whom I've spoken agrees that Earth is dying, slowly and by degrees. Within another generation or two, glaciers will cover most of northern Europe, and in the meantime North America is frying. Much of the Southern Hemisphere is already uninhabitable . . . what hasn't been flooded has turned into desert . . . and over half of the world's wildlife has become extinct."

He looked back at us again. "I don't intend to join them. I want to immigrate to Coyote."

Carlos shrugged. "That shouldn't be difficult. We've worked out immigration protocols for—"

"Yes, yes, of course you have." Morgan waved an impatient hand. "But do you really think I'm going to live in a log cabin and eat . . . what is it you call it? . . . creek crab stew for lunch?" He chuckled, shook his head. "Mr. President, I've become accustomed to certain comforts and privileges, and I'm not prepared to surrender them lightly. I want . . . well, concessions . . . to be made on my behalf."

"Concessions." Carlos raised an eyebrow. "What do you mean?"

"Nothing much, really. Just some real estate I can call my own, and the ability to do with it as I please. Perhaps a small island off the coast of Midland or Great Dakota. Minimal interference from the Colonial Council . . . I won't do anything to harm you, if you won't do anything to harm me."

"That's quite a bit to ask for."

"Not really. Only privacy. In return, you'll have my company's resources at your disposal. Janus quite diversified, with subsidiaries in many different areas. Shipping is our primary interest, but we're also involved in communications, construction, electronics, medicine . . . they're all yours for the asking, or at least at below-market prices. All I want is—"

"Privacy." Carlos glanced at me. We'd been prepared to deal with the Union's form of social collectivism, and over the last week we'd negotiated agreements with dozens of different countries. Yet this was something new: a billionaire capitalist who had everything we wanted, and was willing to exchange them for a private stake. Maybe this was the going price for forty acres and a mule. I didn't know whether to laugh, scream, or just throw up.

"Your offer is interesting," Carlos said, putting on a straight face. "Give us time to think about it."

"Of course. No rush." Again, Morgan favored us with his most charming smile. "When we land, though, I'll show you a gift that may help to persuade you."

"You said that before. What's—?"

"*Shh.*" He raised a finger to his lips, gave us a broad wink. "A good gift is always a surprise. Be patient." The smug smile remained on his face as he glanced at his watch, then he shifted in his seat. "Almost time for my midday nap. Are there any more questions?"

"Just one," I said. "It has nothing to do with anything we've just discussed, but it's something I've wondered about ever since we got here. And since you say you have contacts with the Alliance government . . ."

"Ask."

"When we arrived at Highgate, we saw a new Alliance cruiser, the *Francis Drake*." Morgan nodded, and I went on. "We were told that it was a merchanteer, specifically built to carry freight and passengers through hyperspace, but I noticed that it had torpedo tubes. When I brought this up to Dieter Vogel, he said that they'd been installed to protect the ship."

"Of course, yes."

"But against whom? Union spacecraft? That makes sense if they're preparing for war . . . but despite a lot of chest-beating, I've seen nothing to suggest that the WHU and the EA are ready to start shooting at each other. And even if they were, for a ship designed for interstellar travel to be armed—"

"What happened to the *Galileo*?" Carlos interrupted. I glanced at him, and he raised a hand, hushing me. "It has to do with that, doesn't it? The *Galileo* was the first EA starship, and it disappeared when it went to the Kuiper Belt. The *Columbus* was the second, but it wasn't armed . . ."

"Because it didn't travel through a starbridge." Morgan cupped a hand against his face, hiding his expression. "You're on the right track. Go on."

"Now they've built the *Drake*, and it is. Armed, I mean." Carlos hesitated, then looked at me. "Ana told me about the *Galileo*, but she swore me to secrecy. I'm sorry, honey, but . . ."

"Never mind." This wasn't the first time Carlos had kept a secret from me; he'd also remained quiet about the *chirreep* until Susan had been abducted by them. That had happened many years ago, and it made me angry that he'd hide something from me again, but for the moment all I wanted was a straight answer. "Let's have it, Mr. Goldstein. Tell us what happened to the *Galileo*."

Morgan rose from his chair. "What I'm about to tell you is a secret," he said quietly, clasping his hands behind his back as he paced down the aisle between our seats. "In fact, it's classified information, known only by a handful of government and military officials within the Alliance. As I said before, though, I've managed to cultivate friends in high places, and every now and then something slips through the cracks that gets to me." He stopped to regard us with solemn eyes. "So I'd appreciate it if you kept this to yourselves. No one must know what I'm about to tell you."

"We understand," Carlos said. "Go on, please."

"The first starbridge was experimental . . . KX-1, built by the ESA in the Kuiper Belt in 2288. Once Jonas Whittaker was revived, the EA encouraged him to revive his research into hyperspace travel, with the express purpose of developing a means of sending ships to 47 Ursae Majoris faster than the Union. By then, the necessary breakthroughs had become possible, and so it didn't take his team very long to devise a means of creating artificial wormholes. So an unmanned vessel utilizing diametric drive was launched to the outermost solar system, and once it arrived, robots aboard assembled KX-1 as a prototype starbridge."

Morgan paused by the bar to pour some more scotch. "The starbridge was still being tested when Patriarchs from the Union Astronautica made high-level contact with their counterparts in the European Space Agency. Their lunar radio telescope at Mare Muscoviense had picked up a very strong radio signal from outside the solar system . . . only two light-years from Earth, in fact, about halfway to Proxima Centauri. Not a message, but simply a regular, repeating signal, almost like a beacon. Since it came from interstellar space relatively close to Earth, it didn't appear to be a pulsar. The EA repositioned their own deep-space radio telescopes in the same direction, and came to the same conclusion—"

"A starship." Carlos said this flatly. "Not one of ours."

"Maybe." Morgan shrugged as he walked back toward us. "Maybe not. Further observations didn't detect anything that looked like engine exhaust, yet mass spectrometers revealed a large object containing traces of carbons, dioxides, various heavy metals. Whatever it was, it appeared to be bigger than a ship, but at the same time it was too small to be defined by planet-finders. But if it wasn't a vessel or a planet . . ."

He sat down again. "Well, of course, a mystery like this just has to be investigated. But the Union Astronautica didn't have anymore starships left in its fleet . . . in fact, they'd virtually bankrupted themselves building those five ships they'd already sent to Coyote . . . and they knew that the

EA was building its first manned starship, the *Galileo*, and was preparing to use it to give KX-1 its first operational test. So, in a rare instance of détente, the WHU and the EA agreed to engage in a joint mission. Launch the *Galileo* through the starbridge, then send it out to intercept Spindrift."

"Spindrift?"

"That's what the object was code-named." Morgan absently swirled the ice around his glass. "Of course, what the public was told was that the *Galileo* was engaged in a scientific mission to explore Kuiper Belt plantessimals." A lopsided smile. "Not that many people cared. By then, things were going seriously downhill here on Earth, so most folks thought . . . well, it just wasn't worth thinking about."

He sighed as he stretched out his legs once again. "So, few people noticed or even cared when we lost contact with the *Galileo*. It went through the starbridge on this side, came out the starbridge on the other end, transmitted back some images of the Belt. And that was it . . . that was the last we heard of the *Galileo*. The public was told that it had suffered some sort of catastrophic failure, perhaps a collision with an asteroid, and that's what they believed."

"But you don't," Carlos said.

"From what I've heard, once the *Galileo* concluded its survey, its crew went into biostasis for the intercept mission to Spindrift. The onboard AI sent back a report indicating that all systems were nominal. After that . . ." Morgan shook his head. "Nothing. No one knows whether it even reached Spindrift. By then, though, construction of the *Columbus* had been completed. Its command crew was briefed about the loss of the *Galileo*, but they were instructed not to reveal anything of this to anyone on Coyote." He looked at Carlos. "Captain Tereshkova must think highly of you, if she told you as much as she did."

"We've become friends." Carlos gave me an apologetic look. "I'm sorry, dear. Ana let me know a little, but she made me promise—"

"Sure." I was still sore at him, yet there's a difference between pillow talk and state secrets. I was married to a chief of state; I was used to the idea that, every now and then, there were matters that I really had no business knowing about. Yet there was more to the disappearance of the *Galileo* than what Morgan had just told us.

Almost everyone on Coyote knew the story of Leslie Gillis: the chief communications officer aboard the *Alabama*, prematurely revived from biostasis only three months after the ship had left Earth. Very few people knew the reason why—that it hadn't been an accident, as everyone believed, but because his cell had been sabotaged by my own father—but what had happened afterward had become legend. Gillis had remained alive aboard the *Alabama* for the next thirty-two years, alone and without any company, writing *The Chronicles of Prince Rupurt* as his sole escape from his dreary existence. Those books had become required reading for every child on Coyote. Indeed, Carlos had read them to Susan when she was a little girl.

What was less known about those stories, though, was their source of inspiration. When Captain Lee had read the ledgers in which Gillis had handwritten his tales, he discovered a brief description of a mysterious light Gillis had spotted from the ship's wardroom window: a distant light that wasn't a star, passing the *Alabama* like a ship in the night without responding to any radio messages the communications officer had transmitted.

Leslie Gillis was convinced that he'd seen another starship. Some believed that it may have only been a hallucination. No one knew for sure. But now . . .

"Something to consider, isn't it?" Morgan glanced at his watch again, then yawned and stood up. "Well, we have a long flight ahead of us, and it's time for my siesta. See you all when we arrive."

With that, he went aft to his private stateroom, closing the door behind him. The steward offered me another drink, but I declined. Instead, I gazed out the window at the blue waters of the ocean, wondering if there was a connection between these two mysteries.

And realizing that, if there was, the consequences could be deadly.

Morgan Goldstein's estate was located in the Berkshires of western Massachusetts, in a remote valley northeast of Stockbridge. As the aerocruiser shed altitude, I peered out the window to see low mountains covered by forest, with small ponds and farm fields scattered among the hills. At first, it seemed as if this was one small part of the world that hadn't been affected by climate change, yet as we came closer, I saw vast blackened areas where fires had rampaged through the woodlands, and dry beds where there had once been rivers.

Here and there, too, were refugee camps: great settlements of tents and shacks, where those who'd been displaced from their homes were trying to make a last stand. The decadeslong heat wave that scorched the South had destroyed agriculture and ruined the watershed, forcing hundreds of thousands to flee to cooler regions. They'd made the right decision—for a time, the northern regions had relatively pleasant weather, with shorter winters and longer summers—but even that eventually changed, for when the meltdown of the Antarctic and Greenland ice packs reversed the Atlantic Current, the wind patterns of the Northern Hemisphere had reversed as well. Now New England, too, was rapidly becoming a hot zone; it wouldn't be long before its mountain forests died, leaving behind only barren highlands and mosquito-infested swamps.

But until then, Morgan Goldstein had his own private retreat nestled within the Berkshires. Once the aerocruiser touched down on a paved airstrip at the far end of the estate and Kennedy opened the hatch, Morgan led us down the stairs. For a morning in mid-November, the air was warm and humid; the driver of the electric cart that awaited us wore shorts and a T-shirt, and he regarded us with faint amusement as we pulled off the sweaters we'd been wearing when we left London. Two weeks before

Thanksgiving, and I was sweltering; if I hadn't known better, I could have sworn we'd just landed in Jamaica.

Leaving Kennedy behind to bring our luggage from the plane, we climbed aboard the cart and headed down a gravel road leading away from the airstrip. Morgan took a moment to gaze at a datapad the driver handed him; he grunted quietly, either satisfied or dissatisfied with what he read, then he folded the pad and tucked it into his shirt pocket.

Morgan had done well with his little getaway. Three hundred acres of crops growing beneath elevated irrigation pipes, the water drawn from cisterns and artesian wells. Two wind turbines, along with a solar farm; all the electricity he needed came from his own energy sources. A large split-level hacienda, constructed of bird's-eye maple and granite fieldstone, with separate quarters for guests and a swimming pool where they could cool off. And a ten-foot chain-link fence around the entire area, patrolled round-the-clock by armed security guards; apparently Morgan was just as serious about maintaining his privacy as he was about self-sustenance.

Yet it wasn't until we approached the long pinewood shed that lay near the main house that he stopped showing off his wealth. "Here's where you'll see your gift," he said, then he looked at the driver. "Hit the horn, will you? I want Joe to know we're coming."

I noticed a large paddock adjacent to the shed. It was vacant, but hay bales were stacked nearby, and water troughs had been built within the wooden fence. The shed door opened as the cart came to a halt, and a tall, muscular man wearing bib overalls came out. A native American, his skin was red as copper, his eyes as dark as his long black hair.

"Mr. Goldstein," he said as we got out of the cart. "Good to have you back."

"Good to see you, too, Joe." Morgan offered his hand, which the man shook without hesitation; I'd become so used to bows that this simple gesture came as a surprise. Morgan turned to us. "Allow me to introduce you . . . Carlos Montero, the President of the Coyote Federation, his wife, Wendy Gunther, and their aide, Chris Levin. My friends, Joseph Walking Star Cassidy."

Cassidy nodded, then without another word he sauntered over to us. Carlos offered his hand, but for a moment Cassidy didn't accept it. Instead, he simply stared at my husband, a long and unblinking gaze as if he was searching for something in Carlos's eyes. Carlos didn't say anything; he stared back at him. For nearly a minute, neither man moved or said anything.

"Yeah, I knew it," Cassidy said at last, not looking away from my husband. "You're the eagle. You've got his soul." He clasped Carlos's hand in both of his own, gave it a hard squeeze; Carlos winced a little, but tried not to show it. "You chose well," Joe said to Morgan as he released Carlos, then he turned to the rest of us. "C'mon, let's go inside. Got something to show you."

Carlos glanced at me, but said nothing as he followed Cassidy to the door. Chris followed him, but I hung back a step to touch Morgan's arm. "Mind telling me what that was all about?" I whispered.

"Sorry," he murmured. "Perhaps I should have warned you. Joe's a Navajo. A shaman, in fact. He has . . . well, a certain way of doing things."

The shed's interior was cool and dark, filled with the rank scent of hay, manure, and animal sweat. My eyes were still adjusting to the gloom when Joe flipped a switch on the wall; lights along the ceiling came to life, and now I saw dozens of stalls, arranged in two long rows on either side of a sawdust-covered dirt floor. Bridles and reins hung from support posts, and well-worn saddles were slung across low beams just above our heads.

A loud snort from the stall next to me; I looked around to see a chestnut mare regarding me with solemn brown eyes. Just as startled as I was, she hastily backed away, tossing her mane as her hooves shuffled against the sawdust. It had been many years since the last time I'd seen a horse, but old instincts came back to me. "Hey, easy, easy," I said quietly. "It's okay, girl. You just surprised me, that's all."

The mare eyed me for a few seconds, probably trying to decide whether to trust a stranger. "Here," Cassidy said, stepping forward to give me a piece of dried apricot he'd taken from his pocket. "She'll like this. You feed her by—"

"I know. Thanks." Spreading my palm open, I placed the apricot slice in the center of my hand, then reached over the wooden gate. "C'mon, girl . . . I want to be friends." The horse gazed at me for another few seconds, then reluctantly ventured closer, tempted by the treat. Her coarse lips gently came down upon my hand, then she nibbled at the fruit, and allowed me to stroke the small white star on her nose.

"That's Lady Jane." Cassidy reached past me to give her a scratch between the ears. "She's sometimes skittish, but I guess she likes you." He looked at me. "You've been around horses before."

"A little." When I was a teenager, after my father had sent me off to a government youth hostel, I'd spent time cleaning out the stables at Camp Schaefly. One of the counselors had even given me a few riding lessons, but that ended when he'd tried to take advantage of what I'd first thought was kindness. "She's a sweetheart . . . Tennessee walker, right?"

"Uh-huh. So's Lord Jim, her mate." The equerry nodded toward the stallion in the next stall. "They're a matched pair . . . get one, take the other for free."

"In fact, they're all yours," Morgan said quietly. "Every single one."

"What?" I stared at him. "What are you . . . are you serious?"

"Very much so." Morgan strolled down the aisle, passing stalls occupied by horses that either watched us with equine curiosity or placidly munched at hay. "I told you I had a gift for your world. This is it. Quarter horses, Kentucky thoroughbreds, Percherons, Appaloosas, Arabians, Morgans, Shetlands, even a couple of donkeys . . . a little bit of everything, forty-eight in all. Some colts and fillies, of course, but all are good breeding stock. My most prized possessions. And yes, you heard me right . . . they're yours."

"And you want to . . . ?" Carlos's face showed astonished disbelief. "I don't understand . . . you say you just want to . . . ?"

"Give them to you. That's what I said." Morgan reached into a stall to gently stroke the neck of a dappled Appaloosa pony. "They're my most prized possession, so believe me when I tell you this isn't a casual gift. You're taking something very precious to me."

"I . . . I don't . . ."

"Whatever you're going to say next, please do not let it be 'no.'" Morgan rested against the gate. "Let me explain. So far as I know, this is the last known breeding stock known to exist. Most of their kind are virtually extinct, save for DNA samples. Starvation, heat stroke, disease . . . many have even been slaughtered for food. I've spent much of my fortune locating the survivors, bringing them here, keeping them alive."

He stopped. "For all intents and purposes, they're the last. In fact, you could say the same for Joe himself. It took almost as much effort to locate him as it did to find Billy here." He fondly patted the nose of the pony who nuzzled his shoulder in search of attention. "But they can't stay here much longer. You've seen how bad things have become, and I have no doubt that they'll get worse. On Coyote, they'd have a fighting chance. Maybe they can do what they're supposed to do, instead of spending the rest of their lives cooped up in this shed."

"But how are we supposed to get them to Coyote?" Chris stared at the dozens of horses standing within the stalls around us. "I mean, c'mon . . ."

"You've got the Alliance on your side, and you've negotiated an agreement with the Union. That'll do for a start." Morgan nodded in the direction of the landing field. "Shuttles can land there, and my vet tells me that if the horses are sedated and well-braced for the ride to orbit, we can load them aboard the *Drake*. It's a risk, certainly, and we may well lose a few in transit, but . . ."

"I don't know." Carlos rubbed at the back of his head. "I mean, I appreciate what you're trying to do, I just don't know if horses would be able to adapt to—"

"Of course they can." Cassidy walked forward, his hands in his back pockets. "I've seen the pictures of your planet. Grasslands, mountains, plains . . . everything they've lost here, you've got there. Adaptation has never been a problem for horses. In the Sixth World, they'd survive very well."

"Come again?" I asked. "The Sixth World?"

"There's a story among my people, about how we came to be here . . . this place, the Fifth World." Cassidy leaned against Lord Jim's stall. "You see, First Man and First Woman weren't born here, but in the First World, which they shared with Coyote . . . the trickster, the one you named your planet after. But that place was too small for them, and there was nothing but darkness, so they migrated to the Second World, where they found the Sun and the Moon . . ."

"That's all very interesting, Joe," Morgan said, "but I don't see how—"

"Bear with me, please." Cassidy held up a hand. "But then Sun tried to rape First Woman, so they had to move again. This time, Coyote took First Man and First Woman to the Third World, which was larger than the last two worlds, and there First Man and First Woman found a place of mountains and cool lakes. There were more humans there, so they had many children with them, and it seemed as if they'd be happy. But it turned out that the Third World was ruled by Tieholtsodi, the water monster. One day, Coyote happened to find his children, and he liked them so much that he wrapped them in his blanket and stole them away. When he discovered that his children were missing, Tieholtsodi became so angry that he flooded the Third World, and so the People were forced to leave again."

Cassidy scuffed at the packed dirt floor with the toe of his boot. "They built boats of reeds, and loaded all their children and animals aboard, and when the waters rose they were lifted into the sky, where they found the Fourth World. This, too, was a green and prosperous land, and again it seemed as if the People would be happy. But then men and women began to argue over who was in charge . . . who was responsible for planting crops, who was responsible for hunting, and so forth . . . and they got so carried away with their quarrels that nothing got done. The crops failed and the animals began to die, and soon the Fourth World, too, became un-inhabitable.

"So once again, Coyote had them build reed boats, and once they did, he led them to another place, and that was here . . . the Fifth World. But by then Tieholtsodi had discovered where the People had fled and came after them, and when he found the People he told them that he'd destroy their world again unless his children were freed. So the People opened their packs and showed Tieholtsodi everything that they'd carried with them, until fi-nally only Coyote was left. He unrolled his blanket and revealed the mon-ster's children. Tieholtsodi took his children back and left us alone, and that's how we came to live in the Fifth World."

Attracted by the sound of his voice, Lord Jim prodded Cassidy's shoul-der with his nose. "I know what you're thinking," Cassidy went on, reach-ing back to stroke the stallion's coarse brown mane. "Just an old injun legend, right? But what it means is that people . . . mine, yours, everyone else's . . . never stay in one place for very long. We run out of room, the sun gets too hot, the waters too high. That, or we fight with each other, or the monsters appear. Whatever the reason, sooner or later, we have to leave."

He paused. "Now it's that time again. Time to build the boats and pack up the animals, and follow Coyote to another world."

No one said anything. We'd fallen quiet while Joe told his story; now the meaning of the Navajo myth was beginning to sink in. We'd been so engrossed in the finer points of diplomacy, the paragraphs and subclauses of international treaties and trade agreements, that we'd all but forgotten that greater things were at stake. Humankind, along with its predecessors, had inhabited Earth for millions of years, yet our time was over. The waters were rising and there were monsters among us. We had to leave.

Carlos cleared his throat. "Maybe we can work something out," he said softly, taking my hand. "If we can build stables in Liberty so that . . ."

The door creaked open just then, and Mike Kennedy reappeared. There was a worried look on his face; without a word, Goldstein excused himself and headed outside. Cassidy waited until the door shut behind him, then he turned back to us. "Glad to hear that, but I kinda doubt anyone there knows much about taking care of horses." He caught my eye. "No offense intended, ma'am, but—"

"No, I agree." I stepped over to Lady Jane's stall, petted her neck. This time she didn't shy away from me. "All I know is how to muck out stalls. We've got shags . . . sort of like water buffalo . . . but we're going to need someone there who's got more experience with horses than I do." I gave him a sidelong glance. "Got a suggestion for someone who might want to bring these guys to Coyote?"

Cassidy's expression remained stoical, but a corner of his mouth ticked ever so slightly. "As a matter of fact . . ."

The door swung open again; we looked around as Morgan marched back into the shed. There was an expression on his face I hadn't seen before: anger, like someone who'd just been threatened and wasn't about to back down. "All right, fun's over," he said. "Time for you to get out of here, fast."

"What's going on?" Carlos asked. "Have we done something wrong?"

"You, no . . . me, maybe." Morgan took a deep breath. "One of my people in Atlanta just learned that the government has issued warrants for your arrest. Appears that, even though I'd cleared this side-trip with the WHU embassy in London, the police have been given instructions to take you into custody as soon as you arrive in Atlanta on charges of customs violation."

"Customs violation?" I was stunned. "But we were told we had—"

"Diplomatic immunity, of course. And you're also official guests of Patriarch Amado." Morgan shook his head. "Nonetheless, you're to be detained until further notice."

"What?" Carlos was just as shocked as I was. "But they can't do that! They—"

"Shut up and listen." Morgan's voice was cold. "My contacts got the whole story. The government wants to use customs violations as an excuse to lock the three of you away. Apparently someone high up wasn't satisfied with the deal you made in London. That, or Marcos set you up for a double cross. Either way, as soon as you arrive in Atlanta—"

"We're under arrest." Carlos's face was grim. "Let me guess . . . we'd be held until our government negotiates our release. And that, of course, would mean fine-tuning the trade agreement a little more in their favor."

"I don't know the details, but yeah, that sounds about right." Frustrated, Morgan pounded a fist against a post. "Damn it, I thought I had this whole thing worked out. They weren't supposed to—"

"You say a shuttle can land here?" Chris asked.

"Yeah, it can, but my cruiser can . . ." Morgan looked at the satphone Chris had taken from his pocket. "What's that?"

Chris didn't reply; he was already punching in the emergency prefix Dieter had given him. "Mike, tell your people to get word to Atlanta that we'll be there soon. Tell 'em to say that . . . I dunno, we're looking at horses."

"Don't say that!" Morgan's face went pale. "No one knows about them!"

"All right, then tell him we're having lunch. Dinner. Whatever. Just stall for time." Chris turned away from us; clasping the phone to his face, he murmured something we couldn't hear.

"Do it," Morgan said. Kennedy nodded, then hurried out of the shed. "That should buy us an hour or two. I'll have the field cleared for a shuttle touchdown."

I nodded. It would be close, no doubt about it, but with any luck an EA shuttle would be here before anyone. And I was more confident about making our getaway aboard an Alliance shuttle than Morgan's aerocruiser; the former could make a quick sprint for space, while the latter could be forced down by military aircraft.

"Sorry your trip has to end this way," Morgan said. "Believe me, this wasn't what I'd planned."

Carlos nodded, then he put a hand around my waist. "Don't worry about it," he said, giving both of us an unexpected smile. "This isn't the first time."

I tried not to laugh, but I couldn't help it. Once again, we were fleeing Earth, just one step ahead of the law.

Two days later, we were back on Highgate.

Little more than an hour after Chris made his call, an ESA military shuttle touched down on the landing field at Morgan's farm. Our rescue was a covert operation; the shuttle was a stealth spacecraft with chameleon outer-plating that allowed it to become virtually invisible, its crew trained for black-ops missions such as this. The pilot didn't even cut his engines; a couple of soldiers hustled Carlos, Chris, and me aboard, and we'd barely had a chance to buckle our harnesses before the bat-like craft took off again. Once the shuttle reached high orbit, it rendezvoused with a freighter bound for Highgate. The ride back to L1 was twice as long as the one to Earth, and the freighter's passenger cabin was considerably less comfortable than the one we'd enjoyed aboard the *Von Braun*, but it was far better than the treatment we would have received in Atlanta.

Besides, the long ride allowed the EA to concoct an alibi for our abrupt disappearance. While being shown around Morgan Goldstein's farm, it seemed that I had the misfortune of being bitten by a mosquito. Since none of us had been vaccinated for malaria—a lie; we'd received inoculations before leaving Highgate—and the hospitals in the area had been closed for some time, it seemed only prudent that we return to England at once, so that I could receive proper medical attention. To back up our story, Morgan even sent his aerocruiser back across the Atlantic. It was later announced that the Coyote delegation had decided to leave immediately for Highgate, in order to prevent being placed in quarantine before returning to our world.

As cover stories went, this one was pretty lame, yet the Union wasn't about to call our bluff. If they had, the Alliance could have produced their own intelligence reports regarding our planned arrest, and that would have been even more embarrassing. So we made apologies for cutting short our trip, and they expressed sympathy for my condition; no further questions were asked, and no more lies were given.

As it turned out, though, our sudden departure didn't hurt our mission. The day after we returned to Highgate, the U.N. General Assembly voted in favor of formally recognizing the Coyote Federation. There was a last-minute objection from the Western Hemisphere Union—Patriarch Amado wanted the World Court to take up the issue of the *Alabama*'s hijacking—but that was overruled by the Secretary-General as a historical event that had little to do with current issues. The Union therefore abstained from the final vote, but otherwise it was unanimous.

Some people are just sore losers. It didn't stop us from opening a bottle of champagne. But we also decided that it would be a long time before the Coyote Federation signed any trade or immigration agreements with the WHU.

Carlos and I spent our remaining time aboard Highgate in the EA diplomatic suite, engaged in teleconference meetings with representatives from the various countries with whom we'd negotiated tentative agreements. While the *Von Braun* was being prepped for its trip to 47 Ursae Majoris through Starbridge Earth, thousands of pages of documents were transmitted to us; we went through each one, signed the less binding ones, and put aside the rest for the Colonial Council to ratify. In the meantime, we also received dozens of personal gifts—cases of wine, sculptures and paintings, rare books, clothes and jewelry—that we accepted on behalf of the Federation, then sent away to be packed aboard the *Von Braun*.

Dieter Vogel returned to Highgate, with a surprising bit of news: his government had asked him to be the European Alliance ambassador to Coyote. We gladly accepted his latest diplomatic post, and that called for another bottle of champagne to be uncorked: Coyote had its first official envoy from Earth.

Another surprise came only a few hours later, when Dieter's aide—soon to be former aide, since he refused to leave Highgate—escorted an old friend to our suite. Anastasia Tereshkova arrived wearing a new uniform, this time with a different patch on her right shoulder; she'd been reassigned as commanding officer of the *Francis Drake*, pending completion of its shakedown run. After that, her primary mission would be to ferry passengers and cargo between Earth and Coyote. Ana also told us that, although Highgate would be home port for the *Drake*, she'd been allowed to have a residence on Coyote.

The only sour note came when Ana told us that she and Gabriel Pacino had decided to end their relationship, both professional and personal. Pacino wanted his own command, and once the *Drake*'s sister ship was christened, it was likely he'd be commissioned as its captain. But more than that, she'd discovered that her first officer had informed their superiors that Carlos had once been a guerilla known as Rigil Kent; she thought this piece of information was something that her government didn't need to know about the President of the Coyote Federation. That solved the mystery of how Marcos Amado had learned about Carlos's role in the revolution. One more thing we'd also have to get used to: espionage as a form of diplomacy.

Yet that was the least of our concerns. We spent one more night aboard Highgate; Chris accepted an invitation from the Pacific Coalition consulate to attend a zero-g handball game, but Carlos and I declined as graciously as we could. Instead, we unplugged all the phones and screens, then spent the evening making love while moonlight streamed through the windows of our bedroom. For a few hours, no one bothered us. No receptions or trade negotiations, no ambassadors or envoys. Just two people lonely for each other's company, even though we'd never been apart.

The next morning, with Dieter Vogel at our side, we boarded the *Von Braun* and made our departure from Highgate. I didn't look back at the station as the yacht slipped out of Alpha Dock and fell away from the Moon; I was tired, and all I wanted was to go home. Yet as the starbridge grew close, and the pilot announced the countdown to hyperspace insertion, I craned my neck to peer through the porthole by my seat, searching for one last glimpse of Earth.

My window faced the wrong direction. All I saw were stars, and the darkness of space. Perhaps it was just as well. I was one of Tieholtsodi's children, being carried away from the Fifth World to the Sixth.

Coyote was my stepfather now. This time, I'd never leave.

Part 6

QUARTET FOR FOUR SEASONS

1. WINTER HORSES (BARCHIEL 37, C.Y. 14)

The approaching starship resembled a storm cloud as it passed over the Great Equatorial River, its smooth grey hull casting a long shadow across the waters. Then the roar of its descent engines reached the crowd; they nervously stepped back from the ropes separating them from the landing field, and watched the enormous vessel as it came closer, gradually increasing in size until it seemed to fill the sky above them.

When it was little more than five hundred feet above the ground, the ship's stern swung around, making a graceful ninety-degree turn that oriented its tapered bow toward the river, as recessed hatches along the underside peeled open to allow landing gear to unfold. By now the sound of its engines was so loud that everyone clasped their hands over their ears; awestruck, they watched the giant vessel as it slowly made its descent. A hot blast whipped snow from the grassy field, and in the last moments before touchdown, the starship was lost within a thin white haze. Then the ground quivered beneath their feet as the vessel came to rest, and cheers rose from the crowd when they realized the leviathan had landed.

Carlos waited until he heard the engines being cut back before he removed his hands from his ears. Although he'd known that the *Francis Drake* was capable of atmospheric entry, until this moment he'd thought it impossible that a spacecraft this big could be safely brought to the ground. Yet there it was: nearly six hundred feet long, its streamlined hull faintly scorched here and there, like a mountain that had come from the sky.

"Take a good look," Dieter Vogel said quietly. "You probably won't see something like that too often . . . if ever again."

"You don't think so?" Carlos asked, and Vogel shook his head. "But if they can do it once—"

"Too risky." Vogel shoved his gloved hands in the pockets of his parka, stamped his boots on the frozen ground. "And certainly not very efficient.

The trick isn't getting something this big to land. The trick is getting it to take off again. It'll take almost a week for the fuel converters to extract enough atmospheric hydrogen to fill the port and starboard tanks, and they'll burn every liter of it just get to back into orbit."

"Then why—?"

"To demonstrate that it can be done." Then he glanced at Carlos, gave him a wink. "And, just incidentally, to impress your people."

Whether or not he was serious, Carlos didn't know. He didn't respond, though, but instead turned to gaze across New Brighton's landing field. When it became apparent that Shuttlefield wouldn't be large enough to handle the anticipated flow of passengers and freight—the *Drake*'s maiden flight had proved that, one month ago—the Council decided to grant the European Alliance's request to establish a new colony, provided that it also serve as a colonial spaceport. Alliance surveyors scouted several possible locations, and finally settled upon the north shore of a small subcontinent across the Great Equatorial River from both Great Dakota and New Florida. Albion had the disadvantage of being on the other side of the equator, but it also enjoyed a couple of advantages; its equatorial location made it a prime spot for a large-scale spaceport, and its proximity to the river made it ideal for keelboats and barges traveling south from the northern colonies.

There wasn't much to New Brighton—a dozen or so log cabins, a meeting hall still under construction, a paddock for livestock and a couple of inflatable domes that served as temporary greenhouses until permanent ones could be built—yet Carlos had little doubt that would change soon enough. The presence of the spaceport alone would assure that the colony would grow very quickly. Although the Coyote Federation had imposed strict immigration limits—no more than a thousand new settlers per colony in a twelve-month period—it wouldn't be long before more ships began to arrive through the starbridge.

"We're impressed," he said, "but this can't be the only reason why you asked me to fly down here." Vogel had arrived last month to assume his post as the Alliance ambassador; the EA consulate was located in Liberty, but he'd spent the last two weeks in New Brighton, overseeing preparations for the *Drake*'s arrival. Carlos glanced at his watch, thought about the gyro pilot waiting nearby. "If you've got something to show me . . ."

"I think they're ready to open the hatch." Vogel smiled. "If you'll lead the way, please?"

Carlos sauntered toward the safety barrier. The Proctor keeping the crowd away from the landing site recognized them immediately; he lifted the rope to allow them through. The engine-blast had melted the snow in a hundred-yard radius around the ship, and their boots stuck to the mud of the flash-thawed ground beneath. Eventually, Carlos mused, this entire area would have to be paved. Perhaps some walkways, too, and maybe even a control tower.

As they approached the *Drake,* Carlos saw that a long ramp was being lowered from the cargo hatch on the forward section. Several crew members had disembarked; Ana Tereshkova was among them, and Carlos walked over to her. "Welcome back, Captain," he said. "Hope you had a good flight."

Hearing him, Ana turned around. "Mr. President," she said, giving him a warm smile. "What a pleasant surprise."

"Thanks, but I'm no longer president. My term expired at the end of last month—"

"You're not?" Ana stopped smiling. "And you didn't run for reelection?"

"One term's enough, thank you. Besides, it's hard to run against your own wife." Carlos couldn't help but grin when her mouth dropped open. "Wendy's in charge now. I gave her my endorsement, of course."

"Of course. But I wonder how her opponents must have felt about that."

"There were none. She ran unopposed." Vogel shook his head. "Apparently politics here aren't as . . . shall we say, competitive . . . as they are back home."

Carlos decided to let the remark pass. He'd seen enough of Earth-style politics to last a lifetime. "The landing was magnificent," he said. "Your crew put on a real show."

"Thank you, but I doubt this will be a common occurrence. We mainly wanted to make sure that the *Drake* was capable of making landfall. From now on, it'll probably remain in orbit while we use shuttles instead." She glanced at Vogel. "Besides, as Dieter has doubtless told you, we have precious cargo aboard. Direct descent seemed prudent in this instance."

"Precious?" Carlos looked at him. "You didn't—"

"Forgive me. I wanted it to be a surprise." A sly smile. "Although this shouldn't be one, really. After all, you already knew it was coming."

Carlos was still taking this in when he heard the clomp of hooves against bare metal. Turning around, he looked up to see someone leading a chestnut mare to the open hatch of the *Drake*'s cargo bay. The horse had blinders attached on either side of its bridle and a thick wool blanket; as the man holding the reins gently coaxed the animal toward the ramp, Carlos recognized him as Joe Cassidy, the equerry from Morgan Goldstein's estate in Massachusetts.

And then Goldstein himself suddenly appeared, with his bodyguard, Mike Kennedy, close behind. Spotting Carlos, the entrepreneur raised a hand in greeting, then the two men stepped around Cassidy and the horse to make their way down the ramp. About halfway down, Morgan suddenly stopped, apparently savoring his first look at Coyote. Then, mindful that important people were waiting for him, he continued the rest of the way down the ramp to the ground.

"My God," he murmured, his eyes wide with unabashed delight, "I can't believe how fresh the air is. And how beautiful . . ."

"Glad you approve," Carlos said evenly. "We had it made just for you."

The others chuckled, and even Kennedy briefly smiled. Morgan turned red for a moment, but then grinned at the joke made at his expense. "Thank you very much. Nice planet you've got here. Care to sell?"

Vogel laughed at this, but Carlos felt a touch of irritation. From the corner of his eye, he noted a frown on Ana's face; apparently she didn't appreciate Morgan's attempt at humor any more than he did. Yet if his term as president had taught him anything, it was the art of diplomacy. "Not really," he said dryly, then he glanced up at the cargo hatch, where Cassidy was still trying to lead the reluctant mare to the ramp. "I knew you were coming soon, but this—"

"We decided it was better to bring them sooner than later." Zipping up the front of his parka, Morgan pulled gloves from his pockets. "Seems that the Proletariat isn't very pleased with me just now. In fact, they've taken it upon themselves to annex my farm . . . for the welfare of the people, of course." He let out his breath in disgust, its steam rising from his mouth. "They can take my land, but I'll be damned if I'll give 'em my horses, too."

"But how . . . ?"

"I signed papers bequeathing the entire herd to the Federation. Once I did that, the Union couldn't touch them. At least not without a legal fight, and I didn't give their magistrates time to find a loophole."

"Two of our heavy-lift shuttles landed at his estate three days ago," Ana explained. "By then we'd outfitted the *Drake* with temporary stalls. Once the horses were sedated and blindered, my people loaded them onto the shuttles and transported them directly to the ship." She gazed at the mare Cassidy was carefully leading down the ramp. "I was worried how they'd handle the trip, but they managed to do better than I expected. A few of them are pretty skittish, but—"

"You've got forty-eight horses aboard?" Carlos felt his face lose color. He turned to stare at Morgan. "Have you lost your mind? It's the middle of winter. How do you expect to feed them until—"

"We brought as much hay as we could," Morgan said. "Three hundred bales. Should last them another month or two. By then, I expect you'll have found good homes for them within the colonies. A few here, a few there."

"But we're not prepared for—"

"You'd rather that we left 'em behind?" By then, Joe Cassidy had managed to lead the horse down the ramp. Stroking her mane to sooth her, he brought the mare over to them. "They've been very brave, Mr. President. Just as courageous as your own people have been. The least you can do is welcome them to their new home."

Carlos was about to object when he took a closer look at the mare. He couldn't be sure, but it looked like the same one Wendy had befriended while they were on Earth. "Is that . . . ?"

"Uh-huh. Lady Jane." Morgan took the reins from Cassidy, led the horse a little closer. "Lord Jim's aboard, too. They're yours now. My gift to your family." He paused. "If you'll accept them, of course."

The horse was still glassy-eyed from dope and the transition through hyperspace, and each step she took was tentative, as if trying to cope with the lighter gravity, the more rarified air. Yet she demurely allowed Carlos to pet her nose and didn't protest when Cassidy handed the reins to him. Another refugee, just as he'd been many years ago.

"Yeah, all right." How could he refuse? "Thank you. We'll find a way."

"I'm sure you will." Morgan took the reins back from Carlos and handed them to Cassidy. "And thank you, sir, for your hospitality," he added quietly. "I'm certain that we'll find our arrangement to be mutually beneficial."

It took Carlos a moment to realize what Morgan was saying. "You're immigrating? Now?"

"Do I have much choice? But I think you'll find that the Union's loss will be your gain." Taking Carlos by the arm, Morgan began to lead him away. "Now, if you don't mind, we have some other affairs that need to be discussed."

2. Spring Encounters (Ambriel 62, c.y. 14)

How far they'd traveled, or in which direction, he didn't know. From the moment he was captured, he'd been at their mercy; he'd managed to put up a good fight, and the knuckles of his right hand were still sore from the punch he'd delivered to the jaw of the biggest one, but they outnumbered him by four to one, and in the end they'd won. They'd lashed his wrists together behind his back and thrown a burlap sack that smelled of old potatoes over his head, and then two of them had picked him up and thrown him belly-down over the back of a shag. Then the long ride into the night had begun.

At least the boy got away. The knowledge that whatever these men had in store for him—and he had little doubt that it would be unpleasant— wouldn't be inflicted upon the boy as well gave him some small comfort. It was just luck that he'd managed to escape when the ambush occurred. Yet he was still trying to figure out how the men would've known where they'd be when he heard his rider give a low whistle, then pull back on the reins.

The shag snorted, then came to a halt. Around him, he heard the soft creak of leather as his abductors dismounted from their own animals. The bag over his head had robbed him of most of his sight, yet through the coarse fabric he could make out the flickering glow of firelight, and his nose picked up the faint odor of woodsmoke. A bonfire.

Someone grabbed him by the back of his belt, hauled him off the shag. Ugly laughter as he fell to the ground; he tried not to yelp as his right knee struck a rock. Then someone nearby said something he could barely make out—"Get him up, bring him over here"—and two pairs of hands grasped his shoulders and hauled him to his feet. Stumbling, his boots shuffling through dry leaves and twigs, he was pushed and pulled a dozen feet or so until he felt the dry heat of the bonfire against his clothes.

"Stop," one of the men said, and he halted. "Now sit."

Not knowing where or how, he hesitated. A fist rammed into his stomach. He gasped as his knees buckled beneath him, and he collapsed into the wicker chair that magically appeared behind him.

"Dumbass," the same man said. "I told you to sit."

More laughter, even more cruel than before. Pain lanced through his wrists as the rope sliced into his skin; although he was seated, his posture forced him to bend slightly forward. Taking deep breaths, trying not to retch, he fought to remain calm, yet there was a low roar in his ears as his heart hammered against his chest.

"All right," said the first voice, "take off his hood."

Someone behind him grabbed the top of the sack, ripped it from his head. He blinked a few times, blinded by the fire that snapped and burned only a few feet away. A half dozen men—loggers from the looks of them, big and tough-looking—stood in a semicircle around a stone-ringed fire pit. And on the other side of the fire, seated in a worn-out wicker chair with a jug of bearshine on a rickety wooden table beside him, was Lars Thompson.

"Howdy, Mr. Parson," he said. "Nice night for a cookout, ain't it?"

A couple of men chuckled at this. Although he was tempted to remain quiet, Parson knew that silence wouldn't get him anywhere. "At least it isn't raining," he replied. "Think the sun will come out tomorrow, or—?"

A sudden impact against the left side of his skull, as the man standing beside him slapped him across his head. "Just answer the question."

Parson tasted something like warm copper; he'd bitten his tongue. He spit out blood. "Yeah, sure . . . it'll do."

"Uh-huh." Thompson picked up the jug and pulled out its cork. "Mighty nice night for a fire. And for a little talk, too, wouldn't you say?"

"If you insist."

Another slap, this one almost hard enough to knock Parson from his chair. "Cut it out, James," Thompson said. "I think our friend gets the idea. Just a straight talk, man-to-man, y'know what I mean?" He was looking straight at Parson as he said this, and Parson reluctantly nodded. "Outstanding. I think we've opened the way to a deep and meaningful dialogue."

Parson didn't reply. He'd come to realize that anything he said was grounds for another beating. Not that it mattered very much; this place was somewhere deep in the woods of Mt. Shapiro, several miles from the logging camp, and he was among men who had no pity for him. Begging for mercy was out of the question, for they obviously had none to spare. They could cut his throat and bury him in an unmarked grave, and no one would ever know.

"Parson," Thompson said. "Jonathan Parson. First officer . . . . no, wait, second officer of the *Columbus*. At least until you decided to go native." He tilted back the jug, chugged some bearshine, wiped his mouth with the back of his hand. "Bet you'd love to know how I know this, don'cha?"

Parson remained silent. Thompson stared at him, waiting for a response; getting none, he handed the jug to the nearest man. "Maybe I'm not making myself clear. We know who you are, and we know what you're trying to do. We caught you down by the dam tonight, on your way to try to knock it down again. You had someone with you, but they got away. You didn't, though, and that's what counts."

There was no sense in trying to deny any of this. They knew who he was, just as they knew that he'd been responsible for an earlier attempt to sabotage the spill-dam used to flood the log flume. How they'd arrived at such information was of little consequence just now. The only thing that mattered right now was getting out of here alive.

Parson was still trying to figure out how to talk his way out of this—or, failing that, somehow make an escape—when he heard a faint rustle from the trees behind them. It could have only been an errant breeze stirring the limbs of the mountain rough bark, yet James apparently heard it, too, for he nervously stepped away from him. Now was his chance; Parson cast a wary glance to the right. No one standing there. If he lunged straight for the trees, running as fast as he could, he might be able to . . .

"Keep an eye on him, now." Thompson's voice was calm yet mildly amused. "Our boy's thinking about making a break for it." He idly picked up a stick, used it to stir the fire. "Not that it'll do you much good. We use this camp for huntin', so trust me when I tell you we're miles and miles from anywhere else. No witnesses, no one to hear us." He grinned. "Just you and us, son. You and us."

James returned to Parson's side. He laid a rough hand on his shoulder, pulled him back against the chair. The jug finished making its way around the circle, returned to Thompson; he took another swig, put it back on the table again. "Now, just as I know you're thinking about running away, I also know you think we're planning to kill you. And believe me, we could, and no one would be the wiser. Hell, so far as your own crew's concerned, you're probably just a skeleton, rotting away God knows where."

He shook his head. "But that wouldn't serve no good purpose, now would it? Besides, the way I figure it, all you need is a good lesson. Some proper instruction about trespassing on other people's private property. 'Cause, y'see, this whole mountain belongs to the family business, and I'll be damned if—"

"You don't own this mountain," Parson said.

"Say what?" Thompson cocked his head. "Come again? I don't think I heard you quite right."

Too late, Parson realized that he shouldn't have spoken. Until now, his silence had been his only defense. Yet he'd let his anger get the better of him, and he'd unwisely blurted out his thoughts. But he couldn't take back what he'd said, so he might as well make a stand. "This mountain doesn't belong to you," he went on. "You're just visitors. You've no right to ruin—"

"Aw, dammit, Lars, do we have to listen to this crap?" The logger standing next to Thompson impatiently stamped his boots against the ground. "It's cold. I don't want to spend all night out here."

"Yup. Time's a-wasting. But lemme just make one more point before we get down to brass tacks." Lars picked up the jug, took another sip. "Mr. Parson, I don't give a swamper's ass who you think this mountain belongs to. Last week my family cut a deal with some people back home . . . Earth, that is . . . for the purchase of as much timber as we can cut and carry. That means we stand to make a lot of money, and I'll be damned if I'm going to let you or anyone else get in the way."

He picked up the cork, inserted it into the neck of the jug, slapped it down firmly with the heel of his hand. "Now, I bet you've been wondering all this time how we knew where to find you, and what your story is. And I'd hate to leave you with any lingering questions, so before we get started, I just want to show you that blood runs thicker than water."

He looked past Parson. "Hawk? Come on out now."

Parson felt something grow cold in his chest. He turned his head, saw the boy step out of the darkness behind him, another logger beside him. Hawk was clearly frightened, but the fact that the boy couldn't meet his eye was worse than anything these men had planned for him.

"I'm sorry," Hawk whispered. "I'm so sorry."

Hawk had led him into the ambush. He'd told his father everything he knew about Jonathan Parson; the reasons he'd done so didn't matter, except perhaps that Lars Thompson was right. Blood was thicker than water, and in the end he'd been forced to make a choice.

"It's all right," Parson murmured. "You did what you—"

"That's enough," Thompson said. "James?"

James grabbed the back of Parson's jacket, wrenched him to his feet, then kicked the chair out of the way. Parson had only a second to steel himself before the nearest logger came forward and, pulling back his arm, drove his fist deep into his stomach. Parson's breath exploded from his lungs, but he'd barely doubled over when another fist came straight at his mouth.

"Stop!" Hawk yelled. "You promised you wouldn't!"

Yet it didn't stop, for now the men had begun to take turns—two men holding him while the others worked him over—and soon Hawk's voice came to him from a vast distance, like a fuzzed-out radio signal from a faraway world. Somewhere along the line, he lost his right front tooth; not long after that, his left eye swelled up and closed. By then, though, his pain had become a symphony; he was incapable of distinguishing which part of his body hurt more than the other. Soon they were no longer bothering to try to hold him up, but simply kicked at him as he lay upon the cold ground.

In his last moments of consciousness, before the darkness closed in upon him, he caught a glimpse of something through the blood that seeped down in front of his face. There, among the high branches of a nearby tree, tiny eyes reflected the firelight as they silently bore witness to his ordeal.

He wasn't alone . . .

3. Summer Fires (Hamaliel 12, c.y. 14)

The smoke could be seen from many miles away, a thick brown column that billowed up from the burning grasslands, rising high into the blue morning sky before the wind caused it to flatten out like the anvilhead of a thundercloud. From the distance, it vaguely resembled a tornado, except that the destruction below was more widespread than even a twister could cause.

Susan bit the inside of her lip as the gyro came closer, its pilot bringing in the aircraft for a low sweep over Albion's coastal savannah. Through the thick haze, she could make out tiny figures moving along the periphery of the fire zone, using flamethrowers to put high grass to the torch. New Brighton was protected by the long trench that had been dug as a firebreak; otherwise, the rest of the savannah was being set ablaze. The fires would continue, day in and day out, until everything that lay within their path would be consumed. Acres upon acres of sourgrass, spider bush, ball plants, stands of faux birch and blackwood . . . all wiped out, with methodical indiscrimination.

"Some people down there," the pilot said, his voice in her headset breaking her train of thought. He pointed through the cockpit's glass canopy. "See 'em?"

Susan looked in the direction he indicated. Not far from the trench, a half mile upwind of the fire, she spotted a handful of figures standing beside a tent. A couple of skimmers were parked nearby, including one cargo flatbed, yet that wasn't their sole means of transportation; a few hundred yards in either direction of the camp, men on horseback patrolled the edge of the fire, maintaining a careful distance from the inferno.

"Set me down there," Susan said, pointing to the camp. "I'm going to have some words with these clowns."

The pilot gave her a dubious look, but didn't say a word as he pushed the yoke forward. The aircraft yawed to the left, then glided downward, its nacelles tilting upward as the props shifted to descent mode. Dust and scorched grass tapped lightly against the canopy, then there was a slight bump as the gyro's wheels made contact with the ground.

The stench of burning vegetation hit her as soon as Susan pushed open the passenger hatch, and her eyes started to water before she was ten yards from the gyro. Gagging against the haze, she held a hand against her nose and mouth. Everyone at the command post had seen the gyro come in for a landing; they silently watched as she marched toward them. No one moved to stop her, yet no one offered to help her, either. They knew who she was, and they knew why she was there.

Susan approached the first person she saw, a young man wearing goggles, a bandanna around the lower part of his face. "Who's in charge here?" she demanded, and he pointed to the nearer of the two tents. Not bothering to thank him, she headed toward it.

Rifle shots from not far away. Startled, she turned around, spotted one of the riders pointing a carbine at something in a patch of spider bush that the fire hadn't yet reached. A high-pitched avian screech caused his horse to nervously step back, but the rider kicked the heels of his boots against the animal's sides, then raised his rifle again. He fired once more into the thicket. Another harsh cry, then two more shots brought abrupt silence. Appreciative cheers from the men watching the fire. Susan scowled, then continued walking toward the tent.

The interior was cool and dark; a couple of portable fans had been set up, and several men and women loitered around a folding table covered with maps and aerial photos. A few observed the conflagration through binoculars, while others consulted the maps, coordinating the movements of those in the field and communicating with them via headset radio. No one noticed Susan as she pushed aside the tent flap and stepped inside.

"Who's in charge here?" she demanded.

They turned to gaze at her, but no one spoke. Susan didn't recognize any of them until Morgan Goldstein put down his binoculars and walked over to her. "Ah, Ms. Montero. What a surprise."

"I can't imagine why. You knew I was coming." She made a pretense of snapping her fingers in sudden recollection. "Oh, wait, now I remember.

You weren't supposed to start anything until I arrived. Wasn't that sup-posed to be next Anael, or was it sometime later next week?"

Goldstein shrugged. "My apologies. We decided to go ahead with the controlled burn a little earlier than planned. I know the government wanted to be informed, but—"

"But you decided that the less we knew in advance, the easier this would make things for your guys." Susan was having a hard time control-ling her temper. "Did you really think we wouldn't notice?"

"Susan . . ."

"What the hell do you think you're doing?" She pointed to the long line of fires. "You were supposed to clear just enough to make room for a spaceport, not burn down an entire savannah. From what I can tell, you've already torched two square miles!"

"We have certain requirements."

"Requirements?" She strode over to the table, impatiently pushing aside one of the men. A quick glance at the areas of the maps outlined in red marker confirmed her suspicions. "Good grief, you've got at least four, maybe five square miles marked for clearance!"

"Susan . . ."

"Don't try to play nice with me. You're friends with my folks, but that doesn't mean . . ." On impulse, she snatched up a headset someone had left on the table. "Never mind. I'm calling this off."

Before she could issue any orders—which doubtless would have been ignored anyway—Goldstein laid a hand upon her arm. "Susan, calm down," he said quietly. "Please. You're not doing any good, and you're just making a fool of yourself."

Another crack of a high-powered rifle. Two of the men standing nearby murmured to one another in German; they glanced over their shoulders at her, then one of them chuckled. Without asking, Susan knew what was go-ing on. As the grasslands burned, so, too, did the habitat of every native creature that lived within them. Creek cats, swampers, grasshoarders, swoops . . . and in particular, boids. As they fled the fire, men waited to pick them off, one by one. Horses had given men an advantage above boids in particular; now they could sit up high above the grass where the giant avians lurked, able to see them long before they attacked. And as fast as boids were, a well-trained stallion was even faster.

"We've lost a couple of our people to boids already." As usual, Goldstein was uncannily perceptive. "Creek cats have been a nuisance, too. We can't expand the colony until we've eliminated their nests, and there's only one way we can do that."

"Oh, c'mon . . ." She gestured to the maps. "You're not doing this simply because you want to get rid of boids and cats. Once you've set up perimeter guns—"

"No. No, you're absolutely right. We also need land for crops, for building more houses, for establishing a spaceport."

"This much? What are you planning to do? Build a city?"

"In fact, yes." Morgan smiled as he looked away. "That's exactly what we plan to do."

She looked helplessly at the fountains of brown smoke rising from the grasslands. "You can't do this," she said, forcing herself to calm down. "You signed an agreement."

"The trade agreement the EA signed with the Coyote Federation places limits on immigration and export of raw materials, in exchange for territorial rights." Morgan folded his arms across his chest, his voice assumed a lecturing tone. "There's nothing there about importing raw material from other colonies, or limiting the expansion of our own colony." He gave her a sidelong glance. "Nor does it affect business arrangements made between companies here on Coyote . . . in this case, the one between Janus and Thompson Wood."

Susan's mouth fell open. "You're . . . ?"

"We've been contracted to develop this area on behalf of the EA." Morgan waved a hand at the burning grasslands. "A thousand new colonists a year . . . do you honestly think that they're going to want to live in grass huts or build log cabins when they arrive? Perhaps your parents did, but these people are used to a rather higher standard of living."

So her suspicions had been correct. The European Alliance wasn't content with only a small settlement. Jon had already discovered as much, the night he'd been beaten up by Uncle Lars's men; the last time she'd spoken with him, he was still recovering from his injuries at the farm he shared with Manny Castro. He'd assumed that the EA was purchasing timber from the Thompson Wood Company for export to Earth. So far, though, not so much as a stick had been loaded aboard the cargo transports that rendezvoused with the *Drake* during its now-frequent voyages through the starbridge. Yet seldom did a day pass when barges stacked high with lumber departed from the Clarksburg mills, southbound down the West Channel to the Great Equatorial and, beyond, the coast of Albion.

"As a matter of courtesy, we agreed to let a government representative come down here to witness our operation." Goldstein reached into his shirt pocket, pulled out a piece of cellophane-wrapped candy. "So you're here. I didn't know you worked for the interior department."

"On temporary assignment." No sense in mentioning that the department consisted of exactly six people, including the commissioner and his personal staff. She'd volunteered her services while on summer sabbatical from the university.

"Ah, so." A noncommittal nod. "Any comments?"

"This . . . this is a . . . a disgrace." She struggled to find words for her outrage. "A complete catastrophe. You're destroying thousands of acres of native habitat—"

"On a world with tens of thousands of miles still unexplored." Goldstein unwrapped the candy, popped it into his mouth, let the wrapper fall to the ground. Noticing her expression, he self-consciously bent down to pick it up. "Your objections have been noted. I'll be happy to review your report, if you wish to forward it to me."

From the distance, she could hear more gunshots; the breeze had shifted, wafting more smoke toward the campsite, and she thought she heard of the crackle of the flames. "This isn't the end of this," she murmured.

"Well . . . no, I think it is." Goldstein hesitated, then stepped closer to her. "Susan, I know you're upset, but have a talk with your father. I think he may enlighten you."

She turned to stare at him. "What about my father?"

"Hasn't he told you?" Goldstein gave her a benign smile. "He's one of my major shareholders."

The wind was colder, this close to the top of the mountain. It moaned like a lost spirit as it roamed along the granite bluffs, scattering dry leaves from the branches of the rough bark and faux birch at its base. So late in the afternoon, there was little warmth to be found in the last rays of the autumn sun, now hovering less than a hand's-breadth over the summit. Soon it would be twilight, and the beginning of another long night.

Feeling the chill, Lars pulled up the collar of his shagswool coat. He gazed at the narrow crack within the escarpment, rising along a steep bluff just above the tree line. "This is it?" he asked. "You're sure there's no other way?"

"I'm sure." Hawk pointed to the top of the crevice. "This is the way Jon showed us to get to the ledge." He paused. "It's easier than it looks."

Lars absently sucked at the gap in his teeth where a dentist in Clarksburg had pulled a rotten molar last month. It didn't look easy at all; at least sixty feet, nearly straight up, and he couldn't see the ledge his son indicated. And the light was beginning to fade. If he had any sense, he'd mark this place, then send a couple of his men up here to do the job for them.

"C'mon. You can make it." Hawk cinched the straps of his backpack a little tighter, then stepped over the broken rubble that lay at the bottom of the cliffs. "You said you want to find where they live. Well, here it is."

"Yeah, but . . ."

"You coming?" The boy looked back at him. "Or is this just one more thing you're going to get James to do for you?"

There was contempt in the young man's voice, a mute challenge in his eyes. "Watch your mouth, boy," Lars muttered, pulling his pack tighter against his back. "There ain't nothing I can't do myself."

Hawk nodded, then stepped into the crevice. Without hesitation, he began to climb upward, bracing his back against one side of the fissure, while finding places to put his hands and feet along the other side. Lars watched his son until he was eight feet above the ground, then he took a deep breath, spit in the palms of his hands, rubbed them together, and followed him.

Hawk had turned eighteen only a couple of months ago; hard to believe the squirt grew up so fast. After their falling-out last year, he'd disappeared for a while before showing up at his mother's doorstep, asking to be taken in. But the kid had never been meant for books and school; six months in Clarksburg, then he'd left home again, hooking up with the logging crew when they returned to the Black Mountains for the spring season.

Lars had agreed to take him back, but only on condition that he help them track down the *chirreep*. The boy knew where they were hiding, but his damn cousin had caused him to mix up his priorities. It had taken a lot of persuasion before Hawk had come clean, or at least halfway clean: as it turned out, the *chirreep* hadn't been responsible for all their troubles, but instead shared the blame with someone else. An ex-spacer named Jonathan Parson, who'd moved into the mountains after he'd jumped ship from the *Columbus,* had been the one who'd tried to destroy the spill-dam.

Hawk insisted that he didn't know where Parson lived, but Lars managed to convince him that, if the boy would just bring Parson to some place near the logging camp where they could meet, perhaps the two of them could peacefully settle their differences. He even went so far as to promise that Parson wouldn't be harmed. Just a little parlay between two grown men.

Yeah, well . . . promises are like turds; just because you make 'em don't mean you gotta keep 'em. Maybe Hawk was irate because of what his father's men had done to Parson after they caught him at the spill-dam, but Lars had kept his word: he'd never laid a hand on him. And since then, no one had touched the spill-dam. But the damn *chirreep* had continued to pester the camp—knocking down flume supports, stealing supplies, harassing the big Percherons the company had recently bought to haul logs—until Lars decided that enough was enough.

His son knew where the *chirreep* were hiding. He'd kept that secret for much too long. And two days ago, Lars laid it on the line. *Show me where they are,* he'd said, *or we'll go looking for your friend again. And when we find him, he'll find himself in a hole in the ground.* And, of course, the boy had agreed. Because, after all, blood is thicker than water . . .

The climb was even worse than he expected. The years he'd spent in the mountains had toughened him, yet he'd spent too many days making his guys do all the work, too many nights drinking until he passed out in his bunk. There was a pot in his belly and flabby tissue in his arms and legs; he had to stop now and then to catch his breath, and despite the cold he found sweat running down his face. Meanwhile, his boy was scuttling up the crevice like a monkey in a tree. More than once, he thought he caught a smirk on Hawk's face, one which quickly vanished when he caught his old man's eye. When this was over and done, he'd have to teach the boy some discipline. Perhaps he was too old for lessons from Mr. Belt, but neither was he too young to be reassigned to the tree-topper crew. A few weeks hooked by a belt to the top of an eighty-foot rough bark would remind him to respect his father.

At long last, he reached the top of the crevice. Hawk was patiently waiting for him, sitting on a rock and having a drink from his flask. He didn't offer any water to his father as he silently watched Lars sag against a boulder. Lars glared at him, then pulled his own flask from his pack. "Think this is funny, don'cha?"

"Not at all." Hawk shrugged, put a stopper in his flask. "Kind of feel sorry for you, to tell the truth."

"If you think beating me to the top makes you a better man than me—"

"No, no . . . it's not that." Hawk looked away, gazing down the mountainside spread out below. Although they were many miles from the camp, the extent of the clear-cutting was plain to see: vast patches of naked terrain where dense forest once lay. "You don't have anything left but that, do you?" he asked. "Just a lot of stumps, and your drinking and womanizing."

"You got something against getting drunk and screwing?" Lars smirked at him. No sense in pretending that he had any affection left for his mother, and what a man did when he wasn't on the clock was no one's business. "And those stumps brought us a lot of money, boy. Don't forget that."

"I know." Hawk paused. "And I've tried to overlook it. But you've got a lot of hatred in you, Papa . . ."

"I don't hate no one." Still trying to get his wind, he drank too quickly. The water went down the wrong way, caused him to cough. "Hell, I love everybody."

"No, you don't." Hawk shook his head sadly. "You don't love my mother or my sister, and I know sure as hell that you don't love me. You're just a worn-out old bully, trying to force everyone to—"

"If that's what you think," Lars rasped, "then why'd you come back?" He wiped his mouth with the back of his hand. "If I'm such a mean ol' daddy, then what made you leave your mama and come back here? No one forced you."

Hawk didn't reply. Instead, he looked down at the toes of his boots, letting his flask swing back and forth by its strap between his knees. "I dunno," he said. "The last time I saw you, things went bad between us. But after I got away, I thought maybe . . . maybe if I gave you another chance, things would work out."

"I gave you your job back. What else do you want?" Lars didn't like the way the conversation was going. "You want me to say I love you? Yeah, well, okay, I love you. Happy?"

"Not really."

"Show me what you brought me up here for, and I'll give you a kiss."

Hawk said nothing for a moment. He sighed, stood up again. "Sure. If that's what you want."

The ledge was narrow, and didn't get any wider as they moved along it. Uma had disappeared behind the summit, taking with it what little direct sunlight they had left. Yet Hawk knew the way. He led his father along a trail that became more precarious with every step they took, until they were practically hugging the granite wall. Lars found himself regretting that they'd come up here. If they remained much longer, they'd have to camp overnight, and neither of them had brought bedrolls, food, or anything to drink except for water. The lack of liquor bothered him more than anything else. God, what he wouldn't give for a shot of bearshine just now.

They came around a large outcropping, and now Lars saw that they were in a broad hollow that erosion had carved within the face of the mountain. Sheer bluffs rose up around them; in the wan light, he could see what looked like piles of branches, stacked here and there around the center.

"Here it is." Hawk kneeled to the ground, motioning for his father to do the same. "There's a sinkhole in the middle. It leads down to a cave where they live."

"I don't see anything."

"Keep your voice down." He saw that Lars was reaching back into his pack for a flashlight, and quickly shook his head. "Don't use that. They'll know we're here."

Lars withdrew his hand. He squinted through the darkness. "I don't see it," he whispered. "You're sure it's there?"

"Of course, I'm sure." Hawk sighed in exasperation. He slipped off his pack, laid it on the ground. "I'll get you closer, but you're going to have to leave your pack behind."

Lars hesitated. His son didn't know it, but he'd brought a couple of bricks of plastic explosive, along with a coil of det cord and a battery-powered charger. He figured that once he found the *chirreep* cave, he'd plant the charges and run the cord to a safe distance. With luck, they might be able to bury the critters alive. "How come you want me to—"

"Because you'll make too much noise carrying it. They've got sharp ears." Hawk glared at him. "Just do as I say, all right?"

Lars thought they were being quiet enough already. Hawk had been here before, though, so he must know what he was doing. Besides, once he knew where the sinkhole lay, he could always come back and fetch the equipment. He took off his pack, placed it next to his son's. Hawk nodded in satisfaction; crouching low, he led his father into the hollow.

The first stars had begun to appear in the twilight sky. Bear hadn't risen yet, but if they waited a little while longer, Lars figured that they'd be able to use bearlight to set the charges. Maybe they'd have to spend the night up here—he didn't look forward to picking their way back across the ledge in the dark—but it would be worth the trouble if they got rid of those damn *chirreep* once and for all.

They made their way through the hollow, trying to make as little sound as possible, and before long Lars made out a patch of darkness within the floor of the cove. The sinkhole was smaller than he expected, yet as they drew closer, he spotted what looked like a pair of sticks sticking up from the opening. The top of a ladder, fashioned from pieces of wood lashed together along two long tree branches. That surprised him; he'd never thought the *chirreep* were capable of anything that sophisticated.

"Down there," Hawk whispered, crouching beside the hole. "That's where it is." He pointed to the ladder. "You first."

"You're kidding."

"You said you wanted to find 'em." He gestured impatiently toward the ladder. "C'mon. It's just a short climb."

Lars felt the hair rise upon the back of his neck. The hole was an abyss, leading into the unknown. "You didn't tell me—"

"Oh, for the love of . . ." Hawk let out his breath in disgust. "Just go, will you? We're running out of time."

Hawk was right. If he wanted to lay the explosives correctly, Lars would have to see how far down the sinkhole extended. He sucked at the gap in his teeth. All right, just a quick look-see; he wouldn't have to go all the way down to make an estimate. Then he could go back and grab his gear. And besides, he didn't want to show his son that he was a coward.

Swallowing his fear, Lars crawled around to the opposite side of the hole, then carefully stepped onto the ladder. It creaked under his weight, but it was sturdier than it looked. He lowered his left foot, then his right; now his hands were upon the top rungs, and he was into the sinkhole, his head just above the edge.

A couple of pebbles, dislodged by the ladder, fell past him. It seemed as if several seconds passed before he heard them make a hollow rattle somewhere far below. All right, that was enough. The hole was deeper than he thought. Courage fled him as he raised his left foot . . .

Then Hawk kicked the ladder away.

Lars didn't even have time to yell before he lost his grip. A glimpse of his son's figure, framed against the dim twilight, then he plummeted into hellish darkness.

For a timeless moment, he was suspended in freefall. Then solid rock rose to slam against him. A white-hot shaft of pain shot from his left hip to the center of his brain, and he screamed out loud, flailing helplessly in the cold black that enveloped him.

Obscenities swarmed from his mouth as he tried to clutch at his broken leg. Yet his agony was without mercy; he tried to roll over on his right side, only to discover that his muscles wouldn't obey his mental commands. His horror increased when he realized that his vertebra had been shattered as well. He was paralyzed, utterly helpless . . .

Tasting blood, his eyes swiveled to the mouth of the sinkhole, somewhere far above. For a second, he thought he saw Hawk, a thin silhouette against the stars. Then he vanished, even as Lars tried to cough out a plea for mercy.

By now, there were sounds around him. Things coming from somewhere nearby; voices that chirped and hooted, echoing from a tunnel he couldn't see. He managed to twist his head to the right, and that was when he saw, in dim light that seemed to come from the rock itself, the reflection of alien eyes.

A stray leaf, caught by the autumn wind, drifted down from the sink-hole. Dry and tender, it whisked against his face: a last touch of life. Lars barely felt it, for now the *chirreep* were upon him. He screamed, and continued to scream, until their tiny knives found his throat.

And that was when he discovered that blood wasn't so thick after all.

Part 7

PARSON'S REBELLION

The landing field lay still and silent in the dark hours before dawn, its concrete apron turned a pale shade of grey by bearlight. Nothing moved save for the windsock on a pole near the chain-link security fence, gently ruffled by a cool breeze coming in from the northwest. Not far away, the town slept; only a few lights glimmered on the outskirts within the windows of farmhouses whose residents had risen early to feed the livestock.

Four figures emerged from the tall grass near the edge of the field. They hesitated for a moment, looking both ways to make sure that no one was in sight, before scurrying through the darkness toward the fence.

Jonathan Parson stopped at the gate, glanced back at his companions. Susan was right behind him, as she'd been ever since she rendezvoused with him and the others outside town less than an hour ago. Manny was the slowest, of course; his mechanical body had never allowed him to move very quickly, and what he ironically referred to as his "war wounds"—the lack of sight in his left eye, the loss of full mobility of his right leg—hindered him even more. As before, Hawk was helping him along; the kid didn't need to do so, but somehow Hawk seemed to feel responsible for the Savant, much as if he was an elderly gent who needed tender care.

Manny was far from helpless, yet he'd never complained about Hawk's attention, and this act of caring seemed to help the kid himself. Parson had come to worry a bit about Hawk lately. His father had disappeared a few weeks ago, under circumstances that remained not wholly explained, yet Hawk didn't seem particularly upset. Indeed, it was almost as if he was glad that his old man was gone.

No. He had to focus on matters at hand. Pulling off his pack, Parson withdrew the pair of bolt cutters he'd had Hawk buy for him in Clarksburg. He raised its beak to the U-shaped hasp of the lock that secured the gate chain, then pulled the handles together. A moment of resistance, then a

hard snap as the blades severed the lock. Parson started to put the bolt cutters back in the pack, then reconsidered and instead tossed them aside.

"Don't you want to bring 'em?" Hawk whispered.

"Why bother?" Parson pulled off the lock and threw it away. "Don't
need them anymore. By the time they find 'em, it won't matter."

The night-watch had left the area fifteen minutes ago; by now the
blueshirt would be sauntering through town, making his rounds once more
before returning to the barracks to fill out the logbook and maybe steal a
few winks. Parson almost felt sorry for the poor guy—no doubt he'd catch
hell from someone—yet no one must have ever seriously considered the
possibility of what they were doing now. The fence was there mainly to
keep animals and children away, and the only reason the Proctor came by
was because it was part of his routine.

The gate creaked softly as he pushed it open. Parson looked at the others. "Last chance," he murmured, "if you want to back out."

"Too late for that now," Susan said. "C'mon, we're running out of
time." Hawk danced nervously from foot to foot, while Manny's right eye
glowed like an amber jewel within his cowl. No one was having any second
thoughts. Or if they were, they were keeping it to themselves.

"Right." Parson picked up the pack, pulled it over his shoulder. "Then
off we go."

They moved quickly across the field, saying nothing to each other as
they headed for the closer of the two spacecraft parked on the apron. Now
that the New Brighton spaceport was in service, most shuttles arrived there,
yet the New Florida landing field was still used on occasion, mainly because
of its proximity to Liberty. Of course, there was the URSS *Plymouth*, but it
never went anywhere; long since decommissioned, the old bird simply
waited for the day when it would be towed to an as-yet unbuilt hangar, to
be preserved as a historic artifact. This morning, though, an ESA skiff
rested nearby.

The *Virginia Dare* had landed only yesterday, following the return of the
Drake to the 47 Uma system. Steam rose from vents along its fuselage as
indigenous-fuel nuclear engines converted atmospheric water vapor into
useable hydrogen. The boarding ramp had been raised—its crew had done
that as a precaution, just before they'd gone to the boardinghouse in town
where they were staying—but this was a minor obstacle that Parson had
already anticipated. Kneeling down, he let Hawk climb on his shoulders,

then he carefully stood up, lifting the young man until he was within arm's reach of the spacecraft's lower hull. Using a pocket light, Hawk found a recessed panel; he slid it open, then pushed a button. A faint grinding noise, then the belly hatch opened and the ramp began to descend.

Parson bent his knees again and Hawk hopped off his shoulders. He waited until the ramp touched ground, then he turned to the kid. "Okay, that's it for you," Parson said, and held up a hand before Hawk could object. "We've been through this before. Not enough room for all of us."

"Aw, c'mon, Jon . . ."

"Do as he says." Susan's voice was cold. "You're staying behind. Period."

His feelings more than a little hurt, Hawk looked down, nodded his head. Parson couldn't help but feel sorry for him. The boy had betrayed him, to be sure, and his body bore scars from the beating he'd taken last spring, but he'd come to understand why it'd happened. Perhaps Susan couldn't bring herself to forgive him, but he had.

"Besides," Parson added, "I've got an important job for you." Opening his pack, he produced a satphone. "It's preset to the frequency we'll be using," he said, handing it to Hawk. "Keep it switched on. When you hear from me, I want you to go to the president and give her this." Then he unbuttoned his parka, pulled out a sealed envelope, and gave it to him as well. "But not a minute before. Understand?"

Susan stared at him. "What are you—?"

"Our statement of demands. The one we signed. Remember?"

"Sure, but I thought you were going to transmit it once we—"

"It'll be more effective if it's delivered by hand." Parson looked back to Hawk. "Look, this could be dangerous. They might try to pin the blame on you. If you don't think you can handle it—"

"I can do this." Hawk put the envelope in his jacket, clipped the phone to his belt. He hesitated, then offered his hand. "Good luck."

"Thanks." Parson shook his hand. "You, too." Susan hesitated, then gave his shoulder a squeeze. Hawk gave Manny a quick nod, which the Savant reciprocated in his own spooky way: a brief forward tilt of a skeletal head within the cowl of his black robe, like the Grim Reaper acknowledging his presence. Then Hawk turned and jogged away, heading for the fence.

"You trust him?" Manny's voice was a low purr.

"You trusted me, didn't you?" Parson peered up at the sky from beneath the skiff's starboard wing. The leading edge of Bear's rings had already touched the western horizon. "Sun's coming up soon. Let's go."

The cockpit was tight: just enough seats for the pilot, copilot, and two passengers, with the rest of the interior space reserved for freight. Once he was buckled into the left seat, Parson took a few moments to study the dashboard. Although the craft was a little more sophisticated than those he'd flown before, the controls remained basically the same. Besides, he had backup; while he initiated the prelaunch procedures, Manny took the right seat, then stretched a cable from his chest to a terminal on the panel before him. "Comp interface achieved," the Savant said. "All systems green. We're good to go."

"Thanks." Parson pulled up the checklist on a screen. With Manny's assistance, nothing would take him by surprise. He stole a moment to glance back at Susan. She'd managed to figure out how the seat harness worked, yet her hands trembled as she snapped the buckles shut. She'd never gone into space before; all this was new to her. "Relax," he said. "It's no worse than riding a jet, really."

"I've never been on a jet. Only gyros." She hesitated. "Three times."

"Okay." He didn't know what to say to that. "If it gets too much for you, then close your eyes, put your head against the seat—"

"There's a vomit bag beneath your seat," Manny said. "Please use it."

Parson cast a cold look at the Savant, which his blind left eye was conveniently able to ignore. "I'll be okay," Susan said. "Just get on with it."

Parson returned his attention to the controls. All systems nominal: fuel tanks fully pressurized, atmospheric engines preheated, guidance systems in standby mode. He placed his right hand on the thruster bars, moved them up a couple of degrees; the hull trembled as the engines ignited. Through the windows, he saw house lights begin to flash: Shuttlefield residents, awakened by the unexpected roar of a ship preparing to take off. If he waited a few minutes, he'd hear someone come over the comlink, demanding to know who he was, where he was going.

He was wasn't going to stick around that long.

"Liftoff," he said, then he pushed the bars all the way forward.

The *Virginia Dare* slowly rose from the landing field, its VTOLs burning hot against the cold autumn morning. For a few moments the skiff hovered against the star-flecked sky, its landing gear rolling up within their wells. Then its bow tilted upward and it leaped toward space.

Carlos had just finished making breakfast when there was a knock at the front door. He didn't respond immediately—if he didn't rescue the biscuits at once, they'd burn to a crisp—so he took a few moments to remove the tray from the brick oven and place it on the stove top next to the coffeepot. One day soon, they'd be able to afford one of the new solar ovens that were being imported from Earth; until then, they'd have to continue to make do with wood fire.

The knocking continued, more urgently than before. He heard Wendy yell something from their bedroom. The door was shut, but he could guess what she was saying. "I'll get it," he yelled back, then he pulled off his oven mitt and dropped it on the counter. Whoever was outside was getting impatient. "Calm down," Carlos muttered as he strode toward the front door. "You'd think the house was on fire."

Chris was on the front porch. He apparently noticed the irate look on Carlos's face, for he took an involuntary step back from the door. "Sorry. I know it's early, but . . ."

"It can't wait, right?" Carlos sighed. When he'd been president, he'd let it be known to one and all that he wasn't to be disturbed, save for the more dire emergencies, after Government House closed at six o'clock, or before he returned to work at eight the following morning. This had gone far to preserve the privacy of his home as well as his own peace of mind; there was little that demanded his attention after hours, save for the monthly meeting of the Colonial Council or the occasional late-night budget session. After Wendy took office, though, she'd rescinded that standing order. She'd promised her supporters that, as president, she'd be on call twenty-seven hours a day, nine days a week, 1,096 days a year, and since then she'd been determined to keep that pledge. As a result, they'd often been visited as late as midnight and as early as dawn. Carlos often griped that she was making more work for herself, but she took her job seriously . . . perhaps a bit more than her husband had, he had to admit.

"It's important, yeah." Chris exhaled a tiny cloud; there was a nip to the morning, with an autumn frost upon the dying flowers beside the front walk. "I tried to wait as long as possible, but . . ." He shrugged. "She's up, isn't she?"

"Getting dressed." Carlos stood aside, letting his old friend inside. "Want coffee?"

"Sure. Thanks." Chris walked over to the dinner table, took a seat in the guest chair. Carlos had set the table for three, so he went to the cupboard to fetch another mug; on second thought, he also pulled out a fourth plate and butter knife. Chris was up early, so he probably hadn't had breakfast yet. And besides, he always made more biscuits than Wendy or Susan could eat . . .

Come to think of it, where was Susan, anyway? Her bedroom door was still shut, and although she tended to sleep later than her parents, by now she was usually coming back from the privy, clutching her robe about her, damp hair wrapped in a towel. Of course, there'd been many times recently when she hadn't been home at all, but that was when she'd been away on research, and it had been a while since . . .

"Morning, Chris." The door of the master bedroom swung open, and Wendy came out. "Early for you, isn't it?"

"Madam President." The Chief Proctor gallantly stood up.

"Hey, you never did that with me." Carlos put a mug in front of him, then placed the extra plate and knife beside it.

"Stand up when you entered the room, or address you as Madam President?" Wendy picked up the coffeepot, carried it over to the table. "I like it. Makes me feel all tingly inside."

She was dressed for the office: ankle-length hemp skirt, cotton blouse, wool sweater, all in earth tones. The kind of outfit one expected the leader of the Coyote Federation to wear while conducting the affairs of state. If necessary, though, she could report to the hospital, where she could change into scrubs to deliver a baby or perform surgery; then she was no longer Madam President, but simply Dr. Wendy Gunther, chief of emergency medical services. One job rarely interfered with the other, although the latter paid better than the former.

"So where's the fire?" Without sitting down, Wendy poured coffee for

Chris, then for herself and Carlos. She seldom let business get in the way of breakfast. "Or did someone steal one of your mother's chickens again?"

It was an old joke between them; Chris forced a smile. "No fire, but you guessed half right. Someone stole a bird this morning . . . the *Virginia Dare*, a skiff from the *Drake*."

"Really?" Carlos raised an eyebrow. "The one that landed yesterday?"

"Uh-huh." Chris sipped his coffee. "Don't blame yourself if you didn't hear it take off. Happened around three-thirty, and whoever did it was careful not to engage the main engines until they reached altitude. Woke up a few people, but most slept right through it."

Well, that was serious enough. The European Alliance had landing rights throughout the colonies, but they'd come to use New Brighton as their principal spaceport. Ana Tereshkova had landed in Albion, aboard the *Walter Raleigh*; no doubt she'd be aggravated over the theft of one of her landing craft.

"What about the night watch?" Wendy took a seat, poured some goat's milk into her coffee. "Didn't they see anything?"

"My guy says he'd just walked the area. Didn't see anything. We found a pair of bolt cutters next to the gate, along with the lock." Chris shrugged. "I was tempted to dock him a week's pay, but then I read the log. He wasn't slacking off. Just didn't see it coming, that's all."

"Who would have?" Carlos fetched the biscuits from the stove top. Picking up a jar of strawberry preserves, he carried everything back to the table. "Why would anyone want to steal a skiff?"

"My thoughts exactly." Wendy cast him a hard look. *I'm the president. You're the ex-president. Shut up and serve the biscuits, and let me do my job.* "Did anyone try to make contact with the pilot?"

"Of course. The minute it took off, my officer hustled the radio chief out of bed. Not a peep, from any frequency. Whoever hijacked that thing, they're ignoring all transmissions."

"Uh-huh." Wendy nodded. "But I think you're missing something. Like Carlos said, why steal a shuttle? It's not like you could go anywhere with it . . . or at least, not to any other colony, because it'd be recognized as soon as it touched down. Maybe you could land somewhere else."

"But then you'd have to fend for yourself." Chris nodded. "We thought of that already. I've got my people going to all the shops in town, to see if anyone recently purchased the stuff you'd need if you wanted to set up camp out in the boonies." A pensive frown. "But that doesn't make sense, either. Why steal a skiff if you could just as easily hire someone to fly you wherever you want to go?"

"Got a point there." Wendy used a knife to open a biscuit and spread preserves on it. "You said they dropped a pair of bolt cutters . . ."

"We're looking into that." Chris helped himself to a biscuit. "And that's weird, too. That sort of purchase can be traced easily enough . . . it was Earth-made, and there're only a few shops carrying that sort of hardware. So it's almost as if they didn't care whether we find out who they are."

"Not only that, but how many people here are rated to fly a skiff?" Wendy's brow furrowed. "Five, ten? A dozen at most? I'll have Tomas check the records. Maybe he'll—"

"Where the heck is Susan?" It was an irrelevant question, but amid the discussion of one mystery, Carlos abruptly realized that there was another that hadn't been solved. Her door remained shut, and there was no sound of movement from her room. "Not like her to sleep in."

"Maybe she had a late night." Wendy was paying little attention. "Wake her up, tell her breakfast is ready."

As he walked across the room, Carlos found himself wondering, once again, when his daughter would find her own place. She was an adult now, with a job at the university that frequently sent her out into the field. Very often she'd been gone for weeks on end, conducting research on the native fauna, the *chirreep* in particular. A long absence, then she'd return, sun-burned and exhausted, with clothes so filthy and ripped that they should be burned instead of washed out and stitched.

Not only that, but lately they hadn't been getting along very well. She'd been upset when she discovered that he'd purchased stock in Morgan Goldstein's company. He'd tried to explain to her that Janus stood to make a lot of money from the development of Albion, and now that Coyote had opened trade with Earth there was no reason why their family couldn't take advantage of this. Yet she seemed to disregard everything he said; the last time they'd duked it out, she'd accused him of selling out his principles, of betraying the very things for which he'd fought when he was Rigil Kent. That had hurt, perhaps more than he cared to admit.

Dammit, Carlos thought. *I love her dearly, but she's a grown woman. If she's going to feud with me, maybe she ought to stop living at home with her parents.*

This even as he rapped on the door. "Susie? Breakfast. Rise and shine."

No response. He tried again. "Time to get up." More silence. He turned the knob, gently pushed open the door, peered inside.

Her bed was still made; it hadn't been slept in since yesterday. Her jacket wasn't hanging on the hook next to the dresser, and the calf boots she customarily wore when she was in the outback were missing as well.

"Susan?" Wendy's voice from the main room. "Is she there?"

Carlos strode across the bedroom to her desk. Her field journal, which she always carried with her when she was on an expedition, lay next to her lecture notes. Strange. He opened drawers. No satphone; she'd taken that, though. He turned to the closet. Yet here was her pack . . .

"Where's Susan?" Wendy had left the table, come to the bedroom door; there was motherly concern on her face. "She's not—?"

"No." Carlos took a deep breath. "Gone." Rubbing his eyes with his fingertips, he struggled to put everything together. Susan was missing; she'd disappeared sometime during the night. She had taken her jacket, her heavy boots, her satphone . . . but no pack, no journal.

"Something's going on here." He looked around at Wendy. "I don't know why, but I've got a feeling about this."

STARBRIDGE COYOTE / 1324

"Chief? We've got a skiff requesting permission to dock with us."

Hearing the voice in his headset, Jonas Whittaker looked away from the galley microwave where he'd been patiently waiting for his lunch to warm up. He tapped the mike wand. "Repeat that, please? You said something about a skiff?"

"Uh-huh. Identifies itself as the EAS Virginia Dare, *from the* Drake." The com officer hesitated. *"I don't see anything on the schedule about any craft coming up today."*

The oven beeped, signaling that his Swedish meatballs were ready. "We don't, the last thing I checked. What does the pilot say they're doing here?"

"He hasn't given a reason. Just wants permission to rendezvous and dock."

Jonas held on to a ceiling rail as he opened the oven and pulled out a plastic-covered tray. Wincing as it burned his fingertips, he hastily transferred the tray to the table and clamped it down. This was weird . . . "Can you patch me through, please? I want to talk to the pilot." A long pause, then a soft click in his headset. "Hello? With whom am I speaking?"

"Lt. Commander Jeffery Thomas, executive officer of the Drake.*"* The accent was British, the tone formal and precise. *"May I ask the same, please?"*

"Jonas Whittaker. Chief of operations, Starbridge Coyote. Mr. Thomas, we haven't heard anything about receiving a skiff from the *Drake*. Why are you here?"

"Ah, Dr. Whittaker. Pleasure to make your acquaintance." The voice thawed a little. *"Many apologies for the confusion. We're not coming directly from the* Drake, *rather, but from Albion. I thought someone was supposed to have gotten in touch with you about arranging for a visit."*

Jonas pushed himself away from the table, glided across the galley to the porthole. This section of the gatehouse faced away from Bear, so he was able to see Coyote. The moon was a green-tinted scimitar, its nightside turned toward Bear; among the stars he could make out a pair of red and blue beacons that flashed in sequence. The formation lights of an approaching skiff, less than twenty-five nautical miles away.

Sure took their sweet time about giving us a shout. "No one contacted us," he said. "There must be a mistake. We don't normally allow tours."

"I understand, Dr. Whittaker, and I'm sorry for the inconvenience. It's just that . . ." A slight pause. *"You see, we have U.N. delegates aboard. We've been trying to keep this as hush-hush as possible, so that's probably why someone neglected to contact you. I hope you understand."*

Jonas closed his eyes. That's all he needed: some VIPs barging in, demanding that he and his crew drop everything they were doing to give them a tour. And just when they were getting ready for another hyperspace transition, this time for the passage of the new EAS ship. Didn't these people have any idea how difficult it was to . . . ?

"Dr. Whittaker?" Thomas again. *"We're on final approach. If there's some sort of problem, perhaps we can reach Ambassador Vogel, ask him to clarify the situation."*

"No, that's all right." Dieter was a jerk; the less Jonas had to deal with him, the better. He turned away from the porthole. "Permission granted . . . but Mr. Thomas, please be advised that we're making an exception. The gatehouse is no place for tourists."

An embarrassed chuckle. *"Understood. We'll try to keep it brief and not to get in the way.* Virginia Dare *over and out."*

A second later, the com officer came back online. *"Sorry, chief. I know it's the last thing you want to—"*

"Can't be helped, Sam." Jonas regarded his lunch for a moment, then glided back across the compartment to remove it from the table. "Better let me take care of this," he added, opening the fridge and pushing the tray inside. "Maybe I can get rid of these guys quick so we can get back to business."

A laugh. *"All yours. We'll tidy up a bit before they get here."*

"Please do. Out." Jonas tapped his mike again, then, regretting the lost chance to enjoy one of the better frozen entrees the station had in its larder, he pushed himself toward the hatch leading to the access shaft.

It had been nearly a full Coyote year—a couple of months shy of three Earth years—since the starbridge had become operative, and still Jonas found himself spending much of his time aboard the gatehouse. Too much time, really. By all rights, he should have retired by now; he'd worked hard to train his five-person crews, which alternated each month between two teams, each with their own managers. He had a nice place in Leeport, a rough-bark cabin on the West Channel where he could sit on the front porch, drink ale, and watch barges moving up and down the river . . . a far cry from floating around in a tin can, eating frozen crap as he waited for the next vessel to pop out of hyperspace.

Yet Jonas was proud of his creation. Although he was always careful to say that he'd stood upon the shoulders of giants—Einstein, Hawking, Thorne, and others—the fact remained that he'd managed to transform theory into practicality, and in doing so had opened the stars to humankind. This is not something from which a man could easily walk away. And so he came up here as often as he could, running a hand-picked shift of technicians just so he could see the flash of light from the distant torus as the starbridge opened to allow a spacecraft to vault through hyperspace, bypassing forty-six light-years in the blink of an eye.

The day comes when I'm bored with that, Jonas thought, making his way headfirst down the narrow shaft, *that's the day I start raising tomatoes. Until then, this baby's mine.*

He'd reached the docking module, located halfway down the station's spindle-like structure, when Sam's voice chirped in his ear again: *"Ah, chief, there's something about this . . ."*

"Tell me about it," he grumbled as he pushed a button above the hatch. It irised open, revealing a spherical compartment. "Next time they send us VIPs, it'd be nice if they'd give us some advance warning."

"That's just it. I'm not sure if they did."

Grasping a rung next to the hatch, Jonas swung himself feet-first into the ready room. Four airlocks on each side of the compartment: two leading to docking collars, the other two direct to space. Suit lockers and equipment racks lined the curved walls between the airlock hatches. A small compartment, without much room to maneuver.

"C'mon, Sam, I don't got all day." Jonas did a somersault that oriented himself toward Hatch 2, then peered through a porthole the size of a saucer. Through the collapsed accordion-tube of the docking collar, he could see the approaching skiff. The ring of its dorsal hatch was lined up precisely with the collar; a brief flare every now and then from RCRs corrected the skiff's trajectory. "What's the problem?"

"Look, I don't know if it means anything, but I just checked the Drake's *crew and passenger manifest, and I didn't find any U.N. diplomats registered—"*

"You're right. It doesn't mean anything. VIPs don't always use their titles." The skiff drew closer. Whoever was flying that thing had a nice hand at the stick. No back-offs or second tries, not one wasted motion. Smooth and steady.

"Maybe so, but I don't find any crew by the name of Jeffery Thomas, either. He said he was the executive officer, right? According to my records, the Drake's *XO is Milos DiNardo."*

"Could be a mistake. Check to see if—"

"I did. That's according to the current manifest. The one for the last time the Drake *came through lists Jeffery Thomas as the exec, but—"*

"So they got things screwed up." He let out his breath in exasperation. "Look, I don't have time for this, and neither do you. Let's just get these guys in and out of here, then we can get back to what's important." Like lunch. He was hungry and, God help him, he'd actually been looking forward to those Swedish meatballs.

"Will you listen to me? Please? I just checked the log for the most recent advisories . . ."

Gatehouse crewmembers seldom looked at text messages from Coyote. For the most part, they were routine reports: global weather forecasts, landing conditions at Shuttlefield and New Brighton, technical data meant to be loaded directly into the comps. There was the daily mail from family and friends, which the crew read when they weren't doing anything else, but otherwise most messages was stored in memory until someone found time to weed through all the junk.

"Yeah, and . . . ?" The skiff blotted out the sunlight. The station floodlights reflected dully from its hull, then the collar expanded to mate with the craft's airlock ring. A moment later there was a dull jar as the docking cradle closed around the skiff.

"There's a flash advisory from Liberty. Says that a skiff was stolen from Shuttlefield at about 0330 this morning. Want to guess which one it was?"

Everything the com officer had told him suddenly fit together. "Aw, crap," he muttered. "You gotta be kidding."

"Does it sound like I'm kidding?" In the background, someone was yelling. Kendrick, probably; the traffic officer was on duty the last time Jonas went topside. *"Whoever's on that shuttle, it's not who he says he . . ."*

Jonas glanced up at the panel above the hatch, watched the lights go green. The sleeve was beginning to pressurize. "Keep that hatch shut!" he snapped. "Don't release the bolts until I say so!"

"No can do. They still can open it from inside."

"Then see if you can disable it somehow! And get someone else down here!" Jonas backed away from the airlock, began to look frantically around the ready room. Suits, helmets, gloves, a first-aid kit . . . nothing that could be used as a weapon. *Didn't anyone ever think that we might need a stunner up here?* Of course not. This was a space station. Who the hell would want to hijack a space station?

"Jodi and I are on the way down, chief." Maurice's voice on the comlink. *"Hold the fort till we get there."*

Good. The last time he saw Jodi and Maurice, only fifteen minutes ago, they were in the crew quarters. That was only three decks up, less than a hundred feet away. Of course, neither of them had been fully dressed; Jodi's hair was still wet, and both she and Maurice were wearing robes, indicating that they'd just spent some quality time in the shower together.

They'd have to put on their jumpsuits first. And with both Sam and Kendrick in the com center . . .

He remembered the nearest fire extinguisher, located in the access shaft about ten feet away. It wasn't much of a weapon, but it would have to do. Jonas pushed himself through the ready room hatch, hastily pulled himself up along the ladder until he reached it. The tank was fastened tight against the bulkhead; he had to brace his feet and back against the tunnel and haul at it with both hands until it snapped loose from its breakaway straps. God help them if there was ever an actual fire in this place.

"What's going on down there?" Ninety feet up, Maurice was emerging from a hatch, wearing drawstring pants and a T-shirt that looked as if he'd just pulled them from the laundry sack. "If this is some kind of—"

"Shut up and get down here!" Tucking the fire extinguisher under his left arm, Jonas pushed himself feet-first toward the ready room hatch. Too late, he realized that he'd left it open. He should have closed it behind him. But that shouldn't matter. He'd been gone only a minute. Ninety seconds, tops. There was no way . . .

His feet had barely gone through the hatchway before a pair of hands—not hands, really, but metallic claws, ice-cold and unyielding—grabbed his ankles. Jonas didn't even have time to yell before he was yanked through the manhole. The back of his shirt ripped against the hatchway, then he was slammed against the wall by something stronger than a mere mortal.

Jonas looked up, saw a skeletal face peering at him, one ruby eye gleaming at him from within a dark hood, the other covered by a patch. A Savant. He'd heard of these beings, seen their pictures yet hadn't met any since his revival; they'd come and gone during the years he'd spent in biostasis, becoming creatures that most people in this time spoke about only in tones of dread.

Oh, hell, he thought, *I'm dead . . .*

"Relax. We don't mean you any harm." The voice that emerged from the Savant's mouth grille was oddly soothing. "Did you think there was a fire here?"

"No, I . . ." Then Jonas remembered what he was holding. "Oh, yeah. We thought . . . I mean, we weren't sure, but . . ."

"He wasn't trying to put out a fire." From behind the Savant, another voice, in the direction of the airlock hatch. Before it'd belonged to Jeffery

Thomas, yet even though Jonas knew now that this identity was false, nonetheless it seemed familiar. "Take it away."

A young woman came up beside them. As she removed the fire extinguisher from his hands, Jonas recognized her: Susan Montero, daughter of the president of the Coyote Federation. What in the world was she doing here?

"Chief? Do you copy?"

Jonas started to reply before the Savant ripped the headset from him. "Two more coming," he said quietly. "Get ready."

The Savant pulled away from the compartment hatch, and that was when Jonas saw the third person who'd emerged from the airlock. His hair was longer, and a beard covered much of his face, but Jonas instantly recognized him: Jonathan Parson, the second officer of the *Columbus*. It had been fifteen months, by the LeMarean calendar, since they'd last laid eyes on each other, yet Parson didn't seem at all surprised to see him. A tight smile and the briefest of nods by way of greeting, then Parson moved to the one side of the hatch, with Susan taking up position on the other side.

"Chief?" Maurice's voice echoed down the access shaft. "Are you okay?"

Jonas caught a glimpse of the stunner in Parson's hand. He opened his mouth to yell a warning, but the Savant clamped a claw across his face. An instant later, Maurice came through the hatch. Seeing Jonas held captive by the Savant, he barely had a second to react before Parson leveled the stunner at him and fired.

Maurice spasmed as the charged wires hit his body, then he went limp. From somewhere close behind him, Jodi screamed. "Get her!" Parson snapped. He tossed the stunner to Susan, then hauled Maurice out of the way.

Susan caught the gun, then dove up the shaft. A brief commotion, then Susan's voice came back to them. "She's down . . . but I think they've shut the top hatch."

"They're onto us." Parson reached into his jacket pocket, pulled out a roll of duct tape. "Bring the girl down here," he said as he pulled Maurice's hands behind his back and began to lash his wrists together. "Manny, let go of Dr. Whittaker . . . but keep him under control."

The Savant released Jonas from his steel grip, but continued to hold on to his shoulder. "What the hell are you—?" Jonas began.

"You'll find out soon enough." Parson paused to help Susan drag Jodi's unconscious body from the shaft, then he proceeded to bind her as well. "How many more up there?"

Jonas swallowed. "Six."

"You're lying." Parson glanced meaningfully at the nearest airlock. "Don't make me do something I don't want to."

"Okay, okay. Two." Jonas fought to remain calm. "Look, don't hurt them. They're not—"

"We won't hurt anyone so long as you cooperate." Parson passed Jodi over to Susan, then he took the headset from Manny. "Here's what I want you to do," he continued, holding out the headset to Jonas. "I want you to talk to those two guys upstairs, tell them—"

"They're already making contact with the ground." At least that was what he presumed Sam and Kenny were doing.

"Not my concern." Parson thrust the headset into Jonas's hands. "Right now, though, what I want them to do is open the hatch, let us come in. If they go along with us, I swear that no harm will come to anyone."

"Yeah, I bet."

"That's a promise." Parson's gaze became a cold stare. "But if they don't go along, then we're going to have to start treating you and your crew as hostages. And believe me, you don't want us to do that."

Another meaningful glance at the nearest airlock hatch. Jonas's imagination conjured unwanted visions. On one hand, he didn't believe that they'd seriously consider spacing anyone. On the other, until now he would have considered it just as unlikely that someone would manage to hijack an EAS skiff, fly it up to the Gatehouse, and overcome three-fifths of its crew. He could refuse, and gamble with the lives of his team, or . . .

"Oh, hell." He pulled on the headset, tapped it once again. "Sam, you copy?"

"Chief! What the hell's going on down there?"

"Sam, we . . ." He took a deep breath. "Look, we've got a situation. Maurice and Jodi—"

"Are they all right? We heard Jodi scream, then Ken shut the—"

"I know, I know. They're all right. Sam, we—"

"I've radioed Liberty, told 'em we're—"

"Sam, shut up. Please." Jonas felt his heart hammering against his chest. "Maurice and Jodi are fine. So am I, but . . . look, we've got a major problem here, and it isn't going to get better unless you open the hatch and let us come up."

A long pause. *"I don't know . . . I mean, I can't . . ."*

"Look, just do it." He sighed, shut his eyes for a moment. "On my authorization. If anything goes wrong, it's all my fault. But they've got . . . they've got me and Jodi and Maurice, and I don't think they're taking no for an answer. So . . ."

"Boss, I don't—"

"Damn it, Sam!" He found himself becoming impatient. "Just pop the hatch, all right?"

A click as the comlink went dead. Everyone in the ready room froze in place, waiting to hear or see what happened next. For nearly a minute, there was nothing but silence. *All right,* Jonas thought, *they've already sent a message to the ground. Now what would they do next? What would I do if . . . ?*

Of course. He tried not to smile. Sam was a smart guy, and so was Kendrick. They'd take precautions.

From somewhere far up the other end of the access shaft, there was the hollow sound of a hatch being opened. *"Come up,"* Sam said. *"I hope you know what you're doing."*

"Thanks. So do I." Jonas clicked off, then turned to Parson. "Okay, you're in . . . but I'm holding you to your word."

Parson slowly let out his breath. He looked just as relieved as his captive, and so did Susan; the Savant was unable to register any emotion. "You've got my word. If this works out, no one will be harmed." Then he smiled. "Who knows? Once this is all over and done, maybe you'll thank me for it."

"For what?" Jonas raised a skeptical eyebrow. "Taking us hostage?"

"No. For saving the world."

Government House was a two-story, wood-frame structure, located in Liberty town square next to the grange hall. Built of Great Dakota rough bark, with a clock tower rising from the center of its faux-birch shingled roof, it resembled a town hall from nineteenth-century America. The flag of the Coyote Federation hung over the front door, but other than that the only ornamentation was the life-size statue of Captain R. E. Lee, carved from a block of granite quarried from the Eastern Divide, that stood in the center of the square.

The office of the president was on the second floor, its window overlooking the square. Wendy stood at the window, her hands clasped together before her as she gazed down at the statue. There was a framed photo of Captain Lee above her desk, yet the artisans who'd rendered his likeness had captured him with such verisimilitude that it almost seemed as if he stood outside the building, holding vigil upon the colony for which he'd given his life. More than once since she'd become president, she'd sought solace by pondering his image, carrying on silent conversations with the man who'd led the original *Alabama* colonists to the new world.

Yet it wasn't the statue that caught her attention now so much as the young man who loitered beneath it. Wearing a catskin hat, the collar of his jacket pulled up against the autumn wind, he nervously strolled back and forth, occasionally glancing up at the clock tower before looking away again, almost as if afraid of being observed. She couldn't see his face beneath the wide brim of his hat, but there was something about him that seemed vaguely familiar. Almost as if . . .

"Madam President?"

"Yes, Tomas?" She turned away from the window. Her aide stood just inside the door, a sheet of paper in hand. "They've heard something?"

"Not exactly, no." Tomas hesitated. "There's been no voice contact with the Gatehouse since the duty officer said he was opening the command center hatch. A minute ago, though, we received a text message."

"Let me see it," Wendy said. Tomas walked across the room toward her. "Who else knows about this?"

"Only the guys in the com office." Tomas paused. "Should I get your husband?"

"Yes, please. But don't let anyone else know." When she'd heard that the Gatehouse had been taken over by forces unknown, the first thing Wendy had done was post a Proctor at the door of the communications office on the first floor. She knew that she couldn't keep this a secret very much longer, yet the last thing she wanted were unconfirmed rumors. Sooner or later, the Council would have to be informed, but until she knew exactly who'd assumed control of the Gatehouse, the fewer people aware of the situation, the better.

Tomas handed her the printout, then hurried off to find Carlos. Unfolding the paper, Wendy read:

11.68.14 (CY) 1427 EST / 21932 / UNCODED
FRM: STARBRIDGE COYOTE / GATEHOUSE (ID UNAVAILABLE/UNCONFIRMED)
TO: CFCOM / LIBERTY (ID 128294 CONFIRMED)
CLASS: T/S
SUBJ: (NONE)
BEGIN MESSAGE
WE HAVE ASSUMED CONTROL OF STARBRIDGE COYOTE. ALL GATEHOUSE PERSONNEL HAVE BEEN SUBDUED BUT NONE HAVE BEEN HARMED. NO DANGER WILL COME TO THEM UNLESS FORCE IS THREATENED AGAINST US. WE ALSO ASSUME RESPONSIBILITY FOR THEFT OF EAS VIRGINIA DARE. NO HARM DONE TO CRAFT OR CREW. THIS IS A POLITICAL ACTION, UNDERTAKEN BY FELLOW CITIZENS OF THE COYOTE FEDERATION ON BEHALF OF ALL. STATEMENT OF DEMANDS TO BE DELIVERED SOON BY COURIER. ANY ACTION TAKEN AGAINST OUR COURIER WILL BE CONSIDERED HOSTILE AND WILL BE MET ACCORDINGLY.
WE INTEND NO HARM TO ANYONE, BUT WE WILL TAKE APPROPRIATE MEASURES UNLESS OUR DEMANDS ARE MET BY ALL CONCERNED. RESPOND VIA SAME SATCOM FREQUENCY OR THROUGH OUR COURIER.
END MESSAGE

Wendy read the printout twice, then slowly let out her breath. She wasn't very much surprised; in fact, this was what she'd anticipated. No one knew who was responsible, yet she'd had little doubt that it was the same persons who'd stolen the *Virginia Dare*. This only confirmed her suspicions.

But who'd do something like this? And for what purpose?

Footsteps in the hall, then Carlos marched into her office. "You've heard from the Gatehouse?" Wendy nodded, then handed him the message. Her husband quickly scanned it. "Oh, hell. I was hoping that it might be—"

"A hoax?" Wendy turned away, walked over to a side table. "You should know better. Jonas isn't the type to pull a practical joke." She poured herself a drink from the pitcher of ice water she kept there. "Have you reached Ana?"

"Uh-huh. She's on her way." Anastasia Tereshkova had been aboard the *Raleigh*, the passenger shuttle that landed in New Brighton yesterday; now that she had her own place in Albion, she tended to stay there between missions. "She's good and pissed, I can tell you that."

"I don't blame her." Which was why Wendy had him get in touch with her. No harm in taking advantage of Carlos's friendship with the *Drake*'s commanding officer. "I take it that she's put her ship on alert."

"I didn't ask, but yeah, that's a safe bet." Carlos looked at the letter again. " 'Statement of demands to be delivered soon by courier.' I don't get it. Why didn't they just contact you personally?"

"No idea." Wendy idly spun the six-inch globe of Coyote that rested on her desk. Handcrafted by a Colonial University electronics professor who dabbled in cartography and mounted upon a pewter miniature of a boid, it was a one-of-a-kind piece, presented to her as an inauguration gift. "We'll find out soon enough. Where's Tomas?"

"Don't know. Last time I saw him, he was heading downstairs."

"I need for him to . . ." She stopped, remembering that this was something that Carlos could do just as well. Perhaps even better, since he'd once been president himself; his word would carry weight. "We should alert the Council members. Convene an emergency session."

"So soon?" Carlos frowned. "We still don't know who we're dealing with. Why—?"

"Because we can't keep this secret any longer." Wendy turned away from the desk. "It affects everyone. If we keep the representatives in the dark any longer, they might—"

"Madam President?"

She looked around, saw Tomas standing in the doorway. For the first time that day, her aide appeared agitated; indeed, it was rare that he wasn't utterly calm. Yet now there was someone behind him: the young man she'd spotted hovering around the town square.

"I think this is the person you're expecting," Tomas said.

Of course. That was why he'd been keeping an eye on the clock tower. "Thank you," she said quietly, then raised her left hand to the bridge of her nose, as if to rub an itch. "Bring him in, please."

Her gesture was a prearranged signal: *get the Proctor now.* No one who'd served as president had ever felt the need to have a personal bodyguard, yet nonetheless Chris Levin had insisted that a blueshirt be assigned to Government House at all times. But Wendy need not have bothered, for as soon as the young man stepped into the room, she saw that he hadn't gone unescorted; the Proctor on duty was close behind, his stunner already drawn from his holster.

Tomas stepped aside, allowing the young man to enter the room. As he came in, Wendy barely had time to notice her husband's astonishment before the visitor removed his hat. Even then, she didn't immediately recognize him.

"Oh, lord," Carlos murmured. "Hawk?"

"Yeah, it's me." Embarrassment crept onto the young man's face. "I'm sorry, but—"

"There has to be a mistake." Carlos turned to Tomas. "This is our nephew. There's no way he'd . . . I mean, he couldn't . . ."

"He arrived just a minute ago, asked to see the president." Tomas glanced at Hawk. "Said that he was acting as a courier, and that it was important that he see her at once."

The blueshirt stepped closer to Wendy as if to protect her, but she waved him off. They had nothing to fear from their own kin . . . or at least so she assumed. "You have something for me?"

Without a word, Hawk reached into his jacket, pulled out an envelope. As reluctant as he was about meeting his aunt's eyes, he was even more nervous about handing the letter to her. Wendy kept her expression neutral;

this was her nephew, but just now she had to put personal considerations aside. Tearing open the envelope, she withdrew a folded sheet of paper, read the handwritten message:

Madam President, and whoever else it may concern:

By now, you know that we have assumed control of Starbridge Coyote. With luck, the Gatehouse personnel have not been harmed. Although we are holding them prisoner, they are not being treated as hostages. It is not our intent to do so, and unless any direct action is taken that would put their lives or our own in jeopardy, they will remain safe.

Upon witnessing the events of the last year, we have reached the conclusion that the existence of the starbridge poses a clear and present danger to Coyote— not only its human colonists, but also the native inhabitants. We believe that further colonization of this world, along with the unchecked exploitation of its natural resources, will inevitably result in the same environmental destruction that brought Earth to ruin.

We cannot allow this to happen. Unless they are stopped, the governments and corporations of Earth will destroy the place we've come to cherish as our home. The construction of the starbridges, and the subsequent trade and immigration agreements, were done without consideration of their impact upon Coyote's indigenous life. Since they're unable to speak for themselves, we've taken it upon ourselves to act on their behalf.

Our demands are simple:

(1.) *The annulment of all treaties and agreements made between the Coyote Federation and all governmental or corporate entities based on Earth, regarding immigration and trade.*

(2.) *All official representatives of the European Alliance and other Earth-based countries and coalitions, along with representatives of all Earth-based companies and governments, must leave Coyote within the next 81 hours, or three Coyote days.*

(3.) *All claims to government territory or private property held by said countries, coalitions, or private companies must be relinquished at once, to be returned to the Coyote Federation as unclaimed land.*

If these demands are not fulfilled to our satisfaction, then we will have no recourse but to destroy Starbridge Coyote, and therefore bring an end to any contact between Coyote and Earth for the immediate future.

Please do not doubt that we have the ability to accomplish this, or that we

will hesitate to do so. You may respond either through direct communication
via satphone, or through our designated representative.

    We await your prompt response.

        —Jonathan Parson (Lt. Com, ESA, ret.)

          Manuel Castro (WHU Council of Savants, ret.)

          Susan Montero (faculty, Colonial University, New Florida)

Wendy's hands shook as she read the last signature. "Oh, dear God," she whispered.

"What's going on?" Carlos stepped closer so that he could read the letter. Wendy let him take it; her legs weak, she staggered to the nearest chair, clung to it for support.

Susan. When she'd turned up missing that morning, Wendy had hoped that it was only a coincidence that her absence was concurrent with the disappearance of the skiff. Now she knew better. Her daughter—her own daughter—was involved in this. She was aboard the Gatehouse, and . . .

"What the hell are you doing?" Carlos threw aside the letter, lunged straight at Hawk. Grabbing the young man by the collar of his jacket, he slammed him against the wall. "Who do you think you are?" he shouted, so violently that saliva landed upon Hawk's face. "What are you—?"

"Stop it!" Wendy rushed toward them. "It's not his fault! He didn't—!"

"Susan's up there! Doesn't that mean anything to—?"

"You know it does!" Wendy hauled Carlos away from Hawk. "Now cut it out!"

Hawk cowered against the wall, his eyes wide with fear. Tomas, stunned by what he'd just seen, stood frozen nearby, unable to decide what to do next. Even the blueshirt had been caught by surprise; he'd drawn his stunner, but didn't know what to do with it. If what had been stated in the first communiqué was true, though, Wendy couldn't allow any harm to come to her nephew. Too many lives were in the balance.

"Calm down," Wendy whispered in her husband's ear. "It's going to be all right. Everything's going to be fine." In her arms, Carlos was trembling with rage, yet he let out his breath, slowly nodded. He knew what was at stake.

"I'm sorry." Hawk's voice quivered in the terrible silence. "I didn't know . . . Aunt Wendy, I didn't think . . ."

"No, you didn't." Wendy released Carlos, walked back to him again. It took all her self-control to keep her anger in check. Carlos had lost his tem-per; it wouldn't do any good if she lost her own as well. "How did she get into this? How did you—?"

"She's doing what she thinks . . . what she believes needs to be done." Hawk picked himself off the wall. "No one made her do this, or me either. If someone doesn't take a stand, do something that will make everyone wake up, see what's happening here—"

"You should've come to us." Carlos bent down, picked the letter off the floor. "We could have talked about this. We would've listened."

"She tried that already. You didn't want to listen." A trace of a smirk. "Or maybe you were too busy figuring out how to get rich."

"What are you saying?" Carlos shook his head. "I don't know what you're—"

"Oh, c'mon." Hawk's eyes became defiant. "You think we didn't know about the deal you made with Goldstein? As soon as you left office, you in-vested in his company. Hell, you probably worked this out even before you left Earth."

"That's not true. We're only trying to—"

"We don't have time for this." Wendy turned to Tomas. "Find Ambas-sador Vogel, get him over here right away. He needs to know what's going on." Tomas nodded, then hurried to the door. The EA consulate was only a few blocks away; the last time Wendy checked, Dieter was in town. She re-turned her attention to Hawk. "Who's in charge up there? Is it Susan?"

"No one's in charge. This is a unanimous—"

"Don't give me that." She took the letter back from Carlos, glanced at the signatures again. "There's three names here . . . Susan, Manny, and this Parson character. One guy's the boss. Who is it?"

Hawk said nothing. He put his hands in his pockets, gazed up at the ceiling as if studying the woodwork. "Let's get something straight," Wendy said, stepping closer so that he couldn't ignore her. "Right now, I don't care if you're family. So far as I'm concerned, you're involved in a criminal con-spiracy. That means I can have you locked up for as long as I damn well please."

"You can't do that. I have the right to see the magistrates."

"Yes, you do. But you're also a material witness, and under Colony Law I have the authority to keep you confined until you produce the in-formation I need." She paused. "I saw you hanging around outside just before we received the first message. You were watching the clock, and I bet you're carrying a satphone, too, because that's how you knew when to deliver this letter." She nodded toward the Proctor standing nearby. "But I can have him search you until he finds that phone, and I can also have him put you in the stockade with some of our finest. I'm sure they'd love to meet you."

She was bluffing. She could order the Proctor to put him under arrest, but there was no way that she was going to submit him to rough treatment, or deny him a hearing before the magistrates. She had the lives of those aboard the gatehouse to consider, though, and right now she was willing to bend the law a bit. Hawk was scared; she could use that to her advantage.

Wendy took a moment to let her words sink in. "So what's it going to be?" she added, her eyes locked on his. "Ready to give it up, or do I feed you to the tough guys?"

Her gambit worked. Hawk's lower lip trembled, his gaze wavering between her and the Proctor. "Jon's the leader," he murmured at last. "He's calling the shots."

"Uh-huh." Wendy glanced at Carlos, and he quietly nodded. He was just as relieved that Susan wasn't the ringleader. "And how do they intend to destroy the starbridge? Do they have a bomb or something?"

"They'll deorbit it. Manny knows . . . at least, he says he knows . . . how to gain access to the reaction control system. They'll boost it out of orbit, send it into Bear's rings."

That made sense. The starbridge was positioned in Lagrangian orbit around Bear, held in place by the gravitational pull of both the jovian and Coyote, with RCRs on the ring periodically firing to maintain that delicate balance. If the comps were reprogrammed to misfire in the wrong direction, then the torus would lose orbit, fall toward the planet. Bear's rings would do the rest; chunks of ice the size of this building would destroy the starbridge as surely as if it was a birthday piñata caught in a hailstorm.

"Thank you. You're doing fine." Wendy held out her hand. "Give me your satphone." Hawk hesitated, and she snapped her fingers. "Now."

Hawk reached under his jacket, unclipped the unit from his belt. "The frequency is preset," he said. "All you have to do is—"

"Push the recall button." Wendy took the phone from him. "The next time you talk to Parson, I'll be on the line, too." She turned to the Proctor.

"Take him to the conference room, and put a guard on him. He gets food and water, and a walk to the privy when he needs it, but at no time does he leave anyone's sight. Understand?"

"Yes, ma'am." The blueshirt stepped forward, took Hawk by the arm. The young man didn't protest as he was led away; an apologetic glance over his shoulder at his aunt and uncle, then the Proctor closed the door behind them.

"Oh, God." Carlos collapsed against her desk, rubbing his fingers against his closed eyes. "What did we do wrong? Why did Susan think we—?"

"We'll work that out later." Wendy's skull thrummed with the beginnings of a headache. "Dieter's going to be here any minute, and so's Ana. I'm going to have to explain everything to them, and tell 'em what we're doing to take care of it."

"Yeah. I know." Carlos glanced at her. "Got any ideas?"

Wendy gazed the globe on her desk. "I think so," she said softly. "Ready to take a ride?"

"Where?" Then he caught her meaning. "Yeah. Sure."

She forced a smile. "Thanks. I was hoping you'd say that."

EASS *Francis Drake* / 1749

"Raleigh, *you're clear for rendezvous and docking.*" The voice of the *Drake*'s com officer was a thin buzz in Anastasia Tereshkova's ear. "*CM field inactive, deck crew standing by.*"

"*We copy,* Drake. Raleigh *out.*" Ana glanced at the pilot. "All yours, Lieutenant."

"Thank you, ma'am." The shuttle pilot didn't look away from the controls as he gently turned the yoke, firing maneuvering thrusters to bring the shuttle in proper alignment with the vessel below them.

Ana gazed out the cockpit's starboard window, watched as the *Drake* swung into view. The enormous doors on its upper hull were already open; for a moment she caught a glimpse of the shuttle bay, a florescent circle illuminated upon the landing deck, then it vanished as the pilot brought up the shuttle's nose, matching vector with the starship. A faint whine as the landing gear doors opened, then he fired vertical thrusters and began final descent.

"Are you all right back there?" Ana asked, not taking her eyes from the crosshatch on the center comp screen. "There's going to be a—"

"I know," Carlos said from the passenger seat behind her. "And stop asking me that. This isn't the first time, y'know."

"Sorry." She took a moment to look back at him. Carlos calmly gazed out his porthole, watching the final stages of docking. "I should warn you," she added, "it's a little different from what you've done before. Once we're within three meters of touchdown—"

"You reactivate the field, let gravity do the rest." Carlos took hold of his armrests, then uncrossed his legs and braced his feet. "No problem."

Ana shrugged, returned her attention to the docking procedure. The pilot was murmuring under his breath, carrying on a subvocal conversation with the bay control officer. Through the cockpit windows, the leading edges of the bay doors yawned open on either side of the shuttle. A quick view of the *Drake*'s forward section, with command deck as a camelback hump above the bow, then the shuttle bay rose up around them, figures within the observation cupola carefully monitoring the landing operations.

Gravity came upon them as an invisible hand, materializing from the Millis-Clement field to snatch at the shuttle. A brief rumble as the pilot fired thrusters to brake their descent, then a swift jolt as the *Raleigh*'s wheels touched down. Contact lights flashed, an alarm buzzed; the pilot shut off both, then ran his hands across the controls, rendering the shuttle cold and inert.

"Docking complete, Captain," he said. "All systems safe, bay doors being secured."

"Thank you, Lieutenant." Tereshkova looked up, saw that the doors were already rolling down. She touched her jaw, opening the comlink again. "Bridge, this is the captain. Belay repressurization of landing bay. Prep shuttle for sortie and extend gangway, please." She looked back at the pilot. "Think you can handle another rendezvous and docking in four hours, or would you like to be relieved?"

"No problem, skipper. A bite to eat and quick lie-down, and I'm all yours."

"Good man. Be back here in three and a half." Tereshkova patted his shoulder, then unbuckled her harness. "Mr. President, if you'll follow me . . ."

"Four hours?" Carlos was astonished. "Don't you mean ten?"

"*Drake*'s not a shuttle. We can make it to the starbridge in less than half the time, if we use main drive." She smiled at him. "And I think you'd like to see your daughter soon as possible, *nyet*?"

"*Da*. Thank you." Carlos unclasped his harness, stood up. "All yours, Captain."

The pressurized gangway led from *Raleigh*'s lateral hatch to Deck 2 of *Drake*'s aft section. An ensign waited for Tereshkova just outside the airlock, the captain's tunic in one hand and a datapad in the other. Ana took a moment to exchange the shagswool sweater she'd worn since leaving Shuttlefield for the top part of her service uniform—when she got a chance, she'd return to her quarters and put on the rest of her out-fit—and took the pad from the ensign. A quick glance at its screen told her that the *Drake* was exactly as she'd left it, save for the absence of twelve crew members on shore leave. No time to wait for them to come back aboard, yet she smiled when she saw that one of them was her ex-ecutive officer. If not for the fact that Milos's predecessor had requested paternity leave just before the *Drake* left Highgate, Starbridge Coyote might have been taken without warning. Not that it made that much dif-ference now.

"Ana?" Forgotten for the moment, Carlos caught up with her and the ensign as they headed down the narrow corridor. "Where are we going?"

"Command deck. Unless you'd rather wait in the wardroom." He shook his head. "Then follow me." She paused, then stopped and turned around. "And no offense," she added, her voice low, "but while we're here, I'd appreciate it if you'd address me as Captain."

"Of course. Sorry." Carlos stood aside to let a crewman brush past them. "And thanks for not leaving me in the shuttle. I want to . . . I need to see what's—"

"I understand." Tereshkova briefly touched his shoulder, hoping that the ensign following them wouldn't notice the familiarity, yet he'd deliber-ately looked away, making this none of his business. "Just remember," she added, "this is diplomatic courtesy. You're now aboard an EA starship. Your status as former president of the Coyote Federation—"

"No special privileges. Right." A smile played at the corners of his mouth. "Believe me, I appreciate it."

Trailed by the ensign, Tereshkova led Carlos through the ship's forward section, making their way through narrow passageways until they reached the ladder leading to Deck 3. At the top was a sealed hatch. Tereshkova paused to press her thumb against the lockplate; the diode flashed from red to green, and she pushed open the hatch and walked in.

Drake's bridge was a split-level compartment, with the propulsion, life support, engineering, communications, and weapons stations on the upper deck and the navigation and helm stations on the lower deck. Her command chair, high-backed and fitted with a moveable lapboard, was positioned behind the railing separating the two levels; from here she could see not only the helm and nav stations, but also the broad, wraparound windows that offered a 120-degree view of the ship's bow, along with the data screens arrayed along the rail. The ceiling was low, with hand rungs among the electrical conduits and florescent panels; the lights had been turned down, so the compartment was illuminated mainly by the blue glow of comp screens. The only sounds were the quiet voices of the bridge officers, and the ever-present hum of the ship's engines.

The command deck was utilitarian and cold, and not just a little cramped. In times past, Ana had regarded the *Drake* as her home. She was still comfortable here, but now that she had a cabin on Albion—three rooms, including a den with a fieldstone fireplace in front of which she could curl up with a good book, and a bedroom where she woke up every morning to the sound of roosters crowing—she'd come to regard her role as the *Drake*'s commanding officer as being less of a calling than a distraction. Retirement was a temptation; lately, she found herself thinking about tendering her resignation. It wasn't too late to consider finding a husband, perhaps even having children.

But for now . . .

"Welcome back, Captain." Her first officer, Luigi D'Costa, stood up from the command chair as she walked in. "Hope you enjoyed your holiday."

"It could have lasted longer, thanks." The other officers on duty acknowledged her arrival with brief nods before returning to their jobs; she didn't require anyone aboard to salute her. "May I introduce our guest? Carlos Montero, former president of the Coyote Federation."

"Pleasure, Mr. President." D'Costa offered a courteous bow, which Carlos returned in kind. "There's not much room here for passengers, I'm afraid, but . . ."

"That's fine. I'll just stand over here." Carlos leaned against the rail. He obviously thought he was being out of the way, yet as Ana took her place in the command chair she saw that he was blocking her view of one of the overhead screens.

"Bring a seat up from the crew mess," she quietly said to the ensign. "We'll bolt it down somewhere." The ensign nodded and left, and she turned to D'Costa again. "What's our status? Any further contact with the Gatehouse?"

"None, ma'am. We transmitted a text message, informing them that we're on our way with a government negotiator aboard—"

"You didn't identify him, did you?"

"No, ma'am, as per your orders. We haven't received any response, other than a text-message reiteration of their demands."

"Hmm. Well, then . . ."

"One more thing, Captain." D'Costa handed a pad to her. "Before we lost contact with the Gatehouse crew, there was a transmission from Highgate, via hyperspace com channel. It was meant as an advisory to them, but a duplicate was sent to us as well."

She took the pad from him, but didn't look at it. "Tell me what it says, please."

D'Costa nervously glanced in Carlos's direction. "Captain, it's a priority ESA message. Classified."

She hesitated. Most hyperspace messages from the European Space Administration were fairly routine—lists of incoming immigrants, for instance, or requests for scientific information about the 47 Uma system—yet now and then a classified communiqué was sent to the *Drake* that was not meant to be divulged to the Coyote government. And for good reason. The ugly truth was that, although the Alliance had signed a U.N.-brokered treaty with the Coyote Federation, neither side fully trusted the other.

In this instance, though, a particular message had been so important that Starbridge Coyote was notified as well as the *Drake*. "Coded?" she asked quietly, and D'Costa shook his head. Carlos was listening intently.

There was no way she could evict him from the bridge without raising his suspicions . . . and after all, he was a diplomatic emissary, not to mention a personal friend. "Go ahead. What did it say?"

"The *Magellan* is due to arrive at 2300 CST." D'Costa let out his breath. "Shakedown cruise, nothing more. No passengers, no freight . . . a dry run."

"Oh, hell." She raised a hand to her eyes, gently kneaded the bridge of her nose. She'd been expecting this, of course, but not so soon. And who the hell at ESA decided not to inform her people until the last minute?

"Another ship?" Carlos stared at her. "You didn't—"

"Later," she said quietly, holding up a hand. "I'll tell you in a minute." She looked at D'Costa again. "Do you think the fly-through has been pro- grammed into the Gatehouse AI?"

"I don't see why not. That's probably why they were notified the same time we were. If Dr. Whittaker received the transmission—"

"He probably did. Something like this, he wouldn't have ignored." She let out her breath. "Damn it. Of all the times . . ."

Carlos moved closer to her. "Captain, you can't keep me in the dark like this," he said quietly. "Is there something I should know?"

"Just wait!" she snapped. Carlos shrank back, and D'Costa glared at him. "Inform Ambassador Vogel that the *Magellan* is scheduled to arrive soon," she went on. "I'll leave it to him to inform the proper colonial au- thorities." She tried to ignore the fact that the president's husband was standing next to her. Better let Dieter take care of this himself; diplomacy was his game, not hers, and she had more important issues to consider just now. "Has the hyperspace relay channel been shut down?" D'Costa shook his head. Good. That was something in their favor. "Then inform them what's happening here, and let them know that I . . ."

She stopped to think for a moment. "Advise them that the situation is critical, and that I believe that the *Magellan* fly-through is a bad idea at this time and should be delayed." D'Costa hurried away, heading for the com station. Ana leaned forward to peer over the railing. "Ms. Jones, are we alive this evening?"

"Yes, ma'am. Wide awake and ready to travel." The young woman seated at the helm grinned as she glanced up at her.

"Excellent. Mr. Rollins, I trust you've plotted a trajectory for the Gate- house."

"Plotted and programmed, ma'am." The navigator's hands hovered above his board, ready to do her bidding.

"Then take us there. Full thrust until we reach cruise velocity, then engage the main drive."

Jones's eyes widened. "Main drive? Captain . . ."

"I want us there soon as possible. Work out emergency braking maneuvers, even if we have to drain the reserves." This was no idle request; in order to decelerate from the high velocity of the diametric drive, *Drake* would have to dump most of its deuterium fuel straight into the fusion reactors. Risky business, but it would cut their ETA from ten hours to less than four. They'd limp home on dry tanks, if they had to. "Tell me now if it can't be done."

Jones took a moment to run some figures through her comp. She traded a cautious glance with Rollins, then looked at her captain again. "We can do it, skipper. On your mark."

"Roll with it." Pulling up her lapboard, Tereshkova activated the intercom and the flight recorder, then pressed her jaw. "All hands, this is the captain," she said. "Sounding general quarters. Repeat, general quarters. Prepare for deorbit and max thrust in sixty seconds, with main drive engagement in ten minutes. This is not a drill."

Orange lamps flashed to life along the ceiling as bridge officers snapped their seat belts into place. She studied the screens, quickly analyzing the graphs and bars of information that scrolled down them. All systems operative. No signs of trouble. Her people knew their jobs, even if they had to scramble to—

"Ana? I mean, Captain . . . what are you doing?"

She'd forgotten about Carlos. Obviously bewildered, he anxiously watched the activity around them. The ensign hadn't yet reappeared with the seat she'd requested, and now that they were on GQ he was doubtless at his station.

"Getting us to your daughter, soon as possible." She tried to reassure him with a quick smile. "Don't worry, the field is still active. We won't pull more than a half-g or so. But you might want to hold tight."

Carlos fastened his grip upon the railing, turned his back against the windows. He understood that *Drake* was about to rip out of orbit. "You still haven't told me what's going on. What is the *Magellan*? Why is it—?"

"There's much I need to tell you, but . . ." She shook her head. "Trust me, please," she added quietly. "I'm trying to do what's right."

"All right. I understand." He paused. "But for whom?"

She couldn't answer that. The flight recorder was active; the truth might incriminate her. "Just hold on," she murmured, then she snapped her belt around her waist. "Helm, are we ready?"

"On your mark, Captain." Jones's right hand held steady above her panel.

"Mark."

STARBRIDGE COYOTE / 1828

Susan listened for another moment to her headset, then turned her chair away from the com station. "Bad news. We're going to have company soon."

Jon was standing watch over Whittaker, who was seated on the other side of the command center, his wrists still bound together. They both looked at her. "The *Drake*?" Jon asked, and she nodded. "What's going on?"

"It broke orbit about five minutes ago. Their com officer says the negotiator's aboard. They still want to speak to us, but—"

"So why don't you?" Whittaker asked. "Might as well. After all, they've received your demands. No point in—"

"We'll talk to them when we're ready." Jon was more nervous than his captive. Indeed, Whittaker had finally relaxed a bit, now that he knew that no one was going to harm him. The rest of the Gatehouse crew had been confined to their quarters; they had plenty of food and water, but Jon had carefully searched the compartment, removing anything that might conceivably be used as a weapon, before he sealed the hatch from the outside, using hemp rope he'd brought up for this purpose to bind the lock-lever to a rung of the access shaft ladder.

"Maintain silence," Jon went on, clinging to a ceiling rail, "but keep monitoring that channel. I expect we'll hear from them before they get here." He glanced at his watch. "Should be about four, maybe five hours."

"That soon?" Susan was surprised. "But it took ten hours for us to—"

"We came in on a skiff, remember? If I know Tereshkova, she'll engage the main drive. That'll get her here sooner." Pulling himself hand-over-hand across the compartment, he extended the stunner to her. "Keep an eye on him," he said, then he went over to Manny. "Any luck yet?"

"Luck's not a factor. Only probability." The Savant stood before a console, his feet held in place by a pair of stirrups. A thick cable led from his chest to a dataport; his claws tapped against the keyboard as information flashed across a comp screen faster than the human eye could follow. "I haven't cracked the password, if that's what you're asking. Given enough time to run all the possible permutations—"

"How much time?"

"Best estimate?" The slightest of pauses. "Seven hours. Perhaps eight."

"Not good enough. The *Drake* will be here by then."

"Then we're back to probability." Manny continued to work, the quantum comp in his chest processing all feasible alphanumeric configurations within nine decimal places. "Or luck, if you prefer."

"Dammit, Manny . . ."

"This conversation has involved three megabytes of my capability. That's about two hundred fewer computations per second. A quick game of chess would be less time consuming, and it might help calm you." Manny tapped a couple of keys out of sequence, and a chessboard appeared on one of the screens. "Black queen's pawn forward two. Your move."

Whittaker snickered. He tried to hide his amusement by looking away, but Susan heard him, and so did Jon. He pushed himself off the ceiling, sailed across the compartment to where Whittaker was seated. "Look, are you going to tell me—?"

"Not a chance." Whittaker grinned at him. "Like your friend says, you roll the dice, you take your chances."

Jon slapped a hand against the ceiling, then pushed himself back across the room to where Manny continued to work.

Susan shut her eyes. Taking over the Gatehouse should have been the hard part, but it wasn't. Just before the crewmembers on duty in the command center surrendered, one of them managed to encrypt all major command functions behind a nine-figure password. The fact that she and Jon had been forced to stun both of them hadn't helped the situation either; an hour had passed before they'd regained consciousness, and since then neither one had been cooperative. Like Whittaker, they'd come to realize that any threats to shove them out the airlock were empty at best. All they had to do was wait until the *Drake* arrived.

It's all going wrong, she thought. *How did I ever let myself get talked into this?*

Desperation, yes. She'd seen firsthand the effects of global colonization: the clear-cutting of forests, the burning of savannahs, the slaughter of wildlife habitats, the threatened extermination of the *chirreep*. That, and anger at her father: he'd turned a blind eye to what the Thompson Wood Company was doing to the Black Mountains, then he'd used his presidency to negotiate the rape of her world, and finally he'd invested in Janus even as it made environmental destruction into a profit-making enterprise.

Rebellion ran strong in her family. Her grandfather helped Captain Lee hijack the *Alabama*, and her father led guerilla raids on Liberty. When Jon proposed his scheme, she hadn't hesitated to go along with it. Outrage wasn't her only motivation, though, but also love . . . and not only for Coyote.

No one in her family knew that, all those times she'd gone to Great Dakota, ostensibly to conduct university research, she'd actually been visiting the camp Jon and Manny had built in the Black Mountains. At first, she'd thought she'd only been helping them learn more about the *chirreep*, yet only recently she'd come to realize that something else had drawn her.

Like it or not, she'd fallen in love with Jonathan Parson. She still didn't know whether the feeling was mutual—they'd spent a few nights in bed together, but she'd told herself that this had only been casual—yet she'd been unable to confess her feelings toward him, and even now she wondered if he had any toward her. Nonetheless, she loved him. And now she wondered if she'd let her emotions take her into something she'd never intended.

Damn it, if only her father had listened . . .

"You don't know what you've gotten yourself into, do you?"

Startled, she looked around at Whittaker. The physicist quietly gazed at her, a knowing look in his eyes. He'd spoken quietly, so that the others couldn't hear him.

"What do you—?"

"You know what I mean." Whittaker nodded toward Jon and Manny.

"You're a smart girl. You know you don't have a chance. In a few hours, you're going to have visitors . . . and believe me, they're not going to take no for an answer."

"I'm not worried about the *Drake*." She looked away. "They won't try anything if they think we're keeping you and your friends hostage."

"I thought you said we weren't hostages."

"I mean . . ."

"Yeah, sure. I know." Whittaker shook his head. "But the *Drake*'s not your problem. You've got a bigger one than that." She looked back at him, and he nodded. "Maybe Mr. Parson can negotiate with Captain Tereshkova. You're not going to be dealing with her, though, or anyone else you know."

Susan stared at him. "Come again? I don't . . ."

"Yes, please," Jon said. "Tell us more."

Susan looked up, saw that Jon had overheard them; he kept his distance, yet carefully listened to their conversation. "You've got something to say, Dr. Whittaker?"

"Might as well." Whittaker no longer bothered to keep his voice low. "No point in hiding it. In about four and a half hours, the starbridge is going to open, and a ship is going to come through . . . the *Magellan*, sister ship to the *Drake*, on her first shakedown cruise."

"How do you know this?" Jon asked.

"Received final confirmation from Highgate only a few hours before you showed up. That's when we entered the activation program into the station AI." Whittaker shrugged. "It's all preset. The comps do the rest, right down to charging the torus at precisely the right moment. All we do here is sit back and watch."

"Then we send them a message, tell them to back off."

Whittaker shook his head. "You'd have to open a hyperspace channel, and for that you need the password." He grinned. "Of course, the *Drake* can do that . . . and I have no doubt that Captain Tereshkova is already in touch with them. But as far as you're concerned—"

"Then we'll shut down the starbridge. Prevent them coming through."

"Jon . . ." Manny turned half around. "We can't do that either. Not without the—"

"Oh, bloody hell!" Jon slammed a fist against a console. "What's the password? Give it to me, or I'll—"

"Do what?" Whittaker remained passive. "March me into the airlock?

Space one of my crew?" Again, he shook his head. "You're not a killer. None of you are. And you know it, too."

A long moment of silence within the command center. No one knew what to say next. Susan stared helplessly at Jon; he swore under his breath, turned away from her. Manny returned his attention to the console, diligently continued to try to crack the password. It was all for nothing. The entire effort had been doomed from the beginning. They should have realized this.

A double-beep in her headset. Ignoring Jon's orders to maintain radio silence, she prodded its lobe. "Coyote Gatehouse," she murmured. "Go ahead."

"Susan? Sweetheart, is that you?"

Her eyes widened. Her father's voice.

And she knew, even without having to look at the com station, that the source of transmission was the *Drake*.

LIBERTY / 1917

Night had fallen outside the windows of the second-floor conference room when the Proctor opened the door and let Wendy in. Hawk was taking a nap at the table, his head resting on his arms; he sat up as she walked in, but he didn't speak to her, only regarded her with sullen eyes. "Thanks," Wendy said. "I'll let you know if we need anything." The blueshirt nodded, then closed the door behind her. "Doing okay there? Have you been treated well?"

Hawk gave an absent shrug. Wendy glanced at the dinner tray on the other side of the table; the water glass was empty, but the chicken sandwich and fried potatoes had gone untouched. "Doesn't look like you have much of an appetite," she said. "If you want something else . . ."

Another shrug. Hawk made a pretense of gazing at a watercolor landscape framed on the wall beside the door. "Guess not," Wendy murmured, then she pulled back a chair across from him and sat down. "But, y'know, if the silent routine is supposed to impress me, you're not getting very far. And it's not going to do your friends any good."

A hint of a sneer before he looked away again. He'd been here for nearly five hours now, without anyone visiting him other than to deliver dinner. Long enough for him to mentally rehearse any number of responses to the next person to come through the door. She should have talked to him earlier, but she'd been busy all afternoon, meeting first with Dieter Vogel, then with the Council representatives. Yet when she hadn't been engaged in diplomacy and politics, she'd been working on how to deal with her nephew. And, unlike Hawk, she'd had the advantage of not working in a vacuum.

"You know," she went on, "your cousin's in a lot of trouble. Same for Parson and Castro. Bad enough that they took control of the Gatehouse, but if they'd just give up now, things would go a lot easier for them. I'd be willing to work out something with the magistrates . . . probation, community service, something on those lines. Same for you, if you'll cooperate."

No reaction. Hawk continued to study the painting. "But the longer they hold out, the more impatient other folks are likely to get . . . the EA, for starters. They built the starbridge, after all, and they negotiated treaties with us in good faith. If they believe that we can't be trusted to hold up our side of the bargain, then they may take measures to make sure that it remains operational. Do you understand?"

Hawk sighed, pretending to be bored by all this. Yet Wendy had anticipated such a reaction. "Maybe not. Or maybe you do, but you just don't care. It's even possible that you think I'm lying. If I was in your position, I'd probably think the same thing. But here's the truth."

Leaning forward, she looked him square in the eye. "There is no way we're going to agree to your demands. All treaties are going to remain intact. No agreements are going to be annulled. No one is going to be sent back to Earth. Even if your friends destroy the starbridge, we won't renege on our promises. That's a fact."

Wendy slipped a hand into a pocket of her skirt, pulled out the satphone the Proctor had taken from him a few hours earlier. "Call them yourself, if you want," Wendy said, sliding the unit across the table to him. "Maybe you'd like to give them the bad news. Doesn't matter. Your uncle is aboard the *Drake*, and in a few hours he'll reach the Gatehouse. No doubt he's already in radio contact. Maybe Susan will listen to her father, maybe she won't, but the message will remain the same. No deals. No compromises. *Comprende*?"

Hawk flinched as the satphone came to rest next to him. His hand twitched, as if he wanted to pick it up yet couldn't bring himself to do so. His resolve was crumbling, though, and now it was time for her to play her trump card.

"Mind if I have this?" Wendy reached over to the tray, picked up half of the chicken sandwich. "Haven't eaten yet, and I'm starving." Ignoring the ravenous look in his eye, she took a bite, chewed thoughtfully. "Shame to let it go to waste. Oh, by the way, want to come clean about what happened to your father?"

Hawk's face became ashen, and he quickly looked away. "I called your mother, had a long talk with her," she went on, keeping her voice casual. "Your uncle and I heard that Lars went missing a few weeks ago, of course, but until today I hadn't gotten the full story. That the two of you had gone up into the mountains looking for *chirreep*, but only one of you had come back. You'd said something about you and him getting lost up there, and how he'd fallen into a ravine."

"A sinkhole." Hawk's voice was hollow. "There was a sinkhole, and he fell in."

"That's it. He fell into a sinkhole." Wendy took another bite from the sandwich, brushed crumbs from her mouth. "Then you managed to find your way back to camp, but somehow you couldn't remember where that sinkhole was."

"It was dark." Hawk's hand trembled as he nervously pushed a lock of hair away from his face. "We got lost up there, and we were trying to find our way down the mountain when—"

"The ground just opened up and swallowed him." Wendy smiled. "Sure. 'And only I survived to tell thee—' "

"It's the truth, I swear."

"Swear all you want. I still have my doubts." She tossed aside the rest of the sandwich. "Your father's been living in the mountains since before you were born. He probably knows them better than I know the streets of town. Even in the dark, you think he'd lose his way and fall into a sinkhole he'd never seen before? I doubt it . . . just like I doubt that you'd manage to find your way back to camp, then conveniently forget where you lost your father."

Pushing back her chair, she strolled over to the window. "Marie tells me you vanished from camp shortly after that. Strange, isn't it . . . your father's missing, perhaps even dead, and suddenly you disappear. No one sees you again until this afternoon."

"I had to . . . I had to get away." The bravado had vanished, and he seemed to be disappearing into his seat. "I don't know what happened to him. He just . . . he just . . ."

"Hawk, listen to me." She turned away from the window, looked straight at him again. "I knew your father from way back when. He and your uncle were in the war together, and Carlos didn't trust him even then. I hate to say it, but I know what sort of a person he is. There isn't a decent bone in his body. There's no one he hasn't hurt . . . your mother, your sister, even you."

Hawk's lower lip trembled. Tears slipped from the corners of his eyes. Wendy pretended not to notice, although part of her wanted to take him into her arms. Instead, she sat down in a chair next to him. "If you did what I think you did . . . what your mother thinks you did . . . then you must have felt you had a good reason," she said quietly. "That's something you'll have to work out with your own conscience."

She paused, hating herself for the way she was manipulating him. "But if you tell me everything that I need to know, then I'll talk to the magistrates, let them know that there were mitigating circumstances. It doesn't have to be so—"

"They're not going to destroy the starbridge." Hawk snuffled, wiped his eyes with his hand. "It's just a bluff. All they want to do is get people's attention, make them see what's happening here. That's all."

She let out her breath. "Good. That's what I needed to hear. Now, can you tell me—?"

"I hated him. I know he was my father, and I tried to love him, but . . . oh, god, I hated the bastard. That's why . . ." He paused. "You can understand that, can't you?"

He'd killed him. Her worst suspicions had been confirmed. Wendy knew that she should be horrified, yet instead she found herself thinking of her own father, how he'd betrayed everyone he'd known, including herself. "Better than you know," she said, nodding her head. "Better than I can ever tell."

Then she moved closer. "Now, talk to me."

The airlock opened, and Carlos found himself staring at the muzzle of a stunner. "Easy, now," he heard Parson say from the other side of the hatch. "Come out slowly, and keep your hands where I can see them."

Hardly the most courteous of receptions, but not unexpected. Parson's instructions had been specific; Carlos was to come aboard alone and un-armed, and if anyone else was in the airlock when it was opened, the hatch would be immediately shut and the depressurization cycle would be initi-ated. Carlos raised his hands above his head, then slowly turned, allowing Parson to see that he was the only one inside the airlock.

"Feel better?" he asked.

"A little." Parson moved out of the way. "All right, come on in . . . but don't try any surprises."

"Wouldn't dream of it." Grasping the rungs on the inside of the hatch cover, Carlos slowly pulled himself into the ready room. Parson was alone as well; he carefully backed away, keeping Carlos at arm's length while never letting the stunner waver from his guest.

"Close the hatch and secure it," he said. Once Carlos had done so, Parson gestured toward a hand rung on the far side of the compartment. "Grab that," he said. "Keep your eyes straight ahead. Any sudden moves . . ."

"I got the idea." Carlos took hold of the rung, looked at the bulkhead while Parson gave him a one-handed pat-down. It occurred to him that Parson couldn't do this in microgravity without anchoring himself; he must have put the stunner away for a moment in order to grasp another rung with his free hand. Carlos's legs floated free; a good, swift backward-kick would catch Parson in the groin or the stomach, perhaps give him an opportunity to grab the stunner. Parson may be half his age, but Carlos had years of combat experience; he was certain he could take him, if he wanted to do so.

Yet he wasn't about to take that risk, any more than he'd gone along with Ana's suggestion to put a couple of her men aboard the *Raleigh,* and have them secretly exit the shuttle through the lower cargo hatch. He was there to negotiate with the hijackers, not double-cross them. Besides, his daughter was aboard; he dared not do anything foolish while Susan was in harm's way.

"All right, you're clean." Parson finished frisking him, then pushed himself away. "Now tell the pilot to undock and return to the *Drake.*"

Carlos turned around. "That wasn't part of the deal."

"It is now." Parson nodded toward the airlock. "Do it, or you can climb back in and shove off."

Carlos hesitated, then tapped his headset lobe. "Lieutenant? Mr. Parson wants you to leave."

The pilot's voice came through his earphone. *"I'm sorry, Mr. President, but I'm under orders to remain here until—"*

"Do as I say." When he didn't hear a response, he went on. "I'll take responsibility. Go back to the *Drake* and wait for me there. Do you copy?"

A brief pause; no doubt the pilot was checking with Ana, who was probably monitoring this exchange from the *Drake's* bridge. *"Yes, sir.* Raleigh *preparing for departure."*

Keeping his stunner on Carlos, Parson pushed himself over to the airlock. He depressurized the sleeve, then peered through the airlock window. A few seconds later, a vibration passed through the hull as the shuttle detached itself from the docking collar; Carlos didn't need to look outside to know that the *Raleigh* was moving away from the Gatehouse.

"Little nervous, aren't you?" He tried to keep his tone casual. "You don't need to keep me at gunpoint, you know. Nothing's going to happen to you."

"Thanks for the assurance, but I think I'll keep it handy. Susan tells me you used to be quite the fighter in your day." Parson prodded his jaw. "We're safe, Manny. Is the rest of the station secure?" He listened for a moment. "Very good. We're coming up." He nodded toward the compartment hatch. "After you, Mr. President."

They made their ascent through the access tunnel in silence. As they passed the hatch leading to the crew quarters, Carlos noticed the straps fastened around the lock-lever. The rest of the crew was probably confined to that deck; Parson hustled him quickly past the hatch. He should have relaxed by now, yet he seemed to be even more edgy than before.

Can't blame him, Carlos thought. *The cards are stacked against him. And he doesn't know it yet, but I've already called his bluff.*

The first person Carlos saw upon entering the command center was Manuel Castro. It had been many years since the last time he'd seen the Savant; although he was supposed to be ageless, his threadbare black cloak, his eyepatch, and the scuffed surfaces of his metallic form somehow gave him the appearance of an old man. He stood beside the hatch, his feet fastened to the deck by a pair of stirrups. "Mr. President, welcome. I hope your trip here was—"

"Fine, thank you." Carlos gazed past him. Susan was on the other side of the compartment, holding on to a ceiling rail. Seated next to her was Jonas Whittaker, secured to his chair by a lap-strap, his wrists taped together. She immediately looked away, yet there was no way she could hide the embarrassment that spread across her face. She was an adult now, yes, but in that instant she became a child who'd been caught doing something wrong, and now anticipated the wrath of an angry parent.

Yet he wasn't angry, only afraid. She'd made a mistake; he had to get her out of this before matters became worse. As they would, very soon. He caught a glimpse of a chronometer on the nearest panel: 2238:43. Little more than twenty minutes remaining.

"So, Mr. President, here we are." Parson came up the shaft behind him, his gun still held at his back. "Let's hear your proposal."

"I'd take it as a sign of good faith if you'd put that thing away." Carlos turned around, looked Parson in the eye. "You don't need it. I promise that I won't try to attack you."

"Sorry, but—"

"When my father makes a promise, he keeps it." Susan's voice was quiet. "Put it down, Jon. Please."

Parson hesitated, then slipped the stunner into his jacket pocket. Carlos tried not to look relieved; he gave Susan a quick nod, but refrained from smiling. Castro pushed himself over to a console beneath the windows, where he picked up a cable dangling in midair and plugged it into a chest socket.

"You're right," Carlos said. "I told Susan that if you'd let me aboard, I'd have a proposal that would put an end to this."

"Don't give 'em anything!" Jonas snapped. "They don't have the passwords to—"

"Shut up!" Parson's face turned red. "It doesn't matter if we have them or not. We can still destroy the station anytime we—"

"I think not." Carlos slowly shook his head. "If you had a bomb, maybe, but you don't. And without access to the comps, you have no control of the RCR system."

"We'll soon have access." Castro didn't look away from the console; his fingers continued to work at the keypad. "I've been processing all possible alphanumeric permutations. Within another hour or so."

"You don't have that much time, and you know it." Carlos glanced at Jonas. "I'm sure he's told you already that the *Magellan* is due to arrive at 2300. The comps are already programmed to open the starbridge, and Ambassador Vogel has already used the hyperspace comlink to inform her captain of the situation. I doubt he's going to be in any mood to negotiate."

Jonas had an ill-disguised smirk, and Parson seemed to be chewing his lower lip, but Susan had gone pale. Ignoring the other two, Carlos used a ceiling rail to pull himself hand-over-hand across the command center. "It's all right," he said, reaching down to touch her shoulder. "I understand. You thought you were doing the right."

"Don't tell me what I think!" She angrily swatted his hand away. "You don't know what I'm thinking! You never did!"

Carlos felt something cold wrap itself around his heart. "I'm sorry. I didn't mean to . . ."

"Then what do you mean?" Anger seethed within her eyes as she glared at him. "Come here to gloat, tell us . . . tell *me* . . . that this is pointless? Now we're supposed to give up, let your friends do what they want?" Turning away, she gazed out the window at the distant starbridge. "God, I wished we'd destroyed that thing. It would have made things a lot more simple."

Her words stung, yet Carlos knew he had to be steady. If he couldn't deal with her on her own terms, then at least he could be truthful. "You wouldn't have done that. It was a bluff. We know that now."

"Oh, hell," Parson murmured. "Hawk talked, didn't he? You forced him to—"

"We didn't force him to do anything," Carlos said, "but, yeah, he talked. He told us that your aim was never to destroy the starbridge, only to shut it down for a while." He allowed himself a slight smile. "You know how much depends on it. If it's gone . . ."

"Coyote becomes isolated again, and Earth is left to rot." Pushing himself off a bulkhead, Parson floated across the compartment toward him. "But I know this world, Mr. President."

"Carlos . . . let's skip the formalities, shall we? And believe me, I know Coyote better than you do."

"Sure, but somehow you forgot what this place is about." Parson shook his head. "It's not supposed to be another Earth. We can't allow it to go the same way. I've seen what's happening down there. Forests leveled, native habitats demolished . . ."

"The *chirreep* threatened with extinction." Susan's voice trembled. "They're an intelligent species, Papa. They've got a language, a social structure . . ."

"I was the first one to find them, remember?" Carlos raised a hand. "Look, I agree we need to find some sort of balance, but we still need to—"

"Nice talk," Parson said, "but that's all it is, right? Talk, and more talk. But the fact remains that, when you were president, you negotiated a trade agreement with the EA that allowed them to establish a colony on Albion. And after you left office, you made a private deal with Janus, invested in . . ."

"They needed local investment so they could build a viable colony." Carlos felt his face grow warm. "It wasn't about making money. It was about putting up homes for everyone who comes here."

"Sure." Susan looked at him askance. "And profit never entered anyone's mind."

"If it builds homes, why not?" He gazed at her in disbelief. "What would you have us do? Drop a thousand colonists on New Brighton, let them fend for themselves? That's what the Union did when they established Shuttlefield." He pointed to Castro. "Ask your pal what that was like. He should know . . . he was lieutenant governor."

"Would it help if I admit I was wrong?" Castro replied.

"It might." Carlos looked at Parson again. "So what choice do you have? Social collectivism? We tried that already. See where it led us."

"Study history, and see where unchecked capitalism leads you."

"Then we tighten the rules." Carlos let out his breath. "Look, this is a frontier. We're making this up as we go along. You want to protect the *chirreep*, save the forests, control population growth? Fine. I'm with you. But you have to work within the system, not . . ."

"We tried that already, Papa." Susan's voice was quiet. "You weren't listening."

"I'm listening now." He turned to her again. "If you were trying to get my attention and your mother's, then you succeeded. You believe something's gone wrong? Then help us fix it."

Parson folded his arms together. "Easy for you to say, now that you've got our back against the wall."

"I would've said the same thing even if you were serious about destroying the starbridge and were able to do so." Carlos shook his head. "You can't win this way . . . but if you do it my way, then you'll get a fair hearing, I promise. And I've been authorized to tell you that no charges will be filed against you if you agree to stop this right now."

"You'd do that?" Parson remained distrustful.

"If you agree to my conditions, yes. Or you can wait for Manny to crack the password."

"Actually, I accomplished this sixty-two seconds ago." Castro turned toward Jonas. "2EZ4U2GET . . . a rather clever mnemonic. Your crewman has a rare sense of humor."

Jonas gaped at him. "And you didn't tell us until now?"

"I wanted to hear his proposal." Castro looked at Parson. "I think we should accept their terms. There's no point in continuing this action."

Susan studied her father for a long moment, her expression stoical. Then, reluctantly, she nodded. Parson sighed. "All right," he murmured. "I know when we're beaten. It's all yours, Mr. President."

"Thank you." This time, Carlos didn't try to hide his relief. He gave his daughter a grateful smile. "If you'll patch me through to the *Drake*, please."

With a resigned shrug, Parson pushed himself over to the com panel. Susan went to Jonas, and the operations chief said nothing as she used a penknife to cut the tape binding his wrists together. Carlos turned toward Castro. "I appreciate your judgment. That was . . ."

A shrill *beep-beep-beep* from the ceiling speaker. They barely had time to react before there was a silent light through the windows. Whipping around, Carlos saw that it came from the direction of the distant torus.

"Starbridge's opening." Jonas ripped the rest of the tape from his wrists, then unbuckled his seat belt and propelled himself across the compartment. "Something's coming through the wormhole."

"The *Magellan*." Carlos glanced at the nearest chronometer: 2300:03. Right on time, and not a moment too soon. "Jon, can you get me through to the *Drake*?"

"Affirmative. You're on."

Carlos tapped his headset, heard the welcome hum of carrier-wave static. "*Drake*, this is Coyote Gatehouse, President Montero speaking. Do you copy?"

"*Magellan* is through," Jonas said.

Carlos looked up at a viewscreen above the windows. A camera on the torus captured an image of streamlined shape almost identical to the *Drake*. The arriving starship was moving quickly away from the ring, its fusion engines glowing hot against the cold darkness.

"*We copy, Gatehouse.*" Ana's voice. "*Good to hear you again. What is your situation, please? Over.*"

"EAS *Magellan*, this is Starbridge Coyote." Jonas had found a headset and pulled it on. "Do you copy? Over."

"Situation good, Captain." Carlos cupped a hand over his left ear so that he wouldn't be distracted by the chatter with the *Magellan*. "We've resolved the problem, and the . . ." He stole a glance at his daughter, amended his thoughts. "Our friends have agreed to release control of the station. Over."

Silence. He heard nothing for a moment. Then he overheard Jonas: "That's not necessary, Captain. The hijackers have agreed to surrender. You don't have to—"

"What's going on?" Parson demanded.

"I don't know." Carlos was just as baffled as he was. He glanced at the screen again. The *Magellan* was almost out of sight, yet judging from its position, it seemed as if it was heading not toward Coyote, but instead the direction of the Gatehouse. "*Drake*, this is Gatehouse. Do you copy? Over."

"Oh, god, no." Jonas grabbed a handrail. "*Magellan*, stand down! I repeat, stand down!"

"*Gatehouse, this is* Drake." Ana's voice again. "Magellan *refuses to acknowledge that the situation has been resolved. They're moving in.*"

A new display on the screen: a schematic of the relative positions of the *Drake*, the *Magellan*, and the Gatehouse. The *Drake* was parked five miles from the Gatehouse; the *Magellan* was nine miles away, but rapidly closing in. Carlos grabbed the back of a chair to steady himself. "Ana, it's over! They've given up!"

"*I understand. I . . .*" A pause. "*The EA is assuming military control of the starbridge. Magellan's captain says that he wants all personnel . . . both station crew and unauthorized parties . . . to surrender immediately and allow a boarding party.*"

Carlos gripped the seatback. "Ana, they can't do this. They don't have the—"

"*Mr. President, the captain says that if you don't comply, the* Magellan *will be forced to take drastic measures.*" Ana's voice was terse. "*Stand by.* Drake *out.*"

A sharp click, and then he heard nothing but static.

EASS *Drake* / 2305

"*Captain Tereshkova, have you relayed our message to the Gatehouse?*"

Ana studied the image of the *Magellan*'s commanding officer, displayed on a miniature screen on her lapboard. Gabriel Pacino had changed since the last time she'd seen him; besides the fact that there were now captain's bars on the shoulders of his tunic, he'd cultivated a thin mustache, and there was a hint of grey at his temples. Promotion seemed to suit him well; now that he had his own ship, he'd become more self-confident than when he'd been her first officer aboard the *Columbus*.

"I have, Captain Pacino," she replied, her tone equally as formal, "and I'm awaiting their response. But as I've told you, President Montero—"

"*Former President Montero, you mean.*"

"*President* Montero is aboard the Gatehouse. He was brought there to negotiate a settlement. And, as I've also told you, he's reached a agreement with the perpetrators. No one aboard has been harmed, and the station is intact. There's no need to . . ."

"*Captain, my orders are clear. Assume control of the starbridge and take every-one aboard into custody, pending investigation of this incident.*" Pacino sat stiffly in his chair. *Magellan's* bridge was identical to the *Drake's*; the effect was akin to looking into a mirror, only to find someone else gazing back at you. "*Your responsibility is to assist my ship with the completion of these orders.*"

"I've received no such instructions, Captain, and I insist that this affair has been peacefully resolved. There's no need to—"

"*Ana, please.*" Pacino gave a rueful smile as he attempted to appeal to her through familiarity. "*This is no affair, as you put it, but a major incident. One of the hijackers is Jonathan Parson . . . I shouldn't have to remind you that he de-serted his command. Another is the former president's own daughter. Yet another is a savant, Manuel Castro.*"

"I'm aware of their identities. You've got a point?"

Pacino raised an eyebrow. "*Isn't it obvious? Local control of the starbridge isn't in our best interests. The colonists can't be trusted. If they allow . . .*" He shook his head. "*Look, they've left us with no choice. We need to take control of the star-bridge, at least temporarily, until this matter can be sorted out.*"

"And if they refuse to let themselves be taken into custody?"

"*Then we'll forced to take drastic—*"

"You said that already. What sort of measures?"

Pacino crossed his legs. "*We've been authorized to use tactical weapons to take out the command center while leaving the rest of the station intact.*" He paused. "*I'm sorry, Captain. I've been given no other option.*"

"I see." Ana struggled to remain stoical. "I'll relay this to the Gate-house. *Drake* out."

Her hand trembled as she switched off the comlink, and for a long mo-ment she stared out the bridge windows. The Gatehouse hovered only a few kilometers away, a fragile cylinder that once made up the core section of the *Columbus.* She couldn't see the *Magellan,* yet the navigation screen depicted its position as being six kilometers from the torus. If Pacino gave the order, his ship could open fire on the station within seconds.

She could assist the *Magellan;* indeed, that was what was expected of her. Or she could relay the ultimatum to the Gatehouse, then sit back and wait for events to unfold without any action on her part. Or . . .

"Captain?" D'Costa stepped closer to her. "What are your orders, ma'am?"

Damn it. I'm going to hell for this. She took a deep breath. "Mr. Rollins," she said aloud, "reposition us between the Gatehouse and the *Magellan*. Ms. Jones, initiate emergency thrust." She looked up at D'Costa. "Prepare for military engagement, please."

D'Costa's eyes widened, even as the helmsman and navigator turned to stare at her. "Captain, are you suggesting that we—?"

"It's not a suggestion. Please do as I say." Ana swiveled her seat around to face the rest of the bridge crew. They'd overheard her conversation with Pacino; as she expected, their faces registered shock. "Gentlemen, ladies," she said, trying to remain as calm as possible, "this isn't something I thought we'd ever have to do. The *Magellan*'s captain has been given orders that are unjustifiable, and it falls on us to protect unarmed civilians. I realize that I'm asking a lot from you. If anyone here wishes to be relieved of duty, now is the time."

Uncertain looks flashed from one crewman to another. A moment passed, then the lieutenant at the weapons control station stood up and walked toward the hatch. Everyone else remained at their stations. It may have been out of loyalty to her, but she suspected that it went further than that. Like herself, many of her crew now lived on Coyote; they might be ESA officers, yet Earth was no longer their home. And they knew how much damage an Alliance takeover of the starbridge would cause to Coyote's independence.

"Thank you," she said. "Mister D'Costa, will you assume the weapons station, please?"

"Captain, I . . ." D'Costa sighed. "Yes, ma'am." He turned to head for the vacant seat.

"Firing thrusters, Captain." Jones's hands tapped against her keypad, activating the auxiliary engines, then she pushed a pair of bars upward. Through the windows, Bear slowly moved away, and now the Gatehouse lay directly ahead. "ETA two minutes."

"Thank you, Lieutenant." Ana punched up a tactical display on an overhead screen. The two ships were only a few klicks apart from one another, with the distance rapidly closing as *Drake* moved to protect the Gatehouse. By now, Pacino would have noticed that her ship was in motion. Any second now . . .

"Ma'am?" This from the com officer. "Transmission from the *Magellan*."

"Vox only. Initiate com buffers." There was a chance that Pacino might try to transmit a virus; the buffers would prevent that kind of electronic warfare. She prodded her headset mike. "Captain Pacino?"

"Ana, what are you doing? You're repositioning the Drake.*"*

"Yes, I am." She kept her voice even. "We're putting ourselves between you and the Gatehouse. Do not attempt to fire upon it, or we'll be forced to retaliate."

A long pause. Ana almost wished she could see his face, but she was just as glad that she couldn't. Although she and Gabriel had once enjoyed a brief affair, that had ended a long time ago; it gave her no pleasure to treat him as a possible adversary.

"Ana, don't do this." Pacino's voice was almost pleading. *"It's not worth . . ."*

"You've been warned, Captain. Any further action on your part will be considered hostile. *Drake* out." She cut the channel, the glanced back at the com officer. "Any attempt to hotwire us, Lieutenant?"

"Yes, ma'am. Buffers registered a subroutine piggybacked to that last transmission. It's been spiked."

"Good work." So Pacino was preparing for battle. Time for her to do so as well. Ana flipped a couple of switches; lights within the ceiling panels flashed to amber and a klaxon howled twice as she activated the intercom. "General quarters," she said. "All hands to battle stations. This is not a drill. Repeat, this is not a drill."

All around, seat harnesses clicked as hands swept across panels. The window shutters closed, and a glance at a status panel told her the compartment hatches were being sealed. *Drake* was not a warship, but nonetheless its crew had been trained for combat situations. The time to question or debate the wisdom of her actions had ended; now they could only hope for the best and prepare for the worst.

"Ms. Fleming, cut MC field," she said.

"Aye, Captain." The life support officer hit a couple of switches. The klaxon blared again, warning everyone aboard the Millis-Clement was about to be disengaged. A couple of seconds passed, then she felt her body drift upward from her seat. Ana swore at herself as she grabbed the lapboard, then she hastily buckled her harness. She'd been so distracted, she'd neglected to . . .

"Approaching Gatehouse, Captain," Rollins said. "Bearing x-ray five-point-two, yankee minus oh-nine-point four, zulu oh-niner point oh-five, distance two point two kilometers."

Ana glanced up at the tactical display. The *Drake* was between the Gatehouse and the *Magellan*. "Ms. Jones, match orbit with the Gatehouse and hold position, then turn our bow toward the *Magellan*." She turned to the weapons station. "Mr. D'Costa, arm torpedoes and open weapons bays."

"Yes, ma'am." All trace of reluctance had vanished; her first officer knew his job. "Targeting solution?"

"Drive nacelles only." With luck, she might be able to demobilize *Magellan* only, and cause the minimal loss of life.

"*Magellan* closing in." D'Costa's voice was tight. "Range three-point-two klicks, velocity—"

"Signal from the Gatehouse, Captain."

"Not now, Lieutenant." Ana tapped at her keypad, gazed up at one of the overhead screens. An external camera caught an image of the *Magellan*: bow-first, heading directly toward her ship. She gently slid a fingertip across a trackpad, and the image zoomed to maximum focus. Dark areas along the ship's forward section showed her what she expected: *Magellan*'s torpedo doors had opened wide.

"*Magellan* has acquired us," D'Costa said. "They're locked on, preparing to fire."

"Ms. Jones, bring deflector array to maximum intensity." *Drake*'s outer hull wasn't thick enough to withstand a direct hit, yet its electromagnetic deflectors, designed mainly to ward off interstellar dust, might foul a torpedo's internal guidance system enough to cause it to miss its mark. Or so she hoped.

"Captain, President Montero wants to speak to you. He says it's urgent."

Damn it! "Put him through, Lieutenant," she snapped, then she impatiently slapped her mike. "Mr. President, this is a really bad time."

"*Ana, stop! You don't have to do this!*"

"Sorry, but we're past that." She looked at her first officer again. "Mr. D'Costa, on my mark."

"*Shut up and listen! There's another way!*"

D'Costa's hand hovered above his board. His eyes were upon the screens, waiting to see if the *Magellan* would fire the first shot, yet for a moment they flickered in Ana's direction. A faint nod. Ana hesitated, then nodded back.

"I'm listening," she said. "Make it quick."

"Government House online." Jonas looked over his shoulder from the com panel. "You're on, Mr. President."

Grasping a ceiling rail, Carlos peered out the windows. He didn't need to check the traffic control screen to see where the Alliance ships were positioned. *Drake* hovered nearby, its stern turned toward the Gatehouse; several kilometers farther away was *Magellan*, visible by its formation lights. In the far distance he could make out the starbridge, a small silver ring floating among the stars. A stand-off in space. His hand trembled as he touched his headset mike. *God, I hope this works . . .*

"Wendy, do you copy?" he asked.

A slight pause, caused by the two-second delay in transmission between the Gatehouse and Coyote. *"I'm here. So is Dieter. Would you like to speak to him?"*

"Just a moment." Carlos cupped his hand around the mike, turned to Jonas. "Are the *Drake* and the *Magellan* patched in?" Jonas nodded, and Carlos released his mike again. "Ambassador Vogel, thank you for being here."

Another pause, then Vogel came online. *"You're welcome, but I doubt anything you say will change the situation."* His voice was tight, lacking the affability that had marked their earlier conversations. *"My government requested that you turn the hijackers over to us and relinquish control of the Gatehouse. You've refused to do so. That leads us to believe that the Coyote Federation doesn't intend to abide by the terms of its treaty."*

"We do, Ambassador," Carlos replied, "but I ask . . . I insist . . . that the Coyote Federation treat this as an internal affair. The treaty clearly states the starbridge and the Gatehouse fall under our jurisdiction, not the Alliance's. The EA has no right to assume control of the starbridge. I assume that my wife . . . that is, President Gunther . . . has explained this to you."

Two seconds went past. *"She has. With all due respect, we disagree on our interpretation of the treaty."* A momentary pause. *"Mr. President, this is a minor incident. There's no reason why it should be exacerbated. The Gatehouse crew isn't at fault, so I have no doubt they'll be released promptly. And I assure you that the participants will be treated fairly."*

"And the starbridge? How long do you intend to control it?"

The next pause was longer than before. Carlos could easily imagine the scene in the Government House communications room: Wendy and Dieter, arguing the finer points of the treaty, while aides and staff members nervously lingered nearby. Carlos took advantage of the delay to cup his hand over the mike. "You got a camera on the *Drake?"* he asked Castro.

The Savant pointed to a screen above his head. Carlos looked up, saw a close-up view of the EA starship. "Good. What about the port?" Castro pointed to another screen. Here was an image taken from a camera mounted on the starbridge: formation lights showing the two ships, the Gatehouse behind them, with Bear providing the backdrop. "Excellent. Keep it steady. We'll need—"

"President Montero, I've told President Gunther that we'll retain control of the starbridge only so long as we need to assure that nothing like this will happen again." Dieter's voice was terse, his promise unconvincing. *"But we cannot allow something like this to—"*

Wendy broke in: *"Carlos, do whatever you have to do. We'll stand by you."*

"Thank you." Carlos waited a second, then went on. "Ambassador Vogel . . . and Captain Pacino and Captain Tereshkova, too, since I've been assured that you're listening . . . I agree that this incident shouldn't cause a breakdown between our respective governments. However, neither should it become a pretext for the Alliance to gain control of the sole means of access between Coyote and Earth. We've fought too hard for our independence to sacrifice it now, so there's little else that we can do but prove our sincerity." He paused. "We're transmitting images from the Gatehouse and the starbridge. I assume you see them, yes?"

A couple of seconds passed. *"We see them, Mr. President,"* Vogel said, *"but what—?"*

"Captain Tereshkova, are your weapons locked on the starbridge?"

Ana's voice immediately came over the channel: *"Yes, Mr. President, they are."*

"Fire."

A brief spark from *Drake*'s starboard side. Carlos glanced up at the screens to see a tiny lozenge sprint away from the starship, its engine flaring as it hurtled toward the starbridge.

"Ana!" Pacino shouted. *"What the hell are you—?"*

"Stand down, *Magellan!*" Carlos snapped. "*Drake,* if they fire on you . . ."

"Understood, Mr. President."

He stared at the screens. *Six . . . five . . .*

"Captain Tereshkova!" Vogel was on the verge of panic. *"Are you out of your—?"*

"Shut up, Dieter!" Carlos felt a hand against his shoulder. Looking around, he found Susan standing beside him. *Four . . . three . . .*

Pacino: *"Weapons control! On my mark!"*

He wrapped an arm around his daughter, drew her close. *Two . . . one . . .*

On the screens, a bright flash as the torpedo detonated a kilometer from the ring. There was no sound, of course, yet Carlos could have almost sworn he heard the blast. Looking down from the screens to the windows, he caught sight of a brief, orange-red splotch, appearing less than a finger's length from the starbridge.

"Carlos!" Wendy's voice in his headset. *"What are you doing?"*

"Just a sec." He silenced his mike again. Releasing Susan, he turned to Jonas. "Status?"

"No major damage, so far as I can tell." Jonas was bent over the console, closely studying the ring's sensors. "Fragmentation dispersed widely enough that it didn't damage the torus. We may have to replace an antenna or two, but otherwise . . ."

"Good." Carlos sighed with relief, then unclasped his mike again. "Ambassador, you saw what happened. If the torpedo hadn't been detonated prematurely, it would've destroyed the starbridge. As it is . . ."

"Captain Tereshkova, this is Ambassador Vogel." His voice quaked with barely suppressed rage. *"You're to cease-fire and surrender immediately to the—"*

"With all due respect, sir, we refuse." Ana's voice was eerily calm. *"This vessel is no longer under command of the European Alliance."*

"Ana, don't do this." Pacino again. *"We've got our weapons locked on you. If you don't surrender . . ."*

"Captain, we have a second torpedo locked on the starbridge. Fire on us, and you and your crew won't go home again."

No answer from the *Magellan*. Carlos smiled. Ana had correctly figured out the situation. Her crew might be reluctant to open fire upon another EA vessel . . . but if they fired upon the starbridge, then both ships would be stranded far from Earth. Yet while *Drake*'s crew would be welcome on Coyote, the same couldn't be said for the *Magellan*'s. Pacino knew this. Checkmate.

Vogel again: *"Captain Tereshkova, this is an act of mutiny."*

"Yes, sir, it is." A slight pause. *"Several members of my crew have had no part in this, and wish to transfer to the* Magellan. *The rest of us hereby resign our commissions, and hereby request political amnesty from the Coyote Federation."*

Carlos's eyes widened. This was a surprise. He'd been counting on Ana's friendship to pull them through, yet he hadn't realized how strongly she had come to feel about Coyote. And apparently more than a few of her crew felt the same way.

"Do you understand now?" Until now, Parson had been quiet. "Do you see what this place does to you?"

Carlos had no time to answer that. "Ambassador Vogel," he said, "you've seen what we can do. If you attempt to take control of the starbridge, we'll destroy it. It's that simple. Order the *Magellan* to stand down, or we'll be forced to take drastic measures of our own."

"Then your intent is to abrogate the treaty."

"Nothing of the kind." Carlos let out his breath. "We want peaceful relations with Earth. Believe me, we do. But we refuse to let the EA, or anyone else, dictate terms to us at gunpoint. We've told you this before, and we'll tell it to you again . . . Coyote is our world, and ours alone. Do you understand?"

Silence. Glancing up at the screen, Carlos could see that *Magellan* parked only a few kilometers from *Drake*. Both ships continued to hold position, their weapons still locked upon one another. He could only imagine what was going on back in Liberty.

A tap on his shoulder. Parson had moved up behind him. "Thank you," he said quietly. "Whatever happens next, I just want to say that."

"I'm not doing this for you." Carlos glanced at Susan, found warmth in her eyes that he hadn't seen in quite some time. "You get my daughter into something like this again, and we're going to have . . ."

"Gatehouse, this is Magellan.*"* Pacino's voice returned. *"Ambassador Vogel has advised us to withdraw, pending cease-fire from the* Drake. *Do you copy?"*

"We copy, Captain." Carlos paused. "Wendy, what's the word down there?"

"Dieter has agreed to take the matter before the council." Wendy's voice was relieved. *"*Magellan *is returning to Earth, once . . . um, uninvolved members of the* Drake *crew are shuttled over."* Another pause. *"It's over. It's all over."*

A knot between his shoulders and his neck suddenly relaxed. "We copy," he murmured. "Thank you, dear . . . I mean, Madam President."

He closed his eyes, let stale air escape from his lungs. He turned to give Susan a hug, only to find that she'd wrapped her arms around Parson. It was the first time since she'd been a teenager that he'd seen his daughter kiss another man; he didn't know whether to feel protective, angry, or merely amused . . . and decided to simply feel relief that Susan had finally found someone.

I wonder how serious this is, he thought. But there were other things he needed to consider just now. He turned to Jonas. "Get your people up here. I think they'd like to know what's happened." Jonas grinned as he released his seat belt and pushed himself toward the access hatch. Then he looked at Manny. "Savant Castro . . . ?"

"Manny, please." The Savant solemnly regarded him with one red eye.

"All right. Manny, then . . ." He shook his head. "Do you think you could arrange for a ride home?"

"That shouldn't be difficult, sir. The skiff is still docked with us, after all. And we do have a qualified pilot aboard."

"Oh, right." With all that had just happened, he'd managed to forget about the *Virginia Dare.* He shook his head; it had been a very long day. "Thank you . . . and call me Carlos, please. I hate it when people call me Mr. President."

Pushing himself over to a chair near the window, he settled into it. "Y'know what?" he asked no one in particular, gazing out at the distant starbridge. "I could be wrong, but I think we just had another revolution."

"They sort of sneak up on you, don't they." Still holding on to Susan, Parson turned to him. "And by the way, Mr. . . . I mean, Carlos . . . while I have your attention, there's one more thing I'd like to ask of you."

He saw the smile on his daughter's face. "I can imagine what it is," he replied.

Part 8

WILL THE CIRCLE BE UNBROKEN?

An exchange of vows, a pair of slender gold bands slipped upon fingers. A formal pronouncement made by the justice of the peace. Finally, an embrace and a kiss. As the wedding guests stood to applaud, the bride and groom turned and, arm in arm, stepped out from beneath the rose-decked trellis, smiling bashfully as they strolled down the red carpet laid upon the grass between rows of folding wooden chairs.

From the front row, Carlos watched as Susan was led away by Jonathan Parson, and suddenly realized that his strongest emotion was neither happiness nor relief, but rather astonishment. Had it really been only thirteen summers ago that his daughter was born? No, not even that long; today was Muriel 45, the midmonth Raphael of the third month of spring, and Susan's birthday was Uriel 52, near the end of summer, a little more than four months from now. Where had all the years gone? One minute, she's a baby in your arms. The next . . .

Hearing Wendy snuffle, he looked around to see tears running down her face. "Sorry," she whispered, wiping her eyes with a linen handkerchief. "I'm being silly. It's just that . . ."

"I know." Putting an arm around her, he watched Susan pause to accept a hug from one of her friends. "They make a beautiful couple, don't they?"

Wendy was about to answer when, from the other side of Sand Creek, there was a volley of gunshots. Members of the Colonial Militia, led by Chris Levin, firing their carbines into the air. Although Susan had been too young to fight in the revolution, nonetheless she was the daughter of a veteran—of the legendary Rigil Kent, in fact—and thus entitled to receive the customary seven-gun marriage salute. Although he'd known it was coming, Carlos flinched anyway; this was a tradition he'd come to despise, no matter how many weddings he'd attended. Too many bad memories.

The volley barely interrupted the Coyote Wind Ensemble as they performed Mendelssohn's "Wedding March." Carlos reflected again upon how
many other people from Susan's life were here. Quite a few were original
colonists. Seated next to Wendy, also wiping away tears, was Kuniko
Okada, who'd delivered Susan at birth. There was Dana Monroe, brought
in from Leeport by Paul Dwyer, who'd also furnished the shag-drawn
wagon that carried bride and groom to the river side. Bernie and Vonda
Cayle, Henry Johnson, Lew and Carrie Geary, Sissy Levin, his old friend
Barry Dreyfus and his parents Jack and Lisa . . . all had insisted upon being
here, with a few older ones like Henry and Vonda making the effort to hob-
ble down to the river. This was a special day for everyone who'd come here
aboard the *Alabama*; they'd watched Susan grow up, and they had their
own memories of her as a child.

Yet there were others, those who'd been among the subsequent waves
of colonists. Benjamin Harlan, standing beneath the trellis, serving as justice of the peace. His mate, Allegro DiSilvio, conducting the ensemble as
they wove their way into a reprise of Pachelbel's "Canon in D." Klon
Newall and Fred LaRoux, who'd come in with their families from Midland.

Carlos glanced over his shoulder, caught a brief smile from Morgan
Goldstein, who'd flown in this morning from New Brighton. Indeed, Morgan had paid for the reception; Wendy almost refused, insisting the bride's
family would take care of this. After all, Goldstein had run against her in
the last presidential election on a prodevelopment platform that sought to
put the brakes on the environmental and endangered-species legislation
that her administration had recently spearheaded, only to discover that
most of the colonists sided with the incumbent. He'd lost by several thousand votes, a decisive majority when it came to Coyote's expanding yet still
small population. Carlos persuaded Wendy to accept his offer in the spirit
in which it was intended, as a peace-making gesture, and she'd reluctantly
accepted.

Yet, without a doubt, the strangest member of the wedding party was
Manuel Castro. Standing beside Jonathan Parson, offering Susan's ring at
the appropriate moment, the irony was lost on no one: the former lieutenant governor of Liberty during the Union occupation, now acting as
best man at the wedding of the first child born on Coyote. Yet Jonathan
had been adamant; Manny Castro had offered him sanctuary when he was
on the run, and now he'd have the Savant stand up for him at his wedding.

Many here were visibly uncomfortable by his presence—Dieter Vogel had almost refused to attend, relenting at the last minute if only for diplomatic reasons—but Molly Thompson had taken the occasion to sew a new cloak for Manny, the light brown shagswool she'd selected making him look much less sinister.

Nearly fifteen years since First Landing Day, by the LeMarean calendar, and now the stepchildren of Coyote were growing up. Carlos reflected upon this as he and Wendy joined the procession following the bride and groom from the altar. It wouldn't be long before he'd be a grandfather. He didn't feel that old, yet there was silver in his wife's hair, and on cold mornings he felt a certain stiffness in his shoulders and knees when he got out of bed. *I'm still young,* he reminded himself. *Hell, Wendy gave me a physical just last month, told me I was . . .*

"Tell me this isn't happening." Marie came up beside him to squeeze his arm and whisper in his ear. "Your baby's too young for this."

"My thoughts exactly." Carlos stopped to give his sister a hug, noting that her eyes were red-rimmed as well. "Last time I checked, she was . . ."

"Thirty-six, by Earth reckoning." Wendy had stopped crying. "Back there, she'd be an old maid. Here . . ."

"Call it prolonged adolescence." It wasn't anything no one hadn't noticed before. Perhaps it was the diet or the fresh air, or maybe it was the psychological impact of longer seasons, yet the average life span of a Coyote inhabitant was much longer than someone on Earth. Even without the aid of gene therapy, the most elderly colonists were in relatively good health. And the young . . . "Don't question it. How was the trip over?"

"Not bad. Dana put us up last night at her inn." Marie nodded toward Rain; she was with her Uncle Garth, chatting with Sissy Levin. She hesitated, then added, "I dropped in on Hawk. He's doing better."

"Hmm . . . yeah, I think so, too." This was something the family still didn't care to talk about. Following the incident at the starbridge, Hawk had been handed over to the magistrates to stand trial for his father's murder. The Liberty Compact didn't have capital punishment, yet he might have remained in the Liberty stockade for the rest of his life if Wendy hadn't interceded on his behalf. As it was, he was committed to a rehab farm outside Leeport for the next three years, with parole possible if he successfully went through psychiatric treatment.

The discovery that Hawk was responsible for Lars's death had been rough on Marie and her family, yet the aftermath of the starbridge affair had hurt Carlos and Wendy as well. The magistrates had sentenced Susan and Jon to six months in the stockade, with the last two months commuted to community service. Their punishment did little to assuage the anger of many colonists, who thought that they'd put the lives of the Gatehouse crew at risk for what was essentially a protest action; some claimed that they would have received stiffer sentences if Susan hadn't been the president's daughter. At Carlos's insistence, the wedding was delayed until late spring; by then, the two of them had served their time, and the incident had faded from memory.

"C'mon. The reception line's forming up." Wendy tugged at his arm. "You don't want to miss that, do you?"

Carlos glanced at the tent set up nearby. Rows of linen-covered tables, with fresh-cut wildflowers and bottles of waterfruit wine. On the buffet line, roast pork and red potatoes, steamed greens and goat's cheese, with a wedding cake and casks of sourgrass ale awaiting the party to follow the reception dinner. Even a box of hand-rolled Minnesota cigars, imported from Earth, for those who cared to indulge in such decadence. True to his word, Morgan Goldstein had spared no expense.

"Sure. Let's go." It was worth shaking a few dozen hands. And besides, his daughter was waiting for him. Radiant in her wedding dress, the afternoon sun casting a halo around her veil, she gazed at her father with a certain shyness. A little girl who'd finally grown up, but nonetheless hadn't outgrown her father.

So he went over to kiss his daughter on the cheek, and shake hands with his new son-in-law, and take his place in line to receive the congratulations and best-wishes of the wedding guests. Never once did he glance up at the sky, nor did he suspect that, very soon, something would come from it that would change everything.

The long afternoon wore on. The dinner was splendid, the atmo-sphere relaxed and informal. Carlos had just danced with his daughter and was waiting for her and Jon to cut the cake, when Tomas Conesco appeared. The moment Carlos spotted him, he knew there was trouble.

Tom had received a wedding invitation, of course, but he'd begged off. The Budget Committee was scheduled to meet tomorrow morning to discuss the next quarter, and as Wendy's chief of staff he felt it was more important that he work through the weekend in order to make sure that the executive summary didn't contain any errors. So when Carlos saw Tom standing nervously on the other side of the tent, searching the reception for Wendy, he realized that something more urgent than a glitch in the spreadsheets had brought him here.

Wendy noticed him, too. Seated near Carlos at the head of the table, she interrupted her conversation with Ana Tereshkova to raise a hand. Seeing her, Tom moved through the crowd; he did so without raising much attention, although a few guests looked up when someone not wearing a suit appeared in their midst. Making his way to the president's side, he bent down and whispered in her ear.

Carlos tried to catch what Tom was saying, but the background noise drowned him out. Wendy listened intently; she said nothing, and kept her expression carefully neutral, yet from the look in her eyes Carlos could tell she was surprised. She whispered something to Tom and sent him off, then she leaned across the table to Carlos.

"Something's come up," she murmured. "I've got to go." She stood up, then hesitated and looked at Ana. "Would you come with me, please?"

"Of course, Madam President." Uncrossing her legs beneath her crinoline skirt, Ana rose as well. Since the events of last autumn, she'd become commodore of the newly formed Coyote Federation Navy. It wasn't much of a fleet, to be sure: the CFSS *Robert E. Lee*—formerly the EASS *Drake*—along with two shuttles and a skiff, yet they were what the colonies had purchased from the European Alliance in exchange for renegotiated passage rights through the starbridge. And although Admiral Tereshkova was now a family friend, it was an indication that something important had occurred when she addressed Wendy by her honorific.

Carlos was pleasantly inebriated—three glasses of wine and a fine cigar had put him in a mellow state of mind—but sobriety quickly returned. "I'm coming with you," he said, pushing back his chair. Wendy started to object, and he shook his head. "Don't argue. Not unless you want to cause a scene."

That shut her up, however reluctantly. "Give Susan and Jon my apologies," Wendy muttered. "Tell her . . . I dunno, just tell her something . . . then come with us. We're heading back to GH."

So it was left to Carlos to saunter over to the head table and make excuses to the bride and groom. Although Susan was mystified by her parents' sudden departure, she'd had a few glasses of waterfruit wine herself, and thus was happy beyond the point of caring. Jon was curious, and started to ask questions, yet a stare from his new father-in-law reminded him of his place; he remained in his seat, and poured another drink for Jonas Whittaker. Few people took notice when Carlos slipped away from the reception, and joined Wendy, Ana, and Tom on the dirt road leading from Sand Creek into town.

"All right," he said, "someone want to tell me what's going on?"

"First, Mr. President," Tomas said, "let me apologize for . . ."

"Never mind." Wendy pulled up the hem of her skirt to keep it out of the dirt. "Just tell him what you heard." She glanced back at her husband. "You're gonna love this."

"About a half hour ago," Tomas continued, "a ship came through the starbridge. An Alliance shuttle . . ."

"I didn't know one was scheduled." Carlos sidestepped a clingberry bush. According to the renegotiated agreement, all incoming Alliance starships were supposed to be cleared in advance with the customs department.

"There wasn't." Tomas's voice rose. "When the bridge was activated from the other side, our people on the Gatehouse didn't know what was going on. No prior notification. No data sent. It just . . . it just happened, that's all."

"But you said it was an Alliance shuttle." Carlos was confused. "If it was from—"

"That's the point," Wendy said. "It's an Alliance shuttle, but it didn't come from Earth."

Carlos stopped. "What . . . ?"

"Not from Earth," Wendy repeated, halting to look at him. "Our Gatehouse sent a hyperspace message to Starbridge Earth. They confirmed . . . nothing had been sent through from their end."

"We even linked our comps, to confirm the information." Tomas stopped as well. "The Alliance denies any involvement, and the records prove it. Their starbridge hasn't opened since the *Magellan* went through three weeks ago."

"Then who . . . ?"

"The ship identified itself as the EAS *Maria Celeste*." Wendy's voice was flat, yet there was a note of incredulity. She looked at Tereshkova. "Tell him."

Ana didn't respond immediately. The late afternoon sky was beginning to tint purple with approaching sunset; a thin wind rustled through the high grass around the path. "The *Maria Celeste* was . . . is, rather . . . a shuttle belonging to the *Galileo*," she said at last. "The first Alliance starship. The one that . . ."

"The one that disappeared." Carlos felt something creep up his spine. "What's it doing here now?"

"We'll know soon enough." Wendy walked quickly up the road toward Government House. "Time to have a talk with her captain."

"Or whoever else is flying that thing," Ana murmured.

The communications room was located on the ground floor of Government House. Packed with shortwave radio and satphone transceivers, it served as the major link between Liberty and the rest of the colonies, along with the Gatehouse and the *Lee*, now permanently stationed in high orbit. There was barely room for the four of them, and not enough seats for everyone; the radio operator on duty was clearly irate to have this many people invade his domain, but he said nothing as he pulled out a chair for Wendy, letting the others lean against walls or stand in the doorway.

"*Maria Celeste*, this is Liberty Communications, Coyote Federation. Do you copy? Over." The duty operator listened for a moment to his headset, then adjusted the gain on his board. "*Maria Celeste*, this is Liberty Communications, Coyote Federation. Do you . . . ?"

"*We copy.*" The voice that came from the wall speaker was male, fairly young, with a faint British accent. "*With whom am I speaking, please?*"

Wendy gestured to the headset she'd put on, and the operator nodded. "*Maria Celeste*, this is President Wendy Gunther of the Coyote Federation. Would you please identify yourself?"

A moment of static. "*Theodore Harker, first officer of the EAS* Galileo. *Never heard of the Coyote Federation, ma'am, but all the same we're glad to hear you.*"

A gasp from Ana Tereshkova. Her face had gone pale. "He's right," she murmured. "Harker was the *Galileo*'s first officer. But . . ."

"But what?" Wendy glanced over her shoulder at her. "Tell me."

Carlos knew. The *Galileo* disappeared in 2288, shortly after it jumped through an experimental starbridge to the Kuiper Belt. By Gregorian reckoning, it was now 2344. "How old was Harker?" he asked.

"I don't know." Ana shook her head. "Thirty, perhaps thirty-five."

"Does that sound like someone in his late eighties?" Carlos looked back at Wendy. "Don't you get it? It's been fifty-six years. Where has he been for . . . ?"

"*Liberty, do you read?*" Harker's voice came back online. "*We know this must be a surprise to you, but we're coming in fast, and we'd like to know where we can land. Assuming we have your permission, of course.*"

"He can rendezvous with the *Lee*," Ana said. "I'll get in touch with my crew, tell them to change orbit . . ."

"Hell with that." Carlos looked askance at her. "I want to meet this guy as soon as possible."

"I agree." Wendy glanced at Ana. "Can you send a skiff from the *Lee* to intercept them and guide them here? To Shuttlefield, I mean."

Ana reluctantly nodded, and Wendy turned to the duty operator. "Put her through to the *Lee* on a separate channel," she said, then she touched her mike again. "Affirmative, Mr. Harker. You have permission to land. We're dispatching a craft to escort you to a nearby landing site."

Another pause. "*We appreciate that, Liberty. However, please advise your craft to maintain safe distance. Our drive may interfere with their control systems if they come too close.*"

"I have no idea what he's talking about." Ana's face registered puzzlement. "How could they . . . ?"

"We copy, *Maria Celeste*, and we'll take that under advisement." Wendy hesitated, then spoke again. "Mr. Harker, the *Galileo* has been missing for a very long time. Where is it? And where are you coming from?"

Nearly half a minute elapsed before they received a reply. "*The Galileo has been destroyed, along with most of its crew, including the captain.*" Harker's voice sounded tight. "*Only three survivors, myself included . . .*"

"Oh, my god," Carlos murmured. Wendy shushed him.

"*We made the jump from HD 143761,*" Harker went on. "*Rho Coronae Borealis.*" Pause. "*We're very tired, and we'd just like to land. We'll explain everything once we're on the ground. ETA . . . um, about an hour or so from now. Maria Celeste, over and out.*"

Before Wendy could reply, there was a buzz of static. No one spoke for a few moments; they simply stared at the wall speaker. "Did I hear that right?" she said at last. "Did he just say that he was landing in only an hour?"

"That's impossible." Ana was incredulous. "EA shuttles aren't capable of . . ."

"I think we've just chucked 'impossible' out the window," Carlos muttered.

It was sundown when the *Maria Celeste* landed at Shuttlefield, the burnt-orange glow of the setting sun casting its rays upon the spacecraft as it slowly descended upon the apron. Yet it did so in near silence. No blast of jets, no roar of engines being throttled back; only a low, almost supernatural hum from a pair of oblong pods mounted on the aft fuselage where the nuclear engines should have been.

Carlos found himself trembling as he watched the craft settle upon its landing gear. At first glance, the *Maria Celeste* looked very much like an old-style ESA shuttle. Yet although the hull was weathered, its underside scorched and dented from atmospheric entry, it no longer flew like anything ever assembled on Earth.

Perfect reactionless drive, he thought. *No rockets, no jets. Someone has retrofitted this thing . . .*

Recessed plates on either side of the mysterious pods went dark, fading from the deep blue radiance they'd emitted, and the humming lapsed into silence. A short distance away, the *Virginia Dare* came in for a landing, its VTOLs howling as they kicked up dust. By contrast, the *Maria Celeste* landed so peacefully that only the evening breeze stirred the wind sock upon its post.

"Spooky," Carlos murmured. "Really spooky."

"Uh-huh." Wendy pulled her shawl closer around her shoulders. "I'm not sure if I like the looks of this." Through the cockpit windows, they could see silhouetted figures, backlit by interior lights. She glanced back toward the gate, where a couple of blueshirts had positioned themselves inside the fence. "Do you think we ought to . . . ?"

"Bring them closer?" Carlos thought about it a moment, then shook his head. "No, have 'em stay back. No reason why we shouldn't trust them." He paused, and looked at Ana. "Is there?"

Ana was quiet, studying the *Maria Celeste* with barely disguised awe. "There may be humans onboard," she said at last, "but humans didn't rebuild that ship." She hesitated, "Leave the Proctors where they are. A show of force might make them nervous." A faint smile flickered across her face. "It did for me, at least."

Carlos nodded. Unlike when the *Columbus* had made its unexpected arrival nearly two years ago, no one besides the two Proctors had accompanied them to the landing field. Word had not yet gotten out that an unknown spacecraft was touching down in Shuttlefield, so there were no crowds to be kept back. For all he knew, the rest of the wedding guests were still at the party. Just as well. Until they knew what they were dealing with . . .

A grating noise from the underside of the shuttle, then a belly hatch opened and a ramp began to lower to the ground. "All right, then," Wendy said. "Let's see who's come for dinner."

"At least we're appropriately dressed." None of them had a chance to change out of their wedding outfits. Carlos started to step forward, then self-consciously stopped himself. "After you, Madam President."

Wendy didn't smile. Squaring her shoulders, she purposefully walked toward the *Maria Celeste*, Carlos and Ana following just a few steps behind. They'd just reached the spacecraft when they heard footsteps upon the ramp. A few moments passed, then three figures made their way down from the spacecraft.

Two men—one in his mid-thirties, the other closer to fifty—and a woman in her late twenties. The younger man had long brown hair pulled back in a ponytail; the older man was tall and thin, with a mop of grey hair receding from a high forehead. The woman was svelte and had short blond hair parted on one side. None wore ESA uniforms; instead, their clothes were long robes, off-white yet braided with ornate designs that softly glowed with an iridescence that seemed to come from the fabric itself, giving them an almost angelic appearance.

The three of them hesitated at the bottom of the ramp, almost as if reluctant to introduce themselves, then the younger man stepped forward. "President Gunther?" he asked. Wendy nodded. "Theodore Harker, first officer of the EASS *Galileo*." A slight frown. "Or perhaps, I should say, former first officer. As I told you earlier, the *Galileo* is no longer with us."

"I understand." Wendy extended her hand, which Harker unhesitantly grasped. "This is my husband, former president Carlos Montero, and Commodore Anastasia Tereshkova, former commanding officer of the EASS *Drake* . . ."

"Now the *Robert E. Lee,* under flag of the Coyote Federation. It was our skiff that intercepted you." Although Ana came forward, she didn't offer her own hand. "I've heard of you, Mr. Harker. The disappearance of the *Galileo* has become something of a legend."

"I imagine it has." Harker gave her a rueful smile. "Fifty-six years ago, or at least so I've been told."

"You've been told?" Ana raised an eyebrow. "By whom?"

Harker took a deep breath. "A long story, believe me." He turned to the others. "Jared Ramirez, astrobiologist, and Emily Collins, the *Celeste*'s pilot." Harker took Collins's hand; in that instant, it seemed as if the patterns of their robes changed to a warm yellow hue. "We owe much to her. She's the one who brought us safely here."

"Here from where?" Wendy couldn't hide her bewilderment. "Mr. Harker, you said that you've come from Rho Coronae Borealis. We checked our star charts . . . that system's over fifty-two light-years from Earth."

"And fifty l.y.'s from 47 Ursae Majoris." Ramirez's face was solemn. "We know. We came through a starbridge."

"But not one built by us, I gather." Ana peered closely at him. "Haven't I heard of you before, Dr. Ramirez?"

Ramirez looked away as if in embarrassment; the designs of his cloak subtly shifted to a purple color. "All in the past," he said quietly. "A lifetime ago . . ."

"A lifetime, indeed." Wendy let out her breath. "Look, I'm . . . we're pleased you've managed to find your way here, but you must understand."

"What happened to the *Galileo*?" Carlos couldn't help himself. "Why were you fifty light-years from here? What—?"

"Did you make first contact?" Wendy's voice was quiet, yet insistent.

Harker regarded her with faint amusement, as if she'd just asked an obvious question. Carlos noticed that his robe's designs became scarlet. Apparently some sort of biomemetic feedback. "Of course," he replied. "You haven't figured that out already?"

Before anyone could interrupt him again, Harker raised a hand. "Look, you've got a lot of questions, and we'll answer them all. But . . ." He sighed. "It's a long story, and there's something important you first need to know."

"And that is?" Wendy asked.

The three surviving members of the *Galileo* expedition gazed at one another, as if uncertain who should speak next. "We're not alone," Ramirez said, his cloak's patterns becoming off-white once more. "We know that now. There's hundreds . . . maybe thousands . . . of other races in the galaxy. Most are younger than our own, and many of them are still struggling to survive. A few are more advanced than our own, and some . . ."

"The survivors are the ones who've learned how to leave their home worlds," Harker continued. "The old theories . . . the Drake equation, Shklovskii's and Sagan's principles . . . are correct. A race that develops the ability to leave its place of origin is more likely to escape self-destruction than those who don't. But by the same token, not all races who achieve interstellar travel are ones you'd necessarily want to meet."

"There's good out there," Collins said, her voice low, "but there's also evil."

Something in the way she said this caused Carlos to shiver. "I don't like the sound of that."

"Nor should you." Ramirez's robe darkened. "Believe me, we've seen things straight from your worst nightmare."

"But we've also seen things that give us hope," Harker added. "And that's just it. The elder races . . . the ones who try to keep peace in this part of the galaxy . . . have been observing us for quite some time." He smiled. "Oh, not as long as you might imagine. They became aware of humankind only after one of their ships observed the *Alabama*, not long after it left our system."

Carlos shared a look with Wendy. She, too, remembered the cryptic note left behind by Leslie Gillis. What he'd seen from the *Alabama*'s rec deck wasn't an illusion; he'd indeed spotted an alien vessel. "We've had reason to suspect that, yeah."

"But why haven't they contacted us?" Wendy asked. "Why did they wait so long?"

"As she said, there's evil out there." Harker's smile faded. "The other races have learned to be careful about whom they contact. They watch, they wait, they observe. And when they feel confident . . ."

"They find a way to make contact." Collins smiled. "Which is why we're here."

Carlos stared at her, then at Harker and Ramirez. "I don't . . . I mean, are you saying—?"

"Yes. Exactly." Harker's expression was calm. "They've been observing Coyote for quite some time now. Waiting to see what you'd do with it, how you'd treat another world once you'd settled it. What might happen once you finally developed hyperspace travel. Think of it as a test."

"And we . . . ?"

"Yes. We've passed. They want to talk to us now." Harker paused. "Ready for the next part? Here it is . . . we didn't come here alone."

Carlos stared up at the *Maria Celeste*. "Are you saying . . . ?"

"What you think I'm saying." A sly grin appeared on Harker's face as he turned to Wendy. "One of them is up there. A Coronean, if you want to call them that . . . although they refer to themselves as the *hjadd*. Heshe's a representative, and heshe'd like to have a word with you."

For the first time, Carlos noticed a shadowy form lurking just within the shuttle's hatch. Bipedal, upright; vaguely anthromorphic, yet clearly not human. *My god*, he thought, *it's one of them . . .*

Wendy saw it, too. Her face lost color, and she involuntarily took a step back. "I don't . . . I mean, I can't . . ."

"Yes, you can." Carlos took his wife's hand, and wasn't surprised to find that it was shaking. "You're the president, remember?"

He looked back at Ana, saw that she wore the same expression. The time had come to put away their fear of the unknown; they had to embrace wonder, find a way back to the things that had led them here in the first place. The stars beckoned, inviting them to join a plurality of worlds.

The words of an old song came to him just then, a spiritual he'd heard long ago in his younger days. He didn't know why he remembered it just then, yet nonetheless it was appropriate:

> *Will the circle be unbroken?*
> *By and by, Lord, by and by,*
> *There's a better home a waitin'*
> *In the sky, Lord, in the sky.*

Wendy stopped trembling. "You're right," she said quietly. "It's my job . . . and yours, too." She smiled. "C'mon. Let's go meet the neighbors."

Hand in hand, they walked up the ramp.

EPILOGUE

The boy found the notebook on the wooden bench, its pages ruffled by the morning breeze. "Grandpapa, look!" he shouted, holding it up in his small hand. "See what I found!"

"Oh, really? And what may that be?" His grandfather sauntered across the lawn, careful not to exert himself too much. He was still in good shape for a man in his mid-sixties, at least by Earth years, yet his right knee had been giving him trouble lately. His wife had given him a cane as a Liberation Day present—an elegant accessory, carved from blackwood branch—but he disliked using it when he was out for a stroll with Jorge. Perhaps it was only a matter of pride, but he didn't want his grandson to think that he was more lame than he really was.

"Here! Look!" The boy rushed back to him with his prize, incautiously waving it above his head. "Someone left it behind over there!"

"Now, did they? Well, let's see who it belongs to." Taking the notebook from Jorge, Carlos opened it to the title page. "Oh, I think I know. This is Ms. Cayle's . . . she teaches history at the university."

"History?" A puzzled expression crossed his face. "If it's written by a lady, then why isn't it herstory?"

"Because . . ." Carlos caught the gleam in Jorge's eye, gave him a mock scowl. "Okay, you got me again."

The boy laughed, delighted that he'd once again fooled Grandpapa. Susan was right; for a kid just shy of his second birthday, Jorge was uncommonly bright. Making bad puns was a favorite game between them. "Maybe Ms. Cayle isn't all she professes to be," Carlos added, trying to one-up him, and Jorge rolled his eyes in disgust. "Well, then, perhaps we should return it to her. She's an old friend, and she's probably wondering where she left it."

"Sure. Okay." Jorge continued to eye the notebook. He seemed reluctant to surrender his find so easily. "But don't you . . . ? I mean, what's in it, do you think?"

"Hmm. Good point. Let's see." Carlos walked over to the bench and sat down. Opening the book in his lap, he skimmed the handwritten notes.

Yes, it was all here. The hijacking of the *Alabama*. The arrival at 47 Ursae Majoris. The establishment of Liberty. His mouth tightened as he caught a brief mention of his father and mother as the first casualties—after all these years, he was surprised that the memory of their loss still hurt—and he quickly flipped to another page. The building of the Garcia Narrows Bridge. The beginning of the Revolution.

"Well, it's about . . ."

He looked up, and saw the hjadd. The Coronean stood only a few yards away, a tall figure clad in an environment suit, hisher features hidden behind a faceplate. Even after two years, it surprised him how silently these beings came and went. There weren't many on Coyote, but they still managed to get around.

The hjadd stood beneath the shade of the faux birch, silent and observant, keeping hisher distance. Perhaps a member of the Coronean embassy, out for some exercise; maybe heshe recognized him, and had wandered over to see what he was doing. Even after two years, they were still just as curious about humankind as humans were about them.

Jorge looked around, spotted the hjadd. "Oh, hi," he said, giving the hjadd a short wave. Heshe responded by raising hisher left arm; four elongated fingers danced at the end of a triple-jointed appendage. Indifferent to the alien, Jorge turned back to him. "So what's it say?"

Carlos smiled. He had an audience. No sense in letting them down. "Come over here and take a seat, and I'll tell you."

He moved aside on the bench, making room for his grandson. The hjadd came a little closer as well. Carlos glanced again at Vonda's lecture notes, then closed the book. This was a story he could tell from memory. After all, it was his own.

"It all began a long time ago," he said, "in a place called America . . ."

COYOTE CALENDAR

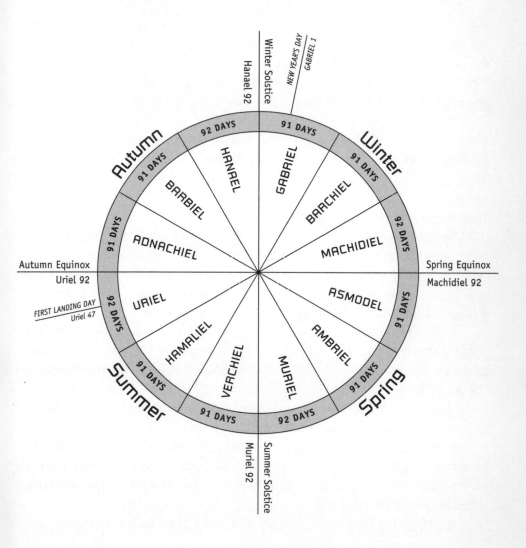

Winter Solstice
Hanael 92

NEW YEAR'S DAY
GABRIEL 1

92 DAYS
91 DAYS

Autumn

Winter

HANAEL
GABRIEL

91 DAYS
91 DAYS

BARBIEL
BARCHIEL

91 DAYS
92 DAYS

ADNACHIEL
MACHIDIEL

Autumn Equinox
Uriel 92

Spring Equinox
Machidiel 92

URIEL
ASMODEL

FIRST LANDING DAY
Uriel 47

92 DAYS
91 DAYS

HAMALIEL
AMBRIEL

VERCHIEL
MURIEL

91 DAYS
91 DAYS

Summer

Spring

91 DAYS
92 DAYS

Summer Solstice
Muriel 92

ACKNOWLEDGMENTS

My appreciation goes to my editor, Ginjer Buchanan, and my agent, Martha Millard, for their continued support. I'm also grateful to Linda Carlson, Gardner Dozois, David Ham, Terry Kepner, Ron Miller, Derryl Murphy, and Sheila Williams for their advice, assistance, and encouragement.

Special thanks to Patrick O'Connor, a longtime fan of this series, for the gift of the Coyote globe that makes a brief appearance in Part Seven.

And, as always, my greatest thanks to my wife, Linda, for insisting that I write this book now rather than later, and for putting up with me for one last trip to Coyote.

September 2003–November 2004
Whately, Massachusetts

SOURCES

(Author's Note: For additional citations,
consult the Sources pages of *Coyote* and *Coyote Rising*.)

Burland, Cottie. *North American Indian Mythology.* 3d ed. New York: Hamylyn Publishing Group, 1973.

Ham, David. "Eludication of Scientific Misconceptions about Global Climate Change." *The Nucleus,* Summer 1998.

Kepner, Terry. *. . . And Remote from Neighbors: A Guide to 105 Known Planets in 91 Star Systems.* Terry Kepner, 162 Onset Road, Bennington, NH 03442.

King, Sir David, ed. "Future Flooding Executive Summary." U.K. Office of Science and Technology, 2003.

Ley, Willy. "Space War" (nonfiction article). *Astounding,* August 1939.

Matloff, Gregory. *Deep-Space Probes.* Chichester, U.K.: Springer-Praxis, 2000.

Neumann, James E., et al. "Sea-Level Rise and Global Climate Change: A Review of Impacts to U.S. Coasts." Pew Center on Global Climate Change, February 2000.

Smith, Joel B. "A Synthesis of Potential Climate Change Impacts on the U.S." Pew Center on Global Climate Change, 2004.

Sullivan, Walter. "New Theory on Ice Sheet Catastrophe Is the Direst One Yet." *New York Times,* May 2, 1995.

Thorne, Kip S. *Black Holes and Time Warps.* New York: W. W. Norton, 1994.

Titus, James G., and Vijay K. Narayanan. "The Probability of Sea-Level Rise." U.S. Environmental Protection Agency, 1995.

Wigginton, Eliot, ed. *Foxfire 4.* New York: Anchor Press, 1977.